THREE ABDUCTIONS AND AN EARL

A STEAMY REGENCY ROMANCE (BOOK 1 IN THE PARVENUES & PARAMOURS SERIES)

TESSA CANDLE

Three Abductions and an Earl

Book 1 in the Parvenues & Paramours series

Paperback Edition

Published by

ISBN: 978-1-77265-008-2

DEDICATION

Three Abductions and an Earl

or Abducto add an Earldom

is dedicated to you, my true reader. You enjoy a good steamy romp with some naughty nobles and a witty heroine—and you only cringe slightly at my horrid Latin puns. Perhaps most importantly, you were one of the very first people to buy Book 1 in the Parvenues & Paramours series. Thank you.

I thought you might be interested in reading one of the novels that Lydia reads in Three Abductions and an Earl. So as a little fun spinoff just for you, I am writing Accursed Abbey, and am almost finished the first draft! It is a steamy Gothic romance, set in the Georgian period.

Hint: if you don't yet know what Accursed Abbey is, it is first mentioned in Chapter 4.

And I will let you in on another secret: when it is finished, **I will be gifting a copy to everyone on my Tessa Candle Updates list**. Sign up now at http://eepurl.com/cPCrI1, or at www.tessacandle.com, which, let's face it, is much easier to remember.

Thank you for being my true reader. You are the person I write for.

ALSO BY TESSA CANDLE

Mistress of Two Fortunes and a Duke, Book 2 in the *Parvenues & Paramours* series —coming very soon! Sign up for updates at http://eepurl.com/clzyVr. I will be sending out a cover reveal...

Accursed Abbey, a Gothic Romance—coming soon! Sign up for updates at http://eepurl.com/clzyVr. Everyone on the Tessa Candle Updates list will be offered a free copy when it is ready for release!

Three Abductions and an Earl, audio book, as read by the author—coming soon! Sign up for updates at http://eepurl.com/clzyVr.

Or you can sign up at www.tessacandle.com.

CHAPTER 1

*L*ydia Norwood was not quite the thing with her freckles and red hair, and she knew it. But Lydia did not want to be a débutante. She wanted to be left in peace in the countryside.

Her mother's eager anticipation of the season had propelled the Norwood family to London in early September while the weather was still warm, and in time to escape the stink of fall agricultural activities at Nesterling Lodge.

Yet Lydia quickly found that she preferred the smell of freshly applied manure to the stench of the ton's superiority over the *nouveau riche*. She preferred her horse to high society, where the company, like the flow of weak tea, was as insipid as it was abundant.

It was getting harder to slip away somewhere quiet to read, but the day's trip with her mother to a pleasure garden outside of the city gave her just such an opportunity. While her mother was engrossed in inspecting the many rare varieties of rose bush within the gardens, Lydia quietly sneaked off down one of the promenades into the woods.

She trailed her fingers over bark and leaves, inhaling the life-affirming sylvan fragrance as she ambled along, finally deciding upon the perfect tree to climb. It had a limb ideally angled for propping her back against the trunk, and from the upper branches she was invisible to the promenade below.

The warm air brought the scent of some flowering bush—she knew not what kind, for she simply could not attend to such irrelevancies, but it was pleasant. She settled into a contented slouch and found her page in *The Necromancy of Abruggio*. Then voices interrupted her solitude.

"Listen, we have not much time, Mrs. Havens. He should be coming along this way any minute. Here are two guineas. You may keep them if you agree to assist me."

"What shall I do, Miss Worth?"

"When we meet him and turn back to walk with him, you will lose the heel to your boot right about here. Bang at it with this rock, that should loosen it. Then I shall send you back to the hall by the fastest path. He might offer to accompany you, but you must refuse all assistance, and be very persuasive."

"Of course, Miss Worth. I understand completely."

Lydia could not help spying on this exchange, and watched Mrs. Havens tuck the coins into the handle of her parasol. She thought it was an incredibly foolish scheme. And what was the point of having a duenna or companion or whatever she was, if she could so easily be bribed to abandon her post. How did this lend countenance to anyone?

The two schemers passed out of her hearing. She dismissed it as more of the stupidity inherent in society, and returned to her novel.

To her irritation, her repose was shortly interrupted again.

"These gardens are heavenly, are they not?" Miss Worth had returned.

"I should say that they fall rather into the realm of *earthly* delights. That is their design, it would seem." It was a man's voice, deep and strong and smooth, and, Lydia thought, quite bored.

Anyone with such a voice would have a distinct advantage in the world, an ability to influence the listener with the pure beauty of the sound. Indeed, she found herself a little spellbound by it. Who was he?

"Oh, quite right. How clever!" Miss Worth simpered. "According to the *on-dits*, the master has actually constructed these ruins and temples that you see scattered around the grounds to lend romance to the landscapes. But they look for all the world like they are authentic. Delightful, is it not?"

Lydia winced. This was just the sort of inane prattle that she was trying to escape, and now she was a captive audience, for she could hardly shuffle out of the tree, excuse herself and scurry away. Could she? No, no. Of course not.

"I suppose the romance is diminished somewhat by the knowledge that they are recent artifices rather than ancient artefacts." The beautiful voice vibrated through Lydia. It was terribly distracting.

"Oh, how you have a way with words, my lord!"

The party was coming into view, and Lydia peeked through the branches of her perch to spy upon them. Mrs. Havens dawdled behind and appeared to be fidgeting with her boot. She was sensibly dressed, with mousy hair, and when she stood up she revealed a remarkably plain face. An ideal companion for the other lady, then.

Miss Worth wore a pink day dress, rabidly frothing with lace, and held a matching parasol, which was unnecessary in the shade of the trees.

The young lady was decidedly pretty—that is, her prettiness was the product of decision. She had some natural appeal, with blue eyes,

3

blond curls, and a slightly up-turned nose, but her hair, dress, bearing, and way of lowering her lashes demurely all fixed her as pretty in a premeditated sort of way.

Lydia wondered if it were having the desired effect on the gentleman, or whether *the romance were diminished somewhat by the knowledge of the artifice.*

"Miss Worth, my lord, forgive me. I am afraid that I must turn back." Mrs. Havens interrupted the tête-à-tête.

"Whatever is the matter, Mrs. Havens?" Miss Worth's mouth formed a dainty rosebud O of concern.

"My boot heel has come free. I shall turn back. Perhaps there is a servant at the hall who might fix it. If so, I shall catch up with you later."

Lydia wished she could see the face of the lord, but as he was a great deal taller than the ladies, any view of his head was entirely blocked. She could not make out anything aside from well-tailored clothes and broad, nicely shaped shoulders.

Not at all to Lydia's surprise, the beautiful voice of the gentleman protested. "Nothing of the sort. We shall walk you back to the hall. In any event, it is not suitable for Miss Worth to be unaccompanied."

Lydia inferred that he meant *not suitable to be alone with me.*

"Oh, but this forest is simply divine. And I shall have your company, my lord. What could be further above reproach than the companion-ship of an earl?"

Lydia smiled to herself. An earl. The young lady had a rather great stag in her sights. His lordship did not seem the least bit interested. He took the arm of Mrs. Havens to lend her his support.

"It will not be much of a retrenchment," said the earl. "And the forest will still be here after we have deposited your friend at the hall and found a suitable chaperone for you."

Lydia remarked that he wore a black armband. In mourning. So the lady's quarry was already wounded. She wondered if she should assist the poor stag, for he could not know that the two huntresses had arranged a trap for him.

But Lydia really did not wish to be dragged into the stupid society from which she sought escape. She wanted to read her book. And anyway, the earl sounded as though he were determined not to be left alone with Miss Worth. All would be well.

"Truly, my lord," Mrs. Havens persisted, "I prefer to avoid such a fuss over me. I can find my way back, well enough. And Miss Worth has so few opportunities for a walk in a proper woods. I should hate to spoil things for her."

"Oh true! I shall not leave for anything, and it would not be genteel to leave me alone here." Miss Worth had discovered a way to make her spoilt wheedling pretty, as well.

What a perfectly formed pout and trembling lip—and another glance up through lowered lashes, just for good measure. Lydia felt faintly nauseous. The poor man.

She sighed, closed her book and cleared her throat loudly. "As you appear to be at an impasse, my lord, perhaps I might suggest a solution."

The party was thrown into confusion, looking about for the woman who had spoken, but unable to see her.

"You are in hiding." Miss Worth did not conceal her displeasure at this intrusion. "It might be better if you show yourself before you presume to address an earl."

"No need to stand upon ceremony, Miss Worth," said the earl. "Though I should like to see the person who offers me counsel."

Could she hear a smile? She wished she could see his face. "I am situated quite comfortably here, my lord."

5

"Then by no means should you bestir yourself on my account." The earl spoke in a lazy drawl.

Was he being sarcastic? She was not certain. "Would you care to hear my advice, my lord, or shall I save my breath to cool my porridge?"

"I think you should." Miss Worth was now looking up. "I believe she is up in one of the trees."

"*I* should very much like to hear your suggestion, Miss." The earl over-rode all objection.

"Very well. I suggest that your lordship can both send Mrs. Havens back to the hall to fix her boot, and stay in the wood to please Miss Worth, so long as you both remain in the vicinity. You see, my lord, she would be chaperoned, after a fashion, for I am here. Of course, your lordship could also assist Mrs. Havens back. For Miss Worth will not be alone, either, if she waits with me."

"Ah. A helpful dryad." His voice was warm, enticing. "These grounds have more romance than was first apparent."

"And who, pray tell, are *you* that you might lend *me* countenance?" Miss Worth's pretty face was now visibly angry.

"It is true that we have not been introduced, but I shall make myself known and available as a witness, should anyone question the propriety of your sylvan amusements." Lydia could not resist further provoking the pink débutante.

She still could not see his face, but the earl's shoulders were shaking with quiet laughter. Lydia was now thoroughly enjoying herself.

"I thank you for the favour," Miss Worth's spine straightened, "but you will pardon me if I do not wish to remain in the company of some unknown woman who goes about hiding in trees and spying on people."

"Of course," Lydia agreed. "That is entirely understandable. One cannot be too careful about the character of those in one's immediate company. Upon reflection, I retract my offer. I shall learn from your example, Miss Worth, and refuse to be left alone with a young lady who gives her companion two guineas to feign a broken shoe so that she might be left alone in the woods with an unsuspecting gentleman. No less than an earl, it would seem, which explains the expense, I suppose."

"That is a vicious lie! We must leave this insulting person and continue on our promenade at once. Let us not permit this nobody to ruin our pleasure."

"And what of Mrs. Havens' shoe?" The earl's voice was calm.

"I will not let my friend be so abused." Mrs. Havens looked a little uncomfortable, as though she knew not what to suggest. "You may both examine my reticule. You will find no guineas."

Miss Worth sighed in exasperation at her companion. Lydia felt a little sorry for Mrs. Havens. The woman must be a bit thick. Thick and plain, truly an ideal companion for a Miss Worth.

And what young lady really needed a companion? Could she not be chaperoned by friends and family in the usual way? On the other hand, her parents might need extra assistance in watching over such a daughter. Lydia hoped the notion should never occur to her own mother.

"That will not be necessary, Mrs. Havens." Miss Worth patted her companion on the arm. "No one seriously believes the slanders of a young woman who hides in trees."

"No indeed. Who would believe a person who was sitting in a position where she could remain undetected and yet have a clear view over this path along which you two ladies just passed, and furthermore who has no motive to lie?" Lydia clicked her tongue. "A most unreliable witness. But in any case, you may as well put your purse away, Mrs. Havens."

"No." The slightly dull woman persisted. Her cheeks were now glow-

ing. "I have been accused and I will show the contents of my reticule."
She opened it and showed it to Miss Worth who pushed it away and
rolled her eyes.

She then extended it to the earl. Lydia wished she could see his facial
expression.

"Your lordship will not find anything in there, for she spirited the
coins away into the shaft of her parasol. The handle screws off, you
see, my lord."

"Does it, indeed?" He sounded vaguely intrigued.

"You must not listen to this awful person. She is only bent on making
mischief. No doubt she has set her cap for you and lain in waiting."
Miss Worth's face was flushing.

Lydia could not help laughing loudly. "The thief suspects everyone of
robbery. My lord, there is a simple way of determining the truth."

"May I, Mrs. Havens?"

"I should prefer that you did not, my lord."

"Yes, one cannot go about ruining a lady's parasol on the say-so of
some," Miss Worth waved her hand, "*tree person.*"

"I shall be very careful," the earl promised.

Poor Mrs. Havens' hand trembled a little as she handed the earl her
parasol. She gave an apologetic look to Miss Worth, whose face now
looked decidedly not pretty.

He shook the parasol lightly, and the rattle of the coins was audible
even from Lydia's position.

"You can hear what condition it is in. Pray be terribly gentle, my lord,
and do not twist it 'round, for the handle is clearly about to fall to
pieces. Have mercy on poor Mrs. Havens, for it is the only parasol she
has along."

Lydia wondered exactly whom this pink-clad fraud thought she was fooling.

The earl gave the handle a twist, and it opened. He poured out the two guineas.

Mrs. Havens' face was beet red as she sputtered, "Forgive me, my lord. I forgot those were in there."

"Quite understandable, Mrs. Havens." The earl handed her the parasol and guineas. "Under the circumstances, it might slip anyone's mind. After all, you were distracted by difficulties with your shoe."

Lydia had to admit that watching this entire scene unfold was better than reading her novel.

"I do not know anything about those coins. *I* certainly did not give them to her." Miss Worth was doing her best to look surprised.

"Miss Worth, it pains me that I must be so direct, but if you are contemplating telling me that this woman has stolen the money, please do not."

"But, *I—*"

"Not another word, if you please. I believe I have had quite enough of the gardens for one day. I shall depart." When the irrepressible Miss Worth made to go with him, he added, "Alone."

He walked a few steps and then turned to face the tree, so Lydia could now see only the smooth contours of his well-muscled calves.

"I am in your debt, dryad. I only wish that I might know to whom I speak. Perhaps we shall meet again under more pleasant circumstances, unless, of course, you would walk with me back to the hall."

"That might be interpreted badly, my lord." Lydia wished she were not such a coward. "But I wish you a pleasant afternoon. I hope we shall meet again." If only she could think of something more clever to say.

She did, truly, hope they would meet again. Something in the polished restraint of his strength, his alluring voice and broad shoulders made her want to be closer to him. If only the other two women were not present, perhaps they might get better acquainted. He was certainly the first man who had seemed remotely interesting to her.

Though, perhaps it was merely that circumstances forced a more entertaining exchange than one generally encountered at tea. But he definitely had wit. It was too bad he was an earl, for they were unlikely to be in the same social circles. She resigned herself to her fate and turned back to her book, as the earl strode away.

"And what have you to say for yourself?" Miss Worth's voice was cold as she stared up at the tree with pure hatred in her eyes.

"Are you still here?"

"Do not think you will get away with this." The pink of the girl's dress now amplified the angry blotches that were forming on her cheeks. Some people really should not permit themselves to become enraged. Lydia knew from personal experience how horridly red a face could become if one did not control one's emotions.

"I have not gotten away with anything. I have merely prevented you from doing so."

"I will have your name."

"Will you? I think not. It is an acquaintance I should rather avoid."

"Coward. Come out and show yourself." Miss Worth scratched at her cheek.

"If you are so intent upon knowing who I am, why do you not come up here? Then we shall see who is a coward."

"I do not scamper about in trees."

"Well, that is settled then. You may go now and leave me to my book."

"You cannot dismiss me. Come down at once. I demand it." The chit actually stomped her foot.

"And you cannot command me. But I can ignore you."

Miss Worth bent to pick up a rock. "I know how to get a rat out of a tree."

Lydia laughed. "You cannot be serious."

"I am. Come down or I shall knock you down." She rubbed her face with the back of her hand.

Lydia took measure of the bizarre young miss. Despite her mother's best efforts, Lydia had extensive experience scrapping with the farm children on her family's estate. She knew how to size up an opponent, and Miss Worth was a weakling.

"I must admit you have audacity," Lydia replied. "But even if you could see me, I doubt very much that you could hit the broad side of a barn with a bucket of slop. Honestly, can you lift anything heavier than a scant cup of tea?"

"I am sure your experience with manual labour makes you feel superior, but I will best you. Come down, or be pelted." Miss Worth was determined.

"I am waiting. Let us see this Amazonian arm."

Miss Worth threw her rock as best she could. It flew into some branches ten feet away from Lydia.

"A little to the left and you might manage to hit your own foot."

The incensed young woman picked up three more rocks and hurled them in rapid succession, each missing worse than the last as Lydia laughed and her assailant grew more angry.

"It is difficult to be certain, but I believe you may be aiming at the wrong tree."

"Miss Worth, someone is coming." Mrs. Havens had to physically restrain the girl from hurling another stone, just as a group of people came around the bend of the path.

Lydia recognized one of the voices. She remained very still.

"Darling! Mrs. Havens! There you both are. Mrs. Norwood, may I present my daughter, Emily, and this is Mrs. Havens. We have been looking for you this last hour, Emily. What have you done to your face?"

Miss Worth rubbed at her blotches. "It feels hot."

"Is that a rock? Whatever are you doing?"

"I just..."

Lydia held her breath. Would the stupid girl risk exposing herself just to spite Lydia?

"I was just," Miss Worth dropped the rock, "looking at interesting rocks. I do not feel quite well." She scratched again.

Lydia realized suddenly that the redness was not merely a product of the girl's anger. Such blotches did not usually get itchy. Hopefully it was some fatal condition.

"If I may say so, Mrs. Worth, those welts look quite serious." It was Lydia's mother. "I think you should get her home and fetch a doctor as soon as may be."

"She is warm. I believe you are right, Mrs. Norwood. Emily, do not scratch! You will ruin your beautiful skin."

The girl complied and lowered her gaze with a meekness that Lydia could not reconcile to the vicious tyranny that she had just witnessed. The party hurried off down the path as quickly as they could, while Mrs. Havens hobbled along behind.

Lydia realized that she would not get to read more of her novel, and had best return to the hall by the long route to give the Worths time to clear out before she reunited with her mother. A meeting with Miss Worth would be too risky.

In fact, rejoining her mother might carry risks of its own, for Mrs. Norwood, no matter how accustomed to her disappearing daughter, would not be best pleased. She set aside *The Necromancy of Abruggio,* tucking it into her satchel with a sigh, and began to climb down from her tree.

CHAPTER 2

*L*ord Aldley stomped toward his barouche. He was oblivious to the sculptures in the Classical Greek style, the shadowy temple ruins, and even the assortment of rare and fragrant flora that lined the walkway.

He preferred to focus his brooding gaze on, and occasionally kick, the rocks on the gravelly path leading from the pleasure gardens to the area where the carriages waited.

The sky was clouding over, but the earl did not care if he got rained on. He could not wait at the hall for the carriage to be brought around, and risk further affronts from the hordes of ambitious women who seemed to lurk in every public venue.

It was insupportable. To have a scheming little chit try to impose upon him and lure him into some sort of compromising situation was not to be endured. But it seemed his lot to be constantly exposed to scheming women. In most cases the mothers were even more mercenary than the daughters, and now that he was actually an earl, and not just the heir apparent, the case was even worse.

He had thought he might have a few quiet moments in some gardens and groves, without having to make the long journey to the family estate at Alderwick Manor that reminded him too painfully of his father. But apparently he was not permitted even this small reprieve.

There was not even a little time to mourn the loss of a beloved parent before he was set upon by the marriage vultures. He had only just transitioned from full mourning to an armband, and this was viewed as an invitation. These society women were reprehensibly ruthless.

Even his mother was determined to marry him off for her own advantage. He was persuaded that she never loved his father, for she seemed entirely unaffected by his death.

She had removed herself voluntarily from Alderwick Manor to take up permanent residence in the London home, perhaps a little sooner than could be considered decent, claiming that she felt he should have full reign at the estates, as he was the earl, now. He did not need his dowager mother in the way of his running things, she said.

And besides, in London she would be in the best position to find him a wife. As though her husband's death should never give anyone the slightest reason for pause in their business. It was unseemly how quickly she moved on. Were all women such plotting, unfeeling creatures?

Yet there was one woman, a total stranger to him, who had tried to help him and protect him from the schemers. And she was disinterested. She made no effort to insinuate herself, although she knew of his rank. She did not even seek an introduction when he offered to make her acquaintance.

And she had made him laugh when she skewered Miss Worth with her wit and sang froid. He wished he could do that, but earls were hampered by the stiff fabric of decorum. Well, perhaps many earls lived a debased life, following whatever whim sprang to mind without regard to correctitude, but he, at least, did not.

This dryad was quite shameless, however, and he could not help admiring it. She did not let social niceties stop her from putting it to the little fraud—although she was rather high up in a tree at the time, so he supposed, as a practical matter, social niceties were not under serious consideration.

Still, had she remained silent, her tree-climbing could have gone undetected, and he might have been entrapped. Perhaps she was not entirely proper, but she spoke like a gentle woman, and she was brave. She was someone he wanted to know.

But he had left without ever seeing her face. He supposed it was hopeless. How could they ever meet now, when he was on the eve of departing for France? He did not know when he would come back, but he had to get away.

He needed time to grieve, far removed from people who hurled their unwed daughters at his head. Someday he wanted something real, not a would-be countess, but a woman of substance who could love him for himself. Was this one luxury an earl could never have?

Lord Aldley reached his carriage, and flung the door open before his coachman, Trodder, could do so. He looked inside, and suppressed a curse.

"Trodder. Apparently this young lady is in some confusion about which is her carriage. I wonder that the coat of arms was not a bit of a hint. Kindly assist her out."

"Yes, my lord." Trodder gave his head a shake, but suppressed the grin that threatened to sprout at the corners of his mouth. He offered a hand to the débutante inside, who pouted among bales of tulle and yellow muslin. "Allow me, Miss."

Aldley pinched the bridge of his nose. He had to get out of ruddy England.

CHAPTER 3

*L*ydia found herself thinking of the earl again, as she made yet another voyage into London at the end of another summer, stuffed into a carriage with her snoring mother and a cache of surplus hat boxes that apparently could not sit up top.

She had not encountered the earl since that day, for she was certain she would recognize his beautiful voice if she heard it again. She wondered if he ever thought of her, if there were any chance that they might meet again.

It was a futile dream, for he was an earl and Lydia could not even claim to be a gentleman's daughter. And she was apparently not irresistible to the opposite sex, either, if her first crack at the London season were held up as an illustration.

Miss Worth had, unfortunately, survived the mysterious pox that smote her that day in the pleasure garden, for Lydia had subsequently seen her in London society. Neither of them let on that they had ever met over a dispute involving trees and rock-throwing, and Lydia could never be certain from her demeanour whether the other young lady recognized her or not.

But she thought not, for Miss Worth had been quite feverish, after all. Yet the illness had not even afflicted the débutante for long, and only marred her face a little, which seemed inequitable. And unlike Lydia, the pretty schemer had been successful in finding a gentleman to marry in her first year out.

Lydia could not repine at this injustice, however, for marriage conveniently removed Miss Worth from London. Nor could she envy the girl. As Lydia was rich, she saw no reason to marry, unless it be for love. And that seemed unlikely.

Mrs. Norwood, however, was not discouraged by the spectacular failure that was her daughter's first season. So Lydia, now nineteen, was left to glumly contemplate her fate as she listened to the rattle of the carriage and her mother's somnolent breathing, and stared out at the passing greenery, wishing she could ride her own horse to town.

Mrs. Norwood stirred and looked at Lydia, rubbing an eye. "I really wish you had not spent yesterday burning your nose like a chestnut."

"I did not do it just to vex you, Mama. A stout breeze took away my bonnet."

"Then you should tie it properly. Red-haired young ladies must be ever so careful with their skin. And indeed you needn't compound the problem of your wild-looking hair by taking every opportunity of running 'round with it falling out of your chignon and full of twigs." Her mother yawned.

She looked at Lydia again and shook her head. "The freckles are bad enough, but I cannot be held responsible for our respectability as a family if you continue going about in all weather with half a forest on your head where your bonnet should be."

"That was just the one time." Lydia tried not to smile at the memory. "Papa was teaching me how to fish, and all the best spots are hidden away behind a bit of bramble."

"Do not remind me." Her mother put a hand to her temple. "I have already had a word with him. No more fishing."

Lydia sighed.

"And you must lose this habit of sighing so much, or it will be taken as a sign of a sullen personality, which is not at all attractive to gentlemen."

When they arrived at their London home, Lydia sneaked into the kitchen. She found Ole Maeb on a stool peeling potatoes over a bucket for Cook.

The eldest servant rose stiffly when she saw Lydia and waddled over to receive a kiss on the cheek. Cook pretended not to see it. Then the beloved old woman leaned to Lydia's ear and said, "The master is upstairs in the library, Miss."

Lydia stole a biscuit on the way out. Cook also did not see this.

When Lydia entered the great, book-laden chamber, she found her father seated in an over-stuffed leather chair.

"So at last you have arrived, my dear. I hope you had a pleasant journey."

She kissed him on the cheek, then slouched into the plump comforts of one of the chairs, inhaling the smell of leather. "Mama was not very forgiving about my nose, nor about our fishing trip."

"No, I can imagine not." His bushy brows arranged themselves in the comical way that always meant secret amusement. "But I have been thinking upon it, and I can see her point. All your mother desires is a good match for you. In truth I have done you a great disservice by encouraging your, um, *country ways*."

"Papa, I despise the city." She tapped her foot idly. "And I do not see what the great fuss about it is, either, if all people do is go about taking horrid refreshments in various parlours and trying to outdo each other."

"But you must be looking forward to the balls, surely."

"I enjoy dancing, but everyone seems to be at their most superior at a ball. I prefer a country dance, where the object is merriment, not making a display. And I so seldom get asked to dance at a ball."

"Well, then, you had best heed your mother's advice and stop burning your nose."

Lydia huffed. *"Et tu, Brute?"*

"I see I should never have let you see any of Shakespeare's plays. It makes you imagine you are clever."

Lydia merely gave him a look.

"No, I think you must make more effort to present yourself well. Mrs. Norwood advises me that there is to be a tea party soon, at the Delacroixs. You must go and make a good impression. For you may then be invited to the Delacroix dinner party, where I understand a countess is to attend. We don't have so many connections to the quality, you know, so you must go and make the most of things."

"Are you really my father, or some very talented imposter?"

"Don't be silly, my dear. Now off you go to pick out a nice frock." He paused and poured himself a drink, grimacing a little, before taking a large gulp and adding, "Wear something pretty, and be charming and such."

CHAPTER 4

*B*y the time of the Delacroix tea party, Lydia was becoming gloomy about her future. Her mother would never give up trying to marry her off to a gentleman of some rank. And what was worse, her father now seemed allied with her mother. Such treachery.

Lydia nibbled an awful tea sandwich, which managed to smell vaguely of wet dog even as it tasted mealy and dry, as she looked about at the garish pink and gold patterned wallpaper. It was one of several recent improvements that Lady Delacroix had enumerated for her daughter's guests, before leaving them to their own scintillating conversation.

She supposed patricide was out of the question.

"And that lace was lovely, I thought. Very expensive," one of the débutantes observed.

Lydia closed her eyes briefly to conceal their rolling back into the sockets. Why had her father insisted on this?

"Oh, it must have been, terribly, I should think. I have heard that Miss Dervish's family is rather well established, and have estates all over the country." Another chit made her contribution to the lively intellectual discourse.

"Did any of you happen to speak with her?" Miss Delacroix's green eyes were animated, and the deep red undertones of her almost black hair lit up as she leaned forward into the ray of sunlight that passed through the great south window, betraying the tiny blue veins at her hairline—a sign of her noble birth, they were given to understand.

"Why, no. We were not introduced," the first débutante conceded.

"No, I do not believe any of us were," came the astonishing revelation from the second maiden, confirmed by a rustle of nodding agreement amongst all the ladies' ribbons.

Except for Miss Ravelsham's ribbons. Her already highly arched eyebrows reached for her golden hairline, as she bit into a cream biscuit with a petite, smirking mouth. She leaned back into the grotesque pink settee with an air of indolence.

Miss Ravelsham's blue eyes sparkled and her petite nose twitched slightly as she enquired, "But what of you, Miss Delacroix? Have *you* made her acquaintance?"

"Well, I have, yes." Miss Delacroix smoothed an imaginary out of place strand of her thick, glossy hair, like a cat preening a whisker.

Of course she had. The other ladies leaned in with a chorus of "oh?", and Miss Ravelsham actually paused in the otherwise relentless shovelling of cream biscuits into her mouth, in order to grin as though enjoying a particularly fine comedy.

After a dramatic pause, Miss Delacroix continued, "And do you know that she came to town with two hundred bonnets?"

A round of titillated gasps followed this comment, and Lydia sunk into deeper despair. Why did her father not call for her quickly, as he promised?

As if responding to an invisible summons, shortly after the cream biscuits were no more, Miss Ravelsham's brother came to collect her and take her to her mother to pick out fabrics for her trousseau.

This gave Lydia an escape plan. "Miss Ravelsham, might I ride with you to the shops? I just recalled that I must purchase a few items. I can send a note to my father to call for me there. It will save him having to accompany me to select ribbons and lace, and the like. He cannot abide such places. You know how fathers are."

"Indeed." Miss Ravelsham's nose twitched again.

"You would be doing us both a great favour."

"I should be delighted to have the company, Miss Norwood. My brother, I should warn you, will probably be in a foul mood, because he hates escorting me around. But that is the lot of brothers, is it not? He will be rid of me soon enough." Miss Ravelsham smiled the complacent smile of the woman who has discharged the great feminine duty of betrothal.

Lydia could smell the sweet scent of caramelized sugar on her breath as Miss Ravelsham leaned in and added, "And perhaps he will be more civil if you come along. So you see, you will be doing me a great favour, as well."

Miss Ravelsham was quite agreeable, Lydia decided. She would remember to send her a large box of sweets as thanks.

"What, is Miss Norwood leaving us, too?" Miss Delacroix broke off from her illustrative discussion of all that could be gleaned about Miss Dervish's clothing from the whisperings of servants and half an hour's acquaintance at a steamy pump room in Bath. "But you mustn't break up our little party."

Miss Delacroix only just managed to avoid stomping her impossibly small foot, but it moved involuntarily and rustled the lace trim of her muslin skirts. "If you go, I shall not have you at our dinner party next week. We shall be entertaining Miss Dervish, herself, you know."

"Oh, why must you torture me with the threat of such deprivations?" Lydia wrung her hands dramatically. "I am only being dutiful, for I must work out a suitable ensemble. My old frocks simply will not do now that *Miss Dervish* is in town. Two hundred bonnets, 'pon rep! I should not wish to shame you. No, I am afraid I must go, even if it costs me the invitation to your irresistible dinner party, though it would pain me deeply. Better not to attend at all, than to make a dowdy appearance. Go I must."

Miss Ravelsham stifled a cough.

"Well, then... Yes, very well." Miss Delacroix seemed to seriously contemplate the matter. "The right attire is ever so important. In that case, I suppose we might let you go."

Lydia wondered if there were one amongst the ladies they were leaving who was capable of fathoming sarcasm, irony, satire, or anything more indirect than what could be communicated with a fluttering fan or a heavily underlined letter. She knew it was bad of her, but could not help her disdain.

With a sigh of relief, Lydia allowed herself to be handed up into an ebony black carriage, embellished with gold leaf and mother of pearl, by Miss Ravelsham's brother, Frederick.

Lydia could not really understand what Miss Ravelsham meant about her brother being in a foul mood, because, though he was quiet, he seemed amiable, and smiled fondly at his sister. This sweet vignette of sibling affection made Lydia wish she had a brother or a sister with whom she could share such closeness.

"What is that fragrance?" The air in the carriage was fresh and invigorating in Lydia's nose.

"It is lemon and orange." Miss Ravelsham patted a sachet hanging from a hook on the carriage wall. "I have scented sachets in all of my carriages, and I like to keep them well aired. I find it stimulates the mind."

"I think you must be right. How clever."

When they arrived at the shop in Sloane Street, Mrs. Ravelsham was already surrounded by seven different bolts of the finest silk. Lydia was not sure how long she could tolerate this degree of fluttering and clucking, so she excused herself to slip over to the shop across the way for "a better look at a pearl-trimmed lace collar."

She only felt a faint pang of guilt over her deception. She knew a good shortcut home, which was only to be taken in dry weather, and of which her mother would have thoroughly disapproved, were she aware of its existence. It also passed the private club at which she was fairly certain her father was whiling away his time at cards, unmindful of the acute torments to which he had subjected his daughter.

As she lifted her skirt to step over a large crack in the dirty street, from which an evil odour of vomit and ale escaped into the humid air, she questioned what possible motivation her father could have for cajoling her into that horrid tea party.

She was accustomed to her mother's inexhaustible enthusiasm for insipid gatherings and balls, but her father had never before insisted on her attending these sort of *female tea engagements*, as he called them. He had been her refuge, permitting her to spend at least her summers running a bit wild in the country.

And he had always taken her side when she was deep in dispute with her mother over attending one or another congregation of clucking hens. There were a certain number of engagements that could not be avoided, of course. But she could not see how today's tea party was so terribly special.

The smell of pipe smoke alerted her that she was passing the back entrance to her father's club. She stopped a servant, who was entering with a crate of vegetables. "You there! Would you get word to Mr. Norwood? I believe he is inside."

The servant was clearly a little confused to see a well-dressed young lady hanging about unescorted in an alleyway near the service entrance of a gentlemen's club. "I believe he is, Miss."

"I am his daughter. Would you please tell him that he needn't call for me at the Delacroix's. I shall be home before he is finished squandering my inheritance at cards."

"Ah, well..."

"You may phrase it more delicately, if you like." She smiled. She could hardly expect him to repeat such a thing to a member.

"Yes, Miss."

She was about to walk away, when a man called out through an open window on the second floor, "So what is your fare, then?"

The servant turned ashen, and coughed slightly, rushing off to discharge his errand.

"Well, how much?" repeated the mysterious cad.

Irritated by the fact that she was blushing at this question, Lydia squared her shoulders, turned her back, and marched off as best she could on the uneven, muddy surface of the alleyway, without so much as a glance at the man in the window.

This was exactly what her mother warned her would happen to girls who scampered about town unescorted. But why must the males of the species make such vile assumptions?

The way home seemed filled with unkempt men who stared and appeared to think evil thoughts, or called out in some incomprehensibly corrupted street cant, as though uttering evil spells through the smoky air of the city.

Shortcuts had always been magical paths through which she could travel undetected by the dragons of *society*. But the enchantment of her childhood was broken and scattered among the gravel and garbage at her feet. Being brave was one thing, but why had she never seen before how dangerous the alleyways were?

She arrived home a little chilled and still a bit nervous, but entirely recovered from her humiliation. Lydia raised a finger to her lips and winked at Ole Maeb, who opened the servants' entrance for her and smiled conspiratorially. Lydia scrawled out a quick note to be delivered to Miss Ravelsham at the shop. It was sure to get there before they left, for the servants knew the shortcuts better than she did.

Unfortunately Mrs. Norwood detected her sneaking daughter as she tried to creep up to the library.

"Lydia."

She froze midway up the staircase.

"You are home from tea rather early. Where is your father?"

"I believe he is at the club. I got a lift with Miss Ravelsham." It was not exactly a lie.

"Miss Ravelsham? This is rather out of her way. Why did you not invite her in?"

"She had to go to the shops for some fabric. With her mother. For her trousseau."

Her mother squinted at Lydia. "Well that is in the wrong direction entirely. I hope you did not put them out."

Lydia decided it was time to change the subject. "Did your new curtains arrive?"

"No. And it is most vexing, for we are to have Lady Delacroix to tea on Wednesday, and I want everything to be perfect for her. Her younger son, Pascal, will be returning to town soon, you know. I understand he has become quite a delightful young man."

Having met his sister, Lydia thought it unlikely. "Oh, indeed? Well I do hope your curtains will arrive shortly."

"Come and sit with me, my dear. We can discuss what you will wear to their dinner party."

Lydia consciously stopped herself from gritting her teeth, and joined her mother in the south parlour.

Perhaps she could coax Ole Maeb into finding her some roast beef later. Lydia had eaten as few of the loathsome tea sandwiches as was tolerably polite—the Delacroix's renowned French cook was apparently on leave—and so she was rather hungry.

They were halfway through an enumeration of all the possible forms of attire Lydia might be oppressed into wearing to the Delacroix dinner, when the tedium was broken by the arrival of Mr. Norwood and an unexpected guest.

It was a man only slightly younger than her father, with hair greying at the temples and somewhat portly of build, but with a pleasant smile that reached up to his dark brown eyes.

"My dears, let me introduce you to Aldus Mortimer. He is the grandson of my father's good friend, Ainsley Truhold. Aldus, here are my wife Gertrude and my daughter Lydia."

Mrs. Norwood rang the bell.

"Not tea, I think, Mrs. Norwood. Order some wine and some roast beef, if you will. The offerings at the club were hardly worth eating. You wouldn't object to a bit of sustenance, eh, Mortimer?

"In consideration of how you have lightened my pocket book at the card table, I believe I shall be happy to eat and drink as much of your fine fare as I am able."

Mrs. Norwood turned her cheek slightly, as she did when she was pretending not to hear or notice something. She liked to imagine that her husband was more cultivated than he was, and that he discussed business, politics and other important matters at his club, and did not, in fact, spend his time there gambling and drinking perhaps a bit more than he ought.

It was odd how different Lydia's parents were. Her father, though brilliant and a great reader, was not terribly refined—at times even a bit coarse. But her mother was the daughter of a country gentleman, and though almost too scrupulous, loved London, but avoided public assemblies and amusements.

In her innocence, Lydia often wondered how they should ever have become interested enough in one another to marry. Now that she had attained the wise old age of nineteen, she understood that people married for much more practical reasons than personal interest, or even than the secret impulses hinted at in her novels.

She was determined to avoid marriage as long as possible. What husband would ever let her be as free as she had been all her young life?

The roast beef and claret arrived, as well as a bottle of brandy, and Lydia set about devouring two large, juicy slices with still warm bread, rich salted butter and a few pickled onions. Her mother turned her cheek.

She dared not partake in any of the brandy, as it was apparently a very firm rule that young ladies did not drink strong liquors—even if they were not, in fact, *ladies*. And the wine was also off the menu, as it made her face go quite red.

The servant brought Lydia a glass of milk. Mr. Mortimer and her father were partaking liberally, however, and discussing the goings on in Knottington Place, Mr. Mortimer's estate.

It was not excessively interesting, and Lydia's mind wandered to the book she had recently purchased, *Accursed Abbey*, which showed great promise of being wonderfully lurid. If only she could find some way of sneaking off to her tree house, she could put a small dint in it before supper.

Maybe she could get Cook to pack up some bread and beef tomorrow, and she could spend the whole day there, under some pretence or another. If only they could have stayed in the country. She had so much more time to herself, there.

After they had eaten, her father asked, "Lydia, would you not like to show Mortimer the rose gardens, while I have a word with your mother?"

In fact, she would not like to at all, but she knew that was entirely irrelevant. What could he have to discuss with her mother that could possibly be so urgent? She stood and smiled. "Certainly. This way, if you please, Mr. Mortimer." She led him through to the east garden.

"Well, these are very lush and healthy plants," Mr Mortimer said cheerfully. "I think it should be quite lovely to sit out here on summer mornings."

"I suppose it might, but I confess I do not come to this garden often. Roses are my mother's great passion, not mine."

"A lady who dislikes roses. That I do not often encounter." There was something in the way that he said it that made her a little nervous.

"I think it is more indifference than dislike. But however I might feel about roses, we are never here for most of the summer. We generally summer in Nesterling Lodge after about May. My mother is quite in love with London, and my father with the country, you see. Although he always has enough business to keep him occupied here. If we return to town just after Michaelmas, my mother thinks it too late, and my father too early. From my perspective, I believe whoever wrote the story of Persephone and Hades must have been thinking of the London season."

He chuckled. "Be careful not to eat any pomegranate seeds. Are you at least looking forward to Lady Delacroix's dinner? Your mother is very enthusiastic about it."

Lydia hesitated. She disliked lying, but such situations called for a delicate rearrangement of the truth. "I am sure it will be quite the thing. Many of the young ladies among my acquaintance are all in a flutter about how to arrange their hair. I believe that is as good a ground as any to suppose it will be a grand success. Though their anticipation of upcoming balls has them in even greater throes of ecstasy."

He smiled and his brown eyes twinkled. "You do not much care for balls, do you?"

She began thinking of a diplomatic reply, but he cut her off. "No, you needn't politely answer. Your father has already outed you as a consummate avoider of society. I should very much prefer to be hunting, myself."

Lydia agreed. She loved to dance, but she hated the stuffiness of London balls and the extreme control she had to exert over her tongue. It was horrid to always feel like you were about to make the social gaffe of the century.

Hunting was much more to her taste. She rather missed her hunter, Ari, who was probably the largest in their county, but leaped like a ballerina and was most intelligent, even for a horse. Her mother advised her, however, that speaking candidly about her love of jumping over hedges was a bad idea.

"So you are here on business, I suppose." She could not think of much else to say.

"You suppose wrongly. I am come to London principally to partake in the balls and assemblies. In fact, I shall attend Lady Goodram's ball, which I understand will be your first ball of the season."

Lydia paused. There could only be one reason why a single, independent man might engage in the season's amusements, if he disliked them so much. But she wished to avoid such a turn in the conversation.

"Yes. I am very much looking forward to spending time with Lady

Goodram. And I do enjoy dancing, but I admit, I should prefer it if the occasion were not a ball. Balls are not really designed to make the daughters of commoners feel at ease."

He smiled. "But surely it must be of some consequence being the sole heiress to a fortune larger than that of all the gentle folk in the room taken together."

"It is of enough consequence that I get invited. I nonetheless enjoy an unimpeded view up a rather lot of noses, which is most extraordinary for someone of my not inconsiderable height. But I suppose we needn't discuss the season, as neither of us is overly fond of it. How long has it been since you and my father have seen each other?"

"Many years, I am afraid. And that is my fault. You can imagine how pleased I was that your father did not apprehend my absorption with improving Knottington Place as a slight, and took up with me as though no time had elapsed. He is one of my favourite people, is your father."

"And also one of mine. In fact, I should say my favourite, but you would be certain to repeat it in his hearing, and he thinks entirely too well of himself as it is." She smiled, but turned away quickly when she saw the way that he returned her smile. He was searching her face for something, and she did not like it.

"If you have seen quite enough of the rosebushes, would you mind if we returned indoors?" Lydia wrapped her arms around her waist. "This shawl is insufficient against the wet cold. I believe I require a cup of tea."

"Certainly. Although I cannot stay, I am afraid. I only meant to make a brief visit today. But I hope I may call again."

"I am sure that would make my father very happy."

He smiled and bowed his head slightly. "Thank you for the tour of the garden. I shall go take leave of your parents now." And he was gone.

Lydia wasted no time, but ran through the empty parlour and upstairs to her rooms, ripping off the shawl and dove grey day dress, and casting away her kid boots—which had mostly been ruined by her detour home.

The grey, light wool dress she pulled from under her bed was a bit stained, but it was warm and just the thing for climbing. Her mother had tried to throw it away on several occasions, but she could always count on Ole Maeb to rescue objects from her mother's fastidiousness.

She tucked her book into the right front pocket of her apron, threw her heavy boots out the window, and shimmied down a sizeable vine growing under the ledge, until she could reach the nearest branch of the oak with her foot. Her arms and legs knew the route by heart, and in a few moments she moved down the tree to the base and had her boots laced up.

As she stood, she heard the sound of hands clapping, and snapped around to see a man's head peering over the west wall of the property. She could not help starting at this sudden appearance.

"Truly impressive," the head said. The voice was vaguely familiar, but she could not place it.

The head was handsome: tanned skin, gleaming blue eyes, and teeth as white as pearls, if rather too sharp-looking to be entirely genteel in appearance. The whole portrait was framed with dark glistening curls.

He even had an aquiline nose, which was her favourite sort of nose, greatly to be preferred to her own small, straight one, which, to her horror, often got called *refined*, when it wasn't too red to politely be mentioned.

However handsome the head, which was still apparently amused, it certainly ought not be suspended above the enclosure of their back yard. No decent man would do such a thing. Lydia resolved not to satisfy the audacious head with any response. She might not be a person of much importance, but one ought not be mocked in the privacy of one's own property.

She left the sound of laughter far behind her, as she trotted over to the trees on the east side and disappeared into their branches. From this point she could move via the ropes and catwalks she had installed between the tree tops, and escape over the north wall into the park behind.

The tree-house was a fairly simple affair. When she was twelve, and hated London even more, though subjected to it less often, she had needed an escape. She had scratched the little hut together with some wood and nails she filched from the workmen her father tasked with making improvements to their London home.

It had taken her some time to sneak the supplies into the park very, very early in the mornings. In truth, the workmen had felt sorry for her, or perhaps were encouraged by her father, who had discovered her plan, and they corrected the most decrepit aspects of her construction.

But in her mind, it was all hers, and she was proud that it was still standing and strong enough to support her. Technically it was squatting, for the park did not belong to her father, but the structure was quite invisible, unless one knew how to look for it.

And her mother would never look for her there. Lydia knew she was well beyond the years when she should be doing such foolish things, but she was loathe to give it up. Trees were her element. London was not. She pulled down the rope ladder, and climbed up to the higher branches, breathing deeply of the evergreen scent.

The little box had seemed quite sizeable, if a bit lopsided, when she was a young girl. But she now had to crawl awkwardly through the tiny door, and carefully uncurl her long body into the space. There were several candles and a mat on the floor. A heavy woollen shawl hung on the wall.

She reminded herself to buy some wool blankets to make for a more comfortable reading nest. There was always lots of money available for lady things—her mother wishfully believed that Lydia would develop an interest in clothing if given a generous allowance. Her father gave her even more money for books. So Lydia bought the occasional bonnet or frock as a cover, and hid away most of the money.

She sighed at her childish need for a tree house, but lay down on her dirty little mat anyway, lit the candles, pulled the shawl around her shoulders, and extracted *Accursed Abbey* from her pocket. She was lulled out of this mortal world by the warmth and heady smoke of candles, and soon embroiled in the strange and fascinating life of Elizabeth Whitely.

Then she heard the sounds of someone walking around the trees below. The hairs stood up on her arms. This tree was well off the path, and no one could have a reason for coming into this area. She hardly breathed as she heard the footsteps grow closer.

Her tree house was invisible from the path, but if he made it to the base of her tree and looked up, he could not fail to see the structure. She thought it must be the strange man who had startled her in the back garden. How could he know where to look for her? He must be looking around in the trees generally to see if she were hiding.

Surely he would not think to look for a tree house. But what kind of man would try to hunt her down in this way, sniffing about like a wolf?

The shuffling sounds moved away and Lydia resisted the temptation to peek out after the intruder. Her tree house no longer felt like a refuge.

CHAPTER 5

*L*ydia sat in front of a dressing table lined with sparkling crystal decanters and mysterious silver boxes, as she viewed the final effect of her toilette in the mirror.

Her hair was knotted high on the crown of her head, and long ringlets hung beside each ear. Her nose was still a little pink, but her décolletée was creamy, almost unblemished by freckles, and framed by cerulean blue silk with gold braid trim.

The puffs at the shoulder were gathered into dainty pleats, and embroidered with a sprinkling of little golden butterflies, and more gold braid separated the bodice from the empire waist. She thought she might just come up to the mark.

Her mother directed the maid to apply a little powder to her nose. "Just this once we shall put a little gilding on the lily. But you must not tell anyone I let you wear powder."

"No, Mama."

"I want you in your best looks. Lady Delacroix does you a great honour in inviting you to this party."

"I am sure she does, but was it really necessary to start this ordeal at one o'clock? Now what shall I do but sit around for hours, trying not to wrinkle this dress and developing a headache balancing this impossible jumble upon my head."

"You should be thankful!" Mrs. Norwood scoffed. "In my day the hair itself could take three hours, and it weighed a lot more than your little pile of curls."

The hair was impressive, Lydia had to admit. Her frizzy curls were tamed into smooth clusters of well-behaved, loose ringlets, and the volume on top had been compacted into a very gentle and civilized little gathering—no one would ever suspect the riotous mass that, left to its own devices, ran rough shod over her head and shoulders.

It was a piece of artwork. And so it should be for the price her father was paying the young woman who accomplished it. Miss Grey was clever and used pomades and potions of her own devising. She was not a household servant, but travelled from home to home only dressing hair.

She was in very high demand, but Mrs. Norwood had won the bidding war. No one needed impeccably sleek or inscrutably complex hair as much as a débutante—or as Lydia now called herself, an *encore-tante*—of indifferent birth.

"I want everything to be perfect. Lady Delacroix's son will be there. He is the younger son, but still the son of a *viscount* is a connection worth pursuing. I am also certain Lady Aldley will be there, and it is very important that you make a good impression upon *her* in particular. A lot will depend upon it, you mark my words. You may read in the sitting room until it is time to leave, but not in any high-backed chairs—and mind you do not slouch or touch your hair or eat anything."

Lydia suppressed a sigh. "Yes, Mama." At least she could indulge in her book, but she should not seem too enthusiastic lest Mrs. Norwood enquired into what her daughter was reading.

The hours flew by in the flow of words and paper. The diabolical Orefados was just about to abduct Elizabeth, again, and seriously compromise her, when Lydia's mother interrupted the evil scheme with a summons to the carriage, and a final command.

"Do not drink claret, you cannot afford to get too relaxed and it makes your cheeks go red, which you know will look horrid and tawdry with your hair colour."

A long row of torches lit the walkway to the Delacroix's, and the flames glistened a little wickedly upon the wet paving stones. It put Lydia in mind of the fiery castle of Orefados, and her cheeks grew warm in the memory of Elizabeth's bewilderingly tempting, and at the same time repugnant, predicament.

Remembering her mothers' counter-indication of red cheeks, she drew a breath, forcing herself to focus on the task of greeting people pleasantly.

Then she was drawn away for various introductions, which were never a comfortable ritual, but she met the unbelievably beautiful Miss Dervish with only a little drop of the jaw. When lucky enough to be introduced to the formidable Lady Aldley, she remembered to curtsey deeply and managed to recite the usual substance-less pleasantries without stammering or betraying a single whiff of personality.

But when she came to be introduced to the recently arrived Mr. Pascal Delacroix, and recognized him as the owner of the mysterious head floating above her garden wall, all the stern maternal remonstrance in the world could not keep her face from turning crimson.

"I hope you are not unwell, Miss Norwood? Only you seem flushed." His lips did not betray a smile.

She entertained a hope that he did not recognize her, until he delivered the stealthiest of winks. She chose to pretend she hadn't seen it.

"No, I am very well, thank you, Mr. Delacroix. Coming in from the cold air always makes my cheeks a bit rosy. *Florid* my mother would say." Lydia was proud of herself for mustering a bland and oblivious demi-smile. "But there is no cause for alarm, I assure you." She turned away as quickly as was polite.

Her next introduction was to the unnervingly tall Mr. John Ferrel, and his lovely daughter Miss Louisa Ferrel, who was, to Lydia's relief, just a little taller than Lydia. With the introductions done, the worst was over, and she had only to avoid Mr. Delacroix for the rest of the evening.

She was seated beside Miss Ravelsham at table. This was also a relief, as she had feared being seated beside Miss Delacroix, or worse, her brother. But apparently the gods of decorum and social ambition prevailed over the gods of perverse luck, and she was seated with *the commoners*. An added benefit of her position was that it gave her an unobstructed view of Miss Dervish.

The long, perfectly curved neck and pristinely creamy skin made Miss Dervish look like the work of some ancient artist, carved out of ivory and adorned with sapphire eyes, ruby lips, and a thick swath of polished ebony hair. She seemed far too divine a sculpture to have come to life and been seated at this mortal dining room table across from an ignoble little rag doll like herself.

Lydia became suddenly conscious of her own overly freckled nose. She swore an oath that the next time her mother insisted upon treatments of buttermilk or strawberries, she would meekly comply.

"They are an otherworldly pair, do you not think?" Miss Ravelsham murmured in Lydia's ear.

"Who?"

"Oh, as if I could be speaking of anyone else. I mean Miss Dervish, at whom you have been staring since you sat down, and that devilishly handsome son of a viscount. I see Lady Delacroix knows what she is about, and has seated her son next to the most beautiful woman in town—though I imagine she is more concerned with the young lady's fortune. I understand she has *sixty* thousand."

Lydia could not help admiring, and being thankful for, Miss Ravelsham's mastery of the barely audible whisper. And for the second time in as many weeks, she found herself liking the humorous heiress.

Lydia smiled conspiratorially. "So how much do they say *I* am worth?"

"Oh well," Miss Ravelsham replied without blinking. "The ton are very stupid, you know. No one can count that high."

Lydia chuckled, then turned back to the handsome pair. "Yes, I see your point. I believe we may displease the gods with so much beauty seated at one table."

"*The gods.* I had no idea you had such heathen notions. And Nemesis shall beset them? Yes, let us console ourselves with the thought. Serves them right for being too pretty. I wonder how they can even stand themselves." The glisten of candle light added an extra sparkle of merriment to Miss Ravelsham's blue eyes. Lydia was charmed.

"Miss Ravelsham, I wonder if you would like to come for tea tomorrow? I mean, assuming I survive dinner and cards."

"If you've another box of those sweets you sent last week, most certainly." Miss Ravelsham contrived to smack her lips in silent theatrics.

Lydia suppressed a broad grin. "I believe it might be arranged."

Mr. Delacroix remained engaged in conversation with Miss Dervish when politeness did not require his attending to Lady Aldley who sat on his other side. To Lydia's amazement, he could smoothly manage the imposing dowager countess, while still dropping the occasional, overly intimate whisper in Miss Dervish's ear.

Could this be the same man who had no scruple but to climb a wall and spy upon her in her own back garden? Lady Aldley could not be aware of his character. There was something very wrong when such a man could move so plausibly in polite society.

Lydia could not help but feel that someone should warn Miss Dervish. But one did not lightly cast aspersions at the brothers of viscounts, especially if one were a person of no consequence.

Dinner was finally over, and there were few enough men that they decided not to linger over their cups, but followed the ladies to the next room.

It was decorated in wall paper of jade green and gold—gold being the apparent thread of continuity within Lady Delacroix's recent improvements. Jade vases stood on side boards, and jade *objets d'art* made appearances on every available surface in the room.

Miss Delacroix also sat in a jade green dress that matched her eyes, singing and accompanying herself on the pianoforte . Lydia only found this grating because Miss Delacroix was actually quite pleasant to listen to—yet another of the young lady's accomplishments.

But Lydia might forgive this one area of superiority, if only the girl would play all the time instead of gossiping and prattling on about her various social advancements and desirable acquaintance, and the latest this, and the most sought after that.

"You are clenching your jaw." Miss Ravelsham suddenly appeared by Lydia's side.

"I am sorry." Lydia relaxed her mandible.

"You needn't apologize. I quite understand. But the competition is rather heated in the marriage market, so I thought you might want to put on your best ingénue face."

"You know, I really do not want to be married."

Miss Ravelsham nodded. "I thought as much. It makes you more tolerable company, really, but it would be selfish of me to encourage you in that direction. My own future marital bliss being secured, counselling my friend to appear as little as possible like a blood-thirsty dragon is the least I can do."

Lydia tried to keep her face from splitting. "You are so good at saying the very thing to make me laugh."

"A valuable asset in a friend. Ladies look five times prettier when they are smiling. And a laugh is in almost all instances much more alluring than a long, murderous stare at the hostess' daughter. But enough about that. I just returned from a chat with Miss Dervish, our sister in the title-less money-pot sorority. She is not half bad, you know, once you get over her unspeakable hideousness. And she has invited us to come play whist with her."

"I do not know how to play." Lydia's mother did not wholly disapprove of cards, but was opposed to high stakes gambling, and forbid her father to teach their daughter any games of chance.

"And you are rich. So a perfect fourth, really. You will learn it in a trice. And Lady Aldley will sit down with us. I believe she wants to assure herself that we are suitable grist for *The Five*'s mill. Or, in my case, that my brother's nearest connections do not make him unsuitable."

"The Five?"

"Surely you have heard of the five Gorgons who guard the entrance to the marriage game in high society? Well, four actually, since Lady Percy succumbed to a heart complaint this August past. No? Perhaps your mother was afraid of scaring you off by telling you how things really work. They are like the seven Gorgons of Almack's, only less obvious and more important."

"I do not know much about those Gorgons, either. I am not really of the correct caste."

"Never mind that, there are plenty of unmarried young gentlemen with more title than money, looking to find a rich wife. Do not think yourself safe. Being a commoner will not deliver you from the gaze of the Gorgons. But the material point is that the countess dowager has designs upon filling the late Lady Percy's position, as soon as she has safely married her last child, Lord Aldley, off to someone appropriate. A member of the royal family might do, perhaps. The Five are not permitted to have marriageable children, you see. A conflict of interest, I suppose. And then Lady Aldley will hold the fate of all your seasons as an unwed maiden in her blue-veined, bejewelled talons." Miss Ravelsham pulled a menacing face, and rubbed her hands together in a sinister gesture.

"Honestly, you must not say such things. Someone will hear you. And besides it is unfair to make me laugh so much. The whole room will think me simple."

"Not to worry, no one is looking at us." Miss Ravelsham turned her gaze, and smiled across the room at Miss Dervish, who was accepting a glass of claret from Mr. Delacroix. "But they will at least be looking in our direction, if we are sitting with *her*."

Miss Delacroix finally stood up, and was replaced by another young lady at the instrument.

"Quick, before Miss Delacroix snatches your spot. She is dying to butter up Lady Aldley."

It was not a difficult game to learn, and Lydia's memory was good enough to raise the ire of Lady Aldley, who sat to her left. She had just decided to stop paying such close attention in the interest of diplomacy, when Miss Ravelsham made her efforts fruitless by dealing herself a grand slam.

"How does one prevail against such fortune?" Miss Dervish smiled and shook her head as she gathered the cards. She was more good natured than her scowling partner.

"If we were not all *genteel* sorts, I should demand an independent dealer." Her ladyship's comment was not at all light-hearted. They might have laughed easily, had anyone else said it.

Lady Aldley's own partner had a pedigree even less distinguished than Miss Ravelsham's, so Lydia could not help but note the injustice of the implied slight. At least Miss Ravelsham's father was well-respected within the London ton, and her mother was very distantly related to the Duke of Wellington.

No one actually knew very much about Miss Dervish's father. It was sufficient to know that no scandal appeared to surround him, and that he was very wealthy indeed. Lydia wondered if Miss Ravelsham had been right, if Lady Aldley were sitting at the card table with the three young women furthest from her station, only to judge their suitability.

"I shall offer my services as a dealer." Mr. Delacroix glided smoothly to Miss Dervish's elbow, pulling in a chair. Unfortunately for Lydia's nerves, he had also sat himself next to her. "Perhaps I can change your Ladyship's fortunes."

"Perhaps you can. The deal is to Miss Dervish."

"And I shall give my chair to you, Miss Delacroix, if you care to play a few hands." Miss Ravelsham stood up as Miss Delacroix approached the table. Lydia flashed her new friend an alarmed look as the treacherous little glutton abandoned her for another glass of wine and a chat with Miss Louisa Ferrel. This was rather like leaving a babe in the woods. Mr. Delacroix began to deal.

"Lady Aldley, I wanted to thank you for gracing our little party with your presence. It really is a kind condescension." Miss Delacroix seized her chance to turn the lady up sweet.

"I should never dream of turning down an invitation to one of your mother's excellent dinners." It was not said with much warmth.

"And I understand your son will soon be in town." Miss Delacroix was unsinkable.

"He is very lately returned from Paris, but has been quite consumed with business matters since he arrived. I think it a very good sign of character that a young man take his business obligations seriously." Lady Aldley briefly raised an eyebrow at Mr. Delacroix. "And not always be off attending his own amusement."

"A very good sign, indeed, Lady Aldley. But then, no one could ever doubt the good and serious character of an *Aldley*." It was an absurd thing for an empty bonnet like Miss Delacroix to say, but she was clearly determined to pass herself off as an expert on serious characters.

When she received only a slight nod from Lady Aldley, she continued, "But still, a young man must have some amusement, too. I suppose we might see him at a few gatherings."

"I believe he will be attending several. And, of course, he will be present at *my* ball." Lady Aldley raised her chin. "There will be many *eligible* young ladies there whom I should like him to meet."

Miss Delacroix pressed her lips slightly. Lydia gathered from the pause that Miss Delacroix had not received an invitation to the Aldley ball. Nor had Lydia, though it was a matter of supreme indifference to her.

She suddenly felt sympathy for Miss Delacroix. After all, she had never been unkind to Lydia. In fact she had made efforts to befriend her despite their difference in social standing. She was a bit irritating, but she did not deserve this intentional infliction of pain.

"Speaking of which, I hope you will be attending my ball, Miss Delacroix." They were almost the first words of conversation that Lydia had spoken since she sat down to the card table.

"I have not yet received an invitation, Miss Norwood," Miss Delacroix replied.

"I do not believe my mother has sent them out yet, but you most certainly shall. I know that you must have a very busy schedule for the season, but I should be very honoured if you came. Lady Goodram and her niece will be attending, so there will be at least one young lady of your social standing. Lady Goodram is a friend of my mother's, you see."

Miss Delacroix nodded and smiled, a little coldly, but at least she seemed somewhat recovered from Lady Aldley's remarks.

Lydia felt Mr. Delacroix's eyes on her and she turned to him, catching a penetrating look, which he sustained for a half moment before it turned into a little dismissive smirk and shake of the head. She wondered about it, but thought it prudent not to ask. Had she said something remarkable?

"And finally we win a hand." Lady Aldley laid down the ace she had been saving, then turned suddenly to Lydia. "So your mother is a friend of Lady Goodram's, is she?"

"Yes, my lady." Lydia would have preferred not to have attracted her ladyship's attention.

"And how do they know each other, pray?" Lady Aldley's question felt to Lydia a bit like an interrogation. Did the countess actually think she was fabricating the connection?

"She is the mother of one of my mother's close friends from childhood. They grew up in the same part of Warwickshire."

"Hmm." It was not clear whether she meant to be disapproving and sceptical, or merely thoughtful on the topic.

"Your ladyship has some acquaintance in Warwickshire, I believe. Is it not so? In Warwick?" Mr. Delacroix wore a smile that was so apparently innocent as to invite suspicion—at least from someone with an inkling of his real character.

"I do not know of whom you might be speaking." Lady Aldley trumped a trick, and led the next.

"Ah, forgive me. I must be mistaken." Mr. Delacroix took the last trick, and tucked it smoothly into Lady Aldley's cache. "I only thought that some members of the Beauchamps family claimed acquaintance with you."

"I suppose they might. Mrs. Wurtherly, for example. However, it has been a rather long time since I have laid eyes upon her." Lady Aldley stood up. "I believe I shall call for my carriage. Perhaps you would like to sit in my place, Mr. Delacroix."

"Thank you, Lady Aldley. It would be my great honour, though I am afraid I cannot fill the void in the company. My mother will be quite devastated. May I walk your ladyship out?"

"No. I shall be attended by my manservant shortly. Good evening." They all bowed their farewells.

"Well, that was a sly move, Miss Norwood." Miss Delacroix gathered the cards and handed them to her brother.

"I am sure I do not know what you could mean." Lydia looked inquisitively at Miss Delacroix.

"Very clever to drop the name of a Marchioness to Lady Aldley. I see you are much more adept than you let on." Miss Delacroix's brittle smile could not conceal her irritation.

"I must confess, my country manners are insufficient in London society, and I do not entirely know what I ought, or ought not say." Lydia wondered what she had said wrong this time.

"Indeed." Miss Delacroix was not convinced.

"No, sister." Mr. Delacroix smiled kindly at Lydia, and Miss Dervish seemed to watch the exchange intently. "I believe your friend is entirely truthful. She may have picked up whist rather quickly, but I think she is not accustomed to the other games that get played at dinner parties. I am quite certain she had no intention of making a display of her connections."

"No! Indeed not!" Lydia was mortified, and there was no restraining the red glow creeping into her cheeks. "Miss Delacroix, I hope you do not think that of me."

Miss Delacroix examined her for a few moments. "No, I certainly do not think anything of the sort. My brother has misunderstood me. I only meant to say that you are a clever girl. Though I am sure you did not seek to impress Lady Aldley, I believe that you did."

"She seemed rather more inclined to disbelieve me." Lydia shook her head. "I do not feel she was impressed in the least."

"You should be thankful that she paid you any attention at all. She had been rather pointedly ignoring me, and it takes some practice to ignore one's whist partner entirely." Miss Dervish looked even more lovely when she smiled. Her teeth were perfectly shaped and milk-white.

"Well then, speaking of cards, I believe the deal is with you, Miss Norwood, now that I am no longer the dealer." Mr. Delacroix's finger tips lingered slightly in contact with her hand as he gave her the cards. And his blue eyes fixed on hers as he added, "I have taken the liberty of shuffling them for you."

CHAPTER 6

*L*ydia's favourite parlour in their London house was small and warm, with a large window and a sizeable fireplace. All the decoratively carved wooden chairs were comfortably worn in and draped with soft wool shawls or sheepskin blankets. They sat out of any order but held their own cheerful assembly in a loose cluster near the hearth.

In the centre sat Lydia and Miss Ravelsham at a small stone table whose inky black surface was polished so finely that one might read one's own fortune in its depths, or examine one's locks in its shallows.

"And how did you enjoy the dinner party, Miss Ravelsham?" Lydia poured tea a little sloppily for her guest, who lounged indolently in one of the larger wooden chairs.

"Oh please call me Tilly. I hope you and I shall be good friends. Especially as your cook makes rather delicious biscuits." She bit one, then popped a sweet in her mouth with the other hand.

"Tilly, then. And you may call me Lydia, as I am sure you are the best friend I have among the young people in London. Is Tilly short for something?" Lydia instinctively moved the sugar bowl closer to her new friend, who placed two lumps in her cup.

"Mathilde. I am not terribly fond of the name, but I do not have to hear it very often. To answer your question, I thought the party was very interesting. Not so much the party, itself, but the interactions between certain people there."

"Oh really? I admit it was the interactions that I found least enjoyable. The pheasant was utterly perfect—crisp skin and moist, succulent meat. And that sauce!" Lydia licked her lips at the memory. "Their cook is from Paris, I understand."

"Ah, you are a gastronome." Tilly savoured a sip of her sugary tea, which turned her smirking face into a caricature of its own impish glee. "Another thing I like about you. But I should just warn you not to let Gaillot ever hear you call him a cook. I understand he is rather snobbish about being a proper chef, with some justification. The braised pork was pure ecstasy, and I was tempted to hide a few of those meringues under my skirt. But I digress from the point. I witnessed something even more delicious than the second course last night."

"I can tell that you fervently wish to tell me about it." Lydia settled back into one of the warm sheepskin throws and smiled. "You do not have to pause for effect, you know."

"Of course I do. What a silly thing to say. Pausing for effect is quite crucial. In any case, when I left the card table, I was standing with Lady Delacroix and Miss Ferrel. We were talking of books, in fact. Miss Ferrel and Lady Delacroix are both very enthusiastic about novels, you see, which makes me almost forgive the latter for her abysmal taste in décor. But I again digress. While we were speaking, Lady Aldley veritably stomped over and took her leave from Lady Delacroix with a frosty air."

Lydia chuckled into her tea cup. "You are a bit of a gossip monger, aren't you?"

"How unkind of you." Tilly feigned shock. "But I do take amusement in laughing at people who think too well of themselves. For a woman of her standing, Lady Aldley really lacks any sort of social grace. She would still be rather handsome if she did not scowl so. But she is all stern superiority without any politesse or intellectual subtlety at all. I cannot help wishing to make a little sport of her. Plus I love a mystery. And it was clear that something put a rather large bee in her ladyship's bonnet. I only wonder what it could have been."

Lydia was disarmed by her new friend's frankness. It seemed intimate, for surely she would not speak so to just anyone. "I wonder if it had anything to do with my foolishly impolitic comments at the card table."

Tilly's eyebrows sprang up to point like a bird dog in a field of ducks. "Oh. Do tell. Did you speculate about the scandalous reasons that her son has been away in France for so long?"

"Certainly not. I should never."

"No, no, of course not. Nor should I, though I have nothing to gain from currying favour with her. I also have nothing against Lord Aldley, having never met the earl. Well, what then?"

Lydia's lips pulled down slightly. "Lady Aldley said something rather biting to Miss Delacroix."

"Not your favourite person, I should say."

"No, but perhaps I have been unfair. I felt for her under the circumstances. Lady Aldley emphasized that only *suitable* young ladies would be invited to her ball and would meet her son, when it was obvious that Miss Delacroix had not been invited." Lydia looked a little concerned. "I believe Miss Delacroix may have some affection for Lady Aldley's son—"

Tilly interrupted her. "An earl who is worth about eighty thousand a year? Yes, I dare say she is violently in love with him, though to my knowledge they have never met."

"Oh surely it is more than that." Lydia searched Tilly's face to see if there were some small trace of seriousness hiding anywhere in its playful character.

"Well, perhaps. But all the best experts of the ton fix him at about eighty thousand."

Lydia could not help laughing, but continued to protest, "You are quite droll, but you know very well I mean that Miss Delacroix cannot only be thinking of that. She seemed very wounded by her ladyship's comments."

"Well, perhaps it *is* more. Perhaps Lord Aldley has had secret dealings with her..."

"No. No indeed! That is not what I meant to say." Lydia laughed at Tilly who had resorted to wildly wiggling her brows. "How do you do that?"

"It is a gift, much like my gift for distorting the kind words of my innocent friend into tinder for a sordid scandal." Tilly slurped the last of her tea, and helped herself to more, and two more lumps of sugar.

"But really, in all seriousness, you must not say such things." Lydia tried to maintain a sober expression. "And whatever Miss Delacroix's hopes are, however little I enjoy her company, she does not deserve to be cut down so cruelly by Lady Aldley."

"Perhaps, but in any case, it is not the sort of thing that would make her ladyship angry, I should think. Cutting down a chit before she has the chance to even lift her gaze to the golden son seems rather more the type of activity that the dowager countess would greatly enjoy. I should hazard a guess that it quite invigorates her."

"Where on earth did you learn to talk this way?" Lydia was diverted. "Please never do so in my mother's hearing, else she will forbid our acquaintance."

"Oh believe me, I know how to address polite company. It is just that I could tell that neither of us is really polite company, am I not correct? Though you are clearly a bit more polite than I. Have you any more of those biscuits?"

Lydia rang the bell. "So, to continue, I felt sorry for Miss Delacroix."

"That was your first mistake. A young lady like Miss Delacroix cannot tolerate pity from girls she considers her inferiors."

Lydia grimaced. "Yes, I see your point. But that is not the worst of it. I wanted to change the subject and make her feel better, so I expressed a hope that she would be attending our ball, and pointed out that there would be some guests of her calibre, like Lady Goodram and her niece, for example."

"Oh dear."

"Is that so very bad?" Lydia looked apprehensively at Tilly.

"You could almost not have said a worse thing—but the fault lies principally with Miss Delacroix's overinflated hopes for the evening. First, you were making a display of your acquaintance in front of a lady before whom she had hoped you would appear inferior. Second, there is a slight implication that you might assist her in society."

"Good Lord! I never intended anything of the sort." A red glow of mortification seeped into Lydia's face. Why did she always put her foot in things?

Tilly lowered her lids and nodded. "I know it. I doubt if someone like Miss Delacroix does, however. She does not appear a very complex creature, but she and her mother have enough cunning to stack a dinner party with a rather lot of commoners who were certain to make her look superior by comparison.

She took a gulp of tea, then continued, "You noted, I imagine, that the *ladies* at the party were all older and mostly married, and that the young women were of no rank and little connection, though all rich enough. And I need not add that there were hardly any men in attendance, which is very bad form. I think it would be difficult for Miss Delacroix to believe that some people are motivated differently than herself."

"—More biscuits, Moll, if you please," Lydia told the servant as she entered. She returned to her story, "Her brother took my part after Lady Aldley left, and I think Miss Delacroix believed him."

"Mr. Delacroix, eh? So he roused himself from the euphoria of staring at Miss Dervish for long enough to defend you. Astounding. In any case, none of this is anything that would give Lady Aldley a moment's unease, much less anger her."

Lydia decided it would be better not to speak of her unpleasant encounters with Mr. Delacroix. "No, but her ladyship did seem upset by something Mr. Delacroix said. He suggested that she had some acquaintance in the place from which Lady Goodram and my mother both come, Warwickshire. She denied it at first. And then confirmed that she had been acquainted with one of the Beauchamps, in Warwick. Then Lady Aldley left abruptly. But I admit, I just thought it was her usual manner to be a bit abrupt."

Tilly perked up. "But then she went directly to take her leave of Lady Delacroix. Yes, indeed, that could be the thing. What was the name of the acquaintance?"

"I do not recall." Lydia thought for a moment. "Mrs. Wurther-something."

"Wurthington?"

"No, I think I should have remembered that name." Lydia tapped her head with a finger. "Wurtherly, I think it was Wurtherly. Nee Beauchamps, I should assume."

"Hmm. No one I know. But it is all very intriguing, is it not?" Tilly sipped her tea happily.

"I suppose it might be. I was just relieved to escape Lady Aldley's interrogation." Lydia shook her head. "It was almost as if she thought I was concocting the connection in order to pass myself off in society."

"From what I have observed, her ladyship's mode of address makes a simple conversation about the weather sound like an inquisition. She may not have meant much by it. It may even have been an attempt at civility." Tilly gave Lydia a mock look of alarm.

"Good Lord." Lydia grimaced. "I hope I am never made the object of her *incivility*."

"Stay clear of her son, then. I believe she has expectations of both wealth and status for his future wife."

Moll returned with a full plate of biscuits, to which Tilly helped herself before the servant had even closed the door behind her.

"I should not think it will be too difficult to avoid her son," observed Lydia with some relief, "as I have not been invited to her ball. And to my knowledge the Delacroixs are my only connection to the Aldleys, and an apparently tenuous one at that."

"You have only been in town for a few weeks, and you only made Lady Aldley's acquaintance last night—though you may be sure that she—" Tilly broke off as Mrs. Norwood entered the parlour.

"Mrs. Norwood. How delightful to see you again. Lydia told me you have been out to call on Lady Goodram."

Lydia marvelled at how completely Tilly's face transformed from the aspect of an incorrigible little mischief-maker to that of a supremely serene and well-behaved young maiden, all in the moments that it took to greet her mother. She even sat up straight so that her back did not touch the chair.

"Indeed I was." Mrs. Norwood sat down. "She has been ill this last week, and I wanted to bring her some fruit and flowers to speed her recovery. She expressed a wish that you had come too, Lydia."

"I thought it better not to overwhelm her with too much company just now." Lydia poured a cup of tea for her mother.

"That is just what I told her." Mrs. Norwood patted Lydia's arm. "But she says she is very nearly cured now, and will be at home on Monday morning, so you may pay her a call then."

"I should be delighted."

"Indeed, Lydia," added Tilly, "You are very fortunate to have such a friend as Lady Goodram. She is a highly respected person, and a rather delightful conversationalist."

"Do you know Lady Goodram, Miss Ravelsham?" Mrs. Norwood beamed.

"I have had the pleasure of meeting her once or twice, though I do not enjoy such a close acquaintance with her ladyship as you and Lydia do." Tilly sipped her tea, primly, without a hint of slurping.

Mrs. Norwood lifted her cup, and then paused before sipping. "She is like a second mother to me, and has promised to assist Lydia in society, which is ever so important, as we are all but unknown among the London ton."

"I do not claim any great experience," Tilly lowered her lashes, "but with the ton, I believe a little mystery can be a good thing."

"Perhaps—yes perhaps." Mrs. Norwood brightened at the thought. "Will you stay to dine, Miss Ravelsham? Cook has got a nice piece of cod, and she is rather a magician with fish, if I may say so."

"I should love to stay but my mother has given me strict directions to be home as we are to entertain my betrothed and his parents. The DeGroens are recently come to town from Amsterdam."

"Oh how very exciting. I am surprised you are not home all a-dither trying to pick out the perfect frock. You are much more sensible than I was at your age."

"It is kind of you to say it, but the truth is that I did all my dithering last week, and my gown is now laid out and ready." Tilly rose. "Of course, I am still anxious to make a good impression with his parents."

"I am sure you shall. They will be delighted with you."

"I hope you are right, Mrs. Norwood. Ah but I hear the bells ringing three, and I should be going."

"I shall ring for your carriage. But I hope you will soon call on us again. It is so nice for Lydia to have made a good friend here. She is not much used to society, and I am sure you will be a great source of guidance for her."

Tilly smiled tranquilly and said, "I shall certainly do my best, Mrs. Norwood."

It was shortly before dinner, and Lydia changed into an evening dress and gloves, and came downstairs to read until her father and Mr. Mortimer arrived. She was intercepted upon the stairs by her out-of-breath mother, however, who excitedly grasped her hand and said, "My dear you will never guess who has come to call on you."

Lydia was puzzled. "I had understood that Papa invited Mr. Mortimer to dinner. Surely no one else is calling at this hour."

"Oh the hour is neither here nor there. *Mr. Delacroix* is waiting in the parlour." Mrs. Norwood clearly ascribed great significance to the event.

"Mr. Delacroix." Lydia felt the blood drain from her face. How could he have the nerve? "I cannot account for his calling upon us, and I do not wish to speak with Mr. Delacroix."

"Of course you do, now off with you." Her mother guided her down the remaining stairs and pushed her into the south parlour, following behind. With a broad smile at Mr. Delacroix who stood to receive them, Mrs. Norwood stationed herself on a chair in the far corner to terrorize an innocently by-standing needle point loop.

"Mr. Delacroix." The tendons in Lydia's neck stood out like pillars supporting the frosty fortress of her face.

"Miss Norwood." He gave her a well-oiled smile. "I hope I find you well."

"Indeed." Lydia kept her voice low, lest her mother should hear, and added, "I have not had to tolerate impertinence from trespassers, recently. I find myself quite refreshed."

He chuckled as though she had said this in jest. "Oh quite. You must be tip top, then. You certainly are in your best looks." He stepped closer and murmured, "Surely you cannot blame a moth for being drawn to such a flame."

Lydia's mouth was a hard line. "I had understood that to be a fatal attraction. And I detest the sight of moths."

"You are such a cruel goddess. Do you not care at all for the feelings of the lowly creatures who seek only to worship you?" His eyes moved unctuously over her form, and Lydia shuddered.

"I do not spare a thought for the debased creatures who only flutter toward light because their tendency to sneak about in the dark makes them indiscriminately hurl themselves at any visible target."

He grasped her hand suddenly, and Lydia snatched it back. "I shall thank you to keep your hands to yourself, sir."

"You will thank me?" His blue eyes glowed coldly and he smiled. "And by what means will you repay me for my forbearance?"

"In case such rudimentary virtue is not its own reward," Lydia replied through clenched teeth, "I shall in return forbear from slapping you in the face and ordering the servants to see you out permanently."

Mr. Delacroix shook his head slightly. "You country girls are so delightfully provincial. No London lady would ever consider a little hand press such an affront."

She refused to meet his gaze. "It is the person, rather than the gesture that is the affront, sir."

"But you cannot refuse to receive me." He laughed and tried to step still closer to her, though she moved away. "Not when our families are acquainted, your mother likes me so well, and your father and I play cards together. You have no say in the matter." He gripped her hand again and pressed it to his lips.

Her stomach shivered. This intrusive behaviour completely defeated his good looks, and she was repulsed. She would have to burn the gloves now anyway, what would a little blood stain matter? But she could not give a beating to a guest, at least not in front of her mother.

So she slid her hand out, and left him holding her glove as she made for the door, calling out, "Mama, I have misplaced one of my gloves. Will you ring for Mr. Delacroix's carriage? He is leaving now. I shall go retrieve a new pair before dinner."

"Oh! So soon?" Mrs. Norwood looked disappointed. "I was about to ring for some refreshments." She sighed. "But, very well, I shall ring for the footman."

"Pray, do not trouble yourself, Mrs. Norwood." Delacroix hurried after Lydia. "My carriage awaits and I shall see myself out."

He followed Lydia through the parlour door. Was he intending to chase her up the stairs to her chambers?

Just then her father appeared in the company of Mr. Mortimer. Lydia greeted Mr. Mortimer and flew to her father's side, kissing him on the cheek and inserting her arm into his.

"Hello, my dear. Are *you* here, Mr. Delacroix?" Mr. Norwood looked surprised. "Do we have some business I have forgotten?"

"Not at all, Mr. Norwood." Delacroix assumed a plausible smile. "I came to call upon your amiable daughter. We were lately made acquainted at my mother's dinner party."

"However he was just leaving." Lydia was not about to let him insinuate himself into the dinner table.

Mr. Delacroix bowed, and as he made to tuck her glove into his jacket, Lydia added, "Oh look, you have found my glove. How clever."

His grin was menacing as he handed it back to her. "Is it yours? Glad to be of service, Miss Norwood."

Her father raised a bushy eyebrow. "Oh aye, and quite a service it is, Delacroix. Stashing away a girl's glove in your pocket. Well, Greenall, as you're here, do show Mr. Delacroix out. Good evening, sir. Send our greetings to your mother and sister."

He grasped Lydia's arm a little more firmly, just as Mrs. Norwood obliviously dawdled her way out of the south parlour to join them and yawned, saying, "Needle work always makes me so drowsy."

As Mr. Norwood led them both to the dining room he whispered in Lydia's ear. "I hope you were not giving Mr. Delacroix your glove as a love token."

Lydia huffed incredulously. "Certainly not."

"Glad to hear it. Those gloves are exorbitantly priced—sets my teeth on edge to think upon it. And I have recently learned that Delacroix hasn't a sixpence to scratch with. T'would be throwing good money after bad."

When they were all seated to dine, her father proposed a toast. "To old friends: may the future draw them ever closer." There was a gleam in her father's eye, as though he attached particular significance to the words. But then, he and Mr. Mortimer were probably half-sprung after their visit to the club.

"Your mother tells me you have made a new friend, my dear." Her father served her some white wine.

"You mean Miss Ravelsham. I made her acquaintance some time ago, but only recently discovered how very amiable she is. And she is patient with me, even though I am so unfamiliar with London manners."

"She is soon to be married, I think?" Her father inquired.

"Yes, to Mr. John DeGroen—though I understand it is to be a long engagement."

"Ah yes," Mr. Mortimer nodded. "I believe his family have made a fortune cultivating plants in Holland and in the colonies."

"And her family has had similar success in plant husbandry, it seems." Lydia felt a bit self-conscious speaking on such a vulgar topic before a guest. "So I suppose the match is well made."

"And you are to be at Lady Goodram's ball next week, are you not?" Mr. Norwood spooned sauce over his cod, and liberally peppered it.

"Yes, Papa."

"Well good. I hope you will wear a very pretty frock." Mr. Norwood's eyes were suddenly wet.

She had never seen her father weep, even a little. Perhaps it was too much pepper, or too much drink, but this was the second time he had been visibly distressed while admonishing her to dress prettily. It was all very odd. She paid special attention to her potatoes and pretended not to see.

He cleared his throat and recomposed himself. "And Mortimer, here, will be there as well, so perhaps you can save a dance for him, eh?"

She was still formulating a polite reply that did not create an obligation, when Mr. Mortimer declared with a chuckle, "Oh don't be a great simpleton, Norwood. You can't go ruining her first ball of the season by filling her dance card in advance with elderly family friends. I shall go and stand in line with all the others."

Mr. Norwood looked aghast. "Lord! If you are *elderly*, I must be near the grave."

"No, old boy, you just smell like it."

Mr. Norwood laughed long and loudly. The awkward moment had passed, but Lydia could not help feeling there was something very wrong with her father.

After brandy and tea and a long chat by the fire, it was at last time for Mr. Mortimer to take his leave. He thanked her parents heartily, then clasped Lydia's hand in both of his, almost like her father would do, and said, "I greatly look forward to seeing you at the ball, Miss Norwood."

"I am sure it will be my pleasure." It was all she could think to politely say.

Was he meaning to woo her? She could hardly think of it without confusion. The man was nearly twice her age, and her father's friend. It seemed unfitting. She knew it was not unheard of for such matches to occur, but she had no feelings for him, save the slight friendship she would feel for any old comrade of her father's.

Not that she had so very much experience with affairs of the heart— in fact she had none. But she had read books, and even if they grossly exaggerated the matter, she could not think their descriptions of the raptures young ladies experienced in the presence of their beaux bore even a passing resemblance to her own feelings about Mr. Mortimer.

CHAPTER 7

*A*fter so much time in Paris, Lord Aldley found himself in the London Aldley house again, waiting in the cold, pristine breakfast room.

The silver on the sideboard was polished to a mirror shine and held vigil over a perfect pyramid of dried fruits. He resisted the temptation to rumple the immaculately pressed white linen cloth that covered the table and formed crisp, straight creases at the corners.

Legally the house was his own, but he had left his mother in residence rather than remove her to the dowager house down the street. Looking around at the perfectly coiffed ornamental plants and the freshly redone, pewter grey and rose upholstery on every curvy legged, overly fussy chair, he did not feel the lack. Bachelor comforts were better provided in his own, smaller dwelling.

He had not even really wanted to come, but he was not one to allow personal preferences to take precedence over duty. A stifled yawn contorted his face. He had not yet recovered from his return journey across the channel.

Lady Aldley entered and gave Aldley her cheek to kiss, smiling sweetly at him. "Welcome home, my son."

He kissed her. "Thank you. You look very well, Mama."

"It is sweet of you to say, and I have had no complaints at all. I find living in London agrees with me. Shall we sit down?"

They sat and busied themselves with choosing among the kippers, sausages, blood puddings, eggs, and breads laid out on the table before them.

Lady Aldley poured the tea neatly and said, "How pleasant it is to breakfast with one's son. I hate to turn to practical matters so soon, but I need to ask you for some money."

"Certainly." Aldley sipped his tea. At least his mother's tea was tolerably strong and had the right balance. He was certain it was of the finest quality. "I shall have a draft made up for you at once. How much do you need?"

"About a thousand pounds should do." Her demeanour was untroubled.

Aldley's eyebrows only twitched slightly. "Very well, I shall see to it this afternoon."

He hoped she had not taken up gambling. As his father had not left much directly to her, Aldley had set up an annuity for her, paid the household expenses, and resolved to always be generous besides. She had grown accustomed to living like a countess, after all.

"Thank you. It is so good to have you here, Thomas. It has been such a long time and is such a relief that you are safely back in England. I do hope you plan to settle down here, now." Lady Aldley spread butter on her roll, then set it precisely in the centre of her bread plate.

"If, by settle down, Mama, you mean *marry the woman you pick out for me*, then I am afraid I must disoblige you."

"You know that my only concern is for your well being and the continuation of the Aldley line. You will not be happy unless you choose a respectable lady, not beneath your sphere, with good connections and an appropriate dowry."

"Such ladies are hardly ten-a-penny." Aldley sampled his omelette appreciatively. The mushrooms were perfectly sautéed. "And I should prefer not to be forced to choose between a pretty simpleton and a lady with teeth as long as the list of her antecedents."

Lady Aldley lifted her chin. "I hope you are not referring to anyone of my acquaintance."

"As do I. But as it is my first morning back in town, let us have a peaceful breakfast together, and speak no more about settling down. I find the topic puts me off English food."

"Off English food?" She dabbed the corner of her mouth.

"I mean that it makes me desirous of a nice *petite Madeleine*, still warm from the *patisserie*."

"Such nonsense. You have only just returned. You have more sense than to immediately go back again."

"Oh well, perhaps not to Paris." Aldley tapped his fingers on his lips, as though in serious contemplation. "But I have always wanted to see St. Petersburg."

Lady Aldley poured her son another cup of tea. "Was there an invite to Lady Goodram's ball awaiting you when you returned?"

"Indeed there was. I admit, I was rather hoping not to be swept into the season so soon. However, I should as soon shoot my best horse as give that lady any offence."

"I do not believe you have any horses to shoot at the moment." She gave him an arch smile. "Unless you have sent word to the estate to have one of the plough animals delivered."

"Oh, but it is terribly amusing that the earl has no equipage. I quite understand your levity. In any event, Lady Goodram's balls are less tedious than most. And I should dearly love a long chat with *her*, even if everyone else there should prove to be intolerably stupid."

"Yes. She is a lady of importance." Lady Aldley left the intonation of the final word hanging in the air while she sipped her tea at length. "But I should warn you that she has some rather liberal ideas, and has invited certain young women who are, perhaps, not entirely suitable company for an earl."

"Indeed?" He should not be surprised that his mother would presume to call Lady Goodram's judgement into question. "Surely, you must be mistaken."

"No. I am afraid she has invited at least one young woman who is not even the daughter of a gentleman—though she may be the daughter of one of Lady Goodram's old friends. I have heard she goes about town unescorted, and has been known to climb trees. *Trees.* The ramshackle. Can you imagine it?"

He took a mouthful of tea to cover his sudden confusion. A tree-climber. How many tree-climbing maidens could there be around London? Surely it was not some sort of fashion that had sprouted up while he was in France.

Was there any chance the young woman could be the same helpful dryad that had haunted his thoughts ever since he left England? It was foolishness to think so. And anyway, he did not know what she looked like. If she were to attend the ball, how would he even recognize her? Foolish obsession. His heart beat faster.

"Who is this young woman?" He tried not to sound interested.

His mother pursed her lips. "I do not recall. But in any case, most unsuitable company for an earl."

"Tree-climber as she may be, I must contradict your assumptions about suitable company for earls. The requirements are quite low, I assure you." Aldley knew his jest would sour her mood, but it seemed fair penalty for presuming to question Lady Goodram's discernment. He found the amusement of trying her nerves irresistible.

"Nonsense. Earls must be particular about their acquaintances." She poured herself another cup of tea.

"No, indeed." He affected an air of noble boredom. "In fact I know of more than one earl who has rather preferred the company of young women known to go about town unescorted, with no ties to the nobility whatsoever—or at least no ties that could be spoken of in polite company."

Lady Aldley flushed deeply, which was becoming in her handsome, though sometimes severe, visage. She deliberately chewed a bite of her roll for longer than Aldley had thought possible, then replaced the bread in the centre of the bread plate, and in a frosty voice said, "Despite your apparent amusement at the erosion of decency, it is most galling to be thrown into such low company against one's will. It leaves one desolate."

"There, there, Mother. Do not let it sink your spirits. It is the stuff of life that we must occasionally suffer the debasement of intolerable society." The alternative being to slip away to the continent.

He finished the last of his eggs and tea, and tapped his mouth with the serviette. "Now I must take leave of you, for I have an appointment with Rutherford."

"Rutherford." Her lips formed a flat, pale line. "I suppose I should be thankful that you paid me the honour of calling upon me before that man."

"Nothing of it. He is my oldest friend, Mama, to be sure, but you are my mother." He did not add *duty before pleasure, or else what would the world come to?* But he gave her a cheeky grin as he said, "And do thank Simmons for breakfast," before striding to the door.

"We do *not* thank servants for discharging their *duties*." Lady Aldley hissed to the broad, disappearing back of her son.

At Rutherford's house, a cabriolet was just pulling away with two pretty young faces tucked into the back. Rutherford bounded down the steps to greet the earl. "Aldley, you are finally come. I cannot tell you how good it is to see you again, my old friend."

"Indeed it is," Aldley warmly returned the greeting. "It has been far too long, Rutherford. I assume those ladies were your guests—or have you fallen on hard times, and are so attempting to conceal the fact that you have let Smythe go, by greeting me out on the street?"

"You have some inkling that I could so easily be rid of him? No, no. I shall never have a hound so loyal to me as Smythe is. And perish the thought that I should ever lose him, for life would be impossible without him, frankly. But yes, that was my sister, Susan, and her governess."

"Little Susan? Have I been gone that long?"

"You were rather too distracted to notice her when you were here last. But forgive my droning on and come inside."

The billiards room was just as he recollected it. The Dark oak panelling that adorned the walls was carved with scenes from classical mythology, and enclave tables of dark marble supported pillar candles that reflected off of the gold framed mirrors at either end of the room.

It still smelled faintly of the late Rutherford senior's favourite blend of pipe tobacco, and even the sideboard appeared to be arranged just as it always was, with cut crystal decanters sparkling in the candlelight and the contents glowing like an array of witch's potions, amber, burgundy and blood red.

"What memories this house holds for me, Rutherford." Aldley finished racking up the billiard balls, and chalked his cue. "It was my great refuge when my father passed. Did I ever thank you for that? I must have been insufferable company."

"No more than usual." Rutherford laughed, and poured them both a drink. "But I know what it is to lose one's parents. And you were certainly no worse company to me than I was to you when your sister married that viscount."

"Lord Essington. Quite. That was my mother's doing. My father rather liked you, you know, he was merely influenced by his wife. And she terrorized Elizabeth until the poor girl gave in. I should have done more. I should have arranged an elopement."

Rutherford put up his hand. "Do not think on it, Aldley. I was a young puppy, probably too young for marriage, anyway. But I do not suppose your mother has kept you apprised of your sister's life."

Aldley lowered his nose into the balloon glass and took a long whiff of the liquid—lightly almondy, dark caramel sweetness. It pleasantly stung his nostrils. "She has only briefly mentioned Eliza in her letters, in fact."

"Ah." Rutherford broke the billiard balls neatly, then returned to his drink.

"Why, do you know something?" Aldley turned his attention from the table.

"It is just a bit of gossip. But it is better that you hear it from me." Rutherford loosened his cravat.

"Good God, man, spit it out. Has something happened? Has she been harmed?"

"No, no. Do not trouble yourself on that head. Lord Essington has been travelling in Venice, and has left Elizabeth alone with their newborn son."

The earl's eyes narrowed. "It is not on business, I take it." He took his first shot and scratched.

Rutherford took his penalty shot and the ball sunk with a satisfying thud into a corner pocket. "If it is, it is the sort of business that has kept him away from Essington Hall for almost a year."

"You mean he left before the babe was born? Why did she not write me about it?" Aldley was ashamed. He had been so absorbed in his own need for escape that he had neglected his sister. "Poor girl. Still, I can only imagine she is more or less relieved to be out of his company."

"Perhaps. But you know how society loves the scent of a scandal. I only know about it because of Randalls—the old gossip. It is like having a woman in the club. I suppose I cannot wonder at Lady Aldley not mentioning it to you."

"No. I imagine my mother would prefer not to acknowledge scandalous talk about her perfect match. This turn of events could hurt her chances with The Five. But you would think she would have some feeling for her own daughter."

Lord Aldley was thoughtful for several minutes, and missed three simple shots, as Rutherford sunk more and more balls.

Rutherford finally laughed. "You are out of practice. Could you not find a billiard table in France?"

"My amusements focussed more on the opera and theatre, and the occasional shooting party." And never a thought for Eliza. Aldley missed his next shot, too. "I must go visit her, Rutherford. She may need assistance. Will you come with me?"

"Yes, I suppose."

Aldley winced. "I beg your pardon, Rutherford. I am a dunderhead. It might have occurred to me that it could be uncomfortable for you."

Rutherford walked to the sideboard and poured himself more brandy. "Not at all, I assure you. I have not the slightest romantic inclination for your sister, or anyone at the moment. The women I meet do not have enough spirit. So if you need my assistance, you shall have it."

"Well, it is not so much your assistance as your set of four greys." Aldley took a sip and eyed Rutherford over the rim of his glass.

"Ah, I see." Rutherford blandly rubbed his eyebrow. "At last we get to the point."

"There is no sense in clomping about the countryside on the back of a hay wagon, is there?"

"I believe there might be a few other alternatives, *my lord*." Rutherford's eyes were amused. "And I suppose you cannot borrow your mother's carriage."

"No. Besides, your nags are faster. I have to be back before Lady Goodram's ball. Look, I am sorry to ask, Rutherford, but I sold all my London horses before I left, as I did not know when I should wish to return. And we have not time to wait until Friday and go about checking teeth down in Smithfield."

"Right then. But you will owe me a rather fine dinner when we return."

"I shall give you two fine dinners." He thumped Rutherford on the back. "And send over a crate of champagne. Perhaps that will put Smythe's nose back in joint."

"True, he will not be happy to be left behind."

Rutherford insisted on driving his own horses out of town, which left Lord Aldley at leisure to survey the London he had left for so long. It was growing. It never stopped sprouting out new neighbourhoods and shops.

As they passed a small park in a fashionable area, he saw, disappearing into the treetop of an evergreen, a slender body in a grey dress and bonnet. This odd person had scampered up the tree as though she were a wild animal. Could it be the young lady he had met so long ago? Could it be the tree climbing young woman that his mother found so unsuitable?

He shook his head and turned away. She was not dressed like a society woman. His fancy was playing tricks on his rational faculties. Perhaps it had been a very large child, or an unfortunate. And yet, she had climbed into his thoughts, and he could not shake her free.

CHAPTER 8

*a*s Lydia arrived at Lady Goodram's on Monday morning and removed her outer clothing, she could hear the muffled notes of a pianoforte.

A man's voice was singing rich and warm. It was beautiful. Though the sound was muffled by the walls, she thought the voice was familiar. Did anyone among her acquaintance have such deep, alluring voice?

Even in its muted state, something about it compelled her, and she followed the footman through the ornately moulded hallways, past the bronze sculptures of portentous angels and noble unicorns forcenés, transfixed as if under a spell.

The music stopped. Lydia hurried to the music room. She met Lady Goodram and a young lady leaving just as she reached the door and the servant was about to announce her.

"Hello my dear Lydia. I am so glad you have come. This is Mrs. Childes. Mrs. Childes, this is Miss Norwood."

"I am pleased to meet you, Miss Norwood."

"And I, you." Lydia turned to Lady Goodram. "I hope you are well recovered now, Lady Goodram."

"Indeed I am feeling much better. A little delightful company will fix me up completely."

"Was that you playing the pianoforte just now, Mrs. Childes?" Lydia could not help indulging her curiosity.

"Yes, it was. Lady Goodram has a beautiful instrument."

"Did I not hear a man's voice as well?" She had to know who it was.

"Oh yes, that was Lord Aldley." Lady Goodram clasped her hands together and grinned. "How I love to hear him sing. He was kind enough to oblige me, though he had just returned from a visit to the countryside to see his sister, and could not visit long. He has only just come home from a lengthy stay in France. He seems to be rushing all about these days, and he left us again as suddenly as he arrived."

"Indeed? I did not see him pass." Lydia tried not to sound disappointed.

"Yes, he dashed out the back entrance to access the hackney more quickly—and I suspect more secretly. He apologized for embarrassing me by showing up in a shoddy hired carriage—as if I cared in the slightest about such trifles! I always tell him he only does these things to make himself appear more fascinating."

Lydia was already a little fascinated. "I am sorry that I did not get a chance to meet him."

"I believe you will have another opportunity some day." Lady Goodram patted her arm, apparently oblivious to Lydia's interest in the earl. "Shall we have some tea?"

Lydia thought, as she followed along, that Lady Goodram had dropped this topic rather too quickly. She shook her head and chided herself for assuming that everyone else should be consumed by the same topics that preoccupied her.

Lady Goodram led them through the main hallway, with its long gallery of gold-framed Goodram antecedents, to a small, warm room on the south side, with a round oak door carved with dragons and other fabulous creatures and fitted with a pentagonal brass door knob in its middle. It was the principle eccentricity of the house, and had always entranced Lydia when she visited as a young girl. It still made her smile.

"I see Brown has not yet prevailed upon you to replace your fairy door." Lydia settled herself into a chair with gilded legs and fat cushions upholstered in purple velvet.

"No indeed." Lady Goodram crinkled her nose as she smiled. "And he never shall. But I suppose I should be thankful that he did not turn mutinous and remove it while I was visiting the continent."

After tea, Mrs. Childes left them, and they pulled their chairs closer to the fire. Lydia settled into a little slouch and squirmed comfortably into the plump cushions, as she drew the wool shawl on her chair back around her shoulders—it was from Lady Goodram that she had borrowed this idea for her own sitting room chairs. Warmth was such an important comfort in London.

Just as Lydia was lulled into torpor by the soothing crackle of the logs and the slight scent of resin and wood smoke, Lady Goodram leaned over and put a hand on her arm. "Now, my dear, I have a serious matter to discuss with you."

Lydia roused herself and asked saucily, "Oh indeed? Do you have some privateering venture you wish me to invest in, or have you heard that I have been making a public display of my needle work?"

"My word! Of course not! Nothing as awful as the grotesque spectacle of your cross-stitch. I told your mother she should burn all your yarns, you know."

"I believe she has given them to her lady's maid."

"Just as well. She has no business with them, either. These deficiencies run in families." Lady Goodram resumed her more earnest face, and continued, "No, but I have heard some gossip about you. I shall not say from where, but a rumour is circulating that you have been spotted climbing trees."

Lydia flushed. "I wish people would mind their own affairs."

Lady Goodram smiled brightly. "That is the eternal wish of the guilty."

"I am not indiscreet, and I see no means by which anyone would know without spying on me." Lydia's thoughts immediately turned to Delacroix.

"London is full of spies." Lady Goodram clicked her tongue. "I know your father has given you rather free rein, but do you not think it is time to stop climbing trees? At least while you are in town."

"I suppose I must. But I confess that I resent it, and it makes me despise London all the more. And furthermore, I believe I know from what quarter these rumours are flying, and may I just say that this person has absolutely no grounds for calling anyone else's propriety into question."

"They never do. But, of whom do you speak?" The lady's gaze was penetrating.

"What, you are not to tell me of your sources, but I must tell you whom I suspect?"

Lady Goodram chuckled. "I rather imagine my source to be a few word-of-mouths removed from your malefactor."

"In that case, there is little to be gained by my giving up tree climbing now, is there? By breakfast tomorrow, everyone in town will know. In the view of society, my character is quite fixed, I imagine."

CHAPTER 9

*A*ldley was a great fool, and he knew it. He had walked around the little park for an hour and a half, and the tree climber he had spied before was nowhere to be seen.

At least he was stretching his legs and getting some fresh air, but the peaceful trees and charming bird songs did nothing to soothe his spirit, and he persisted in searching around every trunk. It was madness to continue this quest, and he knew that he indeed looked like a madman, wandering about and periodically staring up at the same tree. But what if it were the same young lady?

Aldley had to meet her. He had to know if it were her, in the very least to thank her properly. She was very probably married by now. He clenched his teeth. But he could at least express his gratitude. On the other hand, if she were married, would she still be out climbing trees? Would her husband put up with it?

He thought not. It was, after all, rather improper. And although it seemed a charming eccentricity in a young lady he might court, he should not countenance it in a wife. He shook his head. Of course it was a merely hypothetical thought. Only he should very much like to thank her. That was all.

CHAPTER 10

*L*ydia was wearing her mother's pearls and a light, russet silk and tulle dress with a cream sash at the waist and gloves trimmed with copper beads. She was painfully conscious of how ladylike the total effect was.

As she caught a glance of herself in one of the many grand mirrors around Lady Goodram's ballroom, lit by the warm candle light so that the copper in her hair and dress gleamed luxuriantly as though she belonged in this warmly sparkling space, she felt a bit of a fraud. She wondered if everyone there could see the tree twigs and sun-burnt nose behind the façade.

She was once again under admonitions not to drink claret or be always tossing her curls about. It was lucky that she was in no head-tossing mood, though her nerves could use a glass of wine. She wished, as she was introduced by Lady Goodram to this or that person, that she had Tilly by her side to give her courage.

"Calm yourself, my dear, there is no one to fear at one of my balls." Lady Goodram took her hand and pulled her toward the refreshments room. "Let us go find a glass of some cordial to fortify you."

"Thank you, Lady Goodram. You are really too kind to me. I shall try not to shame you." Some champagne would help.

"Shame me! No chance of that my dear, for you are so frightfully pretty—well, perhaps the Duke's daughter over there might be just a bit more beautiful."

Lydia suppressed a laugh. No one would be overwhelmed by the mousy haired girl's personal appearance, but she had fortune and an enviable pedigree as well as connections to the royal family. And she was not plagued with freckles. Lydia could hardly feel superior. Out of respect, she tried to maintain a demeanour as deceptively sober as Lady Goodram's.

"But then," Lady Goodram continued, "one's vision is always affected by the knowledge of her social standing. So who knows but that you might not be slightly prettier after all."

"I am sure all the prettiness in the world cannot overcome my father's not being a gentleman."

"Well, that might be somewhat true, but beauty combined with good fortune covers a multitude of genealogical sins. And anyway, you are only thinking of what engages female fascination. Just remember that what is important to men is rather a different thing than what is prized by the ladies of the ton. It is true that you do not have noble birth, nor do you play an instrument, and your needle work is... well let us not speak of *that*."

Lydia giggled. The cocktail was a bit stronger than she was used to. "Does this have brandy mixed in with the champagne?"

"Yes. A rather lot—do not tell your mother. But as I was saying, along-side your numerous failings, you also have good sense, an improved mind, you read French and German, and far too many intellectual topics, and I dare say you have a very charming personality, when you are not hiding from society—which is, of course, only too tempting. But now you must shine. Share your beauty, your sense and your sweet, unspoiled disposition with the company, avoid the topic of trees, and I assure you more than one man will lose his heart to you."

"I do not really want anyone to lose their heart. I just want to get through the evening without embarrassing you."

Lady Goodram smiled and patted her arm "You could not embarrass me, even if you were trying, my dear little Lydia. I do not embarrass easily. Now, I think you have some acquaintance among this group of young ladies, so I shall leave you to their charming society."

As they approached the group of muslin-and-lace-swathed débutantes, she said, "Miss Louisa Ferrel, I believe you are acquainted with Miss Norwood?"

"Yes, my lady, indeed I am." She smiled at Lydia.

"And Miss Stokes, and Miss Dreydon, may I introduce to you the daughter of my very good friend?" The ladies both expressed their pleasure at the idea, and when all three were introduced, Lady Goodram gave Lydia a private wink and said, "I must now go teach your mother how to lose gracefully at whist. Enjoy yourself, my dear."

Lydia felt the loss immediately, for she did not really know what to say to these girls. Compliments. Her mother said always to lead with a compliment.

"That is a most elegant necklace, Miss Dreydon, and it is very becoming with your complexion." But wait, her mother also said not to comment on personal appearance. Lord, had she made a gaffe already? But Miss Dreydon seemed pleased, and so the little dance of bland pleasantries and civil whiskers began.

They were sweet enough girls, but not nearly as interesting as Tilly. Lydia sipped her champagne drink and chatted, trying to appear engaged, and only surreptitiously glanced about the room. She saw an unexpected face.

"Oh!" Miss Ferrel's mouth opened in surprise. "It is Mr. Delacroix, unless I am mistaken."

"Indeed, I believe you are right." Even from a distance, Lydia could make out the alarming blue eyes, tanned skin and dark hair.

"But, I understood from Miss Delacroix that none of them were invited." Miss Ferrel looked puzzled.

"Yes, that had also been my impression." Lydia tried to maintain a bland expression.

"He is mightily handsome." Miss Stokes played with the finger of one glove, and with a dreamy sort of look asked, "Do you think he bribed a servant and sneaked in through the back entry?"

"I should think not." Miss Ferrel had the facial resolve of a lady choosing to believe the best. "We must have been mistaken, I think. It is not unheard of for only one person from a family to be invited, after all."

Lydia held her tongue. She was rather more inclined to believe Miss Stokes's speculation, though she did not ascribe to it the same romantic veneer which appeared to entrance that young lady.

"Ah, but there is Miss Dervish." Miss Ferrel's sweet smile broadened.

So there was an explanation. Whither that beauty went, there Mr. Delacroix would be drawn like a bee to a blossom. Or a fox to a hen house. Lydia watched as he approached Miss Dervish and took her hand briefly. Miss Dervish averted her gaze and blushed.

"That is Miss Dervish?" The finger of Miss Stoke's glove was now getting completely twisted, and she sighed rapturously. "She has the face of an angel!"

"It almost does not seem fair, does it?" Miss Ferrel's remark reminded Lydia of Tilly. How innocently one person might say something that would be pure mischief from another's lips.

"But I believe we have no cause for repine. It might be a little wrong of us to speak of unfairness when none of us will ever really want for anything. That is more than many can say." Miss Dreydon, though undeniably right, seemed a little prudent for her fifteen years, a little too concerned with the lot of the poor for her conspicuous emerald pendant, and a little too correct in her views to be any fun at all.

A gloom settled over the four, demanding a few moments of silence.

"I say, I believe that is Lord Aldley." Miss Ferrel's eyes were keenly trained on a tall, golden-haired man with broad shoulders and impeccable tailoring.

"The tall man with the golden hair?" Lydia's breath caught a little. So this was Lord Aldley, the man who sang so beautifully. She did not often remark upon clothing, but this man wore his very well, and his tailoring showed his muscular body to great advantage. She could feel her heart beating faster.

"Just the same." Miss Ferrel nodded.

"You know Lord Aldley?" Miss Stokes' eyes rounded a little.

"Not really." Miss Ferrel smiled at Miss Stokes' awestruck face. "But my father once sold the senior Lord Aldley a horse, and the son accompanied him. I spied him from a window. I remember thinking that he was a prince, with the sun shining in his hair, and almost as tall as Papa." She laughed at the recollection. "I was a fanciful girl. But I was not so very far from wrong. He is an earl, after all. And he has a fine bearing."

Miss Stokes sighed dramatically and nodded in agreement.

The man finished his discussion with the older couple he spoke to, and slipped away into the back card room. Lydia wondered if he would turn out to be as disagreeable as his mother—surely not if Lady Goodram liked him so well. But she wondered why Lady Goodram had not contrived to introduce them.

She turned to spy again on Miss Dervish's tête a tête, and realized that while they had all been gaping at the earl, Mr. Delacroix and Miss Dervish had disappeared.

Her curiosity, and the glass of spiked champagne, got the better of her fear of making a wrong move. She resolved to go look for them. "Will you excuse me for a moment? I must go take some air." It was a strange way to excuse herself, for the rooms had not grown hot, but the young ladies acceded without comment.

She walked to the balcony on the south side of the hall. Her novels had educated her well on what goings on might occur on dark balconies and in garden pavilions. Perhaps it was a perverse curiosity about such secret meetings that propelled her out the doors to the balcony, or perhaps it was a particular fascination with Miss Dervish, and a desire not to see her compromised.

She could not say which, or how much of each motivation drove her. But her curiosity went unsatisfied, for the balcony was empty but for the long shadows of plants in urns and classical statues, cast about by a sprinkling of torches.

Lydia breathed the moist cool air, lightly scented by the flowering plants. She should spend at least a little time out there, or it would look odd. She walked to the edge of the balcony, and gazed out at the garden, remembering life in the countryside, where the skies were clear and one could see the stars perfectly.

Lydia had just decided she had been out long enough when a now familiar voice came from behind her.

"There you are, Miss Norwood. Have you... climbed any good trees, lately?"

Mr. Delacroix. She started, but ignored the comment, and fixed her gaze on an oak tree on the far side of the gardens.

"In fact, I see you have spied some future arboreal conquests on the grounds. Ah, you will never turn your gaze to me." He came around to stand before her. "Not since the first time I saw you. It is cruel of you to hide your radiance from a poor besotted creature like myself."

"We were facing each other when we were introduced, Mr. Delacroix." Her voice expressed her extreme displeasure at the meeting.

"Perhaps, but not when we *met*." His smile was a flash of wolfish white teeth.

"I am sure we had not met until the evening of Lady Delacroix's ball."

"Then how should I know that you have a penchant for scampering about unescorted in the alleyways behind gentlemen's clubs?" His arms were suddenly around her waist and his breath against her neck as he whispered, "With your beautiful red locks falling out of your bonnet. Do not worry, your secret is safe with me, my wild little beauty."

She had mixed feelings. On the one hand, her body was responding rather bewilderingly to his touch, to this forceful surprise. She was suddenly thankful for her uncomfortably complex undergarments, as her traitorous nipples hardened slightly beneath her corset and silk slip.

And he was terribly handsome, if at the same time repugnantly presumptuous. And something else. What was it? She searched her memory. Her father's club. He was the man in the window. He had thought she was a woman of easy virtue—his thoughts had obviously not altered much.

His grip was strong, but she had the advantage of anger and surprise. The young man had not the benefit of acquaintance with women who climbed trees for amusement.

She pried his arms off, and when he tried to re-entangle her, she drove her knee into his groin, a trick she learned from the farm children she had played with in her childhood. He cursed and stepped back in a partial crouch. The technique still worked rather well.

She hurried back to the door, and he did not follow her. Taking a breath, she attempted to look calm, but her limbs shook as she stepped back into the ballroom. She decided it more prudent to go check in on her mother than to see the other young ladies right at the moment.

Or perhaps she merely wanted to be somewhere safe, near her mother and Lady Goodram, near the card tables and polite conversation, the symbols of dignified society, as though it might erase this recent shame.

As she neared the table where her mother and Lady Goodram were playing cards, she noticed the tall Lord Aldley, his head inclined in conversation with Miss Dervish, who was seated and playing cards. She had been luckier than Lydia, and had escaped to the card room, where the hostess sat, and where Mr. Delacroix would not likely follow, if he indeed had not been invited.

Her mother was facing the door, and was the first to see her. "Lydia, my dear you are flushed. Are you unwell?"

She knew her mother secretly wished to enquire if she had been drinking the forbidden red wine.

Lord Aldley looked up from Miss Dervish, to take in the view of Lydia's person. His brows raised slightly, and a faint smile played around his lips.

His eyes were a deep, innocent blue which offset the high, chiselled cheekbones and strong jawline that might have otherwise made his face look severe. His hair waved at his temples, and was not golden as she had thought when she first beheld it, backlit by candles. It was rather a deep nut brown shot through with beautiful veins of gold.

But his shoulders were just as broad and strong as she had first thought them, and his perfectly tailored shirt and jacket showed off the movements of lithe muscles in his arms and chest as he straightened to better behold her. It took both of them a moment to realize they had been staring at each other just a little bit longer than they ought.

Lydia felt her flush deepen, but rallied herself. "No, Mama. I am very well. I only came to check on you. Has Lady Goodram reduced us to poverty, yet?"

The lady smiled fondly at Lydia. "Your mother is a sly thing, and more lucky at cards than is entirely plausible."

"She has this in common with you, Miss Norwood," added Miss Dervish with a smile. "As I recall you were also rather good at whist, for an uninitiated player."

Lydia omitted to explain to Miss Dervish that her talent for cards might be more fairly attributed to her father's side of the family. She wondered if Lord Aldley were still looking at her, but disciplined herself to keep her gaze pointed elsewhere.

"Well, I suppose I shall be fortunate to escape with my own pearls." Lady Goodram fingered the heirloom strand possessively. Her mother maintained an innocent look, but appeared pleased with herself. It was not a high stakes game, of which she would not have approved, but she clearly enjoyed the pretence.

"You needn't worry, Lady Goodram." Lord Aldley's voice was deep and strong and smooth. It made the hairs on Lydia's back stand straight up.

She drew in her breath sharply. Lord Aldley's beautiful vocalization would have melted her insides, if it did not throw her into a cold panic, for she recognized it. She could never forget the beautiful voice of the earl she had almost met in the pleasure garden the summer before her first season.

How could she not have heard it previously? She should have recognized that lovely singing voice as the same one that enchanted her before. Did he recognize her?

"I shall front you my best gold watch, if you are too hard pressed. Your pearls are safe." Lord Aldley was grinning rakishly at Lady Goodram.

It made him that much more magnetic, but Lydia smiled and relaxed a little. He could not recognize her, surely. He betrayed no sign that he did. And this playful affection for Lady Goodram was becoming in him—as was his tendency to look at Lydia as often as was polite, although he stood next to the most beautiful woman in London.

In the light cast by the great pillar candles and smaller tapers that lit the room, he looked so angelic. She realized she was staring again, and re-focused her attention on the many fascinations of the card table.

"All I ask in return is that you introduce your young friend." Lord Aldley must be speaking of her, but Lydia could not permit herself to look up.

"Oh my, yes of course! I should have offered to do so immediately." Lady Goodram tapped her temple. "Decorum is the first casualty of losing at cards. Lord Aldley, may I introduce Mrs. Norwood's daughter, Miss Lydia Norwood."

"How do you do, my lord." Lydia curtseyed deeply. His lips curved imperfectly around his slightly crooked teeth, forming into a smile that seemed a bit sideways and boyishly charming. Her stomach fluttered.

Lord Aldley bowed. "Very well, I thank you. I am pleased to make your acquaintance, Miss Norwood."

"The pleasure is entirely mine, my lord." Warmth rushed throughout Lydia's body. She could listen to his voice forever, but she had run out of words with which to prompt him, now that the official formalities were over.

Still, she wanted more than anything to impress this man—or at least not to look like a great simpleton with nothing to say. And yet, remaining silent was the best preventative for saying something unacceptable, like the country-come-to-town chit that she was.

Suddenly she remembered his mother. What might Lady Aldley have said to him? But at least it gave her something to speak of.

Lydia opened her lips and forced herself to say, slowly and clearly, "I was introduced to Lady Aldley at a dinner party last week. Her ladyship mentioned you are recently returned from Paris. I hope you had a pleasant journey, my lord." It was a little banal, but it was something.

"Yes, thank you. The weather was very fine for the crossing. Have you ever been to Paris?"

"No, my lord, but I should very much like to. My father has told me stories about it. He says he has eaten the best meals of his life there."

"I can well believe it. I could say as much, myself. The French understand the proper enjoyment of food in a way we English only play at."

"Careful, Lord Aldley," Lady Goodram cautioned, "or she will think you are not a patriot."

"No, indeed, Lady Goodram." Lydia hated the nervous sound to her laugh. "I should never presume to judge his lordship's love of England. And anyway, I have often thought that the things we truly love, we love in spite of those little flaws of which we are well aware, or perhaps even because of them. It is possible that a patriot who finds himself enamoured of French food, might miss certain English meals, though they be inferior fare, and I dare add even though they be quite dreadful, indeed.

His eyes locked on hers, and she thought she might faint, so she turned to look at the urn of flowers behind her mother.

"My daughter exaggerates for your amusement, my lord." Lydia's mother felt obliged to defend her domestic management. "We keep a very good cook, and I shall vouch for it: she has never had a meal that could fairly be called *dreadful* in all her young days."

Lydia remained silent, but could not help the little mischievous smile that played across her lips. She had no idea of its effect on Lord Aldley.

He moved a step closer to her, almost as though a cord around his waist had suddenly been tugged. "If you are not engaged for the first dance, Miss Norwood, might I have the pleasure of standing up with you?"

Lydia's heart sunk through her stomach. She had not a single name on her fan. Her mother would be disappointed.

But on the other hand, he was really the only man she wished to dance with, and judging by the look on Mrs. Norwood's face, she was most pleased to hear Lydia reply, "You do me a great honour, my lord. I am not engaged for the first, and should be delighted to dance with you."

She wrote his name on her fan with her pretty little ivory-coloured pencil, only just restraining herself from encircling it with hearts and cupids.

Lord Aldley smiled broadly, showing his slightly crooked teeth, which Lydia decided were the new standard for perfection. She hoped he might be about to say something more to her, but then his expression suddenly cooled, and she was alarmed that she had done something wrong, until she realized he was looking toward the doorway behind her.

"I hope you will excuse me, Lady Goodram, ladies. I see someone I must speak to." And he was gone.

Lydia felt as if all the air and light had left the room with him. She shook her head and tried to steady herself.

"Well, Miss Norwood." Miss Dervish smiled slyly from behind her cards. "I believe we may pronounce this ball a grand success for *you*."

"We may, indeed," affirmed Lady Goodram. "I was about to chide you for sitting in here instead of circulating with the young folk and filling your dance card. I can see I need not have worried."

"Stop, I beg of you, or my face will never return to a normal colour." Lydia could not stop smiling, but wished to change the subject. "What of you, Miss Dervish? Your card is already filled, I suppose?"

"Yes, I have been very lucky." It was Miss Dervish's turn to blush. But Lydia noted, with a pang of jealousy, that Miss Dervish's flush was like a kiss of rose petals upon her cheek.

"I should venture to say that it has less to do with luck, and more to do with your incomparable beauty." Mrs. Norwood would not be so honest as to explicitly rank Miss Dervish's beauty before that of her own daughter, though it was undeniably true. But she was not an entirely unjust judge of personal appearance. "And you must have the most fashionable head of hair in London."

"You are very kind, Mrs. Norwood. But I think at least *some* of the young men here prefer red hair and green eyes." Miss Dervish was very likeable, really, in spite of her perfection.

"Perhaps, but do you not think you should go fill your dance card a bit more, Lydia? Everyone here is not quite as handsome as Lord Aldley, to be sure, but still very agreeable and of impeccable character. You shall be quite safe." Lady Goodram squinted at the gold face of the Comtoise clock stationed between the champagne-brocade-curtained windows. "And there is not an hour until the music starts. Your mother and I shall finish this game, and join you."

Lydia rejoined the young ladies in the main room, and did not catch sight of Lord Aldley again, but used her pretty pencil to fill two more names into her dance card fan, one a brother to Miss Stokes, the other a Mr. Frobisher, who was a cousin to Miss Ferrel.

"You are having good luck, Miss Norwood," Miss Ferrel told her.

"It is merely thanks to you ladies. I only wish I had brothers and cousins to introduce you to."

"That is not necessary for my part, I assure you." Miss Dreydon seemed out of sorts.

"I am sorry, Miss Dreydon, I meant no offence by it." Lydia thought she had made yet another faux pas.

"I am sure she did not take offence, Miss Norwood." Miss Ferrel smoothed things over. "But we are to understand, as Miss Dreydon has recently informed us, that she prefers not to dance."

Miss Dreydon nodded. "I find no enjoyment in it, and should greatly prefer having an opportunity to converse with my society, rather than dance with them."

Even if it sounded rather like sour grapes, Lydia was not entirely unsympathetic with the sentiment—though they disliked balls for opposite reasons. Lydia greatly enjoyed dancing, but she would prefer not to go to London balls at all.

They were too grand for her, and she thanked the heavens that her mother could not abide the questionable company at public balls. But she smiled inwardly. She could be persuaded to attend a great many balls, if she knew Lord Aldley would attend. Her thoughts were interrupted by the arrival of Mr. Mortimer.

"Miss Norwood! I am glad to see you here." He was dressed impeccably, and in his best looks.

"Thank you, Mr. Mortimer. I hope you are well."

"Indeed I am. And greatly looking forward to dancing with you, if you would oblige me for the fourth." His eyes sparkled.

"I am engaged to dance the fourth with Mr. Stokes."

"I should have known you would be popular. My loss for not arriving earlier. Well, then, what of the fifth?"

"It would be my pleasure to dance the fifth with you, sir."

"Do I ask too much to beg an introduction to these lovely ladies?" Mr. Mortimer gestured to the little group.

Lydia was unsure, she gave an inquisitive look to Miss Ferrel, who smiled and nodded. She introduced him to the three.

"Mr. Mortimer, there you are." Lydia's mother approached with Lady Goodram and Miss Dervish.

As Lady Goodram introduced everyone, Lydia could not help but notice Mr. Mortimer's long gaze at Miss Dervish, almost as though in disbelief. She could well understand his feeling. She, herself, had not yet grown accustomed to this perfect face. Miss Stokes also seemed quite overwhelmed.

"Well, ladies, Mr. Mortimer, I must take my leave for now, as there are a few guests I must go speak to. I hope I shall see you all dancing soon." Lady Goodram quit their little group.

Mrs. Norwood took Lydia's arm and pulled her aside to view the dances on her fan.

"Hmm. Very good, dear. Has Lord Aldley been back to talk with you?"

"No, and I have not seen him."

"If he should ask you to dance a second time, do not hesitate to alter your card to accommodate him, for he is an earl, and these others are of little consequence."

"But, Mama, would that not be very rude? I do not wish to cause a scene and embarrass or offend any of Lady Goodram's guests."

"Much better embarrass a few young men than slight an earl, my dear. You must make the most of this, you know. You will not have so many opportunities to fall into such society. We are not of the fashionable set, and aside from a few gentlemen friends of your father's and the Delacroixs, Lady Goodram is our only real society connection outside of," Mrs. Norwood's voice hushed to a whisper, "the *nouveau riche.*"

"But what is so very wrong with being *nouveau riche*, Mama?" It all seemed rather stupid to Lydia.

"It would take too long to explain it—but it is very important that you pretend to know, and disassociate yourself from that caste as much as may be possible. In fact, do not even mention the term. No, take my advice, darling girl: do what ever it takes to dance a second dance with Lord Aldley, if he should ask. And whatever you do, be inviting and sweet to him when you dance the first."

"Yes, Mama."

"And also, my dear, I do not mean to alarm you, but be on the look out, for I just overheard something between Lady Goodram and one of the servants, and I believe there is an uninvited—" her whispering was cut off.

"Mrs. Norwood, Miss Norwood, Miss Dervish." It was Lord Aldley who had appeared at Lydia's elbow. "I am sorry to have left so suddenly, earlier. I am only lately returned to town, and there is always one thing or another to which I must attend. I hope that I may be properly settled in within a week, so that I might have five minutes conversation without some interruption."

They all assured him there was nothing at all to forgive. Lydia tried to smile reassuringly at Miss Stokes, who looked as though she were about to faint when Lord Aldley asked Mrs. Norwood to introduce him to the little party.

Poor Miss Stokes would simply have to throw away her frayed gloves after this night. But Lydia's own feelings were hardly calm, either. Miss Ferrel, who was closer, took the girl's arm and steadied her.

The first strains of the orchestra warming up filled the ball room. The milling groups of people cleared the floor, and its highly polished surface gleamed with promise in the candle light, like a great magic mirror.

The earl offered Lydia his arm and led her to the floor, and she felt foolishly like a princess in a fairytale. His muscles were firm against her arm, and made her feel inexplicably safe, and at the same time in great peril—of what she could not say, but it was exhilarating and she did not entirely dislike the feeling.

"I hope you are enjoying your evening, Miss Norwood." Lord Aldley took his place for the quadrille, and the music transported Lydia into the pure enjoyment of dance.

"Yes, thank you, my lord." She steadied herself, and focused her thoughts on the topics of conversation that she had formulated, in case there should be uncomfortable lapses. "I meant to enquire earlier, how things were in Paris, now that Napoleon is tucked safely away, again. Is it the same?"

"I am not as old as I look. I do not know, aside from what I have read, how it was before Bonaparte, or before the revolution— which my mother calls *that recent unpleasantness in France*, when she can bring herself to refer to it at all."

Lydia laughed with him, but not for too long. It was his mother, after all.

"But," he continued, "I imagine that it cannot be the same. It can never be the same, perhaps. But that may be forcing too philosophical a turn to the conversation."

"You mean, my lord, like Heraclitus's river, or the ship of Theseus, I suppose." Lydia relaxed at bit as the conversation became more about interest and less an act of social display.

"Yes, just so." His face betrayed a brief look of surprise. "Order is restored—or at least royalty is restored, for I should not say that Napoleonic rule lacked order—in a way Paris is restored. But is it the same Paris?"

"From what I have heard of the city, it is so full of life and dynamic, I should think it was ever-changing. One might argue that Paris was never the same Paris twice, but in that way change is so essential to her nature that as long as she is changing, she will always be the same Paris, no matter what besets her." Lydia stopped herself, reflecting she might be running on too much in a way that, her mother advised her, made an unfavourable impression upon men. "But, now I am being too philosophical. And anyway, I have never seen *la Ville Lumière*. I apologise, my lord, for running on."

His eyes held a dreamy expression. "Please do not apologise. You may be furnishing me with the most sensible conversation I shall have all evening, apart from Lady Goodram's, of course. I hope you will get a chance to see Paris. It has many diversions, and beyond that, if you get to see beneath the surface, I believe you will find it fascinating."

"I hope that I shall. Are you a traveller, in general, my lord?"

"Well, I have been to *York*." He maintained a serious expression, but she was sure he must be joking, so she permitted herself to look down a moment and laugh a little.

"No, do not do that."

"I beg your lordship's pardon," she blushed, "I should not have laughed, I know, but I—"

"I mean do not look down. You may laugh as much as you like, you have a very pretty way of laughing, only pray do not turn your eyes away from me. I only have a few more moments to look at them before I must return you to your friends. Do not deprive me of their full enjoyment." Lord Aldley's lips curled.

Her heart was beating fast, and she knew that her face must be turning about the same colour as her hair. "Oh." It was all she could say, but she obliged him by meeting his gaze.

The way he was looking at her must mean something. There was a silent connection that passed between them without words, palpable but fleeting, like breath frozen in winter air. For the second time this evening, she felt utterly betrayed by her physicality—a charge shot through her line of symmetry, and her nipples seemed to be humming their own little country tune.

It was the end of the dance. Without breaking his gaze into her eyes, he took her arm, and said, "Alas, I must return you, and stop embarrassing you so by staring at your eyes, or I shall embarrass myself by falling over my own feet."

Lydia smiled nervously, and the moment passed. She felt slightly shaky as they made their way back to her little party.

"I must go fulfil my obligations to dance with some other ladies. But as you dance like an angel, I am compelled to ask for the fifth. Please agree to it." Lord Aldley's blue eyes and beautiful voice were mesmerizing.

For a moment Lydia might have promised him anything. "My Lord," she paused, and found no matter how much her mother would want her to, no matter how much she did not want to risk driving Lord Aldley away, she could not embarrass Mr. Mortimer. "I am *not* engaged for the *sixth* dance."

He chuckled. "Very well. Even better, the sixth is to be a waltz—one of the advantages of Lady Goodram's balls. The lady is fond of a waltz, whereas my mother considers them yet another dangerous revolutionary practice from the continent—she is quite unmovable on the point. I shall be happy to dance the sixth with you, except that it means I must wait that much longer. But," he returned her to her mother's side and bowed over her hand, "I shall eagerly look forward to it."

He strode off across the room to lead the Duke's daughter to the floor, and he looked extremely good doing it. She did not even know that lady's name—for she had missed the announcement. But whomever she was, in that moment Lydia could not help hating the sight of her.

She was luckily prevented from staring too long by the arrival of Miss Ferrel's cousin, Mr. Frobisher. She wondered, as she danced with the quiet, droopy-eyed young man, if he might be a little sickly, for he was rather pale and thin.

She thought it just as well that he was taciturn, for it gave her leave to focus on her own thoughts, and try to catch glimpses of Lord Aldley, when she might. She saw Miss Dervish dancing with a handsome young man whose hair was almost white blond. He contrasted so strikingly with that darkling Mr. Delacroix.

Delacroix. How thoroughly thoughts of Lord Aldley had driven her memory of the horrible encounter from her mind. Her mother had been trying to say something about an uninvited person when Lord Aldley's arrival interrupted her. If she had meant to warn Lydia about an intruder, then he must have been discovered. Hopefully Delacroix had by now been made to leave.

She wished never to see him again, but he would be hard to avoid if she remained friends with Miss Delacroix. She could give no explanation of her desire to avoid Mr. Delacroix without confessing what had happened. It was not the sort of thing that one spoke of. Her father could not defend her honour, and nor would she want him to try. There was no harm done, unless word of it should get out.

"Am I such a bad dance partner?" Mr. Frobisher finally asked.

"No. Not at all, sir." Lydia was surprised at the question. "You do very well."

"It is just that your face was very serious, just now, almost disapproving. I thought perhaps I had trod upon your foot." His droopy eyes were quite in earnest, but his lip twitched.

"No, indeed." Lydia shook her head. "I must apologize, my mind was wandering to less agreeable things. I beg your pardon, sir."

"Not at all. You are such a good dancer that you can focus on other things while you dance. You have quite the advantage over me."

"It is the one aspect of my training that I enjoyed," Lydia confessed. "We all have our natural inclinations, I suppose. I must prefer, for example, that no one look too closely at my needle work, or ask me to play the pianoforte. My efforts in those arts are an affront to the senses." Lydia assumed a theatrical look of terror.

He laughed, and suddenly his face did not look so sickly. "You know, most young ladies take pains to exaggerate their accomplishments. It is refreshing to meet one who frankly disavows her own abilities."

"Should I seem more typical of my sex if I owned that I am rather good at riding horses, and have a reasonable command of a couple of foreign languages? Not that I mean to boast, but my penmanship is also not entirely horrid. However, lest you think me of an artistic bent, I should just warn you that drawing and painting are entirely out of the question."

"Indeed, I feel I am in no risk of inflating your accomplishments. But the ones you possess seem charming enough."

"You are very kind, sir." The dance finished and he smiled as he walked her through the couples leaving the dance floor.

"Thank you for the dance, Miss Norwood. I hope we shall meet again." He left her in the company of her mother.

"You are doing well, Lydia. Your dancing is very pretty, and I see you are making an effort to converse with your partners. Your father will be pleased."

"Thank you, Mama. Do you think I have earned some refreshments? I have not any partner for this lancers."

The refreshments, the polite talk, and the intervening dances all blurred into a single tedium that imposed itself between her and her next dance with Lord Aldley.

She felt a certain sympathy for Mr. Mortimer, who, she was increasingly persuaded, was only playing at being interested as a favour to her father. She certainly detected affection in him, but she could not see in it the passion of a lover. This was a relief to her, though she still needed to sort out what was wrong with her father. She resolved to speak with him about it.

"Do I interrupt your thoughts?" At last Lord Aldley had arrived.

Goosebumps formed on her spine at the warm tones of his voice. "Not at all—or, perhaps, but I greatly welcome the interruption of this dance, my lord." Lydia felt foolish for the way her heart beat madly as they walked to the floor, but could not suppress a little smile.

"I saw you dancing with that Frobisher fellow." Aldley's hand was suddenly at Lydia's waist. He guided her masterfully with a delicate but firm pressure at the small of her back.

"Did you?" His touch sent thrills through her. She had to focus her thoughts to speak and perform the requisite hand movements for the waltz. "I should have thought your lordship would be more attentive to a partner, at least when dancing with the daughter of a duke."

She was feeling bold. Lady Goodram had not exaggerated about the brandy.

"I do not believe I neglected my partner." Aldley's lip curved playfully. "But I most certainly noticed you. Frobisher and I are acquainted, in fact, and I have rarely seen him laugh while dancing. You must have a most diverting wit."

"I was not being witty at all. He was laughing at my enumeration of the many things I do badly."

"Indeed?"

"He advised me that young ladies are wont to overstate their accomplishments, not disavow them." Lydia tilted her head. "So apparently I have been going about things the wrong way entirely."

"Or you may just be exceedingly clever in devising new ways to distinguish yourself." Lord Aldley stared in admiration.

"I should never have thought that distinguishing myself by publishing my inabilities could really be called *clever*. However, if you think it an apt stratagem, my lord, I shall not contradict you. Your lordship possesses greater expertise than I in these matters."

"And what makes you say that, pray?" He looked as though he might have taken her comment seriously.

"Why, because I am a commoner from the countryside, woefully inexperienced with society. But you are an earl, my lord. That must imply a superior sophistication, I should think. I suppose I would do better not to point this out, but as I have made a start at highlighting my defects, I find I cannot stop."

"Well." He chuckled and then frowned slightly. "But you know, I am not so enamoured of the rules of this social fencing—partly *because* I am an earl. In fact I think many of what might be called *social stratagems* are entirely at odds with both decency and the proper conduct of society."

"Ah, that is what I mean. You really do have more experience, my lord. Other than a vague discomfort I have that everyone is drafting a complex diagram of accounts and genealogies in their head whenever I am invited to a social gathering, I do not think I even know what your lordship means."

"I suppose some such calculation is inevitable, but in the extreme it becomes thoroughly vulgar. What I meant to refer to, however, is the extent to which the business of making matches has been taken as leave for every type of grasping and overstepping imaginable."

Lydia nodded thoughtfully. She had her Delacroix and he had his Miss Worth—and probably many others besides. She began to wonder if he could be thinking of the day they met in the pleasure garden. But he had made no mention of it.

"The crush at most venues is only a physical symbol of the horrid social spectacle that underlies it. And I do not think it prudent that the winds of fashion may turn precedence on its ear. It goes against the grain, for instance, to allow a handful of women of inferior rank the presumption of *permitting* me entrance to their substandard club."

Lydia was silent. This line of talk burned her cheeks. Could he be referring to her? Was her own interest in the earl not something of a presumption? He had seemed liberal enough at first, but this sudden concern with precedence suggested otherwise. Had he only been toying with her for his own amusement?

Perhaps she had been too unguarded with her feelings and read too much into his. But her heart would not listen to her head. It still fluttered at the beautiful blue of his eyes glinting in the light of candles, still revelled in how close he was to her, how the touch of his hand and the timbre of his voice warmed her insides.

Lydia swallowed and tried to calm herself. "Your lordship refers, I suppose, to Almack's. And on this topic I must defer entirely to the knowledge of my betters, for I shall never see a voucher for that institution."

"Perhaps, but you needn't be envious. The balls are stinking crushes with unspeakably bad fare—I cannot call them *refreshments*. The ball you are currently attending is filled with people of immaculate character, and is of ten times the consequence in real society."

"Real society?"

"Yes. There is an imaginary society, a thronging mass of the ton who think very highly of themselves, for they have some minor pedigree which permits them to exclude the nouveau riche. And in lieu of taste they have enough borrowed money to pay others to dress them and decorate their parlours according to the latest whim of fashion."

He continued, apparently unaware of the inner turmoil that his words, juxtaposed with his touch and the allure of his voice, threw

Lydia into. "But they only think highly of themselves because they do not understand what real substance and real character are. Real society does understand this. Lady Goodram is real society. Almack's is a self-important gambling den that has reduced the institution of marriage to a Wednesday night horse market."

"So, in spite of rank, we have this much in common, my lord: we shall neither of us frequent that place. You, because it is beneath your lordship's touch, and I, because it is beyond my reach." Lydia had never found Almack's even slightly tempting, but thought there must be some personal reason for the earl's strong feelings.

"You speak lightly of it, and I know I speak with too much heat on the topic. But I should hope that you would avoid that place, even if a voucher were within your grasp." He looked earnestly at her.

"I am honoured that your lordship should take an interest in my social exposure. Though, whatever the evils of Almack's may be, I believe I am safe from them. Even if I should meet the standard, my mother detests large public assemblies and balls."

"I am glad to hear it." Aldley suddenly shook his head slightly, as if to dispel a fugue. "But I am a great fool. I have spent my time haranguing on about inconsequential things, when I should have been trying my best to amuse you. Forgive me, Miss Norwood, please."

"There is nothing to forgive, my lord." She felt relieved at this slight retrenchment on his part. "I honestly have so little experience conversing at these gatherings, much less with an earl, that I have no expectations."

She could feel his hand increasing the pressure on her back, drawing her closer to him. She continued, a little breathlessly, "But I must confess that, if left to my own preferences, I should rather hear your lordship's honest thoughts on any topic, than words politely crafted solely for my amusement. So I thank you, my lord. And I have never heard another speak this way about Almack's."

"You should ask Lady Goodram about it sometime."

"I think I shall." Lydia smiled suddenly. "There is a lady of whose society I could never tire, and, though she is very thoughtful, she always makes me laugh."

"I could not agree more." Lord Aldley's face was very close to hers, so she could feel his breath on her cheek, smell him. He continued, "Indeed, I believe she and my friend Rutherford were the people I most missed, while I was away. Though perhaps, had I then the pleasure of such a delightful dance partner, I might never have left."

"I could form a wish, then, that you had, my lord." She knew she was blushing furiously. The fragrance of leather and orange about him, and the manly scent of his skin as he drew her a little closer were turning her interior to hot liquid.

As much as she wished him to continue such sweet utterances, she thought she would say something foolish or faint if he did. She was both relieved and bitterly disappointed at the end of the dance.

The earl took her arm as they walked off the gleaming surface of the magic mirror dance floor. "I fear I must leave you soon, Miss Norwood. And I do not stay to dine, though I must beg Lady Goodram's pardon for it."

"I am sure you will be greatly missed, my lord. But Lady Goodram is of a forgiving nature."

"It has been a great pleasure." He bowed over her hand.

She found herself wishing that he would kiss it as forwardly as Delacroix had done. But they were as opposite as night and day, and she sensed it was not in the earl's character. If only the one were a little more restrained and the other a little less. His eyes locked with hers as he stood straight again. Then he took his leave.

"Well, Lydia? How did you enjoy your second dance?" Mrs. Norwood's face was so animated and joyful, that, had Lydia not been all too familiar with her mother' feelings on strong drink, she might have suspected her of indulging in the brandy.

"I enjoyed it very well, Mama. It was most enlightening." Lydia felt as giddy as her mother looked. For the rest of her life, she would never forget dancing with the earl at Lady Goodram's ball.

CHAPTER 11

*L*ydia and her mother returned home late after the ball, but her father was waiting up for them by the fire in the south parlour.

They sat in chairs which were French, ornately carved with curving legs, bone white and gold upholstering, and delicate gold detailing at the rounded top of the backs. They were elegant, after her mother's taste. Lydia preferred the more cosy chairs of her own small parlour, but as it was her mother's favourite location, the grander south parlour had become the family room.

"Well, my dear, what of your first ball of the season?" Mr. Norwood blinked fondly at his daughter.

"It was a great success, Mr. Norwood, a very great success." Lydia's mother answered for her. "Lord Aldley danced with Lydia twice. Only think of it!"

Mr. Norwood nodded his approval. "And what of Mr. Mortimer? Did you jilt him for the earl?"

"Oh, I danced with Mr. Mortimer, Papa." Lydia smiled sleepily and sipped her camomile tisane. "But you must not talk of my jilting him. He is a kindly man and he feels affection for me as your daughter, but I wish you would not imply more."

He patted her hand. "Very well, my dear."

They all sat quietly for a while, then her mother declared her intention of retiring. Her father stood, and said, rather gloomily, "If you are not too tired, Lydia, I should like to have a word with you in the library."

It was not that it was an unusual request. They were very fond of each other and often had long *tête a têtes*, discussing books, articles in the paper, hunting, or even occasionally stories of his travels abroad— though she was certain these were heavily edited to be *less unsuitable* for a young maiden's ears.

But this time her father seemed strained, as though he were not looking forward to a visit with his daughter.

Lydia shuddered a little at what might be causing his strange demeanour. Surely he was not ill. He had been eating well enough. And he seemed to have accepted what she had said about Mr. Mortimer, so it could not be that.

The servant lit the candelabra, fixed up the fire and then departed as Lydia sat down sideways in her favourite leather chair with her legs dangling over one arm. It didn't matter anymore if her dress got wrinkled, as her mother told her she could only wear each gown once.

She stared dreamily up at the spines of the many books. She loved how the candle light cast a patina over the stacks, and brought up the sheen of the hand-worn leather bindings. Her father sighed deeply and poured himself a brandy.

"You seem distressed, Papa. What is it that wears upon you so?"

"Ah, I see I am transparent." He grimaced. "I hate to trouble you with it, my dear child, but I must. You are in many ways much more sensible than your mother—indeed, you have almost been like a son to me..." She knew this was meant as a compliment. "So I am telling you first, before your mother, even. You will forgive me if I say this without delicacy..."

"There is no need for that between us, Papa. Pray, tell me what is the matter. Surely you are not ill?"

"No, no. Nothing like that. I am perversely full of good health, so that I may be entirely sensible of the mess that I have made."

"What is it, Papa?" Lydia could not keep the alarm from her voice.

He sat heavily in the leather chair across from her, and took a deep drink from his balloon glass. "I have great cause to be glad for your increasing interest in taking part in society, Lydia. And I find myself extremely grateful for your mother's connection with Lady Goodram, for we shall need it more than ever now... Now that we are destitute."

"Destitute? Surely not! But how?" She regretted that she said it immediately when she saw the pained look on her father's face.

"In the past I have restrained my gambling to the club."

"You could not have gambled away our fortune at cards."

"No, not at cards. I am not so big a fool as that. Unfortunately, as events have shown, I am a big enough fool to speculate heavily on risky investments."

"But surely it is not *all* gone."

"I exaggerated only slightly. Let us say that I lost multiple warehouses in Martinique to fire, and then I tried to cover the loss through buying the cargo already en route on several ships from Brazil. In fact, I liquidated many other assets, mortgaged this house, and bought the lot of them."

He paused and shook his head. "I have been merrily awaiting the arrival of these ships, all the time believing that I should be richer than a prince when they came in. I thought coffee should go sky high because of the shortage created by the fires, which had damaged everyone's warehouses, not just mine. But I was a fool. I did not realize that a defect in the insurance meant that it did not transfer with the cargo. And I have just received word that the ships have sunk —all but two."

He passed a hand over his face. "There is every expectation that the other two are also gone, though no official report has come yet. Even if they made it to England, their cargo would not cover the losses. And so, I have lost a fortune. Why could I never be satisfied with nice, safe five percent returns?"

This miserable confession ended with a refill of brandy, and he began to think aloud. "We still have Nesterling Lodge. But with the encumbrance upon this property, I shall have to choose between them. And I suppose there is a small income from Nesterling. Thank heavens Farleigh is such an excellent manager. We have very little prospect of liquid capital besides, except..." He took a thoughtful drink, then shook his head. "No."

"Except?"

"I have set aside fifty thousand pounds to form part of the settlement, should you marry. It will have to be all of your dowry, now."

"So we are very far from destitute. You must use it to pay off the mortgage, or to reinvest."

"No, my dear, I have had enough of gambling with your future."

Lydia replied more bluntly than she intended, "But I have no immediate prospects for marriage, and little inclination to marry. If we rebuild the fortune, I shall not have to."

"That, my dear, is more precisely what I wanted to discuss with you. I am very well aware that I have raised you, much to your mother's consternation, almost like a son. I have permitted you liberties of action and information that are normally out of the question for young women. And although I was probably indulging my own inclinations—"

"And mine."

He patted her hand. "Be that as it may, in retrospect it may have been the wrong path to place you on. But I always thought that a less typical upbringing would do you no harm. You must believe that. I did not mean to be a bad father."

"But you are not a bad father. You have been the best—"

"No, my dear, I have not. But I assumed our wealth would protect you. You would be an original. You would only marry if you chose it, and unlike men of the quality, most of your suitors would probably prefer a useful, vivacious sort of wife. Or if you had suitors from the upper ranks, they would be of such a bent that a little education, adeptness of mind, and physical robustness would not be viewed as a disadvantage. Only now everything has changed."

"We are really not so very poor, Papa. And I have always preferred the country. We can go and live there quite comfortably." She could not bear to see him so gloomy for her sake. Except for the recent allurement of Lord Aldley, she could happily quit London forever and retire to the countryside. She loved Nesterling.

"We shall not have the money for new dresses, and bonnets."

"I care not."

"Nor for delicacies of the table, nor for books. We shall sell the library over time."

She shook her head, but resolved internally that she could make do without books.

"And the horses—we shall keep only those necessary for the farm." He sighed and finished his brandy in one inelegant gulp. "I fear it is this last item that will most pain you. I shall be forced to sell Aristophanes.

And we shall keep a minimum of servants. In short, our sole income will be from farming, which is not entirely predictable, and we shall live very carefully."

Lydia paled. Not Ari. He was the best jumper she had ever seen. She loved that horse. Surely her father was over-reacting. He acted as though he did not have a surplus fifty thousand pounds sitting in an account.

They would not have to sell the horses immediately. Perhaps something could be done to save them. But if they let the servants go, would that mean Ole Maeb as well? She had rheumatic pains and did not see well. Lydia could not bear it.

"But what of Old Maeb? Remember that she saved my life when I was a babe. Mama says that were it not for Old Maeb's herbal concoction, I should have died of that fever. And she is beyond the years that anyone else will hire her. We cannot cast her off so heartlessly."

The thought was even worse than losing Ari, who might have a good life in someone else's stables, loved and well cared for.

"Do not worry yourself on that head. Her employment with us has been entirely symbolic in these last few years. I shall cease to pay her wages—but as long as we have a home, she will have a place in it. Only none of us will have the level of luxury to which we have grown accustomed."

"I can endure it, Papa. And in time we could earn back our wealth— fifty thousand is no small amount for a starting investment."

Her father shook his head resolutely. "That money shall be your marriage settlement. That is my point, Lydia. Our circumstances have changed and now you must marry. And it will be best if you make a match quickly, before the ton discovers our turn of fortunes, for it will hurt your chances greatly. I had hoped perhaps you would consider Mr. Mortimer. He is a decent man, and kind. And he loves country life as much as you do."

"He is a good man, Papa, but I cannot marry him. I simply cannot. Nor do I believe him to have any deep feeling for me."

Her father sighed.

"How long do you suppose we can conceal the truth of our circumstances?" Lydia's brain began concocting plans.

"The devil won't be at the door for some months. If I sell a few items discreetly, I can cover the payments on this house, so we can remain in London long enough to make a good match for you, I hope. But you must marry a man of some fortune. If I can see you well-married, I shall not have to worry. Your mother and I can live in the countryside without labouring under the expense of spending the season in London—though it will not make her happy."

Lydia nodded sadly. Her mother would be devastated.

"And do not speak a word of this to anyone, my dear." Her father was stern. "Not even your friend, Miss Ravelsham. I am sure she is very trustworthy, but we can take no risks."

CHAPTER 12

$\mathcal{T}$he morning sunlight lit up the butter yellow walls of the breakfast parlour with an optimistic glow that could not penetrate Lydia's gloom. She wished she could be cheered by the sweet fairy design on the teacup, or by the rainbows cast through the crystal inset in the window.

Her mother's eyes were slightly swollen at breakfast, but no omission of toilette or display of emotion suggested that there was anything amiss. Lydia wondered how much her father had told his wife.

Lydia had not cried, but her eyes were shadowed, as she had spent a sleepless night trying to devise a way out of their straits. She had some vague notion that she might invest the small amount of money she had saved from her allowance and help the family that way. It was not such a solid plan that it compensated for her tired eyes and wilted vigour, but it was a start.

She was grateful that their morning visitors would likely attribute their dull looks to the late conclusion of Lady Goodram's ball. Lydia found herself recalling with some sympathy Lady Goodram's frequent observation that morning visits coming on the heels of a ball were an uncivilized abomination. Lady Goodram could simply declare herself *not at home.*

But the Norwood family were obliged to endure it as best they could, for they now relied on cultivating their acquaintance more than ever. Yet Mrs. Norwood managed to leave Lydia alone with the young morning callers when they arrived.

Miss Delacroix contrived to call upon them early, no doubt to get the timeliest possible information about the ball, and possibly also to punish Lydia for having attended a ball to which she had not been invited.

Tilly accompanied her because she had arrived to call at the Delacroix's, only to discover Miss Delacroix leaving to call at the Norwood's. No doubt Tilly wished to lend support to Lydia under the burden of Miss Delacroix's call—though it was also possible that she entertained a tiny hope of Lydia's supplying cream biscuits and news of some sordid happenings.

"And Lord Aldley attended?" Miss Delacroix's face was straining to maintain a pleasant expression.

"Yes, he is apparently well acquainted with Lady Goodram." Lydia smiled a little at the memory.

"And did that lady introduce you?" Tilly could not help twisting the thorn of jealousy which was visibly lodged in Miss Delacroix's heart.

"Yes, she did." Lydia did not really want to be closely interviewed about it in front of Miss Delacroix, but clearly Tilly took great amuse-ment in precisely this activity.

"What was he like? I hear he is very handsome." Tilly cocked her head.

"Yes, he is, indeed," Lydia affirmed. "And his manners are rather different from Lady Aldley's, I should say."

"What do you mean?" Miss Delacroix leaned in slightly, and Tilly shot Lydia a warning look.

Lydia took the hint and amended, "Oh, I do not quite know. I really am not well enough acquainted with Lady Aldley to comment on her mode of expression. But Lady Aldley is truly grand, and I admit that can intimidate a girl from the country. I should just say that Lord Aldley made me feel more at ease."

Miss Delacroix sat straight again. "Yes, well, I have heard that he is very much the kindly gentleman in his ways. I do not believe he would ever attempt to rub anyone's nose in their own inferiority of rank."

"Why yes, I believe you must be right." It was probably not entirely true. But Lydia endured the barb with complacence, because she knew it proceeded from Miss Delacroix's frustration at having never met the earl.

"And did he ask you to dance, or was he as utterly bewitched with Miss Dervish as Miss Delacroix's brother was?" Tilly was not letting the matter drop.

Miss Delacroix fluttered her lashes slightly at this question, but said nothing.

"So you knew that Miss Dervish was to attend?" Lydia did not conceal her surprise. "I did not. I had not known she was acquainted with Lady Goodram."

She was aching to talk to Tilly about Mr. Delacroix's unsupportable behaviour, but she could hardly discuss it in front of Miss Delacroix. She did not wish even to mention his presence, for fear of embarrassing her with the news that her brother had intruded upon a ball to which he had not been invited. If it were, indeed, news to her.

"I do not believe they are well acquainted. I understand Lady Goodram arranged an introduction because she wanted to meet the famed beauty, and only invited her fairly recently. But you are evading my question, I think. He *did* ask you to dance, did he not? You sly thing."

"We danced, yes." Lydia tried to keep her expression neutral, and not grin stupidly like an infatuated school girl.

"That is what I mean by a *kindly gentleman*." A crease was forming in Miss Delacroix's forehead. "He is very attentive to Lady Goodram, I understand. No doubt she suggested he ask you to dance, and he was kind enough to oblige her."

"I do believe he is very fond of Lady Goodram, indeed. Although, in point of fact, Lord Aldley requested the introduction. But then, it is entirely possible that she had suggested it to him earlier." Lydia knew that being agreeable about it would not truly appease, but would only deny Miss Delacroix the one real satisfaction she could take from this conversation, which was to irritate Lydia.

Miss Delacroix nodded.

"And how was it? Did he dance well?" Tilly was grinning.

"Yes. Well, I do not quite recall how he danced, actually, so I suppose he danced well."

"That must mean you were talking," Tilly prompted.

"I thought it was expected." Lydia noted the slight swelling of the fine blue veins at Miss Delacroix's throat and hairline.

"Indeed it is," agreed Tilly. "Did you discuss anything interesting?"

"I found it very interesting, though I could hardly tell you what we spoke of. Paris—we spoke of Paris. And for some reason the Ship of Theseus."

Tilly laughed.

"The Ship of What?" Miss Delacroix squinted at Lydia.

"She means they were discussing philosophical questions." Tilly continued to chuckle.

"Ah." Miss Delacroix, satisfied by this answer, smiled again. "That

certainly does not sound like a topic likely to produce strong contro-
versy, at least."

"I am glad you think so, for I admit that I have very little idea what is
best to talk of, in such cases, for I have never before danced with an
earl. We did speak of Almack's at one point." Lydia could not be so
cruel as to mention his remarking upon her eyes, but she would not
forget it.

"*Almack's?*" Miss Delacroix's superior giggle sounded like a brittle
glass bell. "How did you contrive to discuss a gathering which you
have *never* attended?"

Tilly cocked an inquisitive brow at Lydia, but she was spared further
interrogation by the entry of her mother followed by servants
carrying several long boxes.

"Some of the new dresses are completed, my dear! I thought perhaps
your friends might like to see them. There is a lovely china blue
muslin, with pearl detailing around the bodice, and white rosettes at
the sleeve. It is as light as a cloud."

Lydia thought it a pity they could not send the dresses back and
cancel the orders for the others. The outlay on things for the season
must have amounted to a great sum. It would have been much better
put into an investment.

Her mother was beaming happily, so her father must have concealed
the worst from her, or perhaps she was concealing it from herself. She
did have a way of putting unpleasant things out of her mind.

As they examined the dresses at length, Lydia smiled and gushed
along with the other girls. She would not dampen Mrs. Norwood's
enjoyment of the moment, knowing that it would be the last opportunity for her to bask in all the lace and grandiosity of a London season.

Tilly leaned close to Lydia's ear and whispered, "We must talk later."

Indeed they must. Lydia wanted Tilly's advice on what to do about

Mr. Delacroix's behaviour. And in her heart she more urgently wished to know what Tilly would make of Lord Aldley's words. The earl had occupied her thoughts almost as much as their recent change of circumstances. ⸺

But it was silliness. He was an earl, no matter how much he wished for an unimpeded view of her eyes. He could go about amusing himself and creating vague expectations amongst the commoners as much as he liked, but marriage was another matter entirely. He would marry above her, certainly.

And now that her family's prospects were so altered, she did not even have the fortune to attract a suitor of his calibre. For whatever her father might say, she could not keep a dowry that would leave her parents in such straitened circumstances.

It seemed a perverse fate that right at the moment when she had finally met a man whom she might want to marry, her prospects were so altered as to remove all hope. And yet, she could not help hoping, wishing at least to know him better.

She had just convinced herself to put any thoughts of Lord Aldley out of her head, when Miss Delacroix asked Lydia's mother, "And have you had any visit from Lady Aldley since Miss Norwood's introduction at our dinner party?"

"We are not so fortunate as to have the close acquaintance with her ladyship that Lady Delacroix enjoys. But I hope that may change, now that Lydia has been introduced to her, and to Lord Aldley."

"I do believe that Lady Aldley's inclinations for acquaintance are somewhat different than her son's." Miss Delacroix was clearly enjoying her superiority.

"Yes, that would certainly be quite natural. Sons have their own minds —especially when they become earls." Mrs. Norwood was smiling, unperturbed.

Lydia began to wonder if her mother was actually oblivious of Miss

Delacroix's spite, or whether she might be rather good at these little battles waged with polite words.

"We should not set our hopes too high, therefore, Lydia," her mother continued. "The mother may never call upon us, even though her son dances with you *twice*, though he leaves before the dinner break." Mrs. Norwood played with a violet in the flower vase.

"Twice." Miss Delacroix looked, for a fleeting moment, as though she had just tapped open a rotten egg.

"Oh yes, did not Lydia tell you? You should not play so coy, my dear." Her mother sniffed the violet.

"I do not mean to be coy, Mama. Only I did not realize it was of any great import." Lydia wondered to herself if she had missed a key signal from the earl. All these hidden meanings in the things the ton said and did were like a secret code to her.

Tilly looked from Mrs. Norwood to Miss Delacroix to Lydia, and her petite, full lips curved impishly. "Oh, it is not of such great import, at all, is it Miss Delacroix? But it is a very good sign."

"Yes, perhaps." Miss Delacroix rose. "Well, I see I have stayed longer than is civil for a morning call. I beg you will forgive me."

"Nothing of the sort. I enjoy so much having you young ladies over. It brings me back to my own days as a girl enjoying the London season. Please give my greetings to your mother, Miss Delacroix."

"Indeed I shall. You will look very pretty in your dresses, Miss Norwood. Thank you for showing them to me."

Lydia remarked to herself that Miss Delacroix had a very useful knack of becoming increasingly polite as she grew more irked by a conversation. Mrs. Norwood rang for the servant to see Miss Delacroix out.

"If you are not needed at home, Miss Ravelsham, would you stay to some nuncheon?" Her mother was all beneficent smiles. "If your mother needs the carriage, I can send you back in ours, so you may change before you and Lydia go for your outing."

"That is very kind of you to offer, Mrs. Norwood. But I am afraid I must go call on Mrs. DeGroen. However, I shall certainly return this afternoon, for it looks to be a lovely day for a walk in the park."

By the time Lydia and Tilly arrived at the park, Lydia was fairly bursting to speak to Tilly, but she wandered quietly through the fragrant grasses and trees until they were out of earshot of the servants.

"I have something to tell you," they both blurted out in heated whispers.

"I must speak first." Tilly was determined. "I called on the Delacroix ladies on Friday, and Miss Delacroix was quite beside herself. No doubt she would not have spoken of it to me, had I not come upon her shortly after the events, but apparently—"

"Is it her brother? Has he done something to Miss Dervish?"

"Good heavens, no! I believe you have been reading too many novels —though I am loathe to let the words pass my lips. In fact, forget that I said that. You should read *more* novels. Only do not take them to represent the secret lives of those around you. There are a few supremely sordid people, but only a very few are that interesting, I assure you." Tilly seemed disappointed by this state of affairs.

However, she rallied herself and continued. "In any case, do you want to hear the story or not? Of course you do. So, as I was saying, apparently Lady Delacroix had just dismissed Miss Delacroix's abigail—a faithful family servant and companion to Miss Delacroix these six years."

"I can understand her distress at the loss of such a companion. But why on earth would her ladyship dismiss the abigail?"

"Quite. That, indeed, is the material question. And the answer is that this young woman, *Marie*, if we are to believe that is her *real* name, was suspected to have stolen a pair of her ladyship's earrings—marquise cut rubies set 'round with diamonds. Miss Delacroix had just borrowed them for a dinner engagement, and therefore they were rather accessibly sitting upon her dressing table."

"Such conduct from a long trusted servant! Is it possible?" Lydia was astounded.

"Possible, of course, but exceedingly unlikely. Have you encountered Marie?" Tilly rolled her eyes. "She is sweet and loyal, and as dull-witted as a ball of yarn. The very thought of it is entirely absurd, as any member of the household should know. Which makes me think that Lady Delacroix has another reason for dismissing Marie, or else that she is trying to conceal from the household the identity of the true thief. Or if we are very lucky, both."

"And how should that make us lucky?"

"Why it smacks of a scandal delicious enough to compensate even for the tedium and endless tiny implied insults that are our lot in calling on Miss Delacroix. You are even more at risk than I, now that you have engaged the interest of Lord Aldley. She will jealously seethe against you, but insist upon increasing the acquaintance in the hopes of gaining more intelligence about, or perhaps even meeting, her quarry."

"Do you really think I have engaged his interest?" A little ray of hope pierced the cloud around Lydia's heart.

"Quite possibly. A lady of some rank might take a second dance at such a ball as a sign that a gentleman intended to press his suit."

"I did not say it before." Lydia could not help blushing. "But his lord-ship expressed a desire that I should not look away, so that he might have a view of my eyes."

"Oh my. That *is* something."

"I thought so, too." Lydia looked down at the grass. "But I am not of the quality. Might he not be merely amusing himself with a meaningless flirtation?"

"It is not impossible. But although you have no claim to rank, his lordship's manners should be dictated by the right customs of the nobility. Still, I do not know anything of his character, yet."

"And we cannot assume," added Lydia, thoughtfully, "that noble birth means gentlemanly conduct."

Tilly's eyes narrowed. "What do you mean? Has Lord Aldley taken some liberties with you?"

"No, not at all. I mean, not Lord Aldley." Lydia winced at the air of disappointment in her voice.

"I see. Well then, this is what you wished to tell me, I suppose." Tilly gave her an alarmed look. "I should have let you speak first. Out with it."

Lydia relived the shock, anger and mortification of Mr. Delacroix's affront as she relayed it to her friend. She also included the details of Mr. Delacroix's prior conduct outside her father's club and his forwardness when paying call the day after the Delacroix party.

She decided to omit the bits about her tree-climbing. In the end, she felt relieved to have finally told it all to someone.

"What shall I do, Tilly?"

"Well, first off, you must stop going about town unescorted." Tilly furrowed her brows and shook her head. "I admit I was a little suspicious of the veracity of your note on that day you left us in the shops —though I was relieved you had made it home uneventfully. You and I have no title, no claim even to the ranks of gentle folk, and so we are a little more at liberty than ladies are, but there are limits. In some ways we are more vulnerable than ladies, and London is not a safe place for women in general. There is good reason for your mother's strictures on the topic."

"Are you sure you are truly my friend, Tilly, and not some imposter? I should have thought you would be more sympathetic to my desire for liberty."

"I am entirely sympathetic. But this is not the countryside, and you are no longer a child. London is a cesspool of crime and vice. If you have any interest in Lord Aldley, you must desist in conduct that can only result in the certain death of your chances in polite society, or worse, in the suspicion of your loss of virtue."

Lydia was shocked that her carefree friend was suddenly so deadly serious.

"Very well. You have my word. I shall always have a servant with me, at least, and I shall avoid the alleys on Bond Street." Then, noting Tilly's lifted brow, she added, "I shall avoid alleys altogether, and all streets entirely, unless I have a proper chaperone."

"That will do for a start. But you must absolutely tell no one else of this effrontery. No good can come out of it."

"Not even to warn Miss Dervish?"

"No. It is too risky. And I think she may already be on her guard, for, according to your account of the ball, she disentangled herself from him with some haste."

Lydia's brow creased. "But what of Mr. Delacroix? What shall I do about him?"

"Never permit yourself to be alone with him again. That means you must avoid being alone, even at safe social gatherings in respectable homes, if there is any possibility that he might be present. I also think it advisable that you have both a man and a maid servant with you whenever you set a foot out of doors, unless your father should accompany you. I am developing a rather dim theory of what

Delacroix's interest in you might be, and I suspect it is more than mere dalliance that would tempt him into such bad ton as invading Lady Goodram's ball by stealth."

"Do you think he is fortune hunting?"

"I do, indeed." Tilly's face was very serious again. "His family has some small fortune, but of course his elder brother, the viscount, holds the purse strings. It can be rather hard for younger sons, particularly if they enjoy gambling for high stakes. But I do not think you were his principle prey, as he approached Miss Dervish first. I believe your encounter with him was the product of opportunity, rather than design."

"Yes, I take your point."

"Still, he is acting somewhat desperately. I should think that fox will spring on whichever duck first steps out of the pond."

"That is a flattering metaphor." Lydia feigned an offended look.

"I am pleased you think so. But, upon reflection, perhaps I should have said *goose*." Tilly was unrepentant.

Glad to have the serious mood dispelled, Lydia picked a weed and threw it at her friend.

"Such uncivil conduct will never win you an earl, you know. And anyway—good Lord!" Tilly suddenly exclaimed. "Is that not the earl himself? What the devil is he staring up into that tree for?"

Lydia flushed a deep red. He could certainly see the tree house from that vantage point. "I cannot imagine. But I had rather not meet him just now. Let us turn back."

CHAPTER 13

*A*ldley took in the view of the back gardens from his enormous picture window. He used to love playing with his father in their enclosure as a lad, and the yard at his London dwelling reminded him of it. A rope swing hung from a mossy tree.

He smiled when he remembered his father pushing him on just such a swing. The rope had been rotten when Aldley moved in, so he replaced it. Upon his return from Paris he had also replaced the deteriorating wooden seat, despite the fact that the swing was never used.

He chuckled to himself. If Miss Norwood were here, she might ask whether, if all the parts had been replaced, it was truly the same swing?

He wondered if Miss Norwood would like it. Would she enjoy swinging her little children there, laughing along with them as they experienced the exhilaration of near flight? Where had that thought come from? Aldley shook his head.

Why was he ignoring his guest and musing about a relative stranger? He should be thinking of his sister. He should never have let things get so far out of hand with her awful husband.

He turned from the window and went to the sideboard to pour dark rum into two heavy-bottomed cut crystal glasses. He handed one to Rutherford, who had slung his long body over one of the leather chairs. His friend took the glass gratefully.

"Cheers, Aldley." Rutherford sipped the drink. "Mmm. This is my rum."

"So it is. You have a most discerning palette. Have you heard anything from your connections in Venetia?"

"Not quite. It is too soon yet. My letters will have only recently arrived there. You should calm yourself." Rutherford swirled his drink and admired the light passing through it from the window. "You have already provided adequate funds to your sister, so the worst of the problem has been attended to."

"But the humiliation she must have suffered. I should like to lay a beating on that Essington cur. What kind of man leaves his wife and child without sufficient money to keep house while he is away, and with no reliable means of contacting him?" Aldley clenched a fist.

"Well, far be it from me to defend your mother's hand-picked pearl in the oyster of English nobility," Rutherford rubbed an eyebrow idly, "but the address *was* reliable for the first few months."

"That is not much of a defence, I should say."

"No indeed. But we must not rule out the possibility that he is more a beefwit than a cad, and has merely got himself into some straits. I believe abductions are not entirely unheard of in some parts of that country." Rutherford grinned.

"I should think someone would have received a demand for ransom, if that were the case. It is possible that he fell ill before he could send word of his new lodgings. Or..."

"Or he could be dead." His friend's grin did not diminish.

"Indeed." The thought had crossed Aldley's mind before.

"It is not Christian of me, but I confess I do not find that prospect entirely disagreeable," added Rutherford.

"Nor I. To his health then." They clinked glasses together and drained them. "This rum is heavenly, Rutherford. You shall make a killing off of that cargo."

"It is vulgar of you to say so, *my lord*, but I hope you are right. Then maybe you will permit me to renew my addresses to your sister, when her mourning is over." Rutherford laughed at his own dark jest.

Aldley knew his friend was only joking, but the idea had some appeal. "You know you would have my blessing, Rutherford, though I believe I may demand those four greys as the bride price."

"Much good it would do you, for you could never drive them. And I dare say your sister would not much care for your offering her hand in exchange for horse flesh, however sweetly they go."

"But let us not be precipitous." Aldley laughed along with his friend. "We have not found the wretch yet. And, as Lady Goodram advises me, *weeds do not die*."

"A wise lady." Rutherford drained his tumbler. "And did you enjoy her ball? You are of sturdier stuff than I. After our return journey from Essington Hall, I scarcely had time to swallow a bit of cold ham before I fell into a deep sleep—and I had not so recently made the crossing."

"I only stayed for part of the first half and left before dinner, for which offence I shall owe that excellent lady a case of champagne in penance."

"I hope that is not *my* case of champagne."

"No, indeed." Aldley stood to refresh his friend's drink. "You shall have yours tomorrow. I brought back about a ship full from France." Aldley returned to staring out the window at the swing.

Rutherford interrupted his reverie. "I breakfasted with Frobisher, you know. He mentioned there was one young lady you danced with twice, though she is sadly bereft of the usual accomplishments of ladies."

"She is not, in fact, even a *lady, per se.*" Aldley tried to look bored. "Is it not a little out of character for Frobisher to be gossiping like an old woman? What is his interest in this commoner with too little skill at needle work to meet his exacting standards?"

"As I said, his interest was in your having danced with her twice." Rutherford pulled a stray hair off of his shoulder. "That is quite something for a man who did not stay through the first half. I dare say if you stayed for both you might have dined with her and managed six dances or perhaps even seven, and be well on your way to earning yourself a *nouveau riche* father-in-law."

"Nonsense. If I had stayed for both, I should have paced myself."

Rutherford's lip twitched. "Frobisher also mentioned that she was a tall girl with beautiful red hair and emerald green eyes. Not terribly fashionable, to be sure, but it puts me in mind of another commoner you once showed an interest in."

"Oh, I was a mere lad then, a school boy imagining himself in love." Aldley raised a disgusted brow at his friend's broad smile. "You think you are terribly clever and insightful, but the case is only this: I danced with her twice because she was interesting and more than a little pretty. That is all. I have scarcely thought of her since."

"Fine, then."

"It is only that, fashionable or not, I find red hair and green eyes alluring." Aldley drained and refilled his glass. "Everyone has certain predilections, do they not? It does not mean they are entirely governed by them."

His friend bowed assent, contriving only to smile blandly.

"Rutherford, I've changed my mind: I shall want the four greys *and* your barouche *in advance*, and my sister shall mourn for a full two years."

His friend was seized with laughter, but raised his hand in protest.

"And one more word from you," Aldley continued his proclamations, "and I shall take back the champagne."

"That you have not yet delivered." Rutherford's upper lip quivered.

Aldley ignored this last comment and stood. "Now, I have a matter to look into. I shall meet you at the club in two hours—that is, if you can stop giggling like a bacon-brained school lad and find your way to Pall Mall."

"I believe I may be able to. Just." Rutherford wiped his eyes.

When they met again at the club, Aldley was deep in thought. He scowled at the gleaming black oak table and downed a glass of brandy before commencing with his customary champagne.

Rutherford lit a cigar calmly as he sat down. "I shall assume from your demeanour that the matter you were looking into poked you in the eye."

"You could say that."

"What is it, Aldley? Is there some development in your sister's case?"

"No. Happily it has nothing to do with Elizabeth." Aldley stopped scowling, but he did not look pleased.

"What then?" Rutherford exhaled a long plume of smoke.

Aldley's shoulders slumped. "I believe what most bothers me is not so much a connection to the persons who might be at risk, but a hatred for the villain in the case."

"Your riddles are most theatrical. Pray, have another drink."

Aldley laughed. "You are a deplorable friend to attempt to pry information out of me, and then ridicule the form it takes. But as you insist," he downed a glass of champagne, "there, that is much better."

"Can you not at least tell me who the villain is?" Rutherford snapped his fingers and fresh glasses of champagne were brought.

"Not here. But let us say he is a member of the ton who has recently given me several reasons, and in more than one country, to lay a beating on him."

"This hasn't anything to do with a certain opera singer in Paris, has it?" Rutherford quirked a brow.

Aldley's lips flattened. "That is merely the first instance. And if it were only that he had preyed on her youth and inexperience, I could perhaps overlook it. It was her willing decision to consort with him after all. True, it irked me greatly to see her throw herself and her talent away on such a worthless man, but it was her choice. That much I do not hold against him."

"Ah, then I know what man you are speaking of. When you wrote me of the business with Solange, I admit I doubted your being entirely neutral." Rutherford looked Aldley in the face. "Forgive me. I see now that you were not in the role of a jilted lover."

"No. Ours was a friendship, nothing more. When she took up with him, our acquaintance ended. But shortly after my return to London, I received word from my Paris solicitor that Solange, deserted by the villain in question, had died in childbirth in some squalid place. But she first sent word to the solicitor to contact me and plead for aid for her child."

"He abandoned her entirely? He did not even establish a home for her and his expected child?" Rutherford procured more champagne.

"Yes." Aldley sighed heavily. "I made arrangements to bring the infant to London. But the child was sickly and had died before I even replied to the first letter. I learned of this two days later."

"A sad story. But you know that had you taken this child in, anyone who discovered the fact would assume it was yours." Rutherford extinguished his cigar and slung his arm over the chair back.

"Certainly. But the indignity of gossip is a small thing to tolerate, really, where a greater purpose is served. To add to his offences, the man in question has affronted a lady of my acquaintance by slithering his way into a ball to which he was not invited. Happily, I was there to escort him quietly out. He was upon the point of giving me such an insult as could only result in my demanding satisfaction, but then he wisely walked away. I detest him, but I do not want his blood on my hands."

"Yes. Quite. I am glad of it. I should rather not be your second and be forced to get up before dawn. That would be a grave injustice." Rutherford smirked. "But these are all past sins, what has so recently soured your mood?"

"Suffice it to say that he has attempted to correspond with a young lady clandestinely and in language that could seriously harm her reputation, if discovered."

Rutherford stretched out his long legs and slid into a proper slouch, sighing, "Well, is she involved with him?"

"I believe I came upon the note before she knew of its existence. I apprehend from the content that she has already spurned his attentions on more than one occasion. His intentions are principally dishonourable, though marriage is no doubt his object. I understand she has a considerable fortune." Aldley sunk into sullen thought for a few minutes.

"I suppose you cannot expose him without casting a shadow upon her, as well."

"Indeed." Aldley's brows knit together. "But I have been considering revealing the letter to her father, that he may at least be on his guard."

"That seems a good idea." Rutherford's face brightened.

"I am only concerned that seeking the acquaintance and calling on him will create a suspicion that I mean to court his daughter." Aldley sipped pensively at his drink.

"Did you not just say that you would tolerate the indignity of gossip in the pursuit of a higher purpose?" Rutherford's smile was lopsided.

"This is an entirely different matter. The gossip would not only concern me."

"I dare say a rumour that she were wooed by a respectable gentleman, an earl no less, could not hurt her reputation within the *beau monde*. Perhaps you are more concerned about being trapped?"

"Not at all. Still, it would be good to have some company and to go under some other pretext." Aldley quirked an eyebrow at his friend.

"Well I love a bit of subterfuge. You may count on me. Anything to escape these tedious doldrums you have sunk into." Rutherford clinked his glass against Aldley's.

"Excellent. I have just come across some information that might serve our purpose. As you know I have been looking to buy horses, and Lord Malcolm just told me that the father has expressed an interest in selling his hunter."

"I had understood you were looking to acquire a team for a chaise?" Rutherford looked sceptical.

"Well, yes. But Lord Malcolm is a bit vague—he could as easily have recollected that I was looking to purchase a sheep. And there is no reason I should not enquire after a hunting horse."

"No reason at all," Rutherford coughed, "aside from the fact that you do not fox hunt, nor even ride properly. I concede you are a crack shot, my friend, but a hunter? I dare say you would have a better chance of staying on the back of the sheep. Lord Malcolm's whimsical memory has served you ill, I fear. But do not let me put a damper on your plans."

As he ordered the evening meal, Aldley wondered whether his transportation difficulties would ever cease to amuse his closest acquaintance.

CHAPTER 14

Two days later, Tilly arrived to make a morning call. Lydia, was seated in her favourite small parlour, slouched comfortably in a chair next to the fireplace, a book lying in her lap.

"I am glad you are come." Lydia stretched and smiled at her friend, gesturing Tilly to a chair across from her. "Mama is out paying calls, and Papa has some meeting or other. So we may have a nice snug chat."

"Has Mr. Delacroix given you any more trouble?" Tilly settled into the chair across from Lydia.

"No. Though I have not been out much since we last spoke. I finished *Accursed Abbey*, but I shall not tell you how it ends," Lydia smiled mysteriously, "as I am sure you will wish to read it for yourself."

"Yes, thank you." Tilly looked distracted. "But at the moment my mind is too engaged with more serious matters."

"Indeed? What could be more serious than fine literature?"

"I have just come from paying a call on Lady Delacroix. I shall tell you what the subject matter of that call was, but you must promise not to tell another soul, or let on to Miss Delacroix that you know anything about it."

"You have my word. But this sounds rather serious." Lydia leaned forward.

"It is more troubling than it is terribly serious. You see, I asked my brother to look into the matter of the missing earrings. He found them and redeemed them. The fence claimed he had bought them from a gentleman, not yet thirty, of medium height, with dark hair and complexion, and blue eyes."

Lydia's mouth was hanging open. "Do you think it could have been Delacroix?"

"I think it infinitely more likely than the possibility that Marie stole anything. And when I returned the earrings to Lady Delacroix, I relayed the description of the culprit. It was obvious that the similarity to her own son did not escape her ladyship's notice. But she merely dismissed it, saying it could describe many people. She also claimed she was still convinced that the abigail was responsible for the theft."

The servant brought biscuits, and Tilly immediately began munching one.

"Good Lord, how dreadful! To have your own son steal from you." Lydia shook her head, but was a little distracted by the need to watch Tilly's facial expression. She hoped that her friend would not notice the decline in biscuit quality. The household was now on sugar rationing. Soon there would be no biscuits at all.

"It is perhaps a more common occurrence than you think." Tilly said nothing of the biscuits, but continued her relentless consumption. "I only feel sorry for the servants who inevitably get blamed."

"How do you know about such things?" Lydia was sceptical.

"I have secret sources of intelligence. You will simply have to resign yourself to my superior information." Tilly gave Lydia an arch look.

"Oh, but you are so mysterious."

"In any case," Tilly did not deign to acknowledge Lydia's rolling eyes, "if Lady Delacroix will not take Marie back, I shall give her employment. A servant's loyalty should not be so shoddily repaid."

"Aren't you the revolutionary."

"The royal necks are quite safe from me, I assure you." Tilly smiled mischievously, then continued, "I cannot pretend to be terribly shocked. Lady Delacroix must keep up appearances as best she can, though her younger son has been so recklessly engaging in very bad ton. He seems quite desperate, like someone with little to lose. That can only mean he has run up debts and his brother is refusing to pay them."

"You think he is in debt? Then why has he not simply made an offer for me, instead of behaving so scandalously?" Lydia's face betrayed how unpalatable she found the idea.

"I think he believes, correctly, that either you or your father would refuse him. You, because he mistook you for a bit of muslin on your first encounter—an incivility from which one does not easily recover. And your father, because Delacroix hasn't a feather to fly with." Tilly looked superior as she bit into another biscuit.

"Yes, my father has said as much. So Delacroix's intentions are not to engage my affections, but..."

"Quite. But frankly, he doesn't strike me as a man with a well laid out plan." Tilly pulled the shawl draped over her chair-back around her shoulders.

Lydia cringed a little. They were keeping the fires low now, to save on wood. She hated not being able to offer Tilly the basic comfort of a good fire. Tilly seemed not to notice Lydia's reaction, or the fact that the fire was low. Lydia relaxed again.

Tilly continued, "However, if he is at the point of stealing jewellery from his own mother, he may be desperate enough to contemplate an abduction."

"Lord, you cannot be serious. And you accused *me* of reading too many novels." Lydia chuckled at her friend's far fetched anxieties.

"I hope I am wrong. But you must be on your guard. And I retracted what I said about novels, so you needn't harp on about it. What about ringing for some more biscuits?"

Lydia complied, but hated how she internally winced at the expense, how quickly she fell into cheeseparing.

When Tilly had eaten two or three more biscuits, she sipped her tea thoughtfully and asked, "Has Lord Aldley come to call?"

"No." Tilly breathed deeply. "If he had, I should have told you at once, for I should need to speak of it with someone."

"I take it that you like him a good deal." Tilly was smiling sweetly behind her teacup.

Lydia was relieved to see Tilly return to her usual, playful mood.

"I suppose... being around him makes me feel very queer. It is not entirely pleasant. I feel it in my nerves, but at the same time I feel an irresistible impulse to draw closer to him. I crave him. It is confusing, and yet I dearly wish to know him better and hope that he shares this wish. But he is an earl and terribly handsome. He must have many suitable young ladies admiring him. I fear that indulging my hopes is a mistake, as they are likely to be disappointed."

"Then I shall not counsel you to be hopeful." Tilly's smile was affectionate. "I shall simply be hopeful for you. Wishful thinking is much less dangerous if it is executed by proxy."

"You are a good friend, Tilly. I do not know how I should ever get on without you."

"For one thing, you would have more biscuits." Tilly shoved another in her mouth and crunched it with zeal.

Lydia remarked internally that her friend could not know how right she was, but was spared trying to make some clever, light-hearted reply by the entrance of her father.

"There you are, Lydia." Mr. Norwood rubbed his hands together. "Miss Ravelsham. I hope you are well?"

Tilly was miraculously sitting up perfectly straight. "Thank you, Mr. Norwood. I am, exceedingly. And is the London air to your liking?"

Lydia wished to laugh at how Tilly contrived so quickly to rattle off the blandest, most banal forms of chit-chat. It really was marvellous how she almost passed herself off as dull-witted.

"I make the best of it." Mr. Norwood smiled. "However, I find I must return to the country for short while on some business."

"Indeed, Papa? Surely nothing is wrong at Nesterling Lodge?" Lydia wondered what new disaster might be smiting her family.

"Not at all. It is nothing to worry about, my dear." He patted Lydia's arm.

Sensing it was a good time to depart, Tilly ate the last biscuit, then took her leave.

After Tilly had gone, Lydia turned to her father. "What on earth could send you back to Nesterling Lodge so suddenly? It is not bad news, I hope."

His face drooped. "I am sorry to tell you that there has been some interest in Aristophanes. I have agreed to show him tomorrow."

Her heart felt as though it had been stabbed. So soon. "Then you must take me with you, Papa. Ari will not perform for anyone else, and I want to meet the buyer. I shall only part with him to someone who will treat him well."

"In fact, I am glad to hear you say it, my dear. For the man enquiring after Ari is none other than Lord Aldley."

Lydia's mouth fell open.

"No time to gape like that. Go and tell your maid to pack lightly—but bring the maid, and bring some, you know," grasping for *le mot juste*, he flopped his hand about desperately, "pretty frocks."

CHAPTER 15

Rutherford turned his chaise and four to evade the side of a cart unloading barrels of beer at an inn on the outskirts of London, before finally permitting his coachman to take the reins and joining Aldley inside the cab.

Aldley raised a brow. "You have decided to trust your coachman, at last. It is lucky he is not as prone to moodiness as Smythe, or who knows but that the chaise might fly into a ditch somewhere between here and Nesterling, because the man were in a huff over the slight."

"My coachman is a steady character and will not drive the horses too hard. He will get us to Nesterling Lodge quickly enough, but he doesn't have the hand that I have for navigating London traffic, which is a constant negotiation."

Rutherford fell silent for a few moments and then continued, with a little pique, "You know, you might have told me that the girl you were protecting from Delacroix was the same girl you had been dancing with at Lady Goodram's ball. When you said it was a young *lady*, I thought it must be a peer's daughter."

"I danced with several ladies at that ball. I did not think it was anything to the point." Aldley looked evasive.

"I think it is very much to the point, if you indeed wished to avoid creating rumours about your reasons for visiting her father."

"I think our transaction may not reach the attention of the ton, as we are meeting out in the country. I am only looking to buy a horse, after all."

"Indeed." Rutherford lowered his lids slightly and pursed his lips.

"And you are puzzled at my secrecy? I believe any man would do a great deal to avoid being subjected to such smugness."

"But you mistake me. I am not smug. It merely defies credulity to believe you would go to such lengths for a girl in whom you have no real interest. But as that is your position, I must be silent on the matter or risk your wrathful tyranny."

"Very well, I have some interest in her, of course. But she is a commoner and a bit of a bluestocking, unless I miss my guess. She also has some rather unusual hobbies, which I shall not delve into, but I am not entirely certain she is wholly respectable."

"A bluestocking *and* not wholly respectable? Unusual combination of attributes. Did she say or do something at the ball to make you question her character?" Rutherford unwrapped a crockery bottle of coffee from its swaddling and filled cups for them both.

"Not at all—indeed she seemed a bit stiff at times, but I assume that she was merely nervous. I do not think she is much accustomed to society. She said as much—that she did not know what was suitable conversation." Aldley accepted a steaming cup of creamy coffee, and sipped it.

"But that is hardly a great offence. It should not call her character in to question, surely."

"No. In fact, I must admit, I find her country manners rather charming. I have always thought I might take a wife from among the middling classes. She has clearly been raised with that unfashionable degree of morality which I prefer. It is so hard to find anyone among the nobility who is not almost completely depraved."

"Quite. Hopefully she is less boring than you make her out to be. You need someone to rescue you from yourself." Rutherford tipped some brandy into Aldley's coffee and then into his own. "For you are so maddeningly virtuous that, if I had not known your father, I might even question your claim to being an earl."

"I shall take that as a compliment, Rutherford, though it comes from a scoundrel like you."

Rutherford chuckled. "But as for her being a commoner, if you like her, does it really signify? After all, she is well acquainted with Lady Goodram."

Aldley could not help smiling a little. "In any case, all told I've about an hour's acquaintance with her. It is not quite enough to know my feelings."

"And yet long enough to have given you reservations."

"I was born with reservations, but they can be overcome, in time." Aldley took a sip of his coffee and enjoyed the warmth that spread over him. "I eventually took a liking to you, for example."

"I believe it helped that your mother could not stand the sight of me." Rutherford's smile was sardonic.

"Perhaps a little. But as I recall, you were charmingly adept at cock-a-roosty, and later were too good at bandy-wickets for me to risk letting the other side get you on their team. I had little choice but to befriend you, really. Plus you much later gave me some very good investment tips, so it seemed a useful acquaintance. And you have a cracking team of horses, so I suppose we must continue, really."

"Yes, I am quite indispensable, as you cannot manage to procure a team of your own, much less drive them. And hiring a man is also apparently beyond your reach." Rutherford stretched out his Hessians, and polished a speck of dirt with a handkerchief.

"Speaking of buying horses, what do you know of Mr. Norwood, Rutherford? Have you come across him in town?"

"Not at all. Of course he is a commoner, but the only thing I have heard against him is that he made much of his early living in trade. He has, since then, made other investments and is very widely known to be indecently rich, so a little filthy commerce may be overlooked. I dare say, if he plays his cards right, it will only be a matter of time until he is elevated."

"Then I wonder why he is selling this hunter." Aldley poured himself more coffee.

"Perhaps he hasn't time to ride it." Rutherford thought for a moment. "And he is getting on in years. One cannot chase foxes forever. Or at all, in some cases."

"You needn't let on that I do not fox hunt, or it will ruin the entire pretext for my being there."

"And do you plan on buying the horse without so much as getting on its back?" Rutherford laughed.

"I believe it might be done. Although, strictly speaking, it is not necessary that I buy the horse, only that I go look at it."

Rutherford continued to chuckle as he served them both more brandy.

When they arrived at Nesterling Lodge, Mr. Norwood received them in a well-lit parlour, with a large curio cabinet and a few shelves of books. They gathered instinctively around the fireplace, and settled themselves into the plump leather chairs alongside the hearth.

"My lord, Mr. Rutherford, would you care for a drink before viewing Aristophanes? He is being warmed up at the moment." He handed them each a glass of spirits. "This is our own schnapps—Olah calls it something else that I can't remember. He tends our orchards and is a magician at making these little potions. This one he has aged upon raspberries. It is delicious, say it as I shouldn't."

"Indeed it is." Aldley was impressed. "Very delicate, but still has a formidable kick."

"I am quite taken with the flavouring." Rutherford's face lit up. "I have experimented with various flavourings in my rum production, but so far they have yielded disappointing results."

"You have interests in the West Indies, have you?" Mr. Norwood looked impressed.

"Indeed, I do. Fortunately I have an excellent manager, so I need not travel there often."

"Aye, here is to capable managers—they are a godsend." Mr. Norwood raised his glass and they all toasted.

"And you, my lord, have you also an interest in rum production?"

"I have some investments," Aldley replied, "but I leave direct owner-ship to those who have been so fortunate as to find excellent managers. Do you suppose you might ask your man to show Ruther-ford the schnapps production? I am quite sure he would be very keen to see it, would you not, Rutherford?"

"Indeed I should, if it is not too much of an imposition."

"Not at all." Mr. Norwood looked delighted. "I shall ask Farleigh to take you out to Olah. Old Olah doesn't hardly speak a word of English, but Farleigh and he seem to understand one another."

When Lord Aldley was finally alone with Mr. Norwood, he produced the letter. Mr. Norwood read it through quickly, a crease forming in his forehead.

"I found this in a most unusual spot—a small hut in a tree, in a park, which I understand is adjacent to the back enclosure of your London home." Aldley examined Mr. Norwood's face for any hint of surprise at the description, but saw none.

Aldley surmised he knew of the structure's existence and continued. "It is embarrassing to admit that I was climbing about in the tree hut, but I was curious. I realize this is somewhat awkward, as we have only just met, but I am a little acquainted with your daughter. I could not conceal this from you when I believed that she might be the intended recipient. In short, although this missive is only initialled, I believe I know who the author is. I may refer you to the note itself for evidence of his dishonourable character. Though I could, I trust that I need *not*, add my own testimony."

"Why did Lydia not tell me of this?" Mr. Norwood looked crushed with grief.

"Forgive me! I should have told you from the outset that it is my strong belief that she has never seen this letter."

Mr. Norwood released a breath of relief. "Lord. I am glad to hear your lordship say so. My daughter and I are very close. I am surprised enough that she did not tell me of this young scoundrel's effrontery. I suppose she was trying her best to forget it, that it might be concealed. But to permit a secret correspondence..."

"I believe she is entirely innocent of it. I do not think she knows of this letter's existence at all. In fact, I must have come across it very shortly after it was left there, for I found it in the afternoon on the day after the ball he mentions. This was Lady Goodram's ball, and unless I am very mistaken as to the author's identity, he had sneaked into that ball uninvited. I escorted him out myself. But the letter, distasteful as it is, strongly suggests that your daughter has been entirely blameless and, far from inviting a correspondence, has repelled his advances."

Mr. Norwood's fists clenched. "Be so good, my lord, as to identify him, so that I may put a slug in him myself."

"I understand the sentiment, believe me," Aldley tried to console the man. "But unfortunately neither of us has standing to duel him over this. I, because I am no relation of your daughter. And you, because, although he is an unworthy bounder, he is also the second son of a Viscount."

"Do you mean Delacroix, my lord?"

"You are acquainted?" Aldley caught his breath. He sincerely hoped that Delacroix was not a suitor to Miss Norwood.

"He has once called on my daughter at my home in London. And before that he came to my club as a guest of one of the members. He has probably been suspended from his own club—the man's gambling is clearly out of control. We played at piquet and he put up a deed for the contents of an entire shipment of coffee, still en route—if it is not lost at sea, which I should not put past him. Indeed I shouldn't have let him bet so high, for he was not thinking clearly and was gambling like a madman. But, in all honesty, I had already taken a disliking to him, even before I had so much cause as I now do."

"I know I have no right to advise you, Mr. Norwood, but I believe you should not confront him. Rather, make certain your daughter is always closely guarded. And as he is apparently aware of the treetop hut..."

"Indeed. I know what I must do. That hut is a childhood fancy which I have indulged, but which has become hazardous. Thank you, my lord, for taking the trouble to bring this to my attention. I am greatly in your lordship's debt—but I must beg for continued discretion."

"You have my word that I shall not speak of this to any other person. Rutherford knows of our true reason for being here, but he is also sworn to secrecy. I shall vouch for his silence."

Mr. Norwood nodded and lapsed into quiet thoughtfulness for a few moments, before asking, "Am I to assume, then, that your lordship does not wish to see Aristophanes?"

"No, indeed. I should very much like to see him."

Mr. Norwood stroked his chin and smiled. "Well, then, I should warn you, my lord, that my daughter will be taking him through his paces. He is rather more her hunter than mine."

"Miss Norwood? She is here?" Aldley was not prepared for this surprise, but he could not help returning Mr. Norwood's smile briefly. He was a little surprised at how very much he wanted to see her again.

"Yes, and in light of what your lordship has just told me, I am rather glad not to have left her in London. Though at least for the time being, I should prefer not to discuss this with her."

"I should not dream of raising the topic."

As Aldley accompanied Mr. Norwood out into the pasture, he found Rutherford already leaning against the fence watching Miss Norwood riding a great grey beast of a horse.

Around the green enclosure she raced, jumping obstacles and making rapid turns with an apparent effortlessness. Intermittent beams of sunlight suddenly lit up her face and a single copper tress on her cheek, before receding behind clouds again in a teasing pulse of shadow and light.

Her hair was braided neatly into a coil underneath her riding bonnet, and she wore a wine coloured velvet habit, which clung to her trim figure rather appealingly. She did not ride side-saddle, but astride, the tails of her skirts flying up as she urged the magnificent stallion over pickets.

Aldley felt a deep heat flood his insides. He imagined how she might look loping through the fields on that giant, with her hair loose, tumbling and flowing around her shoulders. He had to stop this line of thought. Her father was standing not ten feet away.

He turned to Rutherford, who had a look of rapt admiration on his face. Aldley found it slightly irritating. Indeed, his friend ought not gape so openly—at least not in front of Mr. Norwood. No, he should not be gaping at all. It was not decent.

He drew close to Rutherford and muttered, "Good Lord, man, try to keep your eyes in your head."

"Why should I not admire such a magnificent creature?" Rutherford replied *sotto voce*.

"Because it is not civil—true it is almost indecent. Her father is standing right there."

"I see. You are cross with me because you think that, instead of viewing the horse which you are supposed to be interested in, I am making calf eyes at a young woman whom you are supposed *not* to be interested in. Is that about it?" Rutherford looked quizzically at Aldley with raised brows and lazily lowered lids.

Aldley coughed. "You are so smug when you think you are crafting a work of satire. How was I to know you were looking at the horse?"

"I believe it would have been obvious to anyone whose thoughts had not been elsewhere engaged."

"Nonsense."

"But now that you mention it, the girl is not bad, either. If you will not make an offer, I might."

Aldley clenched his teeth. He did not trust himself to reply.

"—On the horse, I mean." Rutherford's lip upturned just a little on one side. "Though I dare say we can now do away with the notion that the young lady is a bluestocking."

She finished the course and brought the horse up to the fence where her father stood. She leaned forward and whispered something in the horse's ear. Aristophanes bent his forelegs and lowered his head slightly to make a little bow to her father, then picked a dandelion with his teeth and offered it to him.

Aldley chuckled. She was utterly charming. He could scarcely believe the rapport she had with the animal. She swung gracefully off his back, not waiting for the servant, and produced a carrot from her pocket, which the great stallion nibbled politely from her hand.

"Why on earth is Norwood selling this horse?" He murmured to Rutherford. "It is most obvious that the beast is her pet—she has trained him to do precisely what she likes. And they ride together like they were made for it. It is atrocious to think of separating them."

"I was just thinking the same thing. But it is nothing to the point. You could look for years and never find horse flesh like that, Aldley, and here it is falling into your lap. Her loss is your gain."

"You cannot be so mercenary. Have you no feeling? And anyway, do you think that nag would even let me get near him?" Aldley looked a little nervously at the animal. "He is all sweetness for her, but he has a devilish gleam in his eye when he looks at us. I believe she may have spoiled him for any other owner."

"That is a real concern, seeing as how you cannot ride a hobby horse. Perhaps we should get you a nice elderly mare, instead. It is much harder to fall out of a swayback. *I* shall take on the retraining of Aristophanes."

Aldley thought his friend might be only half joking. He strode over to Mr. Norwood and his daughter, whose skin was alluringly flushed from the exercise, and whose green eyes sparkled as she fed carrots to the stallion.

He could not help smiling at her. She smiled back and his heart skipped a beat. She was perfect, a true original, how could he ever have had any doubts? Mr. Norwood beckoned to Rutherford, and introduced him to his daughter.

"What a marvellous animal. Beautiful and obviously intelligent. And you ride astoundingly well, Miss Norwood." Aldley finally spoke to her, but could not help feeling that his praise was worthless, considering his own inability to ride even passably.

"Thank you, my lord. I have been riding since I was very young. It came much more naturally than needlework, I am afraid."

"We all have our strengths." A stupid smile spread over Aldley's face as he remembered dancing with her, smelling her skin and feeling the luscious curve of her back.

"I should say riding is a much more exhilarating accomplishment, would not you, Aldley?" Rutherford clapped his friend on the back. "And it insures that a young lady gets sufficient exercise, which is a disadvantage of needlework or playing the pianoforte . Do you play, Miss Norwood?"

"I believe it would be un-Christian of me to subject anyone to my offerings on that, or any other instrument. I do enjoy music. That is to say, I appreciate hearing good music far too well to tolerate my own fumbling clamour." Her smile was playful, dazzling.

"Aldley here plays very well, and sings too, if you can get him to do it. So you see, you each have at least one accomplishment that is somewhat unusual for your sex."

"I have had the pleasure of hearing his lordship sing, briefly and unfortunately through a wall, at Lady Goodram's home. I believe I have never heard a finer voice." She looked a little embarrassed at the confession.

Aldley smiled and bowed, resisting the urge to clasp her hand to his chest so she could feel his heart. "You are too kind, Miss Norwood."

"Do not misconstrue the young lady's words, Aldley." Rutherford cocked his head to the side. "I believe she just said it was a pleasure to hear you sing briefly and through a wall."

"No, indeed." Miss Norwood laughed. "I should have wished to hear more. I think his lordship's talent must be a great boon to his acquaintance." Her gaze met Aldley's briefly and she blushed prettily. Aldley wished to draw her close to him, kiss those lovely, smiling lips.

"It would be, if he would ever perform for me." Rutherford gave him a sidelong glance.

Aldley knew he should say something or he would look reserved, but he was terribly distracted. "I should not wish to displace the efforts of the young ladies. They seem to so enjoy any opportunity of performing, that it would be selfish to deny them the pleasure, particularly when it is a matter of indifference to me whether or not I play for an audience."

"These are the kindest of intentions, to be sure, my lord. But do you not also consider that you are depriving them the very great pleasure of hearing you play and sing?" Miss Norwood was smiling at him openly. Did she like him? Did her heart beat like his did?

"No one has complained. And as for my never playing, you only have Rutherford's word for it, and I warn you, he is a rogue and a mischief maker." Aldley made himself laugh a little more easily than he felt.

"Is it not bold of him to defame me to my face? I suppose an earl may take whatever liberties he will." Rutherford assumed an expression of martyrdom.

"Being an earl is nothing to the point. It is only defamation if it is not true." Aldley could see she was now shaking with laughter, which made her look down, as he wished she would not.

And yet, although he was mesmerized by the deep green colour of her eyes, he could not help noticing that her ivory lids curved perfectly over them when she cast her gaze downward. Her lashes were thick and surprisingly dark for a woman of her hair colour.

There was one little freckle on the outer corner of her right eye that was perfectly situated so as to invite his finger to graze over it. He straightened suddenly, and adjusted his already perfectly tied neck cloth.

Aldley turned to Mr. Norwood, who had stood quietly observing this whole exchange and grinning broadly.

"Perhaps we should discuss an offer, Mr. Norwood. For the horse."

At his words, Aldley remarked that Miss Norwood was no longer laughing, but reached out possessively to touch the stallion's neck. He thought he could see tears in her eyes before she turned her face away from the party, and focused her attention on scratching Aristophanes' ears. His heart clenched. How could her father even consider selling the favourite pet of such an angel?

"But, indeed," he added, "I have some scruple that perhaps the animal should not be separated from the one who appears to have trained him so well."

"Perhaps, my lord." Mr. Norwood's heart seemed heavy. "But I think we must sell him. My daughter is now of an age where she must think of marrying and running a household, not jumping over hedges. She will be in London now for the foreseeable future anyway."

During this speech, Miss Norwood kept her back to them. It felt entirely wrong—against Aldley's every instinct to separate her from her favourite horse. No matter how meekly she was going along with her father's scheme, it must be making her utterly miserable.

Despite an alarming desire to remain in her presence as long as possible, he felt it was unkind to be talking of the matter in front of her. "Perhaps we should sit down and discuss it between ourselves. Miss Norwood may prefer to have a proper ride on Aristophanes."

Mr. Norwood took the hint. "Yes, of course, my lord. Won't you and Mr. Rutherford join me in the parlour, again?"

In the end it was settled that Lord Aldley would purchase the horse for the asking price, plus fees for boarding. The stallion would remain at Nesterling Lodge indefinitely, and at the disposal of Miss Norwood.

For, the earl observed, "It is in my best interest that the horse remain under the excellent training he has thus far enjoyed for as long as possible."

Mr. Norwood appeared to accept this arrangement, despite the obvious logical flaw that Aldley would not be able to ride a horse situated so far away. Nor would the *excellent trainer* have much opportunity to do so, as long as she was resident in London. Mr. Norwood very cordially invited them to stay to supper.

"I thank you for your kind hospitality, but I fear we must return to the city," replied Rutherford pre-emptively, to Aldley's great irritation. "I have business that requires my attention, and I believe the earl also has some matters to look into, have you not, Aldley?"

"I do not know what you mean." Aldley wondered what Rutherford's problem was.

"Well, I had assumed you had some involvement in the upcoming ball." Rutherford's face betrayed that he knew how weak this excuse sounded.

"Not at all. It is all my mother's doing, and she does not countenance male incompetence in such important schemes. She would most certainly think me in the way." Aldley tried not to openly scowl at Rutherford.

"Lady Aldley is to host a ball soon, is she, my lord? Yes, well, these matters are perhaps best left to the female sex." Mr. Norwood affected a nervous laugh. "A bit too much blood sport for me, I am afraid."

"You have a point, there. But have you not heard of the ball? Has Miss Norwood not received an invitation?" Aldley could not believe it.

"I could not swear to it, my lord, but I do believe Mrs. Norwood would have mentioned it."

"I shall see to it that one is sent immediately. I apologize for the oversight. Perhaps it just got lost." When Aldley thought about it, there was really no reason why his mother should invite Miss Norwood—quite the contrary, in fact.

There was almost no connection between their families at all, and his mother had already expressed her disapproval of Miss Norwood's rumoured tree-climbing, which he had long since decided was utterly charming. But somehow, he had simply been assuming that Miss Norwood would be at the ball.

Although he had not consciously thought of it, a part of him had been looking forward to dancing with her again. But now that he thought about it, it had been rather unrealistic to leave the invitation up to his mother.

Yet he wanted her at that ball. He should very much like to take the opportunity of chatting with Miss Norwood over dinner now, too, if Rutherford were not being such a wet blanket.

"That is most obliging of you, my lord." Mr. Norwood seemed quite beside himself and utterly ill-equipped to deal with the delicate arts of balls and invitations. "I assure you I keenly feel, as I know my wife and daughter will, the honour your lordship pays us and the kindness of this condescension. I should explain—I mean I am rather sure that your lordship and Lady Aldley have not received an invitation to our upcoming ball. I should like to assure you, my lord, that is only because we did not presume to send one. It will never be such a grand affair as the Aldley ball, of course. However, if your lordship should have any wish to attend, it would make us exceedingly happy to send invitations."

"I thank you, Mr. Norwood. I cannot speak for my mother of course, but I should be very much obliged to receive an invitation." Aldley thought things were going rather well, and would be better still had he not brought gloomy old Rutherford along.

"I shall see to it, then, my lord. It is a shame your lordship and Mr. Rutherford cannot stay, for it is rather late to begin the journey back to London."

"You are exceedingly kind, Mr. Norwood." Rutherford intervened once again. "But I believe we must make a start at least. I've a good team. I think we may make the Stag and Sparrow early enough for dinner. From there it will be a mere hour's drive to London, and we shall arrive more refreshed."

Aldley really wanted to stomp on Rutherford's highly polished Hessians. What on earth was wrong with the man?

They took their leave and departed. But as soon as they were in the carriage and safely rolling down the drive, Aldley could no longer suppress his irritation. "I should very much like to know what business you have in town that could possibly be so urgent that you would decline supper on my behalf."

"Do not be piqued. I should have thought I was expressing your own interest."

"My own interest? Such as my preference for half-warm, stale-larded inn food, rather than a proper meal, I suppose?" Aldley glowered at Rutherford.

"No." Rutherford spoke slowly as if talking to a dull child. "I was refer-ring to your *expressed* preference not to be presumed engaged to Mr. Norwood's daughter."

"What are you on about? It is quite natural to dine with an acquain-tance after concluding business. There is nothing more to it." Aldley straightened his impeccable cravat in frustration.

"That might be true, if you had not as good as purchased an engage-ment gift for the business acquaintance's daughter."

"Nonsense. I purchased a horse and paid boarding fees. It was not a gift of any sort, much less a gift to *her.*"

"Honestly, can you possibly be so blind? Did you not see how Mr. Norwood received your words when you made the offer to leave the horse at Nesterling, and then later, when you invited his daughter to your mother's ball? I should have kicked you in the knee, were it not too obvious."

"It seemed only polite." Aldley hated the way his voice faltered.

"Good Lord, man! For someone who is trying not to create expectations, you are doing everything short of getting down on one knee to do so. Can you not see that?"

"Do you think the father is expecting me to propose, then?" Aldley had to suppress a smile.

Rutherford gave a pained look to the heavens above him. "I certainly should do, in his place. Can you really have forgotten all your tricks for evading matrimony? You were rather adept at it before you fled to the continent."

"I did not flee."

"Perhaps not," Rutherford laughed, "but you might consider it now."

"It is hardly a matter of such desperation." After all, she was lovely to look at and much more interesting than the other young women he had met in society.

She seemed decent in a way that people of his class held in disdain. He had to marry sometime, and provide an heir. Whom did he think he was hoaxing? She was utterly irresistible.

"All I shall say is have a care, Aldley. You do not know what you are about. Unless..."

"Unless what?" It was Aldley's turn to feign boredom. He rubbed an eye.

"Well, unless, of course, you *do* know what you are about."

"I see what you mean." Aldley tried to sound indifferent.

"Do you? Frankly, you *should* court this girl. She is rich, beautiful and charming. I should marry her myself, if the horse was included in the bargain—except that I fear she might just ride better than I do, which would be too humiliating. But you have no such vanities."

"Certainly not. And I dare say there is some merit to your theory, for when you speak of marrying her as though she were a sack of oats to be thrown into a horse market deal, I feel rather inclined to plant you a facer."

"Well, then, that is settled." Rutherford slapped Aldley's shoulder and laughed at him until his eyes streamed.

CHAPTER 16

*L*ydia stood with her mother before the long mirror in her dressing room, trying on gowns. The emerald green silk brought out the green of her eyes, though it also made her nose look a bit pink.

"May I borrow your emerald pendant, Mama?"

"It will be too much green, trust me." Her mother shook her head. "You would do much better with the amethyst. In fact I should very much like to see you in the wine velvet with the amethyst."

Lydia huffed. "But that dress is so heavy, Mama. Will it not get dreadfully hot?"

"What is a little heat? This is not just a matter of amusement, my dear. Though I hope you shall enjoy yourself, your principal duty is to be a credit to your family and to secure a husband—preferably Lord Aldley. Other trifling considerations should fall by the wayside."

"But if I get hot, my skin will turn all horrid and red." Lydia knew it was shameless manipulation, but it was the only way to persuade her determined mother.

"True. It might be better to save the velvet gowns for engagements with no dancing. In fact this new muslin would be better for a ballroom—it floats so beautifully. I wish I had such light fabrics when I was a girl. However, you must be turned out in an expensive fabric for the Aldley ball, so silk it shall be, but in the wine colour."

Her mother pursed her lips thoughtfully. "And the amethyst. Definitely the amethyst."

The ball was not for some time, but Mrs. Norwood was determined to make certain everything was planned out perfectly in advance.

Lydia forced herself to be compliant and attentive. She was only following her father's adjuration to make a good match. This ball was an excellent opportunity, after all. She supposed that all this silly preparation and fixation on appearance was made a little more pleasant by the thought that it might make her more attractive to Lord Aldley.

Perhaps she was a fool to even hope for it, but did his actions not suggest an interest? He had ensured that Ari could stay at Nesterling, that they would not be separated. What man buys a horse and leaves it in the hands of its previous owner?

Surely that was for her. Her heart fluttered. He was her hero. Even if he were not so devastatingly attractive, such evidence of kindness and consideration made her think she would not object to being his wife, to having him draw her close as Delacroix had once done. Such things must be much more agreeable if experienced with the right man.

"Stop gathering wool, darling. Do turn round so I can attach this. Yes. That is just the thing. I have some amethyst hair pins. I shall consult Miss Grey as to their use when she comes tomorrow. Now let Harding get you out of this dress—carefully, mind."

Lydia was relieved when Tilly called shortly after her extrication from the silk gown. She ushered her friend into her little parlour.

"Thank the Lord you are here," Lydia huffed, "for I have not been allowed out of the house since we returned from Nesterling Lodge."

"That may be prudent with Delacroix on the prowl." Tilly seated herself.

"But Father does not know about that, yet he has nonetheless been quite adamant." Lydia omitted to tell her friend about his threat to cut the tree down and bar her window if she sneaked out of her room again. She did not think her father was joking, either. "It seems strange that he is suddenly so severe. He is not usually so."

"Presumably he is concerned that you not be seen behaving like a savage now that there is such an eligible prospect on the horizon." Tilly turned her head to the side and gave Lydia a mischievous look.

She knew her friend was joking, for Tilly did not know the half of it. "I believe you are right. He lectured me almost the entire journey about doing everything I can to secure Lord Aldley. It was as though he were not my father at all, but a man possessed by the spirit of my mother."

He need not have wasted his breath. She was well aware that she had feelings for the earl, but even if those feelings were returned, could he overlook her birth and her relative poverty, should he come to know of it?

"Well, it is a sound plan—for it certainly means something that Lord Aldley extended you a personal invitation to the ball." Tilly nodded thoughtfully. "And I cannot belive he made that arrangement with the horse for any other reason than consideration for your feelings."

"I am so grateful to him for it. True, he is a wonderful, kind man. I could not stand the idea of losing Aristophanes." Lydia shook her head.

"I wonder at your father selling him."

This was a perilous topic. Lydia decided to change it. "He says I had better put away jumping over fences and find a husband. I believe he wishes me to focus all my energy on securing Lord Aldley. But I simply do not know how one goes about securing anyone, let alone an earl."

"I think if the earl has taken an interest in you, as he certainly seems to have done, it must be at least *in spite* of your social ignorance." Tilly looked thoughtful.

Lydia could not help smiling at the offhanded way that her friend insulted her without intending to give offence.

Tilly continued, "It may even be that he prefers your country manners to the extremely calculating refinements that he has encountered among the young ladies of the ton. I have heard he is a bit straight-laced."

"Far better than crooked-laced," Lydia retorted.

"To each their own." Tilly pursed her lips. "But I do not think you should attempt to *secure him*. Only take every opportunity to speak with him and become better acquainted. Of course, I do not know the earl, but I believe it is preferable to appear like you are not trying to catch him."

"Your advice conveniently corresponds to my own feelings in the matter. I should very much like to get to know Lord Aldley better. And, while I admit that I greatly prefer his company to any other young man I have met, I should never wish to throw myself at him."

"Well, it is settled then. But surely you must be less calm than you seem about this last minute invitation." Tilly looked at her with mock suspicion. "I wonder how Lady Aldley feels about this. But no, I do not wish to spoil your enjoyment by thinking on unpleasant topics."

"I view the ball as a necessary evil to be endured for the goal of spending more time with Lord Aldley." Lydia chafed her hands. "The scrutiny of Lady Aldley is the aspect which I least look forward to. I am also a little anxious about the calibre of guests. Surely I shall be the only commoner."

"That may well be. But if you encounter snobbery, simply remember this formula: your allowance tallies up to a good half the annual income of three quarters of them."

"Perhaps." Lydia could not correct her friend on this point, but it stung a bit to think that her one claim to distinction had been her wealth, and those days were past.

It reminded her that she should look into investing some of her saved allowance. Surely she could contact a solicitor to manage it for her.

"But I hope that, at least for an earl, the amount of my settlement will not be an important consideration."

"It might be too much to ask of a mere mortal that he should not think on it at all. However, I have asked around, and the general consensus is that Lord Aldley's principle flaw is not gambling or debauchery or fortune-hunting. In fact, he is something of a prude."

"One might call it having a good character." Lydia scowled at Tilly.

Tilly just rolled her eyes and continued, "His principle flaw, according to the ton, is not vice but rather a somewhat ignoble predilection for closely managing his own investments. This brings him, on occasion, perilously close to the insufferably vile realm of," she mouthed the word, "trade."

"Well, I shall not be the one to hold that against him." Lydia huffed at the stupidity of the *beau monde*.

"Nor I. You see, unlike the ton, *we* are disinclined to judge our fellow man for sins that our own fathers have dabbled in. It will not do, of course. We are simply not hypocritical enough to be genteel."

Lydia's laugh fell a little flat, for she was feeling rather too hypocritical for much levity. Now that her father's finances were so very compromised, she felt her own situation was not entirely unlike that of a fortune hunter.

"But back to Lord Aldley." Tilly dismissed her digression with a wave of her hand. "It seems that as a consequence of his unfashionable approach to money-making, he is astoundingly rich, even for an earl. Not quite as rich as your father, of course, or mine, but still very rich. So I think it unlikely that he would be disproportionately interested in your fortune."

"That is a relief. But wherever do you get all of this information?"

"You must simply resign yourself to the fact that I have ways and means, Lydia." Tilly gave her a look of arch superiority.

"You are mysterious, but I shall not indulge your self-importance by pleading for disclosure. However, talking of taking an interest in investments, would you be very disappointed if I said that I harbour inclinations in that direction myself?" Lydia wanted to talk to someone about her investment plans, and Tilly was really the only person who might understand.

"I should be delighted to hear it—so delighted in fact, that I should refrain from gossiping about it, for it would not help you at all in the earl's circles. What the earl can get away with is very different than what the reputation of a *nouveau riche* female can support. Still, if one is clever and careful, one may do a great many things without detection. But you do realize that women cannot really invest the way that men can."

"Yes, that is my difficulty. I believe I shall need the assistance of a solicitor to start a trust for me and take directions in its management."

"I can see you have some knowledge of these things. That is good." Tilly looked thoughtful.

"And, it cannot be my father's lawyer."

"Quite. But of course, you do not really need to do this."

"Of course not, but I believe I should find it quite diverting." Lydia tried to sound light-hearted. "And, really, though I believe my father will be careful in the structuring of my settlement, it would not be such a very bad thing to have a little something outside of my future husband's reach—should I marry. One hears of so many stellar matches that turn out to be... horribly disappointing."

"Yes, one does." Tilly nodded. "I very much approve of planning against unpleasant future events. And it so happens that I know of just the lawyer for the job. But we must be very subtle and discreet in our planning." She smiled a little, crooked smirk. "It will be great fun. Leave it in my hands for now. I shall arrange a meeting and provide some chaperones who know how to keep their mouths shut."

Not for the first time, Lydia was struck by the strange array of resources her friend possessed. It proved useful, but why would a soon-to-be-married, pampered young woman require silent chaperones, acquaintance with lawyers, and the means of locating and redeeming stolen jewellery?

Tilly's brother was the ostensible agent of the jewellery retrieval, but Lydia had met the mild-mannered brother, and was not convinced. And it was improbable that Tilly would let herself be excluded from any opportunity for intrigue.

"Speaking of keeping one's mouth shut, you have not told me how the Delacroix earring case has turned out. Did Mrs. Delacroix take the abigail back?" Lydia asked.

"No. I have taken on Marie. I had to soothe the feelings of my lady's maid, Browning, of course, but I believe it is settled now. Marie *assists*. She is reasonably good with hair, and fantastic at mending and making adjustments to clothing. And she is alarmingly loyal to me— the poor girl was so grateful. Miss Delacroix's loss has been my boon."

"I congratulate you, but I think your spirit of equity has made you very deserving of the reward. I suppose Lady Delacroix remains silent about the topic, then."

"Oh yes. Most silent. The official story is that Delacroix is visiting family in the countryside. No one has seen him in town for some time. I believe he is hiding from his creditors, but I suspect he remains in town. He does not strike me as a man much predisposed to the quiet amusements of country life."

"Yes, I see what you mean." Lydia's shoulders drooped a little. "I suppose it would be too much to hope for that he had actually cleared off."

"You cannot let your guard down. His disappearance is only evidence of concealment, and therefore desperation, which means he is more dangerous than ever."

"Certainly. I only wish to be permitted out of the house, now and again." Lydia pouted. "I feel myself a prisoner in my own home. It is quite unjust."

"You father will let you out, at least to make calls, I am sure. He doesn't know about Mr. Delacroix's advances. He is merely trying to keep you presentable, now that there may be an earl interested. And you shall attend the ball. In the meantime," Tilly tossed her curls, "I shall not take offence if you do not return my calls. I shall never snub you."

"That is a kindly promise. But you should better choose your friends, for you know I shall not be seen with the likes of you when I become a countess." Lydia pursed her lips, and fixed Tilly with an arch look.

"Quite. I made you out to be just such an infidel."

"Do you fancy a trip to the shops this afternoon?" Lydia was feeling indulgent as she should not be, and little desperate for escape. "I wish to buy something to read. I think if we took your chaise and had servants with us, it would be safe, and must appear respectable enough even for my father.

Tilly agreed to call for her in the afternoon with two man servants, her maid, and the recently hired Marie.

When they were settled in Tilly's rose scented carriage, and well on their way, Tilly squinted at Lydia. "Hatchards? Seems a little dry for you."

Lydia lifted her chin. "I do not only read novels, you know. I like to read educational material as well."

"Indeed. Well, then, do not let me be the one to dissuade a young woman from improving her mind."

Lydia was facing her friend, as they walked into the shop. "I must compensate myself for having spent the entire morning in the tedium of trying on ball gowns."

"So tell me, what are you looking for?" Tilly queried, throwing a hungry look over Lydia's shoulder as she spoke.

"I have heard a small collection of sketches and commentary on the fossilized remains of ancient creatures has been published. A curious woman named Mary Anning has been gathering and assembling these bones. Along with bezoar stones, which, it turns out, are actually fossilized..." She leaned in and grinned at her friend, "poop."

Tilly, though clearly diverted, was still looking over Lydia's shoulder.

When Lydia turned and saw Rutherford approaching, she blushed, thinking he must have been close enough to overhear her words. "Mr. Rutherford. How very nice to see you again so soon."

"Indeed, it is a pleasure, Miss Norwood. Am I to understand that you are fond of books as well as horses?" His smile was wolfish.

"Yes, I am. I do not believe I could give up either. May I introduce my friend?" She watched his face as she made the introductions.

His eyes were fixed and dilated a little as he took in Tilly's features. He smiled at her a little stupidly, but Lydia could not detect any evidence of amusement, so perhaps he had not heard the naughty comment.

It was considered bad breeding to eavesdrop on other peoples' conversations, after all. But perhaps he had just been knocking about with the nobility enough to acquire some of that unwavering sang froid.

"So you are Lord Aldley's friend." Tilly was playing it polite, but she wore an impish smile that Lydia knew she reserved for people that she liked.

"I believe he would own it himself, on most days. We met as school boys." Rutherford was now quite openly staring at Tilly.

"That is a long acquaintance." Tilly breathed in deeply so that her bosom heaved. "You must know him well. And how is he enjoying his recent acquisition?"

"You mean, the stallion?" Rutherford stepped incrementally closer to Tilly. "I believe he is very pleased with the bargain. I admit to being a little jealous of his luck. I dearly love riding and hunting—I am so fond of my dogs that I bring them with me to town, selfish as it is. I should very much like to someday find such a hunter for myself. Aristophanes is magnificent, and Miss Norwood here is an excellent rider. She has trained him very well."

Lydia blushed a little more deeply, but smiled.

"I did not know you were such a renowned equestrian." Tilly turned to her. "We could go out riding in Hyde Park some time, you know. My father keeps a few riding horses in town."

"Nothing would give me greater pleasure, but I had no idea that *you* rode."

"Well, another thing we have in common." Tilly's grin was just a little too enthusiastic. "Although I am afraid I shall not be hopping any fences. Shall we go riding one afternoon—Thursday, if the weather permits? I believe Mr. DeGroen might be persuaded to come out with us."

"That sounds a delightful outing. I hope the weather obliges you." Rutherford looked very pleased with himself.

When Rutherford had taken his leave, Tilly whispered to Lydia, "Actually, I do not ride at all."

"Then why on earth did you suggest it?"

"You can give me some lessons. I could not miss the opportunity of dropping the information of our plans and our whereabouts into the ear of Lord Aldley's good friend. And if Lord Aldley should happen to go riding in Hyde Park next Thursday afternoon, then I believe we shall have to start picking out the lace for your wedding gown."

"Good Lord, not more lace. But you are quite terrifyingly clever. I should never have thought of it."

"You are far too sweet to be conniving. That flaw will no doubt be purged once you have had more experience in town—or once you become a countess, whichever should come first."

CHAPTER 17

The worn wooden bench of the fencing club's toilette room gleamed in the light from the high windows. The air was a heady mixture of manly sweat and the perfumes and pomades administered by the servants. Aldley mopped his face with a towel and let his valet begin dressing him.

He had needed a workout to burn off some of the coal Miss Norwood had lit inside of him. A little fencing was just the thing. Rutherford was a natural athlete, and had almost lazily countered him at every point. Aldley had improved greatly since taking expert lessons in Paris, but he was still no match for his friend.

However Aldley could not repine, his heart was too full for unhappy thoughts and anyway, there were few men in London that Rutherford could not best with foils. Aldley consoled himself that he was still a much better shot than his Corinthian friend.

"I cannot believe you just happened to run into her at Hatchards, of all places. And she was actually looking for a piece on Mary Anning's fossils?" Aldley shook his head at Rutherford, as their valets perfected their cravats and gave a final brush to their jackets.

"Indeed. She was with an acquaintance, a Miss Ravelsham. I was happy for the introduction. And I overheard Miss Norwood explaining the true identity of bezoar stones to her friend, rather humorously." Rutherford laughed. "I believe the pair of them are two little mischiefs."

"A curious mind and a playful disposition. She has so many facets." Aldley could not help the stupid smile on his face.

"She is no longer to be dismissed as a blue-stocking, then?" Rutherford's nonplussed facial expression was designed to mock.

"I should never have said such a thing and I shall thank you not to mention it again." Aldley knew very well that he adored the philosophical turn to Miss Norwood's mind. It was yet another aspect of her sweet singularity.

"Well, just as you please." Rutherford grinned. "Her friend, Miss Ravelsham, is a stunner. She has the face of an angel, but her pert little smile looks just like the devil set his fishing hook at its corner and gave it a tug. And there is a naughty flash in her eye. I admit I am utterly fascinated."

Aldley smiled and shook his head. "I am sure you misrepresent the young lady."

"Anyway," Rutherford continued, unperturbed, "Miss Norwood and all of her many facets will be on glittering display in Hyde park next Thursday afternoon, weather permitting. She and her lovely friend will make an outing, if you are interested."

"Indeed? Her father is not going to let her go out without a chaperone, I hope." It was an alarming thought. In fact Aldley was beginning to think she should have an armed guard.

"The plan is that her friend and her betrothed shall be with her." Rutherford stretched his arms.

"Her *betrothed*?" Aldley suddenly paled.

"Miss Ravelsham's betrothed, that is." Rutherford rolled his eyes.

"Ah."

"Not to worry, Aldley. No one has got there before you."

"Oh do shut up." Aldley could not help smiling. He had completely lost his ability to affect noble boredom and he no longer cared. Anyway, he knew Rutherford was not fooled by his masquerade of indifference, so there was little point in maintaining it.

"Someone has got there before *me*, however." Rutherford's face hardened. "I hope the man deserves her."

"You can speak this way after a quarter hour's conversation in a book shop?" It was Aldley's turn to mock.

"I see what you mean. It is a foolish fancy." Rutherford paused for a moment to sigh and run his hand through his hair, to the visible irritation of Smythe whose fingers twitched. "In any case, I imagine they will also have at least a groom with them, for they intend to go riding."

"Riding. I see." Aldley's good humour dwindled.

"So you could go see her there, but you would be at rather a disadvantage if you were not on horseback."

"I do not believe that falling and breaking one's neck is the best way to make a favourable impression."

"True. Well, you could simply not go." Rutherford permitted Smythe to fix his hair again. "I am sure you have many other things to do, and Delacroix probably will not accost her with so many people around her."

"*Probably* is not good enough. I have some fellows looking into his whereabouts, but no one has yet been able to locate him. I am sure he is still in London, though."

"Not to change the subject, but your speaking of making enquiries has jogged my memory. I have some news from Venice."

"Indeed?"

"My acquaintances have located Essington. He is gravely ill and at times quite delirious." Rutherford grimaced. "He was in some rancid little hovel adjacent an opium den."

Aldley gasped in disgust. "Good Lord. But he is still alive."

"Yes, but getting him to leave may take some doing." Rutherford wrinkled his nose into a sneer. "The fool refused assistance."

"Well, they are strangers to him. I may have to travel there, myself, to retrieve him." The thought did not at all appeal to Aldley.

Rutherford scoffed, "Does he not have friends that might be prevailed upon to travel to him?"

"Perhaps, but discretion is of the utmost importance. Frankly I care not if he rots for the way he has treated my sister, but he must rot by the mode which creates the least shame for his wife and child."

"The timing could not be worse." Rutherford shook his head. "Recollect that you have just invited Miss Norwood to your mother's ball. You cannot leave her there stranded."

Aldley sighed in frustration. "If I leave this evening, I can be back in time."

"If you travelled there, found him, packed him up, turned around and travelled immediately back, with good weather for the crossings, you might even have an opportunity to change your clothes before the ball. A surfeit of time, really. I do not know why there is any question."

"You exaggerate. I do not suppose you would accompany me." Aldley looked hopefully at his friend.

"And leave no one to stand in your stead at the ball, in the," Rutherford laughed, "unlikely event that you do not return on time? Besides, without my assistance, the cur is more likely to die. Only bring some others with you—a doctor and attendant." Rutherford ran his hand through his hair again, and Smythe huffed audibly. "I believe my doctor, Kellerman, might be willing."

"Yes, I can see you are indifferent as to his living or dying. But is it as bad as all that?"

"He has putrid wounds. It is not a case of merely sleeping off his profligacy."

"If you are here, perhaps you could watch over Miss Norwood and her companions on Thursday. I shall have my people who are hunting for Delacroix report to you, if you will be my proxy."

"You may rely upon me. A ride in the park is a bit tame for me, but I should relish an opportunity to see Miss Ravelsham again."

"And meet her fiancé."

Rutherford only pulled a face.

"I knew I could count on you, my friend." Aldley cocked a cheeky brow. "Aside from my valet, there is no one I rely upon more."

"Only take care that you are be back in town before the ball. I do not relish her ladyship's barbs any more than will Miss Norwood."

Aldley's mood was ruined, but one could not shirk family obligations, even under the supreme temptation of the lovely Miss Norwood.

CHAPTER 18

*T*he sunlight warmed Lydia's back, and the birds sang sweetly in the trees lining their path through the park. The air was a little cool, but lightly infused with the green scent of freshly cut grass. Gentle breezes stirred the lace of her bonnet, tickling her cheek as though Demeter were caressing her daughter.

She beamed at Tilly. "What marvellous weather for a ride." It was not as much fun as racing through the woods on Ari, but it was good to be on a horse again. The plodding pace was soothing, and it amused her to see Tilly so out of her element.

"Yes, the *weather*, at least, is marvellous." Tilly shifted uncomfortably in her saddle. "But I cannot fathom how you can find this exercise enjoyable."

"It is far more enjoyable if you are not riding side-saddle. In a world of stupid rules, that must be one of the stupidest. I never ride side-saddle in the country."

"I think polite folk are deeply disturbed by the spectacle of a woman astride a horse," Tilly laughed. "They say it is a matter of decency, but I think they are only uncomfortable with any symbol of physical capability among the fairer sex. It resembles power a little too closely, and undermines the sense of order to which they desperately cling." She assumed a masculine voice of spiritual authority. "If first a woman rides astride, what abominations might then follow?"

"I always thought it was so we could never beat men in a race." Lydia was sceptical.

"Put succinctly, that is just what I said."

"You are quite revolutionary in your opinions. Is your betrothed aware of your views?" Lydia tossed her head at Mr. DeGroen, who was riding some distance behind them with Tilly's brother. "For I am sure you keep them to yourself in society."

"Of course I do. My ideas may be a little wild, but I am no fool. As for Mr. DeGroen, I dare say that he asked for my hand *because* of my views."

"Really?"

"Really." Tilly's smile was self-congratulatory.

"And yet he seems so upright and, well, conforming." Even his attire was almost dull. Lydia could hardly believe there was anything the least bit revolutionary about the man.

"Yes, for he is no fool, either." Tilly's lips formed into her slightly crooked smirk. "I should prefer not to marry a fool, you see."

"I really could not imagine it." Lydia chuckled.

"Just so we do not get arrested for our seditious ideas, I shall change the subject. Were you pleased with the lawyer I found for you?"

"Yes, indeed. He has set everything up just so. It is not a large amount, but I thought I should start small and make increases in the investment as I see how things go."

"That seems prudent."

"I also have recently had another idea for an investment, but it would put me rather perilously close to being," Lydia lowered her voice to a theatrical whisper, "in trade."

"Scandalous. Well perhaps you should discuss the matter with the lawyer, too. There may be some way to distance yourself from direct involvement. Are you going to tell me what this investment will be?"

"Not yet, but soon. I shall want your opinion, of course. Your opinions always seem so well-informed." Lydia gave Tilly a little sideways, suspicious look.

"I am pleased that you think so." Tilly returned the look. "I admit I am rather curious, so to keep myself from prying I shall change the topic again. Have you heard anything from Miss Delacroix?"

"She called very briefly yesterday morning. I was given to understand that she had just purchased the most fetching bonnet imaginable. I have not yet got over it and am still quite beside myself with jealousy."

"As well you should be. She also called on me in the afternoon, for she had just heard some astounding news about Lord Aldley."

"Really?" Lydia's heart beat faster. What could Miss Delacroix know about Lord Aldley? "This she omitted to share with me, but perhaps she had not yet heard this news when she called on me."

"Perhaps. But howsoever that may be," Tilly raised her brows significantly, "she had heard that his lordship left town very suddenly last week, the day after we met Mr. Rutherford, apparently. It is all quite mysterious, she claims, but her new maid has connections to some of his house servants, and it seems he was bound for Dover."

"A crossing? So he was for the continent." Lydia's heart sunk. She had cherished a hope that they might see him in the park.

"Yes. So he shall not be here today, I am afraid. I have suffered the pains and indignities of this bizarre exercise for nothing." Tilly's mouth betrayed that she was not impressed by the earl's sudden travel plans. "We may only hope he was not bound for the colonies, for else he will certainly not be back in time for the ball."

"Whatever could he be up to?" Lydia wondered if he had thought the better of the expectations he might have created and simply left to get away from her.

"Well, it is possible that he is a rather flighty fellow. He is only just back from a long stay in France, after all. But he does not seem so. I think it must be something very particular to take him away. Miss Delacroix is of the opinion that he is returning to a paramour in France. She has heard from a reliable source that there was a pretty young Parisian opera singer that caught his eye. She said that this might put *some* young maids off of his company."

Tilly raised her brows and smiled faintly. "She assures me, however, that such things would not deter *her* from accepting his affections, for, although she is innocent of any particular knowledge, she *understands* the ways of men, in general. Very broad-minded is Miss Delacroix. Who would have known?"

"Has he paid some attentions to her—to Miss Delacroix, I mean?" Lydia hated the slight sound of panic that crept into her voice.

"I think it highly unlikely. It was expressed in the hypothetical. If she had any real cause for hope, you can be sure she would have exclaimed it to us both. And do not trouble yourself about it." Tilly smiled reassuringly. "She only said these things to me that I might relay them to you. Her *reliable source* is almost certainly her brother, who was in Paris at the same time as the earl, but we both know that Delacroix is too smoky by half."

"I wonder at her repeating such things about a man she has apparently fixed designs upon." Lydia's dislike of Miss Delacroix was growing with each encounter.

"She is most likely trying to undermine your confidence in the earl's character, for she cannot get close enough to undermine his confidence in yours. I believe she has heard of your invitation to the ball. Clearly it has made her jealous and quite desperate."

"Why would she not say it to me directly?" She hated all these London games, these foolish, contrived intrigues.

"Do you not see? This way she may feign concern for your feelings, while being certain that the information will reach your ear. And it will seem more credible if she does not say it directly to you, for it disguises her motives. She may deny any mischievous intention, for she did not say anything to *you* about her suspicions."

"Where would she get any idea about my feelings?" Lydia disliked the presumption and the nosiness.

"She is surmising, I suppose. I might as well tell you that everyone in town knows of your last minute invitation to the ball, and of the earl's visit to your home in the countryside. The ton have great ears, though very small wits."

Lydia's face sank. "Good Lord, I am done for. I shall not deny that I like Lord Aldley, but I should prefer not to have my feelings to be the subject of speculation and gossip around town."

"That is unavoidable, I am afraid." Tilly assumed an air of arch dismissiveness. "Tedious people have nothing to interest them but the lives they imagine others to be leading."

"Oh come, you are not so entirely averse to gossip, yourself." Despite her glum mood, Lydia was amused at her friend's superiority.

Just at that moment, before Tilly could formulate a clever reply, a rider approached much too quickly from the side. In fact there were two horses. All Lydia saw was a flourish of black, before someone was holding the bridle of her horse and someone else was pulling her out of her side-saddle. Tilly was already swinging something at the assailant, before Lydia's own instincts had her struggling and clawing at the man who tried to pull her from her mount.

She punched him in the eye, but he recovered quickly. Lifting Lydia off her horse, he swung her over the front of his saddle. The indignity of being treated like a sack of provisions had her cursing and twisting to get free. She heard yelling from the men behind her, but no one reached her in time. Her assailant carried her away, galloping hard to separate her from the protection of her friends.

Lydia dug her gloved fingers into the leather saddle strap, as best she could. She dared not further attempt escape lest she fall off and break her neck. Her skull jounced back and forth with the motion. Blood rushed into her head in a dizzying torrent. In a few minutes, they were slowing. Spots swam in Lydia's vision, but she could make out a covered carriage at the edge of the park. It bore no markings.

This had to be Delacroix's work. She would claw his face bloody if he tried to touch her. In fact, as soon as her feet touched the ground someone was going to get a proper beating.

Probably anticipating her thoughts, the other man dismounted first and pulled her off of the horse, so that she only got one badly aimed swing in, before her arms were pinned. One of them was pinching her nose, so that she was forced to breathe orally as she struggled.

She turned her head this way and that to avoid the bottle that her assailant was tipping into her mouth. More of the fluid landed on her face than made it past her lips, but the man then forced her mouth shut and held it. She was suffocating, but she would not swallow. She would not.

"Ijit. Let 'er nose be." The other man released her nose, and grabbed her with both arms.

"Won't be but a few moments. She'll swallow."

It might be better to play faint. Perhaps they would let their guards down and slacken their grips. She willed herself to relax her body and closed her eyes. The man holding her now had to support all of her weight. He did not set her down however.

The hoof beats of someone fast approaching on horseback were just audible, but she dared not look. Suddenly she felt it easier to relax. The drug must be affecting her, though she still held it in her mouth.

"Get 'er to the rig!"

The two men were carried her, one still clamping her mouth shut. She heard the sounds of punching and a struggle. She opened her eyes just as she was dropped. The sudden jar caused her to swallow involuntarily. She cursed herself for this.

Her eyes were already a little heavy. She was feeling a bit more relaxed than she ought in the circumstances, but she could still make out the back of a man. He was tall and strong, and was tying a pretty good beating on one of the two men who had attacked her.

She tried to stand and assist in the fight. Her first grapple missed badly. One of the men elbowed her in the stomach, which threw her back onto the ground. She tried to stand again, but her body would no longer even sit up right. She lay on the grass and watched with a strange detachment.

The other miscreant tried to escape, but was engaged by Mr. DeGroen and Mr. Ravelsham, who had just arrived. She thought the man fighting nearest her was familiar, but she could not say exactly how. She tried to focus her memory, but recollection evaded her.

She caught a view of the side of his face. Yes, she certainly knew him, but from where? It was Mr. Rutherford. Of course. It felt nice to be rescued, and he was rather handsome. She smiled. Quite comforting, really. Like everything was going to be fine. In fact, the men had things well in hand, so she might just as well have a little nap.

She felt a sudden grasp on the back of her dress. Rough hands hoisted her up and dragged her backward toward the carriage. She tried in vain to gather her legs underneath of her. Then came the thump on the head.

CHAPTER 19

"**G**ood Lord, she is in that carriage!" Rutherford gave a final swing and knocked his adversary senseless.

The other villain, who was restrained by Mr. DeGroen and Mr. Ravelsham, laughed.

"You are lucky I have not time to attend to you, too." Rutherford leapt onto his horse and called out to the others, "I shall send word as soon as I can." And he rode off after the carriage.

Keeping pace was no trouble at all, but Rutherford could only follow them. He cursed himself for not bringing a gun. And yet, who comes armed for a ride in the park? The whole situation was preposterous. It was unthinkable and outrageous conduct.

If he had a gun he might be tempted to ride past the carriage and shoot Delacroix in the face. For it must be Delacroix. A whip would be more satisfying, but he supposed that neither would help the situation.

Miss Norwood's reputation was already in serious peril. If word of the abduction got out, she would be ruined.

Still, he would not let anything happen to her person. If only there were a way of getting word to Aldley, but he was on the continent. With any luck, he would return home in a few days. But in the meantime, Rutherford would have to deal with the situation himself.

Rutherford rode hard for an hour, before the carriage in front of him made a sudden right turn, almost tipping over in the process. It turned onto a smaller road, and the carriage had to slow down to navigate.

Fortunately he had just decided to slow his horse's pace, and leave some distance before him, when he saw a head and arm appear out of the carriage window. Rutherford realized too late that he was staring down the barrel of a pistol. He felt an amused sense of incredulity when the shot rang out.

CHAPTER 20

*L*ydia was still groggy when she opened her eyes, but her first vision was a man crowding her in order to lean out a window.

She could feel the jouncing motion of a carriage. He smelled of whiskey and smoke and sweat, and her throat clenched with revulsion at the stink of him. A loud bang and the smell of gunpowder brought her around.

"What on earth are you doing?" she shouted.

The man sat down next to her, re-holstering his pistol. It was Delacroix. "I am terribly sorry my dear. Just shooting some vermin."

"Where am I?" Lydia put her hand to her head, as though that might steady her vision.

"I think the better question is, *where was I?*" He leered at her. "Ah yes. Your bodice."

She looked down and found herself in the early stages of being undressed. Her outer dress was completely loose around her. Only her undergarments remained in place. He reached for her again. She swung at his face. It was a weak blow, but she scratched his cheek. "Do not touch me, you filthy pig!"

He leaned back and pulled out a knife. "Really, my darling, I thought you were smarter than this."

"I am not your darling." Her eyes were getting heavy again. She fought to keep them open. How could she ever have thought this man handsome? He was utterly revolting, his teeth yellow, his clothing heavily stained and his hair slithering about in greasy coils.

"Surely you understand that you have lost. You cannot possibly evade me now. Look at you, you can barely remain sensible. If you continue to struggle, you will only be hurt. I do not want to scar you." He brandished the blade with a smile that suggested he would enjoy using it.

"But believe me I shall, if it is necessary. Or," he leaned in and traced the blade lightly over the skin of her chest, "you can just lie back and enjoy it. I can be very gentle, dearest. I shall not hold your conduct at our last meeting against you."

She clenched her jaw to stifle an impolitic reply.

His breath reeked of drink. How drunk was he? The gun was in a holster at his side, but it was a single shot pistol and he had not reloaded it. She dismissed any thought of using it on him.

Her thoughts were still scrambled, but the effects of the drug were starting to wear off. She wondered whom he had been shooting at. It must be one of her friends come to rescue her, surely.

"That is better. Relax."

Just then she became aware of a horse approaching close to the carriage. Delacroix was fiddling with his clothing and appeared not to notice. But he snapped to when he heard the sound of someone landing on the back of the vehicle, and scrambling up on to the roof, which made alarming cracking noises.

He cursed and re-fastened his attire. The carriage slowed and there were sounds of struggle. Then the carriage stopped.

Delacroix, still cursing, moved to exit the carriage by the right door. Lydia grabbed the handle and flung the left door open.

Delacroix turned back, and grabbed her dress. "No, no, my little flaming beauty. You stay here. I shall not be long, then I'll give you the full measure in your hot little—"

Lydia dove forward and slipped out of her loose outer garment, leaving him holding her dress, as she rolled from the carriage. She landed in a muddy ditch wearing nothing but her undergarments. But she was free. She had a sensible pair of boots on, so she made quick use of them.

Her legs were still wobbly, but she ran to the nearest tall tree with sturdy looking branches. It would not be the easiest climb of her life, but she was motivated. She thought she heard Delacroix behind her, but she didn't turn.

Heaving herself up to grab the lowest branch, she used her legs to walk herself close enough to swing one leg over, then paused in this ridiculous position to regain her balance.

Every moment she expected to feel rough hands upon her, pulling her back down from behind. But she remained unimpeded, so she hoisted herself up and balanced on the branch carefully, for she did not yet trust her limbs, then reached for the next.

Lydia discovered, when she was well up the tree and dared to take a look below, that Delacroix was not behind her, nor anywhere near the tree. Her limbs were shaking as she climbed around to position herself for a better view of the road.

She could not see the men, but she could hear the sounds of fighting. She climbed a little higher, until she could see over the carriage. Delacroix and Rutherford were at blows. Despite his drunken state, Delacroix appeared to be holding his own.

Then Lydia saw the blood seeping out of Rutherford's arm. She should never have run away. She should have stayed and helped him fight. And now she was halfway up a tree, hiding like a coward.

There was movement at the front of the vehicle. The driver, who had been lying in a heap on the ground, stood up and rubbed his jaw. He stumbled to his seat at the front of the carriage. Lydia thought for a moment that he might simply drive away.

Instead he seemed to be rummaging for something. She strained to see what he was doing. Her breath caught in her throat. He was holding a pistol.

The other two men didn't notice the driver. Rutherford fell back as Delacroix kicked him in the chest, then scrambled to retrieve his blade from the ground. She was sure they would murder Mr. Rutherford one way or the other.

She had to help. She began to climb down, but froze when she saw Delacroix lunge at Rutherford with the knife, just as a shot rang out. Both Rutherford and Delacroix fell to the ground. She gasped.

The driver stumbled back to Delacroix. He rolled the two men apart. Rutherford did not move. He was covered in blood. The driver tried to rouse Delacroix, to no avail. He hobbled back to the carriage, hopped into the seat and whipped the horses into motion, leaving Mr. Rutherford and Delacroix behind in the dirt.

Shaking, Lydia climbed down so fast she almost pitched out of the tree on her head. Her limbs were scraped, bruised and bleeding. She was shivering with cold and fear when she reached the ground, but she could only think of Rutherford, lying there in the dirt, covered in his own blood.

She ran as fast as her wobbly legs would carry her to the man who had tried to rescue her and was lying there dying alone. If he were not already dead.

She reached Delacroix first. His body lifelessly still and covered in blood. His own man must have shot him. Good riddance. She rushed past to kneel beside Rutherford, looking for some sign of life.

"Mr. Rutherford?" She tore open his blood soaked shirt. There were no wounds to his lower chest or stomach. Perhaps some of the blood on his clothing belonged to Delacroix.

She bent her ear to his lips. A surge of relief went through her when she felt a faint breath on her cheek. "Oh thank heavens!" Throwing propriety to the wind, she pulled him gently into her arms. "I do not know how I could live with myself if you died. Please hold on. You just stay alive, Mr. Rutherford."

A further search revealed an injury to his left arm—it looked shallow, a grazing wound. It had bled a lot, but seemed to have clotted. His right shoulder had a deep, angry-looking wound that was still bleeding heavily.

She had read enough medical literature to know that sudden blood loss could render a man senseless. She had to bandage him and get him somewhere warm. But there was no carriage.

Lydia looked around. Her garments still lay in the dirt where Delacroix had discarded them. She tore a few strips from her already tattered underskirt, then quickly dressed herself.

She tended to Mr. Rutherford's wounded shoulder as best she could. She packed it with moss from the trees, as Ole Maeb had showed her, and wrapped the strips of cloth around his shoulder to put pressure on the wound.

She struggled to shift his heavy torso and dragged him over to prop him up against Delacroix's body. It was still warm and would keep Rutherford's shoulder out of the dirt. It might not help very much, but it was something, at least.

Lydia surveyed her inexpert work without optimism. The sound of horse hooves filled her heart with hope. She turned to see that it was not a rider come to her assistance, but a lone chestnut stallion trotting toward her. Of course. Lydia cursed herself for a fool. She had forgotten that Mr. Rutherford had followed them on horseback.

The horse lowered his head and nuzzled Mr. Rutherford's hair.

"Well, my friend." Lydia stood up and introduced herself, stroking his neck and scratching his ears. "Will you help me save your master?"

The problem was, Rutherford was too big to hoist onto the horse's back. Furthermore, she had no idea where in all of the English countryside they were.

CHAPTER 21

Tilly surveyed the landscape as it crept by the carriage window. It was slow going, following the hounds and trying to be inconspicuous about it.

Smythe, Rutherford's butler—and, he assured Tilly, also his closest servant and valet—had insisted on accompanying them. In fact, he had refused the use of the dogs unless he came along, as well. It made the carriages more crowded, but Miss Ravelsham, after some consideration, thought that having some extra domestic servants along might not be a bad thing.

Whatever they did, it had to be plausible. Servants almost always aided plausibility.

They had the advantage of knowing which road out of London Rutherford had taken in pursuit of the carriage. But after they were out of the city environs, there were plenty of side roads that might be taken. So they had brought out the dogs, and plodded along behind them with the curtains half drawn so that any curious persons that might pass could not identify them.

It was a preposterous way to spend a Thursday afternoon, and Tilly would be fully enjoying absurdity of it, were it not for her concern for Lydia. She shuddered to think what might be happening to her friend even now, while they crept along at a maddeningly slow pace behind Rutherford's huntsman, who handled the dogs.

At least they seemed to know where they were going, for Rutherford had taken his own horse, and the dogs knew the scent well. Tilly thanked the heavens that he brought his dogs with him to London, and happened to mention it when Lydia introduced them at Hatchard's.

It was a large coach, but they were crammed in tightly. Mr. and Mrs. Norwood sat across from her, next to her brother. Tilly sat with Mr. DeGroen and Smythe, who claimed he could not possibly fit into the servants' carriage, and who clearly had an elevated sense of his own dignity.

The strange combination of tension and boredom was maddening, and Tilly was just about to risk looking frivolous by suggesting a game of whist, when she felt the carriage turning sharply onto another road. Relieved for the possibility of progress, she looked out the window again.

"I believe this is the road to Dunston Hall, is it not, brother?"

Frederick shrugged. "I am afraid you know more about such things than I, Tilly."

"I believe Dunston is in this general direction, as I recall hearing it from Mrs. Delacroix. It is not ten miles from our own estate, though we are not acquainted with the Viscount." Mrs. Norwood's face looked drawn.

"You mean the estate of her elder son, the viscount? Yes, I believe you are right. I suppose that is a hopeful sign that we are on the right path." Despite these optimistic words, there was a deep grief and anxiety in Mr. Norwood's eyes. He clearly felt even worse than Tilly did.

The carriage slowed and stopped. Tilly opened the door and stepped out to see what was happening, then gasped at the sight. They had found Lydia. She stood, totally dishevelled, in the middle of the road-way, holding the reins of Rutherford's horse. She was pale and bleed-ing, in torn and dirty clothing.

Tilly ran to her friend, who was already being wrapped in a cloak by the huntsman.

"Lydia, thank God you are safe!" She pulled her friend close and hugged her tightly, then stood aside to allow Lydia's father and mother to do the same.

"Never mind me. We have to get Mr. Rutherford somewhere warm and fetch a doctor immediately. He has been gravely injured." Lydia patted the horse, affectionately. "And somebody get this darling half a dozen carrots and a good rub down. You lot only just arrived in time. I was running out of fabric to re-tie the sleigh and I had not the faintest idea where I was going."

Sure enough, behind the horse, the groom and the huntsmen were carefully lifting Rutherford from a makeshift jumble of branches fastened together with strips of cloth from Tilly's habit. The whole thing had two longer poles attached to the saddle, so that the horse could pull it along the ground.

"That is a rather ingenious contraption." Tilly could not believe that they had found them at last. Lydia was safe. Tilly blinked back her tears and shook her head to dispel her mawkishness. "But look, you are chilled. We shall talk later."

After a quick conference, Mr. Norwood sent the huntsman and a groom back down the road to retrieve Mr. Delacroix's body and deliver it to the viscount at Dunston Hall. Then they made re-arrangements in the seating order within the carriage.

Mr. Ravelsham and Mr. DeGroen volunteered to ride up top with the coachman. And Smythe, who was quite beside himself with concern, agreed to squeeze into the servants' carriage, so that his master might not be pressed for space.

Mr. Norwood's manservant rode ahead to fetch a doctor who would meet them at Nesterling Lodge, which, according to Mr. Norwood was less than an hour away.

And so they bundled Rutherford into the coach, wrapped in a wool blanket, and set off as fast as the horses could bear them.

When they were in the carriage, without any servants about to hear them, Lydia could finally tell the party what had happened. When she was finished, they were all astounded.

"Good Lord, what a foul devil of a man!" Mrs. Norwood's face was glowing at bit pink from the story. "And so you hacked away at branches with that fiend's own broken, bloodstained knife to make that contraption for poor Mr. Rutherford? Well, thank the heavens you were wearing your riding gloves. But what effrontery! Whatever shall we do?!"

"My dear, it shall be just as Miss Ravelsham has laid it out for us." Mr. Norwood instructed his wife. "But you must be strong. You must act as if our sole intention in coming out to the country were to enjoy the company of our friends on a hunting party at the estate."

Mrs. Norwood sighed. "Yes, yes. But then what was the rest?"

"The unfortunate business with Mr. Rutherford occurred while he was riding out to attend to some matters in the country. He was then to proceed on to Nesterling to join our party, having sent his servants along with ours." Lydia's father patiently recited the fiction they had agreed upon.

He thought for a moment. "But he came across Mr. Delacroix being attacked, apparently by his own carriage driver. When the driver shot Mr. Delacroix, Rutherford intervened, was stabbed and fell in a dead faint. The assailant escaped in the carriage."

Mr. Norwood took a breath and continued, "When he regained consciousness, Rutherford managed to get on his horse and ride back to the main road, where we came across him, nearly falling out of his saddle. So we made for the nearest place we could treat him, which happens to be our conveniently situated estate. Thank the Lord for that."

"Right." Mrs. Norwood looked unsure.

"And Lydia has been with us this whole time," Tilly added.

"Indeed."

"Thank God the bleeding seems to have stopped." Lydia could not keep her eyes off the pale face of Rutherford. "He was so brave. I should have been—well you would doubtless have a daughter on the point of marriage by now if he had not come to my aid."

"Over my dead body." Her father's eyes gleamed. "I should never let you marry such a man, even had you been caught *in flagrante delicto* by the Archbishop of Canterbury and paraded naked through the streets with an 'A' branded on your—"

"Charles, please!" Mrs. Norwood interjected. "Miss Ravelsham is a maiden and not accustomed to your unusual way of talking."

Tilly kept her lips pressed together, until the impulse to laugh passed. "Not at all, Mrs. Norwood. This experience has taxed us all to the utmost limits of our nerves. However, I agree with Mr. Norwood's sentiment, entirely. Who could condemn dear, sweet Lydia to any sort of connection with such a vile man? No one who loved her."

Tilly grasped her friend's hand, but noted that Lydia stared almost blankly at Rutherford.

Mrs. Norwood wiped her eye and looked out the window.

Mr. Norwood turned to Tilly. "Miss Ravelsham, I must commend you, again, for your quick thinking. And I must thank you. You are a most remarkable young woman, and we are so fortunate that Lydia has found such a steadfast and clever friend."

"'Twas nothing at all. I am only glad, indeed deeply thankful, that Lydia is safe." Tilly tried to catch Lydia's eye, to no avail.

"And he was not daunted by being shot at." Lydia's gaze was still steadily fixed on Rutherford, as though she had not heard this exchange at all. "He came to save me, though he had no weapon to defend himself. And I ran off like a coward to hide in the trees."

"Really Lydia!" Tilly squeezed her friend's hand again. "You must not blame yourself for trying to escape, after such a horrible affront. You were frightened to death and still half drugged! Running away was the only sensible thing to do."

Tilly sighed and shook her head, then added, "And devising a way to remove Rutherford to safety after he was injured was much more than most girls your age would have had wits for."

"Or most men, either, it should be said." Lydia's father smiled, though tears threatened to flood his eyes. "You two really are forces to be reckoned with. I am truly very proud of you, Lydia. And you are blameless in this. Utterly blameless."

But Tilly could see very clearly that Lydia did not feel blameless and that her nerves were so shocked by this whole adventure that she could not receive comfort from her father, from any of the people who loved her.

CHAPTER 22

*L*ydia could only stare at Rutherford's unconscious form where he lay in a well-warmed guest room at her family's estate.

The cheery amber blaze of the fire in the hearth could not dispel the gloom and dread in her heart. Her virtue mattered not at all if the man who had tried to protect it with his life should pass from this world.

"I am sorry to say it, but there is not much more I can do at the moment." The doctor's eyes were shadowed and red.

He had spent most of the night removing the tip of the broken blade from Rutherford's shoulder and observing him. "I shall go home now, but I shall be back to check on the patient after dinner, if that is convenient."

"Of course it is. You may come at any time, Doctor Gant. We are very grateful to you for your close attentions to our friend." Mr. Norwood looked almost as weary as the doctor.

"Is there anything we should do for him?" Lydia was not permitted to sleep in Mr. Rutherford's room and attend him, as she had wished.

But her parents had indulged her feelings of guilt and concern enough to let her check on him regularly.

"No. Nothing more than you are already doing. The worst is over. He has lost a lot of blood, but he should recover from that, fully, so long as he does not develop a fever. I have treated a lot of duelling injuries, and nine times out of ten the fever is more serious than the wound itself."

He looked at Lydia's worried face and added, "But he is young and was clearly in good health before this mishap. I have every reason for optimism. Only now you must excuse me. I shall see you this evening."

They all saw the doctor out, leaving Rutherford to the tender ministrations of Smythe.

Just as the doctor was leaving, the huntsman and groom entered.

"Beg your pardon for the intrusion, Mr. Norwood. Only I thought you would want to hear the news direct, like."

"News? What news?"

Lydia drew closer so she could better hear.

"Well, we went back to tidy up the sled trail, and such, just as you said. Only when we got there, we checked on the body, and Mr. Delacroix, he was still breathin', shallow like."

"Good Lord!"

"We bundled him in our cloaks and onto one of the horses, and made our way to Dunston."

Her father nodded his head grimly. "Yes, yes. You did the right thing. Very good."

"His lordship happened to have a doctor there for one of the farmer's children."

"How very fortunate." Mr. Norwood's lips formed a hard line.

"Yeah. So long and short, Mr. Delacroix is there at Dunston Hall. His brother was very grateful for the service. You should expect his lordship to pay a call in the next few days."

"Very well. And I thank you. The doctor has seen your master, and is hopeful. Our housekeeper has arranged rooms for you in the servants' quarters." Mr. Norwood slipped into deep thought.

After the servants left, Lydia and Tilly joined him in his study.

"I know I should not think this, much less say it to you two, but why couldn't Delacroix just have stayed dead?" Lydia's father rubbed his weary eyes.

"Indeed. I quite sympathize with the sentiment, but on the other hand, he may still die. And in the meantime, it lends a sort of credibility to our version of the facts." Tilly pressed an index finger to her temple. "I only hope that Mr. Rutherford regains consciousness soon. We rather need him to go along with the story, if things are to go smoothly."

It was irritating that her friend took such a mercenary view of her rescuer's recovery.

Lydia's tone was tart as she remonstrated, "I hope Mr. Rutherford regains his health, howsoever it might bode for our official story. I just want him well and I do not care a whit if I am branded as a fallen woman. I should gladly trade my reputation for his life."

"Well, luckily it will not come to that." Tilly tried to sound conciliatory. "Only we must find a way to make what we say seem natural and plausible. And we had better hope that Delacroix has the good sense not to contradict it."

"Yes, let us hope so." Mr. Norwood poured himself a brandy, as early as it was. "Though I cannot say he has shown much evidence of having any goodness at all and very little sense, I believe we may at least rely upon his robust supply of basic self-interest."

Lydia excused herself to look in on Rutherford. Smythe was holding vigil by his bedside. Such loyalty. "Has there been any change in our patient?"

"Not as yet, Miss." Smythe stood up as straight and stalwart as a stone tower. "But he seems to be resting peacefully."

"That is as it should be, I suppose. I can sit by him for a while, if you would like to take a little turn about the grounds."

"Not at all, Miss. I shall stay here as long as I have leave to do so."

She smiled again. "Of course you have leave. I shall have your meals brought to you here, then."

"Be careful what you offer. He eats like a horse." Rutherford's voice was faint and gravelly.

"Sir!"

"Mr. Rutherford!" She rushed to his side. "You cannot imagine how relieved I am. We have all been so worried."

"My appetite is quite restrained, I assure you, Sir." Smythe appeared at her shoulder.

"Yes, yes, Smythe. Once again you are unjustly maligned. But thank you both for your care—where am I?"

"At Nesterling Lodge, my father's estate. Do you remember coming here to see Aristophanes?"

"Yes, of course. But I am rather sparse on the details of this most recent visit. Pardon the indelicacy, but I last remember clamouring about on a carriage, trying to rescue you. And Smythe was decidedly not there."

"It is a bit of a long, complicated tale, I am afraid." Lydia could not help grinning at him, and tears of joy were threatening to make a fool of her.

"You mean, something more complicated than being shot? Good Lord, my shoulder feels like it has been hewn off and stitched back on with vetch."

"That was the result of a knife wound, actually. The bullet only grazed you. Doctor Gant left some laudanum for you."

She retrieved the bottle, and measured out the dose into a cup of barley water. "It will make you sleepy, however. If you can manage to endure the pain for a short while, I believe my father and Miss Ravelsham will wish to speak with you as soon as may be—if it is not too great an imposition."

"Miss Ravelsham is here, too, then?" Rutherford's face formed into a stupid smile. "No, indeed. No imposition at all. But this is all rather mysterious."

When the little group had assembled in his room, they explained the situation as quickly as possible. Lydia blushed when she recounted the tale of her escaping into a tree and then coming back after she thought he had been shot. Mr. Norwood clenched his jaw when he spoke of the news of Delacroix's survival.

Miss Ravelsham calmly outlined the story they had conveyed to Delacroix's brother and the original plan to find and retrieve Lydia, then pretend that they had all merely gone for a hunting trip to the country.

"I must say I am impressed, almost terrified, in fact, at how quickly you devised this scheme and executed it, Miss Ravelsham. Using my dogs was a stroke of genius." Rutherford's good arm moved a little toward Tilly.

Tilly smiled. "Well, you had mentioned that you brought them with you to town. But it was nothing. I think you should be more impressed with Lydia for bandaging you up and cobbling together a sleigh to get you out of there."

"Yes. I am not sure which of you is more terrifying, really." Rutherford looked back and forth between the two of them.

Lydia blushed. "I am, in fact, most impressed with *you*, Mr. Rutherford. For you chose to risk your own life to rescue me—though I am nothing at all to you. I do hope—I pray—you will forgive me for running away in the first place, when I should have stayed and fought with you. I have been cursing myself for a coward ever since."

Lydia could feel her voice giving out at the end of these words, and wished she did not look like a vapourish little fool.

"Lydia..." Her father looked beside himself.

"Please do not trouble yourself on that head," Rutherford reassured her. "You are a most unusual girl for even thinking of joining the fight. I wanted you to run. You did what any sensible woman would have done under the circumstances. There is little you could have done, formidable though you appear to be, against men armed with knives and guns. Or if you had shown me up, I should have died of manly shame much sooner than of these trifling wounds. There is nothing at all to forgive."

"You are too good." Lydia was relieved, but could not meet his eye.

"Only now, I think I really must take that laudanum. Forgive me. Perhaps we can speak more later."

When they all left the sick room to let Mr. Rutherford rest, Tilly pulled Lydia aside. "Are you up to visiting Delacroix?"

"I beg your pardon? What on earth are you thinking?" Her friend must have finally lost her mind.

"Well, not visit him, precisely, for he is no doubt not up to visitors, but we could call at Dunston Hall. Look, I do not know the details of what went on in that carriage, but I should understand if you were afraid of ever seeing him again." Tilly searched Lydia's face.

"Well... things did not get *that* far. But I should prefer never again to set eyes on that vile bit of human filth, unless it is to lay a beating on him, if that is what you mean."

Tilly laughed. "My friend, I love your spirit. But you must conceal your feelings."

Lydia frowned. "Why ever should we go visit him?"

"Is it not obvious? We are the only members of our party acquainted with him—aside from your father, who shall accompany us, but is still a bit too angry to be trusted with delicate social subterfuge."

"But please, what are you speaking of?" Lydia's voice betrayed her exasperation.

"I mean, it is quite natural for people of his acquaintance to pay a call to enquire after his recovery, being in the same part of the country."

Tilly carried on as though Lydia were not staring at her like she was utterly balmy. "And particularly Mr. Norwood, to whose hunting party Rutherford was bound when he came across the robbery. But it would not be natural for someone who had, for instance, been abducted and wronged to show up and pay a visit."

"You mean, in case he makes that claim." Lydia knew her friend had a point, but she did not like where the conversation was going.

"Yes, it is hard to be certain of what he will say. He is probably not even conscious yet. His injuries must have been more serious than Rutherford's, surely. By your account, I can scarcely believe that he is still alive. But a secondary motive for the visit is that we may ascertain how well the vile little wretch is recovering."

Lydia shook her head. "But if he says anything, if he tries to implicate me, what shall I do?"

"You will look innocently confused. It will be the ravings of an invalid. Probably feverish. Having laid eyes on you while still in leave of his senses, a compromised mind might dream up anything... Though it is highly unlikely that he should be able to talk for some time."

"His ability to breathe is a sufficient marvel." Lydia did not add *and a great pity.*

"The crucial thing is to behave normally—as if you are only there to visit a convalescent acquaintance."

"But there is so much at stake for me." Lydia leaned against the wall and tried to control her breathing. It was too much. She could not see him again.

"And nothing for him. I see what you are feeling." Tilly rubbed Lydia's arm. "Be at ease, his brother is probably a respectable man. He will be most eager to believe our version of events, should it come to that. Who would not prefer to believe that his brother was the innocent victim of a robbery, rather than a would-be abductor? In fact he probably already believes us. The story was given to him under compelling circumstances—the delivery of his injured brother. Saving his miserable hide would not be in the interests of the family of the woman he had wronged, would it?"

"Your logic is sound. However, I cannot but apprehend that this will be a most unpleasant visit." Lydia's face was pale.

"I shall be there with you, Lydia. But you must seem like any young woman of the ton visiting a passing acquaintance who is unwell. So you must sound vaguely too curious—as though you might be angling for some gossip."

"Right. That sounds natural."

"Not for you, perhaps, but for a good three quarters of society, it is. He doesn't know you. And we shall wait a day or so before we go. We can practice a bit before we pay the call. Would that help?"

"Probably." She could not help feeling ill, even as she tried to smile for Tilly's sake. "I honestly do not know what we should have done without you in this whole débâcle. But you are oddly capable of such extensive machinations. I really do wonder at you."

"If you keep questioning my character, I think I might require some sweets as compensation." Tilly loved to change the subject.

Lydia lifted a brow but led her friend to the breakfast parlour. "Let us not go right away, however. I shall need to rehearse, and I want to be very sure that Mr. Rutherford is recovering, first."

CHAPTER 23

*A*ldley had taken the best staterooms available on the boat. He had decided that crossing sooner was more important than arriving in grand style, and so had settled for a more modestly outfitted vessel that departed earlier.

Though it was a humbler vessel, the cabins were clean and recently painted. After some of the inns they had taken, the fresh linens of these quarters would be a treat. The smaller vessel was also less conspicuous, which was important, as he hoped to return his brother-in-law home without anyone recognizing them.

They had had no delays for storms in either direction, which was the principle worry which had made him uneasy about returning in time. A surfeit of time, indeed. Rutherford need not have been so worried. As it was, Aldley should have enough time to finally get himself a suitable equipage before his mother's ball.

Unfortunately the crossing was always choppier in this direction. The rolling motion of the boat made Aldley a bit green, but did not seem to affect his wretched brother-in-law in the least. Yet another injustice in the situation.

"Maybe we could bide a while at Dover. I know a rather nice gambling house there—with rather nice *ladies*." Essington winked at Aldley.

"I should think you know of several, but as you cannot even stand without assistance, I cannot imagine what you think you might do there." Aldley was beyond sick of his brother-in-law's endless display of vice.

"I'd come up with something that didn't call for standing."

"See here, Essington, you have engaged in enough entertainments for a whole century's worth of family embarrassment. If you have no concern for your own health, at least consider how your reputation will affect your son."

"I shall be dead and forgotten before he is old enough to worry about things like reputations and consequences."

Aldley decided not to say what he was thinking.

"We have to lay over somewhere. You didn't even let me sniff the air in Calais." Essington was wheedling now.

"I do not think it was the air you were looking to sniff. I shall hire a roomy coach at Dover. You can sleep on the road as well as I." Aldley turned to the doctor who had accompanied them. "I hope that is acceptable to you, Dr. Kellerman."

"Indeed, I am at your disposal, my lord. And I have no desire to make this trip any longer than it must be. In any case, I think it preferable to keep our patient confined and away from public houses as much as may be possible."

"I quite agree."

"Well devil take the both of you." Essington crossed his arms. "You cannot keep me imprisoned forever. You cannot tell a man where he may go and where he may not."

"But we can certainly refuse to carry him there." Aldley wondered how an utter reprobate like Essington conjured up righteous indignation, as though his character should place him beyond suspicion.

Lord Essington merely spat on the floor in reply.

"In my opinion, my lord, you must be ever so careful with your health. There is no guarantee that your lordship will regain use of those legs. If I had not thought a rapid removal the most important priority, I might have taken that left leg off entirely." Dr. Kellerman's concerned expression could not conceal that he knew he was wasting his breath.

"You just try it, leech. Anyway, I shall be as right as ninepence in no time. Then I should like to see anyone try to tell me I can't go to public houses, brothels, or anywhere else I want."

"Will you attend to the patient, Doctor?" Aldley placed a hand on his queasy stomach. Essington's company was not helping the seasickness. "I shall go take some air."

Aldley breathed deeply as he walked onto the deck and closed his eyes. The motion was no better, but at least there was fresh air, and no brother-in-law. Essington was like an insolent young master, and badly in need of a sound thrashing. The wastrel was, unfortunately, too ill for a thrashing.

He had been incontinent for two days when they first removed him from the hovel he was rotting in—and gripped with such tremors that at times they thought he was having seizures. He was in a miserable state and cursed everyone trying to help him to hell for their trouble.

Nothing on his body worked properly except his tongue. After the unpleasant spectacle of the initial subduction of the drug from Essington's body, Dr. Kellerman decided treat him with doses of laudanum, which the good doctor had been steadily reducing during their travels, to the strenuous objection of the patient.

Indeed, there was scarcely a thing Essington did not object to. Their lodgings were beneath his standards, despite the fact that even the humblest inn was several cuts superior to his lodgings in Venice—and Aldley could scarcely even call them *lodgings*. Every meal was unpalatable, and the carriages all had springs made of granite.

The ingrate resisted their aid to the best of his ability. He would not even tell them how his legs had become injured, though the doctor thought the wounds were originally inflicted by a sword or large knife of some kind.

But left unattended to fester in the heat they had turned septic. Dr. Kellerman said he had seen plenty of men die of less in the war. And yet, Essington gave every indication of improving—physically if not morally. *Weeds do not die*, as Lady Goodram always said.

Lady Goodram. All he wanted was to get home, have tea with that excellent lady, and attend his mother's ball. Be in the good company of Rutherford. Dance with Miss Norwood.

Yes, he wanted to do more than dance with Miss Norwood. But he would not think on that now, for he should not imitate his brother-in-law's depravity with his own unchaste thoughts.

He simply needed to immerse himself in the quiet pleasures of decent people, in calm and respectable society. He could even wish for mundane morning calls with the most boring of the ton, just to feel clean again and reassured in the basic character of mankind, by exchanging bland pleasantries and accepting blander refreshments.

But even weak tea seemed like a distant dream. When he returned to England, he would still have to make his way to Essington Hall, return this cretin to his sister's care, and support her as best he could.

If they stopped over anywhere it meant delay. And Aldley had matters to attend to before the ball.

For one thing it was about time he got his own carriage and a proper team—this riding about in a hack was tiresome. He had to return to London as quickly as possible, to prepare for—if he was honest with himself, it was to prepare for marrying Miss Norwood.

He smiled at the thought. They would sleep in the carriage on the road from Dover, as horrid as that might prove to be. He would get this mess over with as quickly as possible, and move on to more pleasant things.

An old newspaper wedged into the door caught his eye. He retrieved it. It appeared to be an illegal, untaxed rag out of London. He gasped as he read the headline: "Viscount's brother left for dead by his own driver!" He read through the article rapidly.

"Good Lord, it is Delacroix!"

CHAPTER 24

The Delacroix estate was quite grand and surprisingly well-managed. The well-tended fields rolled by as Mr. Norwood's carriage moved up the long drive. The Viscount must live a much more regulated life than his debauched swine of a brother. Lydia banished such uncharitable thoughts. They would not help her play the role that she had come to play.

"Are you ready?" Tilly was irritatingly collected.

"As I shall ever be." Lydia did not even pretend to smile.

"Remember, you are appropriately concerned, but otherwise carefree and perhaps just a little too interested in gossip. Giggling helps." Tilly sounded like a governess.

Lydia giggled.

"Good enough. You should get on brilliantly." Tilly smoothed a strand of hair back under the cover of her bonnet.

"What about you, Mr. Norwood?" Tilly turned her scrutiny to Lydia's father. "Can you play the good neighbour?"

"I believe so." His face looked tired and strained.

"Just do not think about Delacroix. It will help. I am sure the Viscount is a good enough man, for all that his brother is worthless. Think of it as a kindness to him."

It was amazing that Tilly could be so charitable to the brother of such a fiend. Lydia stared at her friend. What an unusual mind.

Lord Delacroix joined them shortly after they were shown into the sitting room. After the usual exchange of niceties and introductions, there was an uncomfortable pause before the Viscount said, "I hope you have not been waiting long. I was only just checking on my brother."

"It is we who should apologize, my lord, for I know we have not been introduced. But we all have some passing acquaintance with Mr. Delacroix." Lydia's father stopped himself from clenching his fists, and pretended to flex his hands.

He continued, "When I heard of your intention to call on us—well, I hope your lordship will pardon the irregularity of it. It seemed unkind to stand on ceremony in this case, for I could not imagine that you would wish to be removed from the patient even for the time it would take to pay a call. And having been involved in the discovery of your poor injured brother, I could not rest until I had news of how he gets on."

At a subtle elbow from Tilly, Lydia leaned in slightly, smiling and nodding sympathetically.

"Truly, you should not apologize." The viscount's face was full of concern and deep sensibility. "I owe you a great debt for returning him to me. You have saved his life—I hope, I pray. He has not awakened, except to briefly utter feverish nonsense. The doctor attends him constantly, but says that the fever will be the most serious threat. The bullet seems to have done as little damage as may be expected from a slug to the stomach. It is a miracle that the blood clotted as it did. But he has bled a great deal—I beg your pardon, ladies. I do not mean to be gruesome."

"Not at all, my lord." Lydia seized the chance to play her role. "We are quite eager to hear of his recovery. It is so shocking to have word of an acquaintance being assaulted in this brutal manner. And by a servant!"

"Have the authorities yet apprehended the driver?" Tilly sounded ever so slightly too interested.

"No, unfortunately. It appears he was not my brother's regular driver. I hope, if Pascal recovers his senses quickly enough, he may assist—at least to identify the man. But where are my manners! I have not offered you so much as tea."

He rang the bell and asked the servant to bring refreshments.

He turned back to his guests. "Forgive me. I am somewhat distracted and my wife, who is much better at receiving guests than I, is away visiting her sister. I should have joined them by now, if my brother had not been attacked. I am so thankful, given these events, that business had delayed my departure."

The tea and sandwiches arrived more quickly than Lydia had thought possible. However out of practice the Viscount was, the servants were clearly alert and at the ready.

She could not trace any similarity between Lord Delacroix and his brother. His colouration was much lighter, his features rounder, and his eyes were hazel. Most strikingly, the viscount seemed to be a tremendously kind, almost deferential man. He was not at all haughty —she could almost forget he was titled.

And there was a basic decency about him that belied any blood relation to Mr. Delacroix. She was beginning to feel guilty for her part in the subterfuge, necessary though it was, for she did not like deceiving him. His grief and anxiousness were real. Her concern was entirely a façade.

Lord Delacroix stirred in sudden recollection. "I should ask what news you have of Mr. Rutherford. I have it from your man that it was he who first came to assist my brother and was also injured by his assailant."

"We believe he will recover, my lord." Mr. Norwood wiped his hands on his pantaloons. "He is awake now, but the doctor wants him to remain in bed for some time longer."

"I am glad of it. I shall pay a call on you when my brother is improved, if I may. I should like to thank Mr. Rutherford personally."

"Indeed you will be most welcome, my lord."

Just then the butler entered. "I beg your pardon, my lord, but the Earl of Aldley is here to see you." He extended a card on a silver tray.

"Please see him in straight away, Gibbs." The Viscount looked surprised.

"Lord Aldley!" Her father made the exclamation which Lydia suppressed in herself. What could he be doing here?

"Do you know the earl, Mr. Norwood?"

"We are a little acquainted with his lordship. The earl is a great friend of Mr. Rutherford's."

"Indeed I am." Lord Aldley entered and received their bows. "Thank you for receiving me, Lord Delacroix."

His eyes fixed on Lydia's for a moment—and then a moment longer with a slight air of enquiry. She merely smiled. His eyes were beautiful. How could she explain this? But was it so very strange? She knew the Viscount's sister, after all.

"I am very pleased to make your acquaintance, Lord Aldley." The Viscount smiled. "I understand I need not introduce you to anyone here."

"By happy coincidence, I know Mr. Norwood and his daughter. But I have not yet met this lady—I think it must be Miss Ravelsham, is it not? My friend has mentioned you to me."

They made introductions, and Aldley looked around at the little group, still slightly puzzled, but smiling warmly at Lydia. Her heart beat a little quicker.

"I am pleasantly surprised to find you all here," Aldley said. "I am only just returned to England, and was on my way to my sister's. But I had heard of your brother's misfortune, Lord Delacroix, and I felt I should call and enquire after his health."

"As did we all, my lord," supplied Tilly, shaking her head. "Poor Mr. Delacroix. We were horrified!"

"Yes, I admit I am surprised that my brother has so many friends who are so kindly attentive to his health as to come pay a visit. I am quite touched." Lord Delacroix said this without a whiff of sarcasm. Lydia stewed in her own guilt.

"Indeed! How could we not take an interest? Such an awful ordeal to have befallen him." Mr. Norwood was in good form. But Lydia thought Lord Aldley looked at him very strangely for a brief moment.

Her father turned to the earl and continued, "We were all on our way to Nesterling Lodge for a little hunting party, my lord. Only Mr. Rutherford came across poor Mr. Delacroix being attacked by his driver."

"It was most shocking! And the horrid man did not scruple but to attack poor Mr. Rutherford, too." Lydia hated the sound of her own voice, the insipid stupidity of the remark.

She hated more the surprised look that the earl gave her. She could not fathom why Lord Aldley would be here, as he was obviously not acquainted with the family. And here she sat behaving like gossip-mongering simpleton. It was such wretched timing.

"Rutherford was attacked?" Lord Aldley's face wrinkled in concern and confusion. "And he was on his way to Nesterling?"

"Yes, but he had some other things to do," Tilly supplied smoothly, and waving her hands airily, continued, "You know, *business* of some sort, so he was riding on ahead, and would join us later, only we came across him in a terrible state."

"Oh yes! It was a terror! We were all quite beside ourselves! And then we heard of poor Mr. Delacroix." Lydia effected an expression of wounded sensibility at these sad and horrifying events.

It was pure, excruciating torment to carry on this charade in front of Lord Aldley, whose face looked troubled.

Her father cleared his throat. "Mr. Rutherford was stabbed while trying to defend Mr. Delacroix."

"Good Lord! Is the injury serious?" Lord Aldley's face was now ashen.

"Please do not be alarmed, my lord. He appears to be recovering well and the doctor is very optimistic. Your lordship will be most welcome to come visit him. I am sure Mr. Rutherford would be exceedingly glad for it." Lydia's father looked uncomfortable.

Lord Aldley looked stricken. "He is staying at Nesterling Lodge, then?"

"Yes, upon the doctor's instructions. He is not to be removed, nor even to leave his bed for a while yet." Mr. Norwood wiped his hands again.

Lord Aldley shook his head suddenly. "Forgive me, this is a lot to take in all at once. Lord Delacroix, I meant to ask after your brother. Is he recovering?"

"The injuries are not insurmountable, according to Doctor Hastings, but he has a wretched fever."

"I am sorry to hear that."

"Are you well acquainted with my brother, Lord Aldley?"

"Not exceedingly. We spent some time in the same circles while we were in Paris. And my mother is recently acquainted with yours. But I was most astounded to hear of this vicious attack."

"I think everyone must be. It is demoralizing for such a thing to happen in England—and out in the countryside." The Viscount shook his head. "But the man was not a known servant, merely a hire. That much betrayal we are spared."

"Lord Delacroix, I hope you will accept and convey my best wishes for a quick recovery to Mr. Delacroix. I wish I could stay, but my sister is expecting me and there are others waiting on me." Aldley stood.

"What, in the carriage? Why did you not bring them in? Think of the inhospitality. My wife will have my hide if she hears of it." The viscount was visibly mortified.

"I shall never tell her." Lord Aldley's smile was a little sad. "And though you are very kind to offer, it would be most inconvenient to remove my brother-in-law, as he cannot walk. His doctor and attendant are with him. But it has been a long voyage, and we must carry on to his estate."

Lord Delacroix looked as though he were about to protest further.

But Lord Aldley made for the door and quickly added, "I am to leave the day after tomorrow to return to London. But I hope you will permit me to visit again, Lord Delacroix, the next time I am in this part of the country."

Then he took his leave of them and exited, but he did not meet Lydia's eye.

"My lord, we should not further keep you from your brother, either." Lydia's father looked sincere.

"Yes, I..." Lord Delacroix seemed lost for a moment. "I should go look in on him. Thank you all for coming to call. It is most comforting to know that my brother has such friends."

Mr. Norwood swallowed. "We should thank your lordship for indulging our irregular visit." They all stood and made their adieus, and he added, "We wish your brother a speedy recovery. Please give him our best wishes. And I hope we shall see you at Nesterling ere long."

"Indeed," added Lydia, desperate to make herself feel less like a deplorable fraud, "it would be a great honour, my lord. And beyond that, we should be most happy for the visit." It was awkward, but the most sincere thing she had said the entire call.

When they walked to their carriage, they saw that Lord Aldley had not yet left. He was attempting, with the aid of another man, to lift a third, struggling man into the carriage.

From the state of his clothing, he had been on the ground. So this was the earl's brother-in-law. Lydia averted her eyes, for she thought it must be quite embarrassing for the man to have others witness his inability. They all seemed to have the same instinct, and moved to their carriage without comment.

But as she was handed in, the disabled man turned and yelled, "There's a fine tail. Where have you been hiding this little bit of muslin, Aldley? Why don't you lovelies join me at Essington Hall. Always room for fetching wenches." Lydia actually gasped, and her father's mouth hung open.

Lord Aldley stuffed the man rather roughly into the carriage and slammed the door.

He then turned with a pained look to Lydia and her father, and called, "I beg your forgiveness for my brother-in-law's conduct. He is truly unwell, on laudanum for his legs, and has quite taken leave of his senses. I am afraid it is better if we leave quickly. But it was my great pleasure to see you and your daughter again, Mr. Norwood. And to meet you, Miss Ravelsham. Good day." Despite his stoic politesse, there was colour high in his cheeks.

Her father only bowed.

When they had settled into the carriage, he said, "Good lord, do you know that man is a viscount—Lord Aldley's brother-in-law, I mean— Lord Essington. We've not been introduced, but I know of him. I had not thought I should ever have to protect you from the insufferable affronts of so many upper class bounders."

"I do not blame Lord Aldley, but I must admit that it was shocking. Having recently experienced the effects of laudanum, I cannot believe Lord Essington's incivility to be entirely the result of the drug."

"Indeed," added Tilly, her lips twitching slightly. "And all this incivility comes at the end of a rather bizarre visit. I think I shall find normal social calls utterly dull after today."

Lydia shook her head. "For my part, I think I should greatly prefer a nice dull chat about Miss Delacroix's latest bonnet."

"Well a closer acquaintance may be inescapable now that you have had tea with her brother, the viscount. There may be many such chats in your future, so you will be happy." Tilly chuckled at Lydia's pained facial expression. "But I believe *I* may have to hire someone in London to hurl obscene insults at me as I step into my carriage, else I may expire from the relative tedium of polite morning visits."

Mr. Norwood, unusually inattentive to the diversion of Tilly's wit, remarked solemnly, "At least we know Delacroix has not said anything to contradict our version of things."

"Nor is he likely to, for the time being. These fevers are not to be taken lightly." Tilly was glib.

"No, I recall that Doctor Gant said as much." It was a relief to Lydia.

"We might still have some hope that we shall finally be done with him, then, say it as I shouldn't." Mr. Norwood smiled a little.

"I cannot help but feel sorry for the viscount, though. Is it possible that he could be unaware of his brother's character?" Lydia still felt guilt for deceiving the troubled man.

"I think not. At least not entirely. I believe he is just a kind man and a good brother." Tilly's face looked suddenly serious. "He may be hoping that the experience will make a better man out of Delacroix."

Mr. Norwood huffed. "I should as soon expect a dog's hind leg to turn into a walking stick."

"And we had best pray that they do not ever find that driver." Lydia's stomach turned at the thought. It was unjust that she should have to go to such lengths to hide the crime committed against her.

And what would Lord Aldley think when he found out the truth? Mr. Rutherford was one of his closest friends. He would not wish to withhold the real story from Lord Aldley. Was there any point at all in concealing this blight on her reputation, if it were not concealed from the earl?

CHAPTER 25

*L*ydia walked into the library at Nesterling. She loved the treated leather smell of the bindings and the insulated quiet created by the stacks of books. It was as though she were among a jumble of various friends, some prim, some unruly, but each silently greeting her as she passed.

She made her way to the south corner to bask in a sun-drenched seat by the window and perhaps nap or enjoy a little light reading. Then she saw Mr. Rutherford reaching up for a book in one of the stacks.

"Mr. Rutherford! What are you doing in the library? The doctor has directed you to stay in bed."

"I thought if I were to be condemned to bed rest, I might at least have something to read."

"Why did you not have Smythe assist you?" Lydia knew she sounded like a governess, but she could not help being worried.

"I have sent Smythe back to London to run things there, and to send me some clothes—in truth, just to be rid of his clucking about like a hen with one chick." Rutherford laughed. "So I am on my own, now. But you shan't cry rope on me to the doctor, now, shall you?"

Lydia smiled conspiratorially. "I suppose we are already bound together by our secrets. What is one more little concealment? But could you not have asked someone else to fetch books for you?"

"I know you love books, so I should not have to explain the importance of browsing for oneself to find just the thing." He was still a little pale, but even when sickly, his smile retained its rakish charm.

Lydia smiled back warmly. "I cannot deny that I know precisely what you mean. However, I can see from your face that you are in pain."

He winced. "Well, a bit. One does not realize how much one uses the shoulder in the simple act of walking, for example, or looking up at a shelf full of books." She could see blood seeping through his bandage.

"Oh no. You are bleeding again. Please, you must return to bed. Come, I shall walk with you. I can bring you a selection of my favourites. Would you not like that?"

"Indeed I should." He looked ready to swoon.

They had almost reached his bedside, when Rutherford collapsed suddenly. Lydia caught him under his good shoulder and tipped him to slide onto the bed, but was encumbered by his great weight. She found herself trapped awkwardly under his limp body.

She was struggling to free herself and her skirts from this entanglement, without hurting the patient, when she heard a voice from the doorway.

"Oh, I beg your pardon! Excuse me." It was Aldley. She recognized the voice, the beautiful voice, though she could not quite see him from her current position.

Her face burned with shame as she struggled yet harder to free herself. But her thrusting and pulling had the unfortunate effect of turning and jostling the unconscious form of Mr. Rutherford, so that he appeared to be roiling about on top of her.

This made the situation look so much worse. What an utter catastrophe of humiliation! And Rutherford showed no sign of awakening. She tried to shake him awake gently, but to no avail. Then she realized with fresh mortification that, under the circumstances, the gesture might look like a passionate caress.

She winced. All the blood in her body rushed to her cheeks and ears. Aldley must be shocked beyond speech by such a scene of infamy. Why was he always popping up at the worst possible moments?

She waved her free hand in the direction of the doorway.

"My lord, could you please be so kind as to lend us your assistance?" she called out in a voice muffled by the collection of manly bulk and fabric that pinned her to the bed. "Mr. Rutherford has fainted on me."

"My lord?"

But no answer came. The earl had already gone away.

When Lydia finally managed to disentangle herself, she called for a servant to fetch the doctor. She then rushed to enquire after Lord Aldley's whereabouts.

"He didn't stay, Miss. He said that Mr. Rutherford was sleeping, and that he would come again another time. He left straight away."

Her heart sank, and she covered her mortified face with her hands. What he must be thinking. But irritation soon roused her from this swoon of ruined dignity.

She could not waste time worrying about the earl's feelings, at the moment. If he had helped her instead of running off in a fit of pique, they might have got assistance for his friend that much more quickly.

She returned to Mr. Rutherford's bedside, checking his breathing and looking with worry at the spreading bloom of red at his shoulder. He groaned in pain. She brought him another dose of laudanum.

"Well, Mr. Rutherford, at least you have one sensible friend to watch over you." It was Tilly returned from her walk with Mr. DeGroen.

Rutherford smiled briefly and closed his eyes, as Tilly drew Lydia across the room.

"I saw Lord Aldley bolting for his carriage, just as I reached the house. He did not look pleased. Let me guess, his lordship grossly misinterpreted your attending to Mr. Rutherford?" Tilly smirked and shook her head.

"I am not entirely sure what interpretation he gave events, but he witnessed my trying to prevent his friend from falling in a dead faint onto the floor. I ending up entangled under Rutherford on the bed. And by the way Lord Aldley tore out of here..."

To Lydia's horror, Tilly began shaking with laughter.

"How can you laugh at such a catastrophe?" Lydia glared at her. "I thought I should die of humiliation."

"Do not worry, my dear friend. All will be explained, and he will realize he has been a colossal fool. In the meantime it is a good sign that he is not indifferent to you." Tilly's face glowed happily.

"I sometimes find your perspective on events alarmingly mercenary. I suppose I should be reassured by that, but the whole situation is mortifying. And I find, at present, I am far too worried that Mr. Rutherford has taken a turn for the worse to contemplate how the fractious Lord Aldley's feelings might be soothed." Lydia scowled and walked back to the bed to cover Rutherford properly with the blanket.

"To be honest, if I were you, Mr. Rutherford would probably put all thoughts of the earl out of my mind entirely." Tilly smacked her lips.

"I know what you are implying. And after our most recent encounters

—or let us say social brushes, I am not sure what exactly Lord Aldley is thinking. But I am not throwing myself at Mr. Rutherford."

Lydia sighed and added, "I deeply respect him for his bravery. He saved me and I shall forever be in debt to him. In fact, I hope we shall become very good friends, for I find I enjoy his company. But even to think of anything more seems indecent. And nor should you be speaking this way, for you are betrothed."

"Betrothed, not dead." Tilly was laughing again, shamelessly. "However, as you are so very serious and prudent, I shall not tease you anymore."

It was nearly dinner before the doctor arrived. Mr. Rutherford had awoken once, taken some broth and more laudanum, then gone back to sleep.

Rutherford's mind was foggy, but he was conscious enough to receive a lecture from the doctor, who frowned as he changed the dressing and said, "I do not just give you instructions for my own amusement, you know. You must remain still and rest."

"I am sorry. It is hard to stay in bed. When can I return home?" Rutherford's face was still pale.

"Travelling?" Dr. Gant was aghast. "I must strenuously recommend against any removal for some time. I shall be guided by the rate of healing, of course. We shall know more in a few days. But if you keep reopening your wound, you will not get out of this bed for a very long time."

"I apologize." Rutherford looked sheepish. "I shall try to be a model patient from now on. I only hate imposing on Mr. and Mrs. Norwood."

"You should not think on it." Mr. Norwood spoke firmly. "I will not hear of your removal until you are quite sound. We are all most anxious to do anything to aid your comfort and recovery."

"Yes, most certainly, Mr. Rutherford." Tilly smiled sweetly at the patient. "You should know how very eager we all are to attend to your every comfort."

CHAPTER 26

"*F*or the love of God, go!" Tilly threw up her hands in exasperation and paced across the sickroom to adjust the drapes. Sunshine lit up her curls and travelled on to land on the shoulder wound of the sleeping Mr. Rutherford.

"Are you sure?" Lydia bit her lip.

"Honestly, Lydia, you have become almost morbid, hanging about in this room, drooping over Mr. Rutherford like an apprehensive pall. Ari knows you are here. Go ride him, or you will break his heart."

"And you will watch over Mr. Rutherford and send for me if there is any change?" Lydia implored. "I shall be riding along the north path."

"Indeed I shall, but you know there is no servant that can catch up to you and Ari." Tilly shook her head. "And anyway, there will not be any change. He has only slept, sipped soup and taken medicine this whole morning. He is doing precisely as the doctor instructed. Now go take some fresh air, I beg of you."

"But you are sure that you do not mind?"

"Mind getting this luscious specimen of manhood all to myself?" Tilly laughed. "Yes, it will be a great imposition, but I shall bear it as best I can."

Lydia looked scandalized. "You mustn't talk like that! What if someone hears you?"

Tilly wiggled her eyebrows and waved her hand at the door. "Be off with you! You have your own stallion waiting."

When her friend finally left, Tilly reached into a pocket in her dress and pulled out a small book. "And now I shall read to you as you sleep, Mr. Rutherford. I understand it aids the healing process. And even if you do not find this amusing, I certainly shall."

After Tilly had regaled him with humorous and often utterly filthy poems for a good half an hour, Rutherford stirred suddenly.

"Are you awake, sir?" She tucked the book back into her pocket.

"I am not certain. Either I am awake and hearing a litany of amusing verses which are alarmingly inappropriate reading material for a young lady, or I am having a rather pleasant dream. It is hard to say, the medicine makes one so groggy." His grin was dreamy.

"Indeed. It must be the medicine, for I was reading to you from Fordyce's *Sermons to Young Women*, just now. What sort of naughty dreams were you having?"

"I shall never tell." He winked. "But I am not to be blamed when such a beautiful creature sits beside my bed."

"You are frank. I suppose *that* is the medicine, too."

"Perhaps. It might be better if you do not get too close, for who knows what other effects the medicine might have? What did you call me? A *luscious specimen of manhood?*" Rutherford cocked one brow. "If I am frank, you are overtly inviting. Who could resist such an allurement?"

"I had no idea you were listening, sir." She did not even pretend to

226

blush, and her tongue ran a little over her top lip. "Is it not unfair to use words gleaned from spying against the victim of your espionage?"

"You can hardly call lying in my own sickbed intentionally spying."

"You could have made your presence—or shall we say your *presence of mind*—known. It is as good as skulking about in a closet." She ran her fingers lightly over her collarbone. "But I shall forgive you, if you overlook my girlish indiscretions."

"I should never call them girlish—or you, for that matter. But promise me you will dance with me at the next available opportunity, and I shall almost forget to have heard you."

"*Almost.* So that is how you bargain. Very well, if you recover, and we are ever invited to the same ball I shall dance with you. I suppose I might invite you to my wedding celebration."

He screwed up his face. "Surely you cannot say such things about me and yet still be considering marrying that stupid fellow."

"He is not stupid, and yes, we are still betrothed. That does not mean I do not have eyes in my head." She smiled and took in his form again, which was stellar, even in its current pathetic state.

"Where is he then? If I were your fiancé, I should not give you a moment's peace." His tone was humorous, but there was heat in his voice.

"I believe the steward is giving him and my brother a tour of some of the farming operations."

"That sounds rather tedious. What a fool. But his loss is my gain." He reached for her hand, but she snatched it away.

"He is not a fool, I assure you. I should never marry a fool. But I am sorry to have thrown you into confusion. I am not a coquette, you know. Truly I am not. You just caught me in a private moment with my friend. Girls' silly talk. However, I do hope we shall be friends, now, Mr. Rutherford—now that we have shared in this whole conspiracy to protect Lydia's honour."

"I shall always think of you in friendly terms, I believe, Miss Ravelsham. That will not be a problem. Speaking of Miss Norwood— where is she?"

"She is off riding Aristophanes, while she still may, as he now belongs to your friend."

"Yes, but I think Aldley will be more than happy to leave the horse at Nesterling for the foreseeable future." Rutherford rolled his eyes.

"I hope you are right. He was here, you know. To visit you."

"Was he? You should have wakened me."

"I mean, he was here yesterday. Right before your turn for the worse —or should I say, at the precise moment of your turn for the worse." Tilly gave him a meaningful look.

"Really? So it was while I was insensible. That laudanum knocks me out."

Tilly sighed at the man's obtuseness and tried again. "I believe, in this case, it was the pain or the bleeding that knocked you out. You were walking back from the library with Miss Norwood. When you began to fall, she tried to direct you to the bed, so you would not be further injured."

"I hardly remember it."

"I imagine his lordship has a rather fresh recollection, however." She emphasized her words.

"Was he there? I do not think I saw him." Rutherford rubbed one eye.

Tilly shook her head. He was lovely to look at, but a bit thick. She hoped it was just the laudanum.

"But he saw *you*. Mr. Rutherford, as we have now shared so much frankness, I believe I should just tell you directly, that when Miss Norwood tried to assist you back to your bed, she ended up being pinned underneath of you on the bed for several moments, during which time Lord Aldley arrived in your chamber, hoping for a little visit I should imagine."

Still seeing no spark of understanding, Tilly added with a significant look, "However he left rather abruptly, while she was still trying to get out from underneath of you."

She looked him in the eye, her brows raised in expectation, hoping to see a glimmer of realization.

Rutherford's mouth dropped open, then shut with a snap. "I see. Oh dear."

"Yes. *Oh dear*, indeed. Far be it from me to interfere, but I think it might be helpful with regard to my friend's reputation, and I dare say your own, if you were to explain to his lordship what really tran-spired." Tilly smiled sweetly as if to reward the progress of her slightly slow pupil.

"I shall get dressed and go to him immediately." Rutherford began to sit up. She pushed him back down, gently, causing a stupid smile to spread over his face.

"Don't be silly. It is not such an emergency as all that. And you would be half dead by the time you reached him."

His smile twisted into a grimace of fresh pain. "Yes, I take your point."

"Perhaps when you have recovered a bit, you could write him a letter." She gently brushed a lock of hair off his forehead. "In the meantime, take this and go back to sleep."

He drank obediently. "I should like not to abandon my current dream." He smiled and took her hand as she pulled back the empty tumbler from his lips. She slipped her hand out of his grasp, but also smiled. "But you must. Now rest well. I shall be back to check on you very soon."

"What a sweet promise."

CHAPTER 27

*L*ydia rode as fast as Ari would carry her. He was as eager for a gallop as she was. The trees rushed past in a streak of green and sable, and the wind beat against her face until her breath felt fused to it, and her being merged in one great ocean of movement and colour and rich woody scent. It was an ecstatic trance.

They cut across the back field and jumped the hedge, rejoining the north path and engulfing it rapaciously within Ari's massive stride. It felt good to be back on her favourite mount. But now Lord Aldley owned him.

Would he still leave Ari in her care, now that he had witnessed her squirming about on the bed beneath his best friend? Her face grew hot at the recollection. What he must be thinking? The worst was that she was so powerless in the situation.

She could not merely ride over to Essington Hall and declare to the earl that it was all a great misunderstanding. That would be as good as throwing herself at him, and in any case would probably only make her look more guilty.

And Rutherford was in no condition to travel or even write, so he could not clear things up. All these rules that allowed men to be forthright, and confined women to waiting about for them to do so, were stupid and tremendously inconvenient.

And Lord Aldley was not even yet aware of what really transpired with Mr. Delacroix. But at least in that she was blameless. Even if the earl could not accept the damage it might do to her reputation, he could not think her morality was at fault in that débâcle.

What he might believe—*probably* believed about her and Mr. Rutherford was so much worse. It was scandalous behaviour for which she would appear wholly responsible. And there was nothing she could do to correct this misapprehension. She had never before had less use for the rules.

It would be a miracle if he did not retract her invitation to the ball. But she had to attend, if only to preserve the false impression there had been no abduction, that nothing were amiss, when in reality almost everything was amiss.

She did not see how Mr. Rutherford would be recovered in time for the ball. She would have the agonizing choice between abandoning him, or missing what might be her last chance with Lord Aldley. Perhaps her last chance with anybody, as they would soon be giving up the London house, whether she married or not.

Only the thing was, she did not want *anybody*. She wanted Aldley. It was a bit confusing, but the thought of being pinned to the bed under *the earl* was rather appealing. She was quite sure she would enjoy it, but now he seemed further out of reach than ever.

Lydia urged Ari on and dreamed of the earl.

CHAPTER 28

*L*ord Aldley bitterly considered his fate as his hard-soled boots clacked across the flagstones of the shadowy courtyard, through the ivy-clad stone arch of Essington Lodge, and finally carried him into the sunshine and away from Essington's odious company. He gritted his teeth as he climbed into the hired rig.

His brother-in-law was now ensconced in a home he did not deserve, with a wife he did not deserve, probably drinking away the last of an unfathomably robust health, which he also did not deserve, and singing the chorus of yet another raucous drinking song.

The man was an utter embarrassment. He could not have much of a mind left, and yet could still call forth an endless repertoire of vile ditties.

That worthless specimen was reaping the benefits of Aldley's thankless sacrifice in retrieving him from Venice, while Aldley was left to have all the dire consequences of it. Here he was, stuck in a carriage on his way back to London to attend a ball which would probably be painful, when he should be back at Nesterling calling out his best friend, whom he currently could not stand the thought of.

And a good part of his misery was the fault of his own, worthless brother-in-law, whose profligacy and dissipation was the reason that Aldley had not been there, had not been the one to spend time courting Miss Norwood.

Worse still was Essington's behaviour toward her. It was utterly humiliating to have such relatives. What she must be thinking. He had hoped for a chance to apologize more thoroughly to her and her friend for his brother-in-law's conduct, but now that seemed pointless.

He was not only shamed by his relatives, but his own friend had utterly betrayed him. He could easily see it happening, a young woman falling in love with a dashing young man. If her heart needed any encouragement, then surely the time spent watching over him and worrying for his recovery would do the trick.

He was certain that there was more to the story of the attack on Delacroix. It seemed quite probable that Rutherford was acting to protect Miss Norwood, but he wondered how much she knew about it.

Surely she must be ignorant of Delacroix's schemes, for she seemed quite at ease paying call on Lord Delacroix. In fact, very oddly at ease —he might even say *inappropriately light of heart.*

And even if Rutherford were not such a tempting catch, certainly any romantic thoughts she might have had for Aldley would have disappeared when she was subjected to that foul verbal abuse from his brother-in-law. He should strangle Essington.

And he should stab Rutherford—as soon as he was recovered. The infidel.

Aldley knew he should have seen it coming. Why had he been so foolish as to ask Rutherford to protect her? Hadn't Rutherford practically stated his intention to make an offer for her when they had gone to see Aristophanes?

They were, after all, perfectly suited for one another: both active, horse-loving, hunter sorts. Both loved to read and were too attractive for their own good. Both were a little adverse to the normal rules of decorum.

No, that was unfair. They were neither of them nobility, why should they be overly nice about propriety?

He laughed at himself for the thought, as if the nobility were not the usual culprits when it came to rolling about on beds with paramours. He had thought Miss Norwood's middling class morality would have put her above that sort of amusement, however.

He clenched his jaw. His own friend, doing that, with that lovely, delicious creature. He clenched his fists. Doing that and what else? Had he compromised her? It was nothing he hadn't imagined doing, himself.

Ever since that day watching her ride the great stallion, he had not been able to get the thought of her spreading her legs and sliding astride him...of grabbing that slender waist and pulling her down onto his manhood.... all her flaming hair falling around him as he thrust into her. Yes, he had been overcome with lust. He should be ashamed.

And yet he could blame Rutherford for taking a few more innocent liberties—he hoped they were more innocent—when he himself had spent many an hour dreaming of tearing her clothes off.

But it was the betrayal that irritated him. He did not care in the slightest if Rutherford gave a pretty girl a green dress every day of the week, but it should not be *his* pretty girl. Aldley had run out of things to clench and so pressed his lips together.

Rutherford *had* to know what Aldley's feelings were for Miss Norwood. True, he had not explicitly stated them. He had, in fact, more or less denied them, but Rutherford gave every indication of understanding his true interests quite well.

And yet, after the first visit to Nesterling, had his friend not tried to prevent Aldley from staying? Had he not seemed bent on preventing him from creating marital expectations? In fact when he had asked Rutherford to come with him to Venice, hadn't his friend declined, claiming that someone had to stand in Aldley's stead at the ball?

Stand in his stead *with Miss Norwood.* How could he not have seen it before? How convenient to have the principal competition out of the way, off chasing errant relatives on the continent, while Rutherford stayed comfortably in England and chased after *his* fiancée.

Well, she might as well be his fiancée, though technically he had not yet asked her. Or asked permission of her father. Or done much more than dance and flirt a bit at a ball.

Though he sincerely wanted to kick the chair out from under his invalid brother-in-law and punch his best friend very hard in the teeth, the person with whom he was most angry was himself. What a great idiot he had been.

There was only one thing to be done about it. He would have to confront Rutherford. He was sorry that it should have to occur under Mr. Norwood's roof, but it had to be done. He reached out and tapped his cane on the driver's bench.

"My Lord?"

"A change in plans. Take me to Nesterling Lodge. We shall proceed on to London from there."

"Yes, my Lord."

Rutherford was sleeping when Aldley arrived at Nesterling. Miss Ravelsham stood up from the chair by the bed, tucking something into her reticule, as she greeted him in Rutherford's chamber.

"He has not had any laudanum for three hours now, so he will be waking soon." Miss Ravelsham stretched. "I have just been reading to him."

"That is very kind of you, Miss Ravelsham." Aldley forced a smile, but he knew it looked false. "I have been very worried for him."

That much was true. As much as he had his own murderous fancies regarding his friend, he did fervently wish him to recover. The idea of losing him was unbearable. The idea of losing Miss Norwood to him, equally unbearable.

"As have I. He has been very brave, you know."

"Has he? Yes, I am not surprised. The man has a lot of nerve."

"Let us just say that there is more to the story of his injuries than what you have heard. But I shall let him tell you of that when he wakes. I am sure you will have much to talk about."

There was no trace of emphasis in her voice, but Aldley thought for a moment that the turn of her countenance suggested an added significance to her words. However, he might have imagined it. It was not uncommon for people to expect everyone else's thoughts to be occupied with the same subjects as their own.

When she left, he sat for several moments staring at his friend's pale face. He thought about reading to Rutherford, but saw that Miss Ravelsham had not left the book.

So, instead, he took his friend's hand and said, "You must recover. I cannot bear to see you like this, whatever your recent behaviour toward a certain young lady. You are my dear friend."

"Aldley." Rutherford's eyes were still closed, but he smiled. "I am so glad you are here."

"Are you? I thought perhaps you would prefer not to see me."

Rutherford laughed dreamily. "Why on earth should I not want to see you?"

"I should not wish to interrupt your enjoyment of certain female company."

"Ah yes. Where is she? Delightful girl."

Aldley clenched his teeth. "You can say that to me, so calmly?"

"Sorry, old chap." His words were slurred. "I took some laudanum not long ago. *Calmly* is about all I can muster."

"Miss Ravelsham said that was hours ago."

"I woke up and took some more while she was out. The pain... You retrieved Essington, then?"

"Yes. The swine is back with Elizabeth. What really happened with Delacroix? Can you tell me?"

"No one has told you?"

"Just that you saved him from an attack by his driver."

"That is the official story. But in truth, the bastard abducted her."

"I suspected something of the sort."

"Only I caught up to him. We fought. The driver accidentally shot Delacroix, then left us both for dead."

"And yet you are both alive." Aldley did not sound entirely happy about this.

"Yes, but I think I need to sleep again..."

"What of Miss Norwood?"

"She saved me."

"You saved her, and she saved you?"

"Yes, fashioned a contraption from branches, and got my horse to pull me behind. Amazing girl. *Someone* should marry her."

He resisted the urge to bite his friend's head off. "And then you somehow met up with the rest of the party, I take it?"

"Yes." Rutherford's breathing slowed, and his head sank into the pillow.

"You cannot just fall asleep. We have not even addressed the matter of your infamous conduct with the lady in question."

His friend opened his eyes a little and smiled. "Not so infamous. She is tempting, though. Don't like the idea of someone else marrying her."

"Is that so?"

"Especially.... someone... so undeserving."

"What?!"

"Someone who just... leaves her alone with me all the time... too busy gadding about the countryside with the stupid brother."

"Yes, how foolish." Aldley was indignant. "You know some people have a sense of familial responsibility."

"Shouldn't waste herself on such a beef-witted..." Rutherford's head flopped back and he began to drool. Aldley poked him not too gently in his good shoulder, but got no response.

"Sleep well, my faithless friend."

So that is how things were. Rutherford's senses were somewhat compromised, but his feelings were clear enough.

He thought the jab about *gadding about* with his brother was rather unfair. Retrieving Essington from Venice was a plan they had devised together, and it was hardly a pleasure trip. What, did Rutherford expect that Aldley would leave his brother-in-law in Dover to find his own way home, and just rush off to pursue Miss Norwood?

No, the man was merely making excuses for his own betrayal. Perhaps Aldley had not acted as quickly as he ought to make his intentions known to Miss Norwood and her father, but he did not deserve to have his own best friend sneak about and take advantage of the situation.

The only thing left to wonder about was how premeditated Rutherford's betrayal was. Was it just that admiration sprang spontaneously from the experience of their saving each other? No, that was the wrong question.

The thing to wonder about was what Miss Norwood's feelings were. It was still an open question, no matter how things looked.

She might not have been a willing party to the encounter. She was alone, caring for him and he was drugged. Rutherford was a bit of a rake. He might have taken liberties. And would Rutherford speak of her marrying another if he were assured of her affections?

It might end in embarrassment, but Aldley knew what he had to do.

"Sorry, old boy." He lifted a mocking brow at the sleeping form of Rutherford. "I cannot let her marry someone unworthy. You know, not the type of beef-wit who would lay about in bed sleeping and let her spend time with another man. Stupid fellow like that does not deserve her, would not you say?"

Aldley spoke to Mr. Norwood before he left Nesterling.

"I hope you found Mr. Rutherford in good spirits, my lord." Mr. Norwood was all amiability.

"Yes, though perhaps a bit too relaxed for a proper visit." Aldley thought Mr. Norwood seemed very pleased to see him, not at all awkward. That was a good sign.

"Ah, indeed. The doctor says the pain should become more tolerable in a few days."

"However, he did more or less explain to me the nature of what actually transpired with Delacroix."

"Yes. I suppose he would." Mr. Norwood's brow darkened. "You must know that nothing happened—that is to say—"

"Please, Mr. Norwood, do not distress yourself. I am only glad that Rutherford managed to rescue her." Aldley's clenched jaw belied the

THREE ABDUCTIONS AND AN EARL

veracity of the statement. Aldley should have been the one to rescue Miss Norwood.

"Yes, indeed, my lord. Only, I must beg your lordship to keep this all in confidence for the sake of my daughter's reputation. She was completely blameless. If only I had warned her. I never told her about the letter, you see. I thought that there was no point in embarrassing her, if I could just keep her safely guarded. But who could have known she would be unsafe while attended by friends and servants in Hyde Park in the middle of the afternoon? I know not what the world is coming to."

"I am certain she was completely innocent. And you may depend upon my absolute discretion. However, I must know..."

"My lord?"

"I hate to leave so abruptly, but as you know, I have to attend my mother's ball three days hence. I had hoped that your daughter would also attend, if she can tear herself away from our invalid friend for a day's pleasure." He winced at the bile that soaked into his voice.

"My lord, I apologize, but with all that has happened, the ball had completely slipped my mind. I shall remind my daughter of the engagement and send her back to London with her mother. True, Lydia would never dream of missing your mother's ball. I shall stay with Mr. Rutherford. I am not so worried about watching over her every moment now that Delacroix is bed-ridden. Yes, I am certain Lydia will be most anxious to take advantage of your lordship's kind invitation."

"Has she mentioned the ball to you?" Aldley looked hopeful.

"No, my lord, but things have been rather overwhelming, just lately. And young ladies are coy. I am sure she thinks about it all the time."

"I am sorry to do this in such a rushed manner, deeply sorry, but I must know, has Miss Norwood had any other suitors?"

"Em, no, my lord. Though I should never call Mr. Delacroix a suitor..."

"Certainly not. That is not what I meant. I meant... Forgive my directness. Has Mr. Rutherford asked for her hand?"

"Mr. Rutherford?! I should think not. No, indeed, my lord. I do not believe anything of that nature exists between them, and I hope he has not given your lordship that impression."

Aldley frowned. "He did not say anything directly."

"There, you see, my lord! It must be a misunderstanding. Lydia has been very concerned about his recovery, but so have we all. We are so grateful for his bravery. There is nothing more to it. I hope your lordship will not harbour misgivings about Mr. Rutherford. Truly your lordship must be mistaken."

"I am sure you are right. Forgive me for rushing off, but I must return to London. I hope you will convey my warm greetings to Miss Norwood. Please tell her how much—" he emphasised the words, "I look forward to seeing her at the ball."

Mr. Norwood smiled widely, both bowing and shaking Lord Aldley's hand. "We are *all* very grateful for the invitation, and *approving* of her attendance, my lord."

Outside, Lord Aldley told the driver to waste no time and almost leapt into the remise. There was much to do and much to put in place before the ball. He was deep in thoughts of his plans, when he noticed the carriage lagging. Irritated, he poked his head out to speak to the driver.

"What is the matter? Why are we slowing?"

"There is a carriage in the ditch up here, my lord, and a young lady. I thought we should stop and check after them."

"Yes." Aldley could not conceal his impatience. "Of course. We cannot leave her. She might be hurt." He knew it was uncharitable, but he privately cursed the endless interruptions of his plans by the problems of others.

CHAPTER 29

*L*ydia and Ari had both worked up a proper sweat as they swept along the north path.

How good it felt to ride, to smell the fragrant resin at the wood cutter's cottage, to watch the great trees fly past her until they were a lattice of green lace spinning off in the periphery. The path seemed to stretch ever onward, now in shadow, now in light, as though perusing a magical course to Faerie.

But the spell broke as they reached the main road. It required more cautious speeds, as there was some risk of meeting traffic. She slowed Ari to a trot and patted his strong neck.

Her problems, though unresolved, seemed so distant now. As she turned a sharp corner, she started at the sight ahead. A carriage sat in the deep south ditch, with another carriage behind it, pulled as much off the road as was practicable.

The carriage on the road looked like Lord Aldley's hired coach. It appeared to be the same team, too. Just then the earl himself emerged. A young woman crawled out of the capsized carriage and ran along the road with astounding haste for someone who had been in an accident.

She threw herself on the neck of the earl, who looked startled and displeased. When the earl made to disentangle himself, the lady's body went into a limp faint, so that he was left holding her up awkwardly as Lydia brought Ari to a halt before him.

"My lord, I am surprised to see you here." Lydia was painfully aware that her hair must have utterly forsaken her bonnet and was probably impersonating Medusa's serpentine locks.

"I am surprised, myself." Lord Aldley looked uncomfortable. "Particularly under these circumstances. Do you know this young lady?"

Lydia was about to deny any acquaintance, but when she looked into the face of the woman, it was all too familiar. "Why it is Miss Delacroix—sister to the viscount and Mr. Delacroix. What is she doing here, I wonder."

"Perhaps she has come to the countryside to visit her brother."

"Yes. Perhaps." Lydia began to entertain suspicions which she thought prudent to keep to herself. Were Miss Delacroix eyelashes flickering?

She dismounted from Ari. "But she is rather out of her way, here. Surely we should lay her down in your lordship's carriage?"

"Quite." The earl shook his head. "Yes of course. I am sorry I have lost my presence of mind, only I am surprised to come across this accident."

He gave her a penetrating look. "And to come across you, here. And then to have this lady be someone of your acquaintance. It is all very odd..."

"It certainly is." Lydia's eyebrow twitched involuntarily. "I cannot account for it. For where are her servants? Where is the driver? Surely she was not out in her carriage alone?"

"Yes. That is indeed strange, now that you mention it."

They positioned Miss Delacroix as comfortably as possible across one seat in the earl's remise.

"She does not appear to be injured," Lydia observed dryly.

"No, I suppose I should be relieved about that." Then he turned to look into Lydia's eyes. "But at the moment I can only think how pleased I am to see you, Miss Norwood."

She looked down, blushing. Surely he knew this was an awkward time to say such a thing. But she was so pleased to hear him say it. After everything he had seen, all the misunderstanding, he was still happy to see her. She resisted the urge to reach out and touch him, lean against him, as Miss Delacroix had so recently done.

"In fact, I was just at Nesterling to call on Rutherford. I had hoped I should also see you. I spoke to your father... Are you coming to the ball? Please say that you are..." His eyes sought out hers, again.

"I... had not thought..." She blushed when she considered that he must now know the story of what really happened.

And yet, he was not shunning her. She realized it was not something she could discuss in front of Miss Delacroix, whose faint she found unconvincing. "I am sorry. With everything that has happened with Mr. Rutherford, I hope you will forgive me for being distracted."

"Yes." His jaw clenched. "But I believe Rutherford is well on the mend. Please say you will come."

At that moment Miss Delacroix sat up and poked her head out of the carriage. "What happened? Where am I?"

What an inconvenient acquaintance the Delacroix family was turning out to be.

"You have been in an accident, it would seem. Where are your servants?" Lydia tried to sound sympathetic.

"Miss Norwood? What are you doing here? And where are your servants, I might as easily ask?" Miss Delacroix did not seem confused. She seemed irritated. She then looked pointedly at the earl and fell silent, as though waiting.

Lord Aldley sighed. "May I ask you to introduce your friend, Miss Norwood?"

As they went through the absurd dance of the introduction, Lydia decided that the circumstances were suspicious enough that she would have to make sure she chaperoned Miss Delacroix until she could be returned to her brother's estate.

It was a hard to believe that any of her sex would set up such a situation just to make the acquaintance of an earl—or worse, to be compromised by one—but Lydia's recent encounter with Delacroix had left her in some doubts about the sister, too.

And her very first encounter with the earl suggested that he had this effect on young ladies.

Lord Aldley appeared irritated by the interruption, but agreed to lend the use of his carriage. Lydia suggested that it would be more proper for appearance's sake that Lord Aldley should to ride up top or upon Ari.

He opted to sit next to the driver—despite Miss Delacroix's protests that she would feel safer if he were sitting with her, and that it was not fitting for an earl to ride up top.

Ari walked sedately behind the carriage, untroubled by any of the human intrigues contained within it.

"So you were out riding alone on your horse, without servants?" Miss Delacroix's smile was thin and unsuccessful at hiding her irritation.

"Yes. I am in the habit of doing so, as none of the servants can keep up with us. Ari runs like the wind and no one can touch him. My home is not two miles from here." She felt like adding, *unlike yours.*

Had Miss Delacroix actually feigned to be the victim of a carriage upset, just to meet Lord Aldley? Somehow the experience of having to struggle alone to save herself and Rutherford had drained the last dregs of her patience for the bland half-sentiments and bald-faced dishonesty of polite conversation with contemptible people. This would be a most trying journey.

"I see." Miss Delacroix turned her gaze out the window.

"And how did you come to be riding in a carriage alone out here? You are a long way from Dunston Hall."

"I must have taken a wrong turn. I cannot recall. Perhaps I hit my head in the accident."

"Perhaps." Lydia kept her doubts to herself. "We shall have you home to your brother's estate soon. I am sure that the viscount will want the doctor to examine you. And how is your other brother recovering?"

"I do not know. I think he is getting better, but he still spends most of his time asleep. I should mention that I had meant to call on you, to see that you were quite well." Miss Delacroix gave Lydia a feline squint.

"I am, thank you. But I am not the one who has had an accident." Lydia practised her sang froid.

"I only mean that I *had* heard there was some unpleasantness in town —in the park the other day."

"Had you? I am afraid I do not know what you mean." Lydia yawned and rubbed one eye.

"I heard there was an *abduction*."

"Ah well, perhaps, but it is nothing that I have heard about. We have been visiting the countryside, however, so I have not heard much of the town gossip."

"Only that is what I heard. That *you* were abducted." Miss Delacroix gave a significant look over her shoulder, as if there were someone there who was in on the secret.

"That *I* was abducted? Well, I suppose the price of fast news is that one cannot always rely on its accuracy. As you can see I am quite well, safe on my family estate and not at all absconded with." Lydia could not believe what she was hearing.

"I had thought my source rather good."

"Well, there can be no better source than the ostensible *offended party*." Lydia raised an eyebrow. "But I wonder who *your* source might be."

"Oh, no one in particular. It is just what I have heard around town."

"Well then, my account must be preferred to that of *no one in particular*, do you not think?" Lydia smiled with a poisonous level of sweetness.

"Yes, of course. I was only concerned that you were quite well. Such a shock would quite destroy my nerves."

"No doubt, but as I have had no such shock, I find myself very well, thank you." Lydia managed the sort of serene look that suggested she might have a sharp knife in her habit pocket.

"So you will be equal to rejoining society, then, to attend parties and balls..." Miss Delacroix would not give over.

"Yes, quite equal."

"Well, that is good. I only thought that you might be *concerned* about how people will view this incident." Miss Delacroix's lips flattened as if she disapproved of how lightly Lydia was taking the situation.

"There has not been any incident. Unless you mean that there is some stigma attached to having come across an acquaintance alone in an overturned carriage, and acting as her chaperone to return her to the care of her brother? If so, I am not sure anyone's reputation could meet such high standards. But if you believe it to be so, then perhaps you should be more careful about going out in your carriage on strange roads without any servants."

"I dare say *my* reputation will remain intact." Miss Delacroix did not sound entirely happy about this fact.

"Then I do not suppose mine can suffer harm from lending you assistance."

"I only meant—"

Lydia interrupted the indefatigable débutante, "Now if someone has actually committed an abduction, such a perpetrator, and members of the perpetrator's family, *their* reputations would be in very great danger, once things were found out. Assuming, of course, that someone actually were abducted." Lydia waved her hand dismissively, as if she greatly doubted any abduction had occurred.

"I imagine in such cases, the abductor and his family have little reputation to be concerned about." Miss Delacroix was trying to distance herself.

"I should tend to agree that they have little *character* to begin with. But as for reputation, we shall see who they turn out to be."

It was pretty rich for Miss Delacroix to sit and make insinuations about an abduction that her own brother had attempted. And doubly so when she was freshly caught trying to ensnare Lord Aldley.

Lydia was not sure which aspect of this grand hypocrisy most angered her. But upon reflection, she decided it was the lady's designs upon Lord Aldley that made Lydia fervently wish to drag her along behind the carriage by her well-coiffed hair.

Such pleasant thoughts made the trip slightly less drawn out.

When they delivered Miss Delacroix to Dunston, and had finished all the polite conversation and explanations necessary in returning a second errant sibling to the viscount's care, Miss Delacroix expressed her great joy in having made Lord Aldley's acquaintance.

She tried to persuade him to stay. But at the insistence of her brother that she lie down to await the doctor, she rather sullenly took her leave, claiming she would retire to her chambers with a meaningful look back at the earl.

Before he left, Lord Aldley took Lydia aside and said, "Now you have saved me from what would have at least been an embarrassing situation. It appears you cannot help saving all the young men around you."

"I believe I know what your lordship refers to, but it would be well for us to remain silent on that topic, for the time being." She felt a bit giddy.

"Yes, quite. But I hope you will come to my mother's ball and allow me to show you how grateful I am to you for saving me." He moved closer to her.

"You would tempt me away from watching over your dear friend, my lord?"

"Your father said he would stay with him. Rutherford will be well cared for. And if you miss my mother's ball because you are attending Rutherford, think what the ton will infer from it..." He let the statement dangle and looked intently in her eyes, searching for something there. "Unless that is what you want the ton to infer?"

"Why no, it is not. If I may speak frankly, my lord, I am about at the point that I do not care a jot what the ton thinks. But I do care about my friends and my family, and those members of my acquaintance to whom I have recently had occasion to grow closer. About them, and about what they think, I am very much concerned. It would trouble me greatly if any of them got the wrong impression about my feelings for Mr. Rutherford, to whom I owe much, and whom I shall always regard as a friend, but for whom I can profess no *other* attachment."

"I believe that is frank enough." He pressed her hand to his lips.

He stared in her eyes for several moments. "It is forward of me to say it at this time, in this unusual circumstance, but you could not have made me happier in your expression of platonic feelings toward my good friend," his smile reached up to his eyes, "unless you were to express a preference for me."

He moved toward her then, as though about to take her in his arms, but he stopped himself. "You must come to the ball."

His voice resonated through her. He was standing so close. She could smell his scent of orange and leather and musk. His warmth reached out to her. She could feel it on her cheeks. She wanted him to take her in his arms and hold her closer still.

"Promise me," he implored again. "For I shall not go, myself, unless I know you will be there. Say you will."

She was almost breathless, and a warmth was spreading over her entire body. "I shall."

He again moved to embrace her, then restrained himself. "I wish I did not have to leave you now. I wish I could see you safely back to Nesterling Lodge. But I have many things to attend to, and am already much delayed."

He pressed his lips to her hand again. "Adieu until the night of the ball."

And then he was gone.

The heat in her face was like a bewildering fever. Her thoughts spun about in such a flurry that she nearly missed hearing the rustle of a skirt around the corner.

Had someone been listening in on their private conversation? She was almost too elated with the earl's near profession of love to even care if Miss Delacroix or one of her servants were sneaking about eavesdropping.

And yet her heart was plagued with worry. Lydia's own feelings were obvious to her, but Lord Aldley did not know of the recent decline in her material circumstances. If he felt the same way as she did, it should not matter, but would it not be wrong to enter into an engagement under false pretences?

CHAPTER 30

*L*ydia sat next to a plain pine table in the small library at Nesterling Lodge and stretched her legs out to prop her feet on a little leather-covered footstool.

It had been a flurry of activity for Lydia to say her goodbyes and get packed. She, her mother and Tilly were to depart for London early the next morning. Mr. DeGroen and Mr. Ravelsham were to follow soon, and Mr. Norwood would remain in the country with Mr. Rutherford.

Tilly and Lydia had sneaked off to the library, where they would be out of the way of the incessant flitting about of her mother to add *just one more thing* to her packing. Lydia wished to discuss the events of the previous day, privately, and Mrs. Norwood's *one more thing* was never a book.

"It is perplexing." Lydia wriggled her feet about as she mulled over the problem in her mind. "I sat up thinking about it last night, but I cannot conceive of how Miss Delacroix could have known that Lord Aldley would be travelling on that road, at that time."

"She had to have accomplices." Tilly lay on a méridienne and dangled one arm over the side. "She did not turn that carriage into the ditch by herself. I do not know that it has anything to do with this latest intrigue, but I have formed a surmise. I do not like to say it, until I can prove that it is true, for it involves the character of a servant, whom I had thought much more trustworthy."

"Really?" Lydia thought a moment. "Ah yes, I see what you mean. But surely..."

"Quite. One would think that Marie would be more thankful toward her current employer, and not wish to betray her trust. But on the other hand, she had been not just a servant to Miss Delacroix, but a companion for so many years."

Tilly looked contrite for a few brief moments, then continued, "Yes, I have been blind to think that would change just because of her new situation—however shoddily she was treated by the mother."

"The communication between them could never be so quick as that, when she was in London and Marie was out here in the country. Surely we are mistaken." Lydia knit her brows.

"I think Miss Delacroix got the information about when Lord Aldley would be leaving Essington Hall through the viscount. If you recall, just before he left, Lord Aldley told Lord Delacroix when he would be leaving for town. And you know that once Miss Delacroix learned that the earl was in the area, she would have extracted all the information she could from her brother."

"Yes, true. Then what is it that you suspect Marie of doing?"

"I was not thinking so much of Miss Delacroix's plotting. I was thinking of what happened in London."

"Hmm?"

"Did you not ever wonder why Delacroix was waiting with his henchmen in the park that day?" Tilly cocked her head to one side. "Surely he does not just idle about the area in his carriage of a

Thursday afternoon, on the off chance that you, or some other rich heiress, would show up."

"Yes." She was stunned for a few moments. "I never thought upon it— so much has transpired since then, and I suppose I wanted to forget. But of course you are right. Of course he must have known in advance. So you think it was Marie?"

"I think Marie may have passed the information to Miss Delacroix. But that must also mean that Miss Delacroix told her brother."

"That little witch. She knew what his plan was. That is why she claimed to have *heard* I was abducted. She knew about the scheme all along." Lydia had never liked Miss Delacroix, but she felt deeply betrayed that the girl would conspire to have Lydia so assaulted. "Shall you at least dismiss Marie?"

"Certainly not. Now that I have an inkling that she is something of a spy, think how useful she might prove."

Lydia shook her head. "I cannot imagine how having a faithless servant could prove useful."

"That is because you are not devious enough. But you are intelligent and unconventional. Given some time, I think you will come along nicely. In the meantime, let me just give you this hint: whatever you want Miss Delacroix to believe, all you need to do is say it in front of Marie. Think what fun!" Tilly giggled with glee.

Lydia grimaced. "My recent experiences have left me with a strong disinclination to think of anything involving the Delacroix family as *fun*."

"Do not let it make you bitter, my friend. I mean, just think how far recent catastrophes have advanced your cause."

Lydia crossed her arms, as her mother always told her not to. "I do not see what you mean."

"You have made a very near connection with Lord Aldley's closest friend. That would be valuable, in and of itself, but you have also inadvertently made the earl jealous." Tilly wiggled her eyebrows.

"There was no reason...none at all—"

"Yes, yes. The fact that it was a misunderstanding, and completely unintentional, just makes it that much better." Tilly played with a cluster of curls on her forehead. "Have you spoken to Mr. Rutherford lately? Did he clear things up with Lord Aldley?"

Lydia looked hopeful. "I believe so. When I checked in on him last night, he told me of his visit with the earl."

"What did he say?"

"Well, he did not recall very much, but he said he told Lord Aldley what really happened with Delacroix."

"But what of the little tussle on the bed?" Tilly's eyes squinted into an inquisitor's gaze.

"It wasn't a tussle."

Tilly waved her hand as if to swat away her friend's irrelevant objections. "Do not be so missish. Did he clear up that misunderstanding?"

"He said that he did not quite recall the whole conversation. They apparently spent some time talking about you..." Lydia blushed. "I think you must be careful not to break poor Mr. Rutherford's heart."

Tilly smiled. "And what of my heart? Have you warned him to be careful of mine?"

"No. And as you are an engaged woman, I could hardly make such a suggestion. I only told him to be careful of appearances." Lydia looked very seriously at her friend.

"Oh dear. You are becoming so terribly dreary. I see that you will not take your own prospects seriously because you are too busy worrying about mine. I shall have to take matters into my own hands." Tilly walked to the door.

"Where are you going?" Lydia looked at her friend in disbelief.

"I need to have a little chat with Mr. Rutherford before we leave—and I do not care if he is sleeping."

The next morning Lydia wanted to ask what Tilly said to Rutherford, but the presence of her mother in the carriage prevented any very interesting conversation. Her friend gave her a playful wink that made her hope all was well. Otherwise they were reduced to occasional meaningful looks.

"I have managed to procure Miss Grey to arrange your hair for the ball, my dear." Mrs. Norwood adjusted her pretty pink bonnet and looked pleased with herself.

"She is terribly clever, and she works quickly. I am glad to give her my business, but was she not already engaged?"

"Not precisely *engaged*. That is to say, she was to do Miss Delacroix's hair, but I managed to persuade her to come to you in the morning, first—Miss Delacroix most obligingly agreed to having her hair done later in the day."

"So I shall have to mind my hair all day until the ball in the evening?" Lydia complained almost out of habit, for she would endure a great deal to assure she looked pretty when she next saw Lord Aldley.

"Yes you will. It is ever so important that you are in your best looks." Her mother was stern.

But Lydia wondered why Miss Delacroix had been so obliging. Perhaps it was because she believed that Lydia would be neatly abducted away by the time of the ball. The ruddy little heifer. How could someone so tedious be as despicable as this?

"Did Miss Delacroix say what the occasion was that merited the special coiffure?" Tilly was apparently also suspicious.

"No. I suppose she might have been hoping for a last minute invitation to the Aldley ball. Did she not strike you as being particularly interested in the earl?" Her mother's smile held a fleeting moment of smugness.

"Yes, I see what you mean." Lydia nodded. Her mother did not know the half of it. "But it seems to be betting on rather long odds."

Her mother turned her cheek slightly. "I hope you will not use such gambler's cant when you are at the Aldley ball. It will not give the right impression."

"Miss Delacroix has a fairly wide acquaintance, perhaps she has another important engagement." Tilly's face belied any true belief in that possibility. "Did Miss Delacroix change her mind suddenly about lending you Miss Grey's services?"

"In fact she did. Just before—well, just before *our trip to the country,* shall we say, she sent me a note. She said she had been thinking the matter over, and felt sorry to deprive such a good friend. The note arrived while you were out in the park. With everything that happened, it quite slipped my mind."

Lydia resisted the desire to give Tilly a meaningful look. She was amazed that so soon after the abduction, her mother could discuss Delacroix's sister with such equanimity, and without the least suspicion.

But Lydia's instincts told her it was better that her mother remain in the dark. "Well, that was generous of her. And I have every confidence in Miss Grey's genius."

"Yes," added Tilly, "Miss Grey's powers are legendary. I think she must be doing rather well for herself."

Tilly sank into thought for a few moments. "May I come over and sit with you while she arranges your hair?"

"Of course." Lydia was certain that her clever friend had some deeper purpose in mind. "I should be most grateful for the company, in fact."

"Oh, and I have changed my mind about your dress, my dear." Mrs.

Norwood tapped her head. "I consulted Floren yesterday, and she said she had a vision in which you were in white when you received your proposal. You shall wear the ivory silk, I think, with the pink ribbon on the bodice."

Lydia wanted to roll her eyes, but merely smiled her acquiescence. She was accustomed to her mother's habit of consulting with the old soothsayer who lived in one of the west cottages at Nesterling. It had resulted in some rather bizarre predictions, which Mrs. Norwood found a way of believing had come true.

How much money had her mother spent on these oracles? She was not indifferent to how she looked, but thought the matter should be left to the superior taste of her mother. Referring the decision to a medium was foolhardy, especially when they were facing retrenchments.

Thinking about the retrenchments inspired Lydia with a greater urgency to get working on her investment idea. If only she could chat with Tilly about it now. She needed to do something.

Her agitation about her family's financial situation was also spoiling her anticipation of seeing Lord Aldley. How much should she disclose to him? Would it not be better to be completely honest?

There was a sudden commotion outside. Their carriage slowed and moved toward the rougher going on the shoulder of the road.

"Good Lord! What now?" Her mother instinctively grasped the edge of her seat.

The reason for their manoeuvring became apparent, as another carriage flew past them. Their own carriage driver halted the horses until the other coach passed, then proceeded to carefully navigate back onto the even roadway.

"Some irresponsible young coxcomb out for a rollick and indifferent as to whether he drives decent folk into ditches!" Mrs. Norwood was irate.

260

Although Lydia more or less shared the sentiment, she could not agree with her mother's sketch of the villain. She was quite sure she had seen a flash of the Delacroix colours on the side of the carriage, but Mr. Delacroix was too much of an invalid for any carriage sport, nor would the viscount be inclined to leave his convalescent brother to go racing about the country.

Surely the passenger was Miss Delacroix—which might explain how her carriage overturned the day before, if Lydia were not already convinced that it was no accident.

The little schemer was in a rather great rush to get back to town.

CHAPTER 31

*L*ady Aldley was resplendent in a deep blue silk morning dress and cap trimmed with bantam feathers. She sat perched in a sunbeam, on a gold silk upholstered chair in the south corner of her parlour, pretending to work at fancy sewing.

"I see you have finally procured a set of four horses and a new carriage," She observed. "It is a rather smart rig, although I observe that it does not have the Aldley colours. Still, I am glad you have given up trotting about in those embarrassing hackneys. Is there some occasion for this new found extravagance?"

"There need not be any occasion. I have been wanting to acquire equipage since I returned home from Paris, but merely lacked the time to attend to it. I should hardly call it extravagant, but I am pleased that I shall arrive at your ball in style."

Aldley smiled indulgently at his mother, then added, "Albeit without the Aldley colours. But I shall remedy that omission as soon as may be."

"I am glad to hear it." She played with the silky, chestnut curls at her temples, then placed another stitch before resting the loop idly in her lap. "I do not suppose you have taken my advice and uninvited that young Norwood person."

"Certainly not. Were it not for the very great pleasure I shall have in seeing her at the ball, I should have stayed in the countryside to be nearer to Rutherford."

"Rutherford. Yes, is he not staying with *her* out in the country? I thought I heard they were soon to be married. A patched up business, no doubt." She pursed her lips in disapproval.

"If you are listening to gossips for your information, you deserve to be as grossly misinformed as you clearly have been. There is nothing to patch up, and they are not to be married."

Aldley tried to give a force of conviction to his words that he did not entirely feel. "Mr. Rutherford is merely convalescing at Nesterling Lodge, where he stays as a guest of Mr. Norwood."

"Well, at least I shall be spared *Mr. Rutherford's* company." She looked at her loop and placed another stitch, then set it down again. "Oh but how you *will* put your interest in the most worthless people before your family obligations. What on earth sort of person gets themselves involved in a shooting?"

"He is the nephew of a duke. I fail to comprehend your disdain."

She only sniffed in reply.

Aldley picked a hair off his cuff, and continued, "And I should have thought that getting stabbed while rescuing the brother of a viscount would lend my friend some distinction, among any but the least generous of the ton."

"It is a suspicious business," Lady Aldley scoffed. "I see it as singular, not distinguished."

"Well then, you will be most alarmed to hear that when I dragged *your* opium-addled son-in-law out of a mean, putrid shanty in Venice, it was apparent that he, too, had sustained an injury. But I very much doubt that it had anything to do with trying to effect a rescue."

His mother's jaw fell open. "I do not wish to hear disparaging speculations about our family members."

"No, I can imagine not. You also did not seem to take *family obligations* seriously enough to have informed me when my sister was abandoned and left to scrape for herself and her child without access to funds. Yes, I can well imagine that you do not want to hear about it. Well, just as you wish."

Aldley drew a breath and calmed himself before adding, "Only I thought you might want some advance knowledge that he has been returned home to Essington Hall. He expressed a wish to attend your ball, in fact. I tried to dissuade him, but clearly I misapprehended your feelings on the matter. Perhaps I should discharge a rider with a quick note. If he left tomorrow morning he could still make it in time."

"I should not wish Lord Essington to inconvenience himself," she said through clenched teeth. Then she regained her composure and scrutinized her loop, adding, "particularly when his health is delicate."

"True. He *has* lost use of his legs. That may slow him down enough to keep him out of your way during the ball. But do not deceive yourself. He is not of a mind to stay quietly retired in the countryside. And when he slithers his way to London, you shall have to decide whether your own reputation can sustain such an acquaintance. But I leave the matter entirely up to you."

She pressed her lips together, and rang the bell for tea. "I am sure you exaggerate the situation."

"I do no such thing, as you will soon be aware. But as for me, I have put him on notice. One more scandalous misbehaviour and I shall cast him off."

"And what of your sister?"

"Oh, now you care about your only daughter," Aldley scoffed. "Now that you have married her off to that beast of a man, then left her to fend for herself when he abandoned her. Be assured that I shall sustain my sister and nephew in any way I can and lend her my countenance, if she should choose to leave Essington Hall."

"She is too well brought up to think of it." She pulled another stitch through.

"Perhaps." *Too cowed* would be a better description. "But she must also think of the child. In any case, as you can see, I am discharging my family obligations, as you call them. And I shall be at the ball, but I do not say what I shall do if your hand-picked son-in-law should make an appearance."

"I do not like your tone."

"I do not like your unremitting commentary on my choice of acquaintance. We all have our crosses to bear."

"You are a most unfeeling son." She set down the loop and pressed her hand to her temple, shaking her head. "All I think of is what is best for you, and all I receive in return are insolent criticisms—" Her further thoughts on the topic were interrupted by the entry of one of Aldley's servants.

"Begging your pardon, my lord, my lady. Only an urgent message is just now come for your lordship, so I came here straight." He handed over the message. "Shall I wait for a reply, my lord?"

"No, Mills, I shall go home now and read it on the way."

"But we were not finished our conversation. We have not yet had tea. Surely you are not leaving."

"Ah, but I am. I shall see you at the ball." He took his leave.

He had warned her of Essington's return. His duty was discharged. If she insisted on wearing blinders and ignoring the problem, that was all a piece to him.

He did not open the letter until he was in the carriage. It was written in French, and rather ill—the explanation given was that it had been composed while inside a fast-paced carriage, in anticipation of posting it at the next stop. He thought, however, that the poor quality of the hand appeared more the product of a determined effort than a jouncing carriage.

A man, who claimed to work for Aldley's solicitor in Paris, would be arriving in London within a few days, bringing with him the infant child of Solange Dupres. The author asserted that the child, though previously thought dead, was still alive.

"How is this possible?!" He read on to find no additional explanation. But he was to expect further contact as soon as the author, an M. Boulanger, arrived in town. The man also assured his discretion.

Aldley had never heard of this Boulanger fellow. At least the letter was written in fluent French—that much appeared authentic. Still, it must be some scheme to extort money from him, otherwise his lawyer would have sent word and vouched for this stranger. He would have to look into the matter.

If it were a fabrication designed to extract money, he would bring the full force of the law to bear on the perpetrator. Aldley had had quite enough of bad characters and underhanded scheming in the past several days, and these plotting frauds would feel the consequences of it.

CHAPTER 32

*L*ydia sat in Tilly's spacious coach and inhaled the scent of cinnamon and cloves. She laughed in disbelief. "I am not sure why my mother is so quick to trust you. I am sure if *I* had told her we were just going down to the shops to look for a new bonnet, she would never have believed me."

They were safely back in London, and there was a whole day free before Lydia had to think of such things as balls and hair and dresses. She certainly would not choose to waste her time shopping for clothing, and it was astounding that her mother would believe such a story.

For that matter, she would not have wasted the money on any frivolous purchase. She had plans for all her saved up pin money.

She had just been lamenting the visible reminders of her family's current financial situation—the disappearance of most of the furniture in the north parlour, about a third of the paintings in the house, and worse, half of the books in the library.

She knew that the official story was that they were simply redecorating, but she wondered how long they could keep up the pretence.

"Oh be assured, my friend," Tilly straightened her skirts, "in this case she would have believed you. And anyway, it is quite natural for a young girl in love for the first time to have an insatiable need for new bonnets. Or so I am told."

"What do you mean *in this case?*"

"Ah. That. You see, I learned a few things while I was at Nesterling—in particular, that your mother always consults this *Floren* woman for her fortunes, and such."

"True. It has been so since I was a child." Lydia sighed.

"Indeed? A long standing arrangement, then. So, I went to visit Floren, myself. She is delightfully practical for being such a magical person, and accepted a small token of my appreciation in exchange for giving your mother some opportune advice."

"You bribed my mother's medium to lie to her?" Lydia did not approve, but could not be entirely surprised.

"She is not exactly a medium, and I should never call it a bribe." Tilly tapped her fingertips together. "I merely gave her some hints on what the mystical voices might wish to tell your mother. That you should spend more time with me, for example, and that a new bonnet would be a good omen for an auspicious marriage proposal."

Lydia shook her head.

"Oh do not look at me like that." Tilly wagged a finger theatrically. "It is not as though you have never told your mother a fib to get out of the house. And if you have such a bad conscience about it, we can go back and say you changed your mind."

Lydia rolled her eyes. "Using her own soothsayer to deceive her is going a little far."

"I truly do not see the difference between telling your mother a little white lie, and getting someone else to tell her a little white lie." Tilly waved Lydia's scruples away with her gloved hand. "You are safe enough now, with Delacroix gone. Anyway, here is your new bonnet, so it is not even a lie." She handed Lydia a hat box from the carriage seat, beside her.

"Thank you," Lydia said, without much enthusiasm.

"Please do not mention it. Now, let us waste no more time on guilty consciences and such stuff. We have more important matters to attend to."

"Such as?"

"I have arranged a meeting with your new lawyer, again, as you requested." Tilly squeezed one of the scent sachets to release more of the spicy aroma into the carriage. "I hope you will tell me why. But of more immediate concern to me is Miss Delacroix. She has been acting almost as desperate as her brother."

"I admit, I was incensed at her so-called carriage accident." Lydia scowled. "And to hear you say that she has had Marie spying on us—it is beyond intolerable. I am persuaded that she assisted her brother. I do not see what we can do about it now, however."

"We shall see about that. But I do not believe her schemes are finished, yet."

"What more can she do?"

"A great deal more than you might think. Honestly, although it is very vexing that she is clearly trying to ensnare your future husband—"

"We should not presume that he is my future anything." Lydia was quick to correct her friend.

"Hmm. But as I was saying, however vexing her schemes are, I must admit I find her so much more interesting now. I thought her spoiled, conceited and a little ill-bred, but otherwise rather boring. I had no idea she was this devious and audacious. I am quite diverted. It almost makes me like her better."

"You are diverted by bad character." Lydia stared at Tilly, then shook her head.

"Most certainly—so long as it is of an interesting variety." Tilly chuckled.

"There is no cause for you to be proud of the fact, you know."

"I do not try to hide it from my true friends, but it is not something I am proud of, exactly. There is no point in being proud of things that are no accomplishments of our own. This character trait comes quite naturally, I assure you. I cannot take credit for it, so taking pride in it would be absurd—though no more absurd than ladies taking pride in their beauty, birth or wealth, I suppose."

"You are very philosophical. But I admit that I am also diverted by your vices, so I shall not attempt remove the mote from thine eye."

"It is amazing how virtuous you are." Tilly rewarded her pious friend with a sideways smile. "It would be tiresome if it were not so novel. Very few of your fellow Christians would hesitate to remove the mote from mine eye, I assure you—though their own eyes were veritable lumber yards. So I suppose I find virtue somewhat diverting, as well."

"What do you suggest we do about Miss Delacroix?"

"I do not think there is much to do, exactly. Not until we know precisely what she is up to. And believe me, I shall work on finding out. I have a guess that she still has designs on Lord Aldley. Perhaps she plans to take a page from her brother's book and sneak into the Aldley ball."

"I should think that would be a little harder for a lady to do." Lydia's brows furrowed.

"I do not see why it should be—so long as the lady is resourceful and a little ruthless, which she gives every appearance of being. Or should I say *ruthless and a little resourceful*? I wonder if someone should warn Lady Aldley."

"I should not like to have that task. And all we have are suspicions."

"True. And Miss Delacroix is the daughter of a viscount, whereas we are only filthy *nouveau riches*. Let me think on it. Speaking of Lady Aldley, I have made a discovery about your future mother-in-law—yes, yes, I know you will object. Very well, the *Dowager Countess Aldley*." She gave Lydia a knowing look.

"Oh? What can you have discovered?"

"Do you remember at the Delacroix dinner party, how she seemed to be disturbed by the mention of a certain acquaintance with the Wurtherly family in Warwick, when Delacroix—accursed little brute — mentioned it?"

"Yes. I remember we puzzled about that a bit. What have you discovered? Is there a shadow on that fine lady's past?" Lydia could not help being curious.

"Only look how quickly you have become a gossip monger! We shall make you into fine ton material yet."

"You needn't crow over your success in corrupting me. What have you to report?"

"It seems as though her ladyship was once an impressionable young lass, if you can imagine it. She fell in love with, and was abducted by—or perhaps it was a failed elopement—a certain handsome young rake in the neighbourhood by the name of Beauchamps. Although this man had neither rank nor fortune, he had some good connections. He was, indeed, a cousin to Lady Aldley's childhood friend, Helen Wurtherly (*nee* Beauchamps). There is the connection to the name, you see."

Lydia's brows rose with realization. "Ah yes. That is why she became so bilious when Delacroix mentioned Beauchamps."

Tilly continued, "It seems Mr. Beauchamps had the audacity to aspire to Lady Aldley's hand—or to Elizabeth Halton's, as was then her name. Her parents did not approve. Fortunately her father caught up with them before they could marry, extracted his daughter, and hushed the whole matter up."

Lydia was amazed. "You would never guess by talking to her now that there could be any such blight on her past."

Tilly nodded and tapped her head "You see? Once again hypocrisy saves the day."

She assumed a more serious pose and continued, "Her family contrived to relocate to London. The next year, she was safely married off to the late Lord Aldley. Beauchamps, by and by, became a lawyer, came into some inheritance, made a small fortune in some very lucky investments, and was later knighted."

"How did you discover all this?" Lydia looked inquisitively at her friend.

"I made some enquiries. You should know by now that I have considerable resources. But I never reveal my informants." Tilly's eyes twinkled with mischief.

"Well, all this is quite fascinating," Lydia shook her head. "But I do not think we should repeat any of it."

"Certainly not. But I found it very interesting to discover that Beauchamps—shall we call him Sir Gerard? Is currently living in London. Apparently also a widower." Tilly's nose twitched.

"I wonder if Lady Aldley would be a kinder, less grand person if she had married Beauchamps."

"I suppose we shall never know how the turn of history affected their personalities, but it seems to me that the separation of the two proved of great advantage to both, viewed prudentially. For she went on to marry an earl, and I rather doubt that her former beau could have attained his fortune and knighthood so easily with a wife and family in tow and more than a whiff of scandal about his person."

"Probably true."

Tilly was silent for a moment, then went on to a fresh topic. "So, now will you tell me what you wish to discuss with your lawyer, or is it to be all a hugger-mugger, even from me?"

"I am sure you have many secrets from me, so it would serve you right." Lydia gave Tilly an arch look.

Tilly wiggled her eyebrows at her. "So you keep saying, but it is only for your own good. And anyway, I know you want to tell me all about it, or I should not have asked."

"You are so all-knowing. Perhaps you should set up shop in Floren's line of work."

"I should never repay her assistance by such a bad turn as going into competition." Tilly held a hand up to ward off such an unthinkable suggestion. "That my friend appreciates my gift of otherworldly vision must be enough for me. Now do not make me resort to reading your tea leaves. Tell me all."

"I know that I must maintain a discrete distance, however I am contemplating an investment in the talents of Miss Grey."

"Miss Grey?"

"She is not just a veritable magician with hair, she also makes her own pomades and treatments. And she is most sought after—all the ladies know of her skill. But, she can only dress so many heads of hair. On the other hand, if she could make her hair products in quantity, I believe they would fetch a fair price." Lydia looked apprehensively at her friend, unsure what her reaction might be.

"I think it is a wondrous scheme!" Tilly clapped her hands. "Have you discussed it with Miss Grey?"

Lydia gave a little smile of relief. "No. With everything that has transpired recently, I have not yet had the chance."

"Well, her involvement is crucial. The products have to bear her name. And they must be exquisite in appearance. Fortunately for you, I have an acquaintance in the glassware business, who makes some of the most sought after crystal jars. The sort of thing a lady would love to have upon her toilette."

"Of course you do. But will not that drive the price up rather high?"

Tilly huffed at such a trifling consideration. "You will be selling to ladies who want to display their status and superior style. It must be the most expensive hair pomade in England."

"I am not sure I have the capital to support such a high cost, initially."

"But I think you do. Or if you do not, I can arrange more financing."

"I thought it might be better to start small." Lydia needed the venture to make money, not create debt—especially not to a friend who was to know nothing of her father's straightened circumstances.

"Believe me, if you want to sell to the bon ton you must be the best, and give every appearance of being expensive and exclusive. You may start small in number, but not in stature."

Tilly's blue eyes lit up so intensely that she looked a bit mad, as she paused to think. "Yes. Better to sell a dozen pomades in pots made of diamonds, and leave every débutante's mother frothing at the mouth because she cannot get one, than to sell one hundred pots at a reasonable price."

"I think we may rule out diamond pots." Lydia laughed nervously. "I know I do not have capital for that."

"It is merely a figure of speech. You needn't be so literal. Anyway, I see we have arrived." Tilly let the servant hand her out of the carriage. "Let us see what Mr. Fromme has to say about your plan."

CHAPTER 33

*T*he sun streamed through the window, framed by sage green curtains, and lit up the spines of books on a small shelf in Aldley's office. He sat at a pedestal desk of black walnut, sprinkling powder over his freshly written missive.

He sealed the letter and hailed his servant to post it. His solicitor in Paris could testify to the facts surrounding Solange Dupres, should the fraudster reveal himself.

"This must be posted without delay."

When the servant left, Aldley turned his mind to Miss Norwood— Lydia. He wished they might call each other by first names. He hated the formality between them. She had only ever called him *my lord*. It was quite proper, as his mother would remind him, but entirely unsatisfying.

She should speak to him in the most intimate terms. When they were not speaking, they should exchange knowing glances and smiles, as he had seen her do with her father and Miss Ravelsham.

When they were not around other people, he wanted to extend that intimacy, to explore the wildness that he had seen in her. Climbing trees and galloping about astride great horses—how might she perform in the bedroom?

"Pardon me, my lord."

He almost knocked over his chair, he made to stand up so abruptly. But then he as quickly decided to sit down again. "What is it, Brown?"

"There was a person here, just now. She left a note."

"Was it a young lady?"

"Yes. Well, not a *lady*, my lord."

"A young woman then. Was it Miss Norwood?"

The man looked puzzled. "My lord?"

Aldley huffed in exasperation that the stupid man should not know the name of his goddess. "A beautiful girl, with red hair?"

"No, my lord. I reckon she was a servant."

"Well, I suppose I might as well read it." He sighed and took the missive. It was certain to be more of the recent intrigue concerning Solange's child. But it was too soon to start demanding money. He read it over hastily.

I write to you because I believe you are on the point of making a most disadvantageous match. I thought someone should warn you that the young woman you have fixed upon is highly unsuitable.

Not only has she recently been the object of an abduction which should have destroyed her reputation, had her family not hushed it up, but her father is also on the verge of bankruptcy.

She will very soon be without a dowry or any good reputation, particularly if she does not marry the man she has been in constant, unsupervised contact with at her family estate in the country.

In every way her conduct and situation in life court scandal and ruin.

I know you must be unaware of her true character and circumstances. Although I am sure this is a blow, I believe in time you will be grateful for the intelligence which must spare you a great deal of unpleasantness and embarrassment.

Sincerely,

Anon.

He leaned back in his chair. In the very first instant, he considered that it might be written by his mother, but he soon discarded the idea. It was not her way to write him notes, and she would have had to disguise her handwriting.

She also had too good an opinion of her importance and influence to try to pretend to be an impartial source. If she knew of Delacroix's abduction scheme, she would have spoken to him of it directly when he called upon her, and would have been most adamant that he should sever all connections with Miss Norwood.

The letter was an affront, an unforgivable piece of presumption. It was obviously just malicious gossip, but it could still hurt Miss Norwood. He must not let that happen.

How had news of the attempted abduction got around? Perhaps the servants had been gossiping. It was something to think on. It was wretchedly frustrating, but he could see no direct way of protecting her reputation. He could only hope that such rumours would be quelled by news of their marriage.

He had been planning to propose at the ball, but now that he thought of it, there was no need to wait. The ball was the following evening— surely she would be returned to town by now. Delaying in making his intentions clear had already almost cost him his opportunity.

He rang for his valet. He would go to her straight away.

CHAPTER 34

*A*s Lydia and Tilly's carriage pulled up at the Norwood house, a very fine carriage and four was pulling away.

"Do you think that was Lord Aldley?" Tilly strained her sharp eyes after the equipage.

"I do not know, I admit I did not remark on the passenger. Did it look like him?"

"I thought so. It would be a shame if we missed him."

"Indeed." Lydia swallowed and her stomach cramped. It was strange how the prospect of being around someone that she liked so well had such an apparently adverse affect on her physiology.

When barely inside the door, they had to listen to her mother's rapid account of the visitor they had just missed, who was indeed Lord Aldley. He had waited for over two hours.

Mrs. Norwood seemed even more smitten by the earl's attention than Lydia was. And she was strangely smug, as though she knew some grand secret about the matter.

"True, it is a great shame that you were not here to receive him, Lydia. Still *new bonnets* are important." Mrs. Norwood gave her daughter a knowing look.

So it was the bonnet. Floren's convenient oracle. No wonder her mother was congratulating herself. She thought she had magically pulled a noble son-in-law out of a new *chapeau*.

She handed her mother the hat box with a slight pang of guilt. "How do you like it, Mama?"

Mrs. Norwood opened the box and with a cursory glance declared, "Why, I believe it is the most beautiful bonnet I ever have beheld! Try it on for us, my dear." When Lydia obliged her, she added, "Yes, it is just the thing. A *perfect match*, would not you say, Miss Ravelsham?"

Tilly smiled a little slyly. "I quite agree, Mrs. Norwood. I declare, it is almost as though this bonnet were destined to be yours, Lydia." She was rewarded with smiles and vigorous agreement from Lydia's mother.

CHAPTER 35

*L*ydia experienced a strange combination of nervous energy and lulling torpor as she contemplated her future, and inhaled the sweet herbal scent of hair treatments that bloomed in the warm air wafting about her toilette.

A box of jewels sat beside the potions and powders that lined the surface of the table, and a pair of iron tongs heated on a brazier full of burning hot coals nearby.

Lydia could not help thinking that somewhere amid this paraphernalia of ritual preparation there was a metaphor for the exquisitely contrived hell of grand social gatherings.

As Miss Grey dressed Lydia's hair for the Aldley ball far too early, Lydia discussed her business plans with her. It was a welcome distraction, for otherwise Lydia would have been terribly nervous about the ball itself.

Tilly sat nearby, quietly watching the fantastic work of Miss Grey, and earnestly listening to Lydia's proposal.

"So, if I understand you, Miss," Miss Grey set aside the tongs and took up a brush, "you are asking for the biggest share of the profits for my pomade. I reckon my work in making it, and having the recipe and all should give me about half."

"Well, you may think about it." Lydia had anticipated a counter offer, but she was determined to stand firm. "But recollect that you will not be making all of it by hand. Once we get established, we shall have workers. And bear in mind that I am taking on all the risk and all of the cost. If the business is not a success, you have lost nothing."

"Except my recipe. How are we to keep these workers from stealing it and making up their own pomades to sell?"

"We can work around that by keeping the production of the most important ingredients your secret, perhaps to be shared with one or two trusted people. Workers can combine the more common ingredients with the batches of ready made secret ingredients."

"I know you are offering me a fairer bargain than I might get elsewhere." Miss Grey brushed out a last curl, then reshaped it using pomade. "And donnay think me blind to how much you honour me by this. Only I shall need to think on it awhile."

"In the meantime, will you please keep our discussion secret?" The last thing Lydia needed was to be the topic of another morsel of gossip about town.

"By your leave I'll discuss it with my solicitor." Miss Grey's face was thoughtful.

"You—" Lydia tried very hard to force the note of surprise out of her voice, "have a solicitor. Very good. Yes, that is just as it should be. Of course he will keep your confidence, but I should prefer that you do not discuss it with others."

"Aye, I'll be silent. I donnay much care to have folk in the know about my business affairs and such. You cannay imagine how full of gossip and nosiness every household servant is when they hear of a girl—one from the north, and all—who hires out her hair dressing services to the highest bidder. But your Ole Maeb has been kind to us, and she speaks highly of you and all, Miss. I am sure that is because she cared for you while you were still a babe. But she is a sharp old soul, and I think she kens folk well."

"Then it also speaks well of you that she has taken a liking to you." Lydia felt this was a great confirmation. "I should like to include her in the business, if she is interested, for she knows a great deal about preparing herbs and decoctions and such."

"Oh yes, she is famous, is Ole Maeb. When rich folk get sick they call for a doctor, but respectable poor folk that know her always go to Ole Maeb."

Lydia's heart was lightened by the prospect of giving Ole Maeb employment, for she knew she was no longer earning a wage from Lydia's father, though she was still living in the servants' quarters, in which there were now many empty rooms. And she could trust Ole Maeb to keep quiet.

"There are few people I should trust more, with my health or otherwise. She would be an ideal assistant."

"Only I hannay decided yet about the business plan, and you must give me my head. I always think on decisions."

"Of course, I should not have it any other way." It was a lie. Lydia would have preferred Miss Grey to leap at the opportunity. But then, the young woman's caution spoke well of her judgement. If they were to go into business together, it was better that she be a thoughtful person than an empty bonnet.

"And how do you like your hair, Miss?" Miss Grey smoothed a final tendril and stepped back from her work, as they both examined it in the large, gleaming mirror.

It was a little too sophisticated, Lydia thought, pulled rather high on top of her head in a mass of cascading ringlets. A bit grand, really. She was not sure that she could wear such a glistening, coiled crown with sufficient conviction, but Miss Grey had crafted the coif perfectly.

"It is beautiful work, Miss Grey. You are a talent beyond all reckoning." Lydia smiled her approval.

Tilly broke her silence to chime in, "Stellar! You look like royalty, Lydia."

"I am glad you are pleased, Miss. I should go to Miss Delacroix, now."

"Indeed, do not let us delay you." Tilly stood. "However, I had another matter I wanted to chat with you about. Might I accompany you to the Delacroix's? We can take my carriage."

"Certainly. I should be glad of the company, Miss, thank you."

"What, are you abandoning me to my nerves?" Lydia gave Tilly an alarmed look. "This is only the biggest social engagement of my life, after all."

"Of your life *so far*. I believe you will have much grander social engagements in your future—in your near future, in fact." Tilly smiled knowingly.

"You see, Miss Grey," Lydia squinted at Tilly, "she thinks she is a clairvoyant, now. But I know she is a great fraud, and bad friend for abandoning me."

Miss Grey laughed and shook her head. "A storm in a tea kettle, Miss. You've nowt to worry on. You'll be the toast of the ball, with hair like that."

Tilly smiled her crookedest smirk. "Say it as she shouldn't. And anyway, I shall be back soon to console you in your hour of need, you great vapourish simpleton."

With that, Lydia was abandoned to the aggravating task of sitting up straight and minding her hair. It would be many hours before she could put on her gown. Ivory white silk. Definitely no red wine tonight.

Perhaps she should find a book. She discarded the idea, as it would involve a depressing trip to their diminished library. And she had purchased no novels since she learned of her father's losses, so she sadly lacked anything new and diverting.

She supposed she should be more curious about what Tilly wished to discuss with Miss Grey, but her friend was simply always making connections with people. It explained a lot about why she always knew someone who could do this or that, find stolen jewellery or manufacture diamond pomade pots, and only heaven knew what else.

She was probably trying to charm Miss Grey into saying yes to the proposal. Lydia doubted Tilly would have any success, because Miss Grey seemed like a very prudent, sensible young woman, who would make her own decisions based on reason.

Lydia admired Miss Grey's mind and her self-assurance. She worked hard. She had even trained herself out of most of her northern brogue, though it slipped out more when she spoke at length. And she had found a way of being the mistress of her own fate, despite her disadvantages.

That had taken courage, one might even say *audacity*, which many others of her class clearly resented. And although she had never been impudent, she still seemed to think herself no one's inferior. There was a sort of nobleness of mind there. Lydia looked forward to getting to know her better.

She pulled out the business plan she had drafted up with the lawyer to look at it again. If she was honest, it was actually a little more exciting to her than the prospect of the ball.

Of course the prospect of seeing the earl was terribly exciting, but the ball itself was intimidating. If only she had some of Miss Grey's audacity.

And what of the earl? He was giving a very strong indication that he had serious intentions. Her mother was certain that, had Lydia been at home when he called the day before, he would have proposed. It was very hard, with her mother, to separate the actual state of affairs from the wishful thinking.

But if Lord Aldley was on the point of proposing, should she accept? She wanted to spend more time with him, that was certain. She even thought she wanted to marry him. But would his feelings remain the same when he really knew her?

What if he knew, for example, that until very recently, she had spent a few days of every week hiding in a dirty little tree house reading novels? And what if he knew that she was the cheeky tree-climber who intervened in Miss Worth's scheme so long ago, and that she was concealing the fact from him?

How would he react if he knew that her fortune was now greatly diminished? Could she ever reveal to him her plans to start a business that would directly involve her in trade, no matter how she disguised it as an investment?

There was still a great deal to be uncertain about.

He knew so little about her. And how little did she know about him? He was, decidedly, the most attractive man she had ever seen, and extremely charming. The sound of his voice drew her in like fairy magic. And from the first day that she encountered him, while perched in a tree, she had felt an almost irresistible pull toward him.

She needed to impress him. It was almost embarrassing how much he made her care about keeping her appearance as pleasing as possible, which was an entirely new interest.

She felt, with a pang, that in some way she was betraying that wilder, younger self that hid in tree houses and ran about without a bonnet, making shortcuts out of back alleys. Was it traitorous to forsake those amusements for the greater, more adult allure of—what, exactly was it?

She had read scholarly books about amorous congress and babies, but the entire thing sounded rather unpleasant. Yet the thoughts she had, the way her body responded to him was bewildering. Not at all unpleasant, though.

Except for the wear on her nerves. No matter how ambivalent she once was about marriage, she was now in love. The thought of it amazed and thrilled her, but filled her with anxiety. Could she really afford to be in love with a man so far above her reach?

Her thoughts were interrupted by a knock. She quickly gathered up her papers and locked them in her drawer. "Yes?"

"There is a letter for you, Miss."

"Thank you, Greenall."

There was no indication of the sender on the envelope. She opened it.

Dear Miss Norwood,

I write to you because I believe you remain uninformed about the true nature of the man who has secured, or is on the point of securing, your affections.

As you may know, he is recently returned from Paris. What you may not know is that, while there, he had a tryst with an opera singer.

This affair resulted in a child, but the mother died during the birth. You should be aware that, although he abandoned this child to its fate when he returned to England, a concerned party has brought the child here to London, to prevail upon him to do what is only his duty.

If he has any character at all, he will take the child into his protection, however unpleasant that might be for a future wife.

I know you must be unaware of his true character. I am sure this must shock you, and I am sorry for it. But I believe in time you will be grateful for the intelligence.

Have a care. An alliance with such a man will not bring happiness, and will, far from elevating you, be a blow to your reputation.

Sincerely,

A concerned friend.

Her cheeks burned. Who would send her such a letter? Was a word of it to be believed when the author was too cowardly to even give a name?

And yet, was it not entirely plausible that a young man of means would seek out such an arrangement while in Paris? She was not so naive as to think Lord Aldley completely innocent, though it tore at her heart to think of him with another woman.

She did not really care about the existence of a baby, or of the scandal, but the idea that he could simply abandon his own child was abhorrent. What sort of man could do such a thing? And especially when, financially, it would be such a small matter for him to set the child up with caretakers.

Lydia felt the happiness and hope drain out of her. She had been a great fool to think that Lord Aldley could be as wonderful as he seemed. When were things ever as good as they were made to look?

Everyone was hiding some secret—Lady Aldley, certainly the Delacroixs, even her own family. The perfected veneers of society were a great collection of lies.

She shook her head. Surely she was judging the matter too hastily, for she did not know that the accusations were true, and the irregular manner of their conveyance should allow of at least a small doubt.

In fact, the letter had a certain whiff of malice about it. It was certainly not written to protect her from an imprudent match.

She chastised herself that Lord Aldley's character, as she had seen it so far, made him worthy of her faith in him. But if this letter gave her nagging suspicions, might not the ton believe such a rumour entirely?

Perhaps she should burn the letter. Foolishness. It would do nothing to prevent gossip. She could do nothing to protect him.

She had read the letter over several times by the time Tilly returned.

Her normally jovial friend sighed deeply when she read the missive. "I hope you will not let this letter give you a moment's unhappiness, Lydia."

"It has already given me several moments of unhappiness. What if it is true? And if it is not true, what if such a rumour circulates? Will that not hurt Lord Aldley?"

"I should say not," Tilly scoffed. "Even if it were true, it would not really hurt him. He has title and means and such goings on are very common among the nobility."

Lydia resisted the urge to scratch her head. "Surely it is not approved of."

"It might be considered, perhaps, a little hard that even a fairly selfish nobleman should not provide for his side-slip," Tilly conceded. "But the ton does not care one jot about such as these. It could hurt the person circulating the gossip much more than the impugned nobleman."

Lydia could feel the truth of her words, unjust as it was. A nobleman could get away with a great many things.

"And no one," Tilly firmly added, "would consider it a valid reason for turning down a marriage proposal from an earl, so it could not hurt your reputation, either. The very suggestion is absurdly naive. Or it is preying upon what the author knows of your quaint country prudishness."

Lydia winced. "Am I that bad?"

"I am not much for judging people, except that sack of horse dung who tried to make off with you, of course." Tilly's brows knit together.

"Well, and a few others. But I do not think I should ever interpret an innocent mind as such a terribly *bad* thing."

"I am not so innocent, really."

"You are a curious blend of virtue, knowledge and irreverence. You seem to think social conventions quite silly, and occasionally do things which could have the appearance of evil. But actual evil, you avoid. I do not think I have ever met anyone more unsuited to London society, really. Here people rely heavily on using polished appearances to conceal actual vice. But in any case, whoever wrote this letter—and I have very strong suspicions who that was—knew something of your character."

"You think it was Miss Delacroix." Lydia had entertained her own suspicions on that front.

"Yes, I do. It was she who first advanced the notion that an affair with an opera singer was his reason for departing suddenly for the continent. And now that she has apprehended that her gossip has had no effect, she may have assumed that I did not repeat it to you, and so sent this letter."

"That is true. She has told this story before, in less detail." Lydia wondered if she should fear a woman who showed such determination. At the moment it only made Lydia wish to slap her.

"In fact I am almost certain it was her." Tilly shook her head in disappointment. "I usually have a pretty light hand with my servants, but since I discovered Marie's treachery, I have kept an eye on her. Just before I came to you, I received a little report on her activities."

"You have had her followed?"

"It is really only for your sake that I am watching her."

"It seems a bit extreme." Lydia wondered why any of Tilly's actions surprised her anymore.

"Extreme precautions can save a lot of trouble. I trusted her once and

I believe you almost paid a very heavy price for it." Tilly looked down for a few moments. "Anyway, do you want to know what she did, or are your moral sensibilities too disturbed by the idea?"

"Of course I want to know." Lydia leaned forward.

"Fine then. Among other things, she had a little meeting with her former mistress—Miss Delacroix, I mean. And then where do you think she went?" Tilly looked pleased with herself.

"I have not the faintest notion." Lydia impatiently waved her stalling friend on.

Tilly gave Lydia a significant look. "Why, she went over to the home of Lord Aldley for a very brief call."

"Lord Aldley? Whatever business could she have with the earl?"

"None at all if we are speaking of legitimate business. But I can only imagine that she has been on the same sort of business as whoever delivered the letter to you. I doubt Marie delivered your letter, however, as all of your servants would recognize her straight away."

"You think she took a letter to Lord Aldley?" Lydia did not like to contemplate the probable subject matter of a letter from that quarter.

"I think that she delivered a letter that was more or less designed to sully your character to his lordship. And I think the author of both letters was Miss Delacroix. Who else is as desperate to put an end to your romance with Lord Aldley?"

"His mother, probably." Lydia sighed.

"Certainly, I suspect that she would not look upon the match with a kind eye. But she is the last person I should expect to circulate information that cast the slightest shade on her son's reputation. She might happily impugn your character, but not Lord Aldley's."

"I wonder what lie Miss Delacroix might have told about me." A little storm crossed over Lydia's face. "But of course, this is all conjecture. We have no proof."

"Actual proof, no. But I wish you would just accept that this letter is her doing, and that she is only making up lies. I truly wish I could ease the distress that this malicious document has given you. It is really not worth thinking on little things like this."

It was not a little thing to Lydia.

"Do not frown so. Let me distract you with some other tasty morsels that I gathered while I was away." Tilly's smile was all mischief. "I admit it is not a perfect distraction, for it involves our favourite acquaintance."

"What have you heard of Miss Delacroix?"

"It seems that she has received an invitation to the ball. Can you imagine? After Lady Aldley cut her down like that at the Delacroix's dinner party, suddenly she is to attend. Odd, do you not think?"

"Yes, I do. I cannot account for it, can you?" Lydia also could not see how Tilly thought this news would be diverting.

"Well I doubt it was Lord Aldley's idea, so I can only think of two explanations." Tilly tapped her fingertips together pensively. "Perhaps Lady Aldley has invited any reasonably attractive member of the quality she can think of, hoping to distract her son from you—which suggests he is about to propose. The other possibility is a little more scintillating."

"Well, do not hold me in suspense."

"Is it not possible that Miss Delacroix, or perhaps Lady Delacroix, has found something to hold over Lady Aldley's head?"

"Such as Lady Aldley's secret, you mean." Lydia nodded. "Mr. Delacroix certainly seemed to know something."

"So you do not think I am being too conspiratorial?" Tilly's face betrayed not the slightest concern as to what Lydia thought on the matter.

"My experience with the family has taught me to put no limits on their audacity. Still, the simplest accounting is that her ladyship is trying to attach her son to someone other than a social nothing like me."

"You are not a nothing, no matter what the dowager countess thinks. But you are right, that is the less far-fetched explanation. Oh, do not look so downcast. It may seem like a curse, but if you were only just a little less virtuous, you would look forward to rubbing Miss Delacroix's nose in your successful conquest of the earl." Tilly tried to induce Lydia to smile by wiggling her brows.

"I cannot share your optimism." Lydia chafed her hands. "I am looking forward to the evening with a great deal of trepidation."

CHAPTER 36

*A*ldley stood before the mirror in his dressing room and surveyed his formal attire with an appraising look. His valet gave his clothing a final brush, and dabbed some scent on his kerchief before offering gloves to his master.

Aldley's garments were new, sleek, without flaw and without ornament except for his gold watch and cravat pin. Every stitch of clothing was perfectly tailored—exactly how he wished to look on the evening that he proposed to his future countess. He walked to the door.

He was less than half an hour away from happiness. He would finally be able to tell Miss Norwood, *Lydia*, how she made his heart feel.

He scarcely had words for it, but he did not want to merely rehearse something. That was too impersonal. When they were together, when they finally had a chance to talk, it would flow naturally. Still, a drink would not hurt.

His valet helped him on with his cloak, positioned his hat, and handed him his silver-topped walking stick. Aldley was just stepping out the door to meet the carriage, when a messenger approached him with yet another letter.

He resisted the urge to tear it into pieces and grind it under his feet immediately. Instead he merely drew a deep breath and tucked it into his pocket.

He was not going to read any more unsolicited correspondence. He would not let any more scheming gossips ruin his mood. His every thought was for Miss Norwood, who would soon be his dearest *Lydia*. And then, to the devil with everyone else.

When he arrived at the ball, he ignored good form and sneaked in through a private entrance, to avoid the tedium of standing with his mother to receive guests.

He discovered that there were many eager young ladies already there. He was surprised that his mother invited some of them—the ravishing but title-less Miss Dervish, for example. And Miss Delacroix.

His lips flattened. He thought his mother had taken a disliking to the Delacroix family, though he knew not why, precisely. It was possible that she had learned enough of Mr. Delacroix's character to turn her against all his relatives. And yet, here was Delacroix's sister, decked out in a deep wine silk.

She turned and smiled at him as she bowed from across the room.

He sighed. Leave it to his mother to contrive to place a big fly in the ointment. The Duke of Grendleridge made his way over to Aldley, his daughter on his arm.

Or, perhaps there were an entire horde of locusts in the ointment. He drew a hand over his face. The thought was unworthy. He respected the somewhat eccentric duke immensely, and his daughter, though unattractive, was sensible and a decent conversationalist.

He should not let his love make him entirely uncivil to everyone but its object. If only Miss Norwood would arrive soon. He threw back a quick glass of champagne, and readied himself to greet the two highest ranked guests in the room.

As they were chatting, Aldley saw, or perhaps first felt, Miss Norwood enter the ballroom. She stood next to her chaperone, Lady Goodram, who caught Aldley's eye and winked, then whispered something in Miss Norwood's ear before sailing merrily off to the card room.

He wanted to catch Miss Norwood's gaze, but she did not see him. She was radiant and beautiful. She looked like a queen with her hair piled up high on her head, and decked out in a virginal ivory silk and lace gown that showed off her perfect collarbone.

He caught his breath and stared, resisting thoughts of unpinning that hair, running his finger over the delicate edge of that clavicle, over the curve of a blossoming breast. Aldley swallowed and fought to restrain his ardour. He had to talk to her, to make her his own.

But before he could politely detach himself from the duke and his daughter, he saw Miss Delacroix, with a speed he had not thought possible within the confines of a ball gown, hasten directly to Miss Norwood's side.

The conversation was left to his imagination, but Miss Norwood's smile looked like the product of monumental effort and facial control. Aldley chuckled to himself, which confused the duke, who was speaking of his new plans for a very large orangery with a glazed roof.

"An orangery strikes you as amusing, does it?" The duke squinted one eye as he sipped his champagne. "Is this some fashionable new form of wit blown in on a fresh wind that has escaped a sheltered old cheese like myself?"

"I beg your pardon, Duke. I am a little distracted." Aldley was already engaged in the unsupportable rudeness of casting about the room to find to Miss Norwood's face. "Terrible manners, forgive me. I hope you will excuse me, but I see someone I simply must speak to."

"Of course, Aldley." The duke waved his hand in a flourish of sparkling rings. "I am accustomed to your cavalier indifference to precedence. We can resume our chat later. Quite at your leisure."

Aldley chuckled at the duke's castigation. But when he had turned again to walk to where Miss Norwood had been, she was gone. It was vexing, but he was not of a mind to let her go so easily. He moved through the crowd to the place where she had stood and began searching for her.

His eye caught sight of Miss Ferrel.

"Miss Ferrel." He received her bow almost with impatience. "I am sorry to disturb you, but have you seen Miss Norwood. She was just here a minute ago."

"Yes, my lord. So she was. I was just about to come greet her, when Miss Delacroix swept her away suddenly." Miss Ferrel looked as bewildered as Aldley.

"Did you happen to see where they went?"

"Toward the card room, I believe." She gestured.

"Thank you, Miss Ferrel. Please excuse me." Aldley dashed off. He knew he was not demonstrating the best breeding tonight, but he was desperate to find Miss Norwood.

There were many people in the card room—including Lady Goodram, who could not resist the allure of so many rich adversaries—but none of them was Miss Norwood.

"So good to see you, again, Lord Aldley." Miss Delacroix appeared suddenly at his shoulder. "I hope you are well."

"Exceedingly well, thank you, as I hope you are." He cut her off before she could entangle him with more pleasantries. "Have you seen Miss Norwood this evening?"

"Miss Norwood?" She looked surprised. "Well, yes. I was just speaking with her. Only she did not seem very well."

"Where is she now?"

"I am not sure, she left rather abruptly, I think perhaps she went outside again."

He got the impression that the chit was being intentionally vague. "Excuse me, Miss Delacroix." He made to leave.

"Shall we not have a glass of champagne and chat? Surely you will see her in the course of the evening. Unless of course she has sneaked off with your charming friend. What was his name? Mr. Rutherford? I hear they were quite inseparable out at Mr. Norwood's little farm."

"Did you? Well, whatever quarter you heard that from, I suggest you stop frequenting it, for that is only idle gossip, and entirely untrue. It is not becoming for anyone to repeat lies about a member of their acquaintance. Nor is Mr. Rutherford in attendance this evening."

He spoke with more heat and candour than was truly acceptable at a ball. But he was sorely provoked—probably by intention, if he understood anything about the young lady's character.

He forced himself to assume a calmer demeanour. "If you see her, please tell her I am looking for her."

"Of course, Lord Aldley." Miss Delacroix procured two glasses of champagne from a passing servant, and offered him one with an inviting lick of the lips. "But are you sure you would not rather wait here with me? I am certain she will be back."

Her laugh was disdainful as she added, "A girl with no status and low connections would never allow herself to miss such a gathering as this. It must be the high point of her life."

He clenched his jaw. The young lady gave the impression of being more than a little fast. "If I were you, Miss Delacroix, I should remain silent on the topic of low connections. Excuse me." Miss Delacroix inclined her head. She smiled and lifted a flute to her lips in a single smug gesture of serenity, as Aldley strode away.

CHAPTER 37

*L*ydia stood in a poorly heated back chamber behind the ballroom, where, she supposed from the various supplies stored on the shelves about her, servants did laundering and repairs to clothing.

She had no idea where her lady's maid had gone. The house servants had dabbed at her gown, trying to remove the red wine from the fine fabric, but it was pointless.

Miss Delacroix had done it on purpose, she was certain. She even smiled at Lydia as she did it. Then she feigned that she was sorry and mortified and whatever other polite profession she could heap onto the humiliating moment after the fact.

It had been all Lydia could do not to plant that nasty little minx a facer. They would never shift the wine stain. The servants seemed to feel the need to try, but it seemed pointless to Lydia to pretend that the gown could be rescued.

The evening was off to a very unpromising start—so much for the soothsayer's visions of white dresses. Her mother should have saved her money.

Lydia remained shivering in the cold room as the servants left. Only one of them remained.

"Would you like to send for a new gown, Miss?"

"Yes, that would be best. I shall write a note to my mother." There was no need to disturb Lady Goodram's card sharping. Sending for new clothes directly would be faster.

"Shall I send this dress back too, Miss? Perhaps your servants can save it if they start to cleaning it straight away."

Something about the way she said it made Lydia pause. And it was odd to suggest an arrangement that would leave Lydia with nothing to wear, standing in a distant acquaintance's house in her undergarments.

And it was perfectly clear that a wine stain of this size on white silk would never be gotten free without ruining the finish of the fabric, whether one started a heartbeat after the wine was spilled, or whether one started a fortnight later. The dress was unsalvageable.

She gave the servant a strange look. "I shall keep this dress until I receive a replacement. Only bring me a pen and paper."

"Oh, but what a shame it would be to lose such a lovely gown, Miss," the servant wheedled.

The hairs on Lydia's neck stood up. There was something wrong with this servant. London servants in noble households did not back-talk their superiors. What did she know about this maid? Was she an extra hired for the party?

Many guests brought servants with them, as she had done, if only she could find her itinerant lady's maid. Was her anxiety just a case of nerves that had been frayed by recent events? Was she seeing conspiracies where there were none?

"Never mind." Lydia was not in the mood to speak longer to this person. "I shall go send the message myself."

"No, no, Miss. Let me. The servant almost bolted for the door, but Lydia was fast and got there first. The audacious servant actually tried to get ahead of her and herd her back into the room.

"Oh, Miss, please, don't be seen like this in the ball. Please, I shall fetch pen and paper to you."

"I care not how I am seen at the ball. Recollect your place and stay away from me." Lydia's instincts were now on high alert.

The servant's face changed. "You'll get back in that room and stay there, or you will be very sorry."

"No one in my family has ever raised a hand to a servant." Lydia's pulse raced, but she kept her voice as even and commanding as she could. "But if you do not step away from me this instant, I will put you in your place, make no mistake. Do not take me for a meek little weakling like the London ladies you are used to. I could leave you in a heap, just as I could that scheming little witch you work for."

The servant looked taken aback, but only paused slightly before attempting to grapple Lydia.

It was enough time for her to anticipate the attack. Lydia evaded the servant's grasp, ducking under her arm. She seized the woman's wrist as she passed and twisted it around behind her.

The servant struggled to free herself, but Lydia gave a sound kick to the back of her knee, knocking her off balance. She wrenched the woman's arm up, eliciting a screech of pain, and pinned it behind her back.

"If you struggle, I will break off your arm." She wrenched the servant's arm up further to prove the point.

"Mary, mother of Christ!" The woman shrieked in agony. "Right! Enough! If you break it I'll never find work again."

"Finding work will be the least of your worries. Tell me where Miss Delacroix is."

"I don't know who you're talking about."

Lydia wrenched the arm further.

"For the love of God, don't break it! She's over there." She gestured with her left hand toward a closed room at the end of the hall. "In that one. I was supposed to bring her your dress."

"What does she want with my dress?"

"I dunno. She paid me to take you into this room and lock you in. But then she changed the plan suddenly, and she wanted me to get your dress, too, and deliver it to her in that room. I don't know nothing more, 'cause I don't ask questions about things what don't concern me."

"I assume you have a key to the room you were to lock me into."

"Yes." She reached sullenly with her left hand into her apron pocket and produced a key. "What are you going to do with me? I was only trying to get a little extra money to help my family, Miss. I am no criminal."

"I shall decide that later." She flung the servant into the room and locked the door.

It felt odd to be getting into physical struggles and locking people into rooms while dressed in a ballgown. Lydia was strangely out of time and place, scrapping like one of the tenant children on her father's estate, when she should be downstairs filling her dance card.

She hadn't even seen the earl yet. But first she had to decide what to do about Miss Delacroix. She wished she had a key for that room, too, so she could lock in the odious young lady and leave her there.

"Lydia, there you are! Thank the heavens!"

She turned to see Tilly, dressed in a servant's uniform.

"But whatever are you doing in the back rooms? Should you not be dancing with Lord Aldley?"

Lydia's mouth hung open for a moment. "Tilly! You are a fine one to talk. You should not be here at all, much less dressed as a servant. What is the meaning of it all?"

"I met with Ms. Grey again, after you left for the ball, and received some information which made me believe you might be in need of assistance—you and Lord Aldley. As I told you before, it is just as easy for a woman to sneak in to a ball as a man." She appeared to be enjoying herself much more than Lydia was.

Tilly looked down at Lydia's dress. "Let me guess, Miss Delacroix accidentally spilled red wine on you?"

"If that was an accident, I am the queen of Spain." Lydia clenched her fists.

"It seems we both have some stories to tell. Me first."

CHAPTER 38

*A*ldley found himself in the absurd situation of skulking about in the back rooms in search of Miss Norwood.

He had already searched outside, to no avail. He began to doubt Miss Delacroix's scant information. He hoped she was not on the path to becoming as bad a character as her brother.

Lady Goodram, who had ensconced herself in the card room, had not seen Miss Norwood, either. He had been reduced to questioning the house servants.

"I believe I saw her, my Lord."

Finally Aldley had found a servant who might be of some assistance. "Well, spit it out, man!"

"Apologies, my lord. Your description sounds just like the young lady that some servants took back here to try to shift a red wine stain from her dress. It seems that someone had spilled it on her—beautiful white silk dress, too. A real shame."

"Show me where she went." Aldley's voice was a little more terse than he had intended, but he was growing increasingly frustrated with the night's events.

The servant led him into the back hall, where a small room stood to the right. "I believe they took her into this room. It is where they do the washing and mending." He paused to open the door. "That is odd. This room is locked."

"Miss Norwood, are you in there?" He knocked on the door. "Miss Norwood?" He put his ear to the door, but there was no answer. "Shall I fetch a key, my lord?"

"Yes. No, send someone else to fetch it. I want you to stay and tell me exactly what happened—everything you can remember."

"Aldley! So good to see you!"

The earl gritted his teeth and turned to see Lord Essington sitting in a wheelchair next to a handsome older gentleman.

"Lord Essington." He forced himself to unclench his jaw. "I did not think you were to attend."

"What? And miss such a grand affair? Never! And only look who I met down at the club. This is my old friend, Sir Gerard Beauchamps. We knew each other when we were young bucks, didn't we, Beauchamps?"

Beauchamps looked embarrassed. "Pleased to meet you, Lord Aldley." The bows were stiff. "Please pardon the departure from ceremony. Lord Essington expressed a desire that I conduct him here. I am afraid I did not realize—I should not have dreamed of intruding upon a ball."

"Please do not let it trouble you." Aldley forced himself to be courteous. "I thank you for your kindness to my brother-in-law in conveying him here safely."

"I shall take my leave, then." Beauchamps made to quit them.

"No, no, no! Why you cannot go now, Beauchamps!" Essington's arm flapping threatened to upset his chair. "You haven't even greeted Lady Aldley. We can't let him leave now, eh, Aldley? Why, he and your mother are old acquaintances after all."

"Then I am sure my mother will welcome a visit," Aldley addressed Beauchamps. "But perhaps you would both prefer a time when you can have a good chat, without the constant interruptions of a ball." It pained Aldley to speak of constant interruptions.

"Indeed, my lord. It is just as you say. And really, it was a very long time ago when we last saw each other. She was a friend of my cousin's." Beauchamps's ears were turning quite red.

"Oh that is laying it on pretty thick." Essington tried to slap Beauchamps' back, but could not quite reach high enough from his wheelchair, and, with no compunction, patted his backside instead. "A *friend of your cousin's*, indeed."

"Perhaps you would like a servant to find you a room, so you can change for the ball, Essington." Aldley had to end this excruciating spectacle.

"Not at all. I have travelled light, you see, with the post. No change of clothes."

"With the *post*?!" Aldley could scarcely conceal his shock.

"Yes, well, there was a problem with my carriage." Essington winked at Aldley.

The earl knew very well that the servants at Essington Hall had been instructed and bribed to make any excuse not to take Essington to town.

Essington went on, "But when I arrived at the club, Beauchamps was obliging enough to give me a lift here. I just thought I should step in for a glass of something and greet your mother, and then step back out to the club for some cards."

"It is good of you to interrupt your evening's amusements to call on my mother." Aldley was not fooled. This was Essington's way of embarrassing Aldley as revenge for the officious interference of saving the miserable bounder's life. "I am sure she will be most pleased, but I have not yet seen her, myself."

"Well, I do not wish to intrude." The viscount blinked innocently.

"No, of course not," Aldley forced a smile.

"She has her obligations to the guests, of course," the wastrel cheerfully continued.

Clearly Essington just wanted drink and a mode of travel about town, with the added delight of humiliating his relatives. The knave cared not about visiting his mother-in-law.

"However," Aldey said, "I have another matter to attend to at the moment. Perhaps one of the servants can bring you a glass of champagne, while I get Mills to fetch a carriage around for you. If I see my mother, I shall ask her to come to you."

"That would be most obliging." Essington smiled broadly, revealing his sparsely populated gums. "Perhaps we might make that a bottle of champagne. Riding post is thirsty travel."

"Of course." Aldley turned to Beauchamps. "Sir Gerard." They bowed their adieus, and Beauchamps left.

Aldley went to instruct the servants. "Bring Lord Essington a bottle of champagne, then assist him to my mother's carriage and take away his wheelchair. Lock him in that carriage, and get Collins to drive him back to Essington Hall, immediately. No stops."

"Yes, my lord."

Aldley paused. "On second thought. Give him a bottle of whiskey to keep him company in the carriage. But make sure you secure the doors before you leave."

Just then another servant came with a message. "The messenger said it was urgent, my lord."

It was trying Aldley's last ounce of patience not to yell at the servant that he should not deliver any more ruddy messages. But he constrained himself.

It was not as if the servant had any idea about the prior missives. And it was not the servant's fault, after all, that the entire world was conspiring to prevent Aldley from proposing marriage to Miss Norwood. He had to find her. But first he had to deal with Essington.

When Essington was safely on his way to the carriage and merrily drinking his whiskey directly from the bottle, apparently in the happy belief that he would be driven to the club shortly, Aldley relaxed, slightly. At least this one of many frustrations was almost out of the way.

He only wished that they had not brought around the carriage with the Aldley colours on it, for he would have preferred to be more discreet in the removal of his unwanted relative.

But he did not care to risk relocating his brother-in-law to another carriage, lest the little rat should escape somehow. Much better to get him out of London as quickly as possible. He wondered where the driver had gotten to.

While he waited, Aldley stepped back into the torch light by the steps to read his missives.

The most recent message, that was apparently so urgent, was another letter from M. Boulanger, again in French.

This time the man claimed to be in town, desiring to visit him immediately, and proposing to do so at his mother's ball, which he assumed the earl would be attending. He proposed to keep the consultation private by meeting discreetly in Aldley's carriage.

The entire thing stank of a fraudulent scheme, for how should a man so recently arrived in town have any idea that Aldley would be at his mother's ball? And for what cause could the meeting be so direly urgent?

However, the earl was angry enough to want to meet the scoundrel. The challenge would be to limit himself to merely turning him over to the authorities, and not exacting his own punishment first.

He looked at his watch, it was a quarter of an hour to the proposed meeting time. He hailed a servant to have his carriage brought around.

In the meantime he read the other letter. It was from Rutherford. He cursed himself for not reading the address before shoving it in his pocket earlier.

My dear friend,

I am not sure whether to apologize for not properly clearing up this misunderstanding before (though I was practically on my death bed, in case you had not noticed), or to further blacken my image in your mind by informing you that you are perhaps the greatest of all the bacon-witted fools I have ever met.

Let me simply state the facts as they are, and let you come to your own surmises about whether you deserve the apology or the insult.

On the day that you first came to call on me at Nesterling and left without seeing me, though I was gravely ill (infidel), you clearly came at an inopportune moment which led you to a most erroneous conclusion about Miss Norwood and myself.

What actually transpired was that I had been foolish enough to disobey the doctor's instructions, and went wandering about the library. This resulted in a reopening of my wound and a sudden bleed (which a more caring friend might have noticed).

Miss Norwood, who was helping me back to my chamber as quickly as she could, was not quite strong enough to support my full weight when I fainted (which was not very manly of me, and you are forbidden to ever speak of it).

This resulted in the entanglement that you witnessed just before you ran off in a huff like a spoiled little school lad.

On your second visit I believe you completely misinterpreted what I was saying—or rather, of whom I was speaking.

In short, you do a grave injustice to the character of Miss Norwood, and indeed to mine (but having been your friend all these years, it is the kind of shoddy treatment I have come to expect from you).

I hope this clarifies the situation, and that, by now, you have gathered the small amount of wits you possess about you, and have proposed to Miss Norwood.

I believe you owe me another case of champagne, but I am willing to forego this debt, if you promise to invite both me and the delicious Miss Ravelsham to the wedding.

Don't invite the fiancé, though. He is a very stupid fellow, most inattentive to her, and, frankly, wholly undeserving. I intend to steal her right out from under his oblivious little nose.

Try not to get married until I am able to remove to town again. The doctor says it should only be a few days.

Until then, I remain always your faithful, mistreated friend,

William Rutherford.

Aldley chuckled to himself as he refolded the letter. So it was Miss Ravelsham that Rutherford was chasing.

The insult was definitely what he deserved, and he could not but be diverted at his friend's words. He felt such a great giddy surge of relief and of care for jolly old Rutherford. It was good for an earl to have someone who sets him on the right path when he is being an idiot.

Of course Rutherford would be invited to the wedding. If Aldley could ever find his prospective bride, that is.

The earl's new equipage rolled up. His plans for marital felicity would have to take yet another detour while he dealt with this swindler, whoever he was.

"Go get another two servants, preferably big lads, and wait at the back for further orders. Be at the ready. I may need sudden assistance." Aldley would be prepared for this miscreant.

He settled himself into the carriage to wait for the scoundrel to reveal himself. He would prefer to have this person safely on his way to prison before he proposed to Miss Norwood. Aldley wanted no shadow cast upon the moment.

He smiled to himself as he returned to thoughts of her lovely red curls tumbling around her bare shoulders.

CHAPTER 39

*L*ydia angrily paced the worn stone floor near the servants' entrance of the Aldley ballroom.

She was incensed by the story Tilly had just told her. Miss Delacroix had actually purchased a red wig and paid Miss Grey to style it in imitation of Lydia's hair. Unbelievable, insufferable, scheming little minx.

Tilly waited with Lydia for the delivery of a second gown, calmly admiring the artwork on the ceiling which was in the renaissance Italian style, and depicted popular Biblical vignettes.

Lydia's maid, who had been led off on some pretext by another of Miss Delacroix's assistants, had found her way back to Lydia, and stood quietly in attendance, concerned about her mistress' mood.

"It is quite a grand household that decorates even the servants' areas with such exquisite artwork." Tilly rubbed her neck, which was sore from staring upward for so long.

Lydia was oblivious to Tilly's comment, and scowled as she paced. "I still cannot believe the audacity of that little witch. When she spilled claret on me, I thought she was just being a spiteful beast. But to have ordered up a wig and embroiled Miss Grey to imitate my coiffure, all so that she might impersonate me to the earl—it is reprehensible!"

"Yes." Tilly smiled despite obvious efforts not to.

Lydia frowned. "Try not to sound so enthralled, or I shall think you have mixed allegiances."

"I understand your anger, truly I do. But really, this is sort of exciting, is it not?"

"I cannot look at it that way."

"No. I suppose not." Tilly sighed. "In any case, it does no good to fume. Her scheme, though somewhat elaborate, is dreadfully ill-conceived. It was never very likely to succeed. You will soon have your revenge. Let her pursue her mad obsession and make a total fool of herself."

Just then the Norwood servants entered, burdened with the gown and other parcels.

"At last!" Lydia went to the locked room, and opened it.

"Don't worry." Tilly waved Lydia into the room. "I shall take care of Miss Delacroix's hench-woman."

Lydia and her lady's maid went inside the room to attend to the wardrobe change, and Miss Delacroix's accomplice stepped out, looking apprehensive.

"Do not think of running." Tilly's face was stern. "We outnumber you, and things will not go well if you do."

The woman looked down.

"What is your name?"

"Mary Wheeler."

"Well, Mary Wheeler," Tilly tilted her head, "I propose a way in which you can help yourself out of a trip to the nick."

"What did you have in mind?" Mary Wheeler did not look convinced.

"We shall give you the dress. You will take it to Miss Delacroix and pretend as if nothing is amiss. If she asks about the delay, just tell her Miss Norwood wanted to wait for her other dress to arrive. Then you will leave. And you will never try something like this again."

Tilly thought for a few moments. "Miss Delacroix may not be very forthcoming with the second part of your payment—I assume she did not pay you the full amount in advance?"

"No, she didn't."

"How much is outstanding?"

"Twenty quid."

"Twenty? You drive a hard bargain. Very well." She handed a card to the woman, who looked at it and then at Tilly in disbelief.

"I know I look like a servant," Tilly sniffed, "but I am not. I have the means. Come see me at this address at seven o'clock on Sunday, if you are not too busy attending an evening mass."

"I shan't be." The servant looked hopeful and oblivious to Tilly's sarcasm. "Thank you, Miss. I don't know how to repay this kindness."

"By doing as I say." Tilly waved an imperious finger. "And by using the money to help your family, as you said you would."

"That I shall." Her mood had lifted enough to bob a curtsey.

When Lydia emerged, she looked only a little bit flustered. The deep wine coloured silk gown suited her very well indeed. If only she had been wearing it in the first place, the claret stain would hardly have shown.

Lydia handed the stained white dress to Mary Wheeler, who looked sheepish, but bobbed another curtsey, and made to the other room where Miss Delacroix was concealed.

"Now you go back to the ball and find the earl." Tilly grinned. "Try to enjoy yourself. I shall keep a discreet eye on Miss Delacroix."

It was difficult for Lydia to pry herself away. She was more than a little curious about what Miss Delacroix would get up to next. It was surely a disastrously stupid scheme, but it was fascinating. Was Tilly's influence really corrupting Lydia after all?

She entered the refreshment room, accepted a glass of champagne and drank it more quickly than was entirely proper as she scanned the adjacent ballroom. She procured another glass and continued to inspect the occupants as she walked into the ballroom, but she could not see the earl.

The dance floor was clearing and the orchestra was making ready. Lydia suddenly spied Miss Ferrel among the flocks of milling guests, and thanked heaven for a friendly face. She made her way through the crowd, examining the people around her. No sign of Lord Aldley.

"Miss Norwood! Lovely to see you again." Miss Ferrel looked very fetching in her canary and cream ensemble. "I was beginning to think I might not get a chance to greet you."

"I am most happy to see you here, Miss Ferrel." Lydia was completely sincere. "It is a relief to meet someone from my acquaintance. If I had known you would be here, I believe I should not have felt half so anxious about attending such a grand affair."

"I was invited rather last minute," Miss Ferrel grinned, "but was very thankful for the inclusion. I have it from Miss Stokes, Miss Dreydon and Miss Dervish that they were also invited, though I have not yet seen them. I have never been in a private ballroom this size. There are so many people."

Miss Ferrel looked around her and then continued, "We were all quite surprised by the invitation. I see you have changed your dress."

"Indeed—did you see my white gown before Miss Delacroix spilled her claret on it?" Lydia tried not to scowl.

"Ah, Miss Delacroix you say? She spilled her wine on you? That explains why you left so swiftly, before I could make my way to you."

"Quite." Lydia tried not to clench her jaw. That detestable schemer would get what was coming to her. She would find a way to see to it.

"She certainly made straight for you with some determination. But I have not seen her since."

"Hmm." Lydia thought she should add some levity, lest she reveal her true wrath. "Well, I am not entirely certain I wish to see her further, unless she constrains herself to champagne."

Miss Ferrel laughed. "But did you know that Lord Aldley was looking for you?"

Lydia's heart leapt. "Lord Aldley? No I did not."

"I did not see his lordship for long, either, come to think of it. Everyone seems to be disappearing this evening." Miss Ferrel looked a little puzzled. "I saw him step outside not long ago, but I thought he would surely return after he had taken some air."

"Did he go into the gardens?" Lydia wondered if she should go looking for him.

"No, out to the entranceway. In fact, he seemed rather determined as well. Now that I think of it, there are a lot of serious faces, for it being an evening of pleasure." Miss Ferrel smiled and shook her head.

Lydia became self-conscious. "I am sorry. I believe mine must be one of those faces. Only I have started things off on rather an evil foot."

"Miss Ferrel, will you not introduce me to your charming friend?" A grand-looking man, wearing a cream evening jacket with black velvet lapels and a vast collection of sparkling rings that encircled almost every finger, arrived suddenly before them.

"Your grace." Miss Ferrel bowed. "May I present my friend, Miss

Norwood. Miss Norwood, this is His Grace, the Duke of Grend-leridge."

She was rather impressed that Miss Ferrel was acquainted with a duke. Lydia had certainly never spoken to one, herself, and she had expected that any duke would be far too superior to wish to meet her.

He was an older gentleman with a kindly face and a look of merriment about his eyes.

Lydia took a liking to him immediately. She remembered to bow deeply. "Your grace, I am very pleased to make your acquaintance."

"The pleasure is all mine. So what are you two gossiping about over here, or is it a great secret, not to be disclosed to strange old fellows who intrude?"

"No gossip, your grace." Miss Ferrel immediately joined in the levity. "We are far too virtuous for that. Though I admit that we were rather impudently wondering about the whereabouts of a gentleman who is our superior."

"One in particular," he winked, "or were you asking yourself, in a general way, whether or not such a man might be found in an assembly such as this?"

"No, indeed!" Lydia could not help laughing, even as she blushed. "Miss Ferrel only means that Lord Aldley was here earlier, and we were pondering where his lordship might have gone, for he has been away some time now. I hope that is not so very bad of us, your grace."

"Not so very bad? Aye, I suppose I have seen worse characters about town—though only a very few. But I am surprised to hear that Aldley has left his mother's ball. Are you certain he is not just taking some air?"

"That is what I thought, at first, your grace. But his lordship went out the front entrance, not into the gardens." Miss Ferrel gestured at the doorway. "I have not seen him return."

"No, I have not seen him recently, either." The duke rubbed his chin. "And he did quit our conversation rather abruptly, earlier. I had thought it was to talk to you, Miss Ferrel."

"In fact, we only spoke briefly. His lordship was looking for Miss Norwood, it seems." Miss Ferrel's lips curved into the perfectly bland smile of an ingénue.

"Ah." The duke raised one brow. "And did he find you, Miss Norwood?"

"Unfortunately, no, your grace." Lydia tried not to look as unhappy about the fact as she felt.

"Hmm. That is most intriguing." The duke played with one of his rings.

"She had left to change her dress, after another guest spilled red wine on it, you see, your grace."

"What?! Which young clod-hopper spilled wine on you?" The duke's chest puffed out slightly as he looked about the room for the offender.

"It was Miss Delacroix, your grace. I am sure it was an accident." It pained Lydia to speak this falsehood, but it seemed socially necessary.

"Hmm." He examined Lydia. "This is a very pretty dress, in any case."

"It is most kind of your grace to say so."

The duke twisted a ring around his finger a few times, then said, "I had thought of asking one of you to stand up with me, but I now find that I should much rather take some air. Would you two grant an old man the pleasure of your company for a turn outside—through the front way?"

"It is a little unconventional, but I should never disoblige you, your grace." Miss Ferrel allowed her arm to be taken.

"Unconventional certainly, but we are only following the earl's example. And in any case, I find dukes rarely get reprimanded for being unconventional." He pursed his lips into a comically supercilious smirk.

"I shall gladly oblige your grace. I find myself quite in need of a turn outside." Lydia liked the duke better by the minute.

He led them, one on each arm, toward the front doors, which were opened with bows and silence by the two doormen. As they stepped outside, the damp, cool air went straight through the silk of Lydia's gown. Her teeth chattered a little.

"I say, look there! That woman's hair looks just like yours." The duke was staring toward a carriage parked nearby.

Lydia gasped as she saw a woman in her white gown, sporting what she knew to be a wig, disappearing into the door of the carriage. Miss Delacroix. Why had she entered that carriage?

"That is rather odd, do you not think? That there should be two of you with the same hair—colour and style and everything?" He pursed his lips.

"Yes. Very odd." Lydia's heart was beating in her throat. Her stomach clenched into a ball of dread. Could Lord Aldley be in that carriage? Had the scheming little witch got her way at last? And here stood a duke witnessing this compromise of the tart's ostensible virtue.

Lydia groaned internally. She was a great fool. Why had she not run out of the ball to find him as soon as she had heard he had left? Why had she listened to Tilly? Why had they not locked Miss Delacroix in that room, or knocked her senseless, instead of letting her continue with her scheme?

A servant, previously not visible from his position on the other side of the carriage, came around the back of the coach, rolling a wheelchair toward the path to the servants' entrance. He paused to lock the carriage door.

Then the driver, who had also been out of sight on the other side, climbed up to take the reins and drove suddenly away.

Lydia involuntarily took a step toward the departing carriage. It had the Aldley colours.

A feeling that she had not before experienced came over her. She feared her legs would not support her. At the same time she wanted them to run after the carriage so she could drag Miss Delacroix out of it, light her wig on fire, and beat her like she had stolen something.

As she had done. Something irreplaceable.

"Is that not Lady Aldley's carriage?" Miss Ferrel seemed intrigued.

"Yes, it is, most certainly. Well, I suppose she has summoned it to take some guest home early. Very courteous of her. Why, Miss Norwood, are you unwell?" The duke patted her arm and looked concerned.

Lydia realized that she was leaning all her weight on him. She straightened. "No, your grace." Her voice was hoarse.

"True, you look a bit pale. I hope you will not want to go back inside so soon, for I believe that is Lord Aldley's new carriage right over there. A smart equipage, is it not? I am rather jealous of the four whites. They step sweetly, I shall vouch for it."

"Yes, they are beautiful horses." Hope glimmered in Lydia's breast. Surely he would not take his mother's carriage, if his own were standing right here. But why was it standing at the ready?

The Duke squinted. "I wonder why it is pulled around. Shall we go see if his man has seen Lord Aldley?"

"Yes, your grace, let us do that—if you feel up to it, Miss Norwood?" Miss Ferrel's face showed her compassion.

Lydia nodded, and tried to look more composed than she felt. Surely he would not have been in Lady Aldley's carriage. Surely. The breath hissed out of her like a weak, little prayer, as they walked toward the vehicle.

"You there! Have you seen Lord Aldley?" The duke addressed one of the men who stood in waiting.

Lydia almost fainted when the earl, himself, stepped out of the carriage.

"Duk—Miss Norwood! I have been looking all over for you!" Lord Aldley's face was aglow in the torch light.

"Well, if you do not mind my saying so, Aldley, the inside of your carriage is a rather daft place to look for this young lady." The duke pushed his chin back so that his waddles protruded.

Aldley swallowed. "Indeed it is. Quite right, Duke. Daft is precisely the word." He looked directly into Lydia's eyes. "I have been an utterly distracted idiot. I hope you can forgive me."

She was so relieved to hear his hypnotic voice, to see him there, safe from the snares of Miss Delacroix. She herself was still feeling the strain of combating that lady's intolerable scheming. She willed herself not to cry. She could not look like a red-faced blubberer at a moment like this.

Her voice shook as she replied, "My Lord, there is nothing to forgive. I am—we are only very happy to have found you. Miss Ferrel informed me that your lordship was looking for me."

The earl only nodded, still staring into her eyes.

The duke and Miss Ferrel exchanged a glance. "I should very much like to dance the next with you, Miss Ferrel, if you are free."

"Indeed I am, your grace. It would be my pleasure." Miss Ferrel inclined her head.

"In that case, we shall return inside. Have you something to say to this young lady, Aldley?" the duke inquired.

"I do." Lord Aldley's eyes had not left hers.

"Well, then, I am entrusting her to your care and good character. If we do not see you inside after the dance, we shall come looking for you again." There was a certain sternness in the duke's smile.

When they were gone, Lydia began to shake. Lord Aldley moved nearer to her. She could smell faint wafts of his scent, leather, wool, vanilla, orange, a faint sub-tone of musk.

"You are cold. I am a beast to keep you out here, but I so long to talk to you. It was my sole purpose in coming to this ball. The thing I have been trying to do ever since I arrived."

"I am not so much cold as… would it be unrefined of me to admit that I am nervous?" Lydia tried to keep her teeth from chattering.

"I do not call it unrefined. I believe you cannot be more nervous than I am." His blue eyes were smiling at her.

"At the risk of incurring my mother's wrath for using gambler's cant, I should take a wager that I am."

He grinned. "I love your honesty."

She smiled back at him, feeling the heat rise in her cheeks so that she became blissfully unaware of the cold.

He took her hand. "In fact, I lo—"

Just then a carriage rushed past them at a mad pace.

Aldley started. "What a lunat—my God, that was my mother!" He stared in disbelief.

In a sudden movement, he pulled Lydia by the hand to his carriage, almost pushing her in.

He hesitated a moment. "Will you come with me? I do not want to lose sight of you again this evening. But someone has abducted my mother, for that is not one of her carriages, and she would never leave in the middle of her own ball."

Lydia found herself quite willing to go with him, dismissing a brief cloud of guilt that what they were about to do was more than a little improper.

"Yes, I shall." Her breath almost abandoned her as she said it.

"Bigsby, follow that carriage, and do not lose sight of it!"

CHAPTER 40

*T*illy stepped out of the shadows where she had been watching Miss Delacroix and the later arrival of the others. The torchlight lit up her amused face in a flicker of amber and shadow.

Everyone had departed—the duke and Miss Ferrel into the ball, the scheming Miss Delacroix off for parts unknown, and Lydia with the earl, just as should be.

Hopefully they would have a bit of fun on the way. She was sure he had been on the point of proposing, anyway, but he was an honourable man, tragically virtuous, really. He would have to marry her after the unchaperoned romp in the carriage.

And he was following Lady Aldley—alarmingly not in her own carriage. So whom had Miss Delacroix rode off with in Lady Aldley's carriage? Tilly chuckled. The whole evening was better than being in the middle of a Roman opera.

It was clear that Miss Delacroix had meant to make off with the earl and be *compromised*, while horribly badly disguised as Lydia—probably relying on the darkness inside the carriage. But she had simply got into the carriage that had the Aldley colours on it.

To her misfortune, it happened to be Lady Aldley's carriage and not the earl's.

But why had it taken off so suddenly? Had the earl learned of her stratagem and planned to have her removed? He looked puzzled enough when he stepped out of his own carriage—it seemed unlikely that he knew anything of Miss Delacroix's plan.

And now he was safely tucked into a carriage with Lydia. They could both use a little compromising, if they were not to become insufferable bores.

Yes, she would leave her friend in the excellent company of the earl, and see if she could instead find out whither Miss Delacroix was destined.

The little minx was not getting more than she deserved, but Tilly did not wish to see her come to actual harm. It would be hard to catch them without knowing where they were going. She would find her own servant and send for her carriage.

In the meantime, she would find the servant who had removed the wheelchair, and see what he knew.

She laughed suddenly. The wheelchair. It must belong to Lord Aldley's crippled brother-in-law, mustn't it? She had to find that servant to be sure. Miss Delacroix would not spend a dull evening, it seemed.

CHAPTER 41

*T*hey were flying over the glistening cobblestone streets in Aldley's new equipage, and despite being in a carriage with the finest suspension made, it was still a little jarring.

Lydia was comfortable with speed, but she had always reckoned horseback to be the safest way to get about quickly—much safer than anything on wheels. The sense of danger added to her nerves, but she was also excited. It was an adventure, and she was finally alone with Lord Aldley.

He took her hand suddenly, then let it go.

"Miss Norwood, I want you to know that although I have whisked you away in my carriage, my intentions are entirely honourable." He knew this was not quite true, but they were as honourable as any man's could be, while passionately in love.

"I do not doubt it, my lord. I understand you think your mother is in that carriage. Is she in some sort of danger?"

"First off, will you please call me Thomas?"

"I do not wish to be improper..."

325

"It will not be improper, and if you wish, you may call me by my name only when we are alone. But, as you are totally alone with me in this carriage, going Lord knows where, it might be a little late for considerations of propriety."

Lydia paled. She was reminded suddenly of Delacroix's assault on her person, of being trapped in a carriage with him, *going Lord knows where...* of the very great risk to women, when first propriety is abandoned. "I..." she forced herself to take a deep breath, and then release it slowly.

"Are you so nervous? Very well, you may call me whatever you like. Do not be afraid. Only look, you are shivering." There was a fur wrap beside him. He picked it up. "May I?"

She permitted him to drape it around her shoulders, and she clutched it tightly to her.

When she recovered a little she said, "Please do not think me of a vapourish bent, Lord Aldley—Thomas. It is just that the last time I was whisked away in a carriage, I was not in such pleasant company as now."

"Ah, yes." He clenched his jaw and fists, then drooped into a helpless posture. "Forgive me. I am a great bumbling oaf. Please know, Miss Norwood, that I should never harm a hair on your head. I am truly sorry that you find yourself in this uncomfortable situation. But I am thankful for your trust. I shall not betray it. Only I could not risk losing sight of you again, for you cannot know how I have been plagued by the myriad intrusions that have frustrated me these past weeks."

"Yes, of course." Lydia suppressed the desire to ask what a rich nobleman could know about frustrated plans. In her experience, they did whatever they liked, and everyone else made it easy for them.

On the other hand, Lord Aldley was different. He was beautiful, kind, principled. "I believe I understand. You may call me Lydia, if you like."

"I do like." He clasped her hand. "Lydia. I like it very much."

She smiled at him. His hand felt good, reassuring. He was a gentleman. She was safe with him. This was not the same situation. "Do you know where your mother may be going?"

"I have no idea. I expect the culprit is after some ransom, for I have been receiving strange notes, which I believed to be fabrications, intending to orchestrate some blackmail or swindle. Now it seems likely that they were designed to distract me so that my mother might be abducted."

"Blackmail?" She wondered what he might be blackmailed with.

One had to have some sort of secret to be susceptible to blackmail. She remembered the letter she had received. They had assumed it was from Miss Delacroix, and if so, almost certainly a lie.

But then again, if Miss Delacroix were planning on posing as Lydia at the ball, why would she then send such a letter? How would it serve her purpose to drive a wedge between them, if their mutual attraction was what she was planning to exploit?

She supposed it was possible that Miss Delacroix was jumbling multiple strategies together. She was bent on scheming, but that did not mean that she was good at it. "Whatever could anyone have to blackmail you with?"

"Nothing at all, I assure you. But there are people who flinch from the mere threat of a scandal—however undeserved, and so are easily extorted. I am not one of them, but I should very much like to find the person or persons responsible and make them greatly regret their actions. Of course, I do not know that the same culprit is involved in taking my mother, but the timing is extremely suspicious. He sent me a letter asking to meet in my carriage outside the ball."

"That is certainly unusual, and suspicious enough by itself. Whatever could have induced you to indulge such a request?" A knot of fearful suspicion was constricting her innards.

327

What if he really did have something to be ashamed of, even if he was not a man whose character would make him feel it?

"Ah, I see the way you are looking at me." Aldley looked pained. "Lydia, the letter asserted things which I do not believe to be true. But the assertions are no shame of mine—no matter what conclusion everyone else might leap to. I am innocent in the matter."

She did not feel assured. She knew she should trust this man if she had true feelings for him. Didn't she love him? And if she did, was she a fool to do so? She was certainly a fool to have put herself in this position if she were not in love with him.

"Perhaps, if you just told me the whole story. Or do I presume too much?"

He stiffened. "No, you do not presume too much. Indeed, there is nothing I should keep from you, so I shall tell you the story, though it is not exactly an appropriate conversation to have with... well, our entire situation will require some flexibility about social proprieties, I suppose. I shall not attempt to conceal that your doubt pains me and disappoints me a little."

"It is not so much that I doubt you." Lydia shook her head in consternation. "I only want to understand. Let me just say that I have been put in some extremely unpleasant situations in recent times, and all at the hands of people whose station in life should have made their vile conduct impossible to contemplate. I find myself very confused. Will you please be patient, and explain this?"

"Yes, as best I can. And as I tell you, please bear in mind that if I were not blameless in this matter, I should never have brought it up in the first place." He then relayed the whole story of Solange Dupres and her child.

"So it was out of pity for the innocent victim of his mother's folly and his father's depravity," he concluded, "that I had attempted to assist this child. I am sorry the babe died. He deserved a better fate. But he was not mine."

"And you are quite certain that this child did not survive?"

"I trust in the word of my lawyer in Paris. He was very thorough in his report. In any case, there would be no reason for anyone to claim that a child who was apparently an orphaned and penniless bastard had died in the streets of Paris, when he had not. Particularly when there was the possibility of a trust, if the child were alive."

He looked at her as though willing her to see the truth. "So when I lately received a letter from the so-called *M. Boulanger*, claiming the child lived, I was extremely suspicious. When the second letter asked for this unusual meeting, I was determined to bring the scoundrel to justice."

She felt the veracity of his words and was stricken by a pang of shame for having doubted his character. "I suppose that the same person may have written my letter."

"You received a letter, too? What did it say?" Aldley's lips flattened.

"Put succinctly, it said that you were the father, and had abandoned the mother and child. The author claimed to wish only to put me on my guard that I might not partake of your shame."

His face darkened. "I should like to get my hands on the person slandering my name—particularly to you. But do you not think that it must be a different person? Surely the motives for the letters are quite different."

"Yes, I see what you mean." She could not help scowling. "But it could also be one person who is too deranged to keep schemes from crossing purposes."

Aldley nodded, and fell silent for a time. "You did not believe it of me, did you?"

"In truth, I knew not what to believe." She burrowed herself more deeply into the fur wrap. "I am sorry. Only your words ring true to me, now. And I do believe you."

"I am glad to hear it. But you should know that I also received a letter suggesting that you were ruined both socially, because of the abduction, and financially."

Lydia shifted uncomfortably.

He continued, "Of course I dismissed it, as I already knew that you were the blameless victim of a man whom, by then, I had great reason to despise. I knew it to be gossip-mongering interference. But I made no connection between the two letters, for the handwriting was different, and one was anonymous, whereas the other was signed."

"Yes, perhaps it is mere coincidence." Lydia was not convinced. "Only I have reason to suspect someone amongst our acquaintance."

"Whom do you suspect?"

She smiled a little self-consciously. "You will not think me a slanderer, myself, if I share my suspicions, will you?"

"No. Certainly not." Aldley drew a little closer to her.

"Do you recall meeting Miss Delacroix under the unusual circumstance of your happening upon her, alone beside her overturned carriage?"

"Yes. That was odd." Aldley's mouth showed his suspicion.

"And do you recall her behaviour?"

"Well, it is not genteel of me to say, but she struck me as someone angling for an introduction." He paused to think for a few moments. "Do you really suspect her? Trying to arrange an introduction, however artfully, is hardly the same thing as slander, fraud and blackmail."

"What you do not know is that this very evening she executed a scheme to spill wine on my dress and take it from me while it was ostensibly being cleaned. She in fact enlisted the aid of a young woman to pose as a house servant and lock me in a room. She had earlier procured a red wig and had it coiffed to look like my hair."

"The locked room. Good Lord, she is as bad as her brother."

"Not quite."

"Yes." Aldley's mood blackened with the memory. "I beg your pardon. Not quite."

"But bad enough, for you also do not know that just as his grace, Miss Ferrel and I were coming out the front entrance, I saw Miss Delacroix in the wig and my dress getting into a carriage bearing the Aldley coat of arms, just before it sped off. I thought the vehicle to be yours, though it turned out to be your mother's."

"My God."

"Yes, I know not how things actually went, but I assume her intention was to disguise herself as me and to meet someone in that carriage. And based on what you have now told me..."

"You think that someone was me. And I can easily see her writing that letter using slanders she obtained from her brother. You might as well know that the real father of Solange Dupres' unfortunate child was Mr. Delacroix."

"Ah. I am not shocked. Does it not seem likely that Miss Delacroix was behind all the letters? That she was trying to arrange a meeting with you, disguised as me so that you might stay with her in the carriage just long enough to compromise her?"

"At the risk of sounding like I think too well of myself, yes, it does seem likely. And she would not be the first young lady to try that stratagem to trap me. Although, this is certainly the most bizarre scheme I have heard of, and—"

Lydia was puzzled when the earl suddenly threw his head back and laughed almost like a maniac.

His eyes were streaming with tears and it was some time before he regained his composure.

"Pardon me, please. I know I must sound like a mad man. You may understand my mirth when I tell you that the carriage Miss Delacroix climbed into contained a bottle of whiskey, no doubt firmly attached to the face of my odious brother-in-law, Lord Essington."

He laughed again, then said, "You had the misfortune of briefly encountering him at the Delacroix estate—forgive me for reminding you."

Lydia smiled broadly. "Really."

"Oh yes!" He wiped his eyes.

"Is it wrong of me to feel gratified by this news?" Lydia allowed herself a malicious smile.

"I should think not. God, himself, and all the heavenly host must be laughing. Even better, the servants were under orders to lock Essington in and take him back to Essington Hall this very evening. So Miss Delacroix is in for a lengthy rendez-vous, though not the one she had in mind."

It was Lydia's turn to laugh long and hard. She wiped her eyes. "And to think, I was only wishing to light her wig on fire. This is so much better." Then she blushed, realizing that this was not quite the thing to say.

The earl laughed again and kissed her hand. "Lydia, you truly are a jewel. I hope you will always be this unguarded and honest with me."

Lydia knew her cheeks were burning. She hoped the gloom of the carriage would conceal it. She felt a little ashamed. Should she tell him about her father's turn of fortune? Should she tell him of their first meeting? Would he not change his mind about her?

"Is there something wrong, Lydia?" Aldley clasped her hand tightly.

"Yes, there is. Only I wish I did not feel obliged to tell you." She chafed the fabric of her dress with her other hand.

"You can tell me anything, dearest."

"Am I your dearest?" Lydia tried to calm herself.

"Have I not all but declared it by being in this carriage with you?" Aldley's voice sounded hurt.

"All but, yes. But you would not be the first in the nobility to have a dalliance with an untitled maid." Lydia wished she did not sound so bitter. But he must realize the truth of her words.

He recoiled as though he had been slapped, unconsciously removing his hand from hers. "I see. You think me a cad, merely toying with your happiness for my own amusement. I wonder what I have done to deserve such a castigation."

"I do not castigate you. Truly I do not. It is only that you have never declared your intentions to me." Lydia sighed. "And when you hear what I have to say, you may not wish to."

Aldley cursed himself. She was right. He had not declared any intentions to her, and had merely expected her to take it on faith. Why had he not? Was it he who was still in doubt?

"Please tell me what you have to say, Lydia. You wrong me with your doubts, but I have also wronged you with my reserve. I wish there to be no secrets between us."

She drew a breath. "That anonymous letter you received refers to an abduction which, as you know, was thwarted, but nonetheless did happen. It seems Miss Delacroix knew of her brother's plans in advance—but I digress. The other accusation is also true. I know it is well known about town that my father is very wealthy, but he has recently lost most of the fortune. We are not forced to withdraw abruptly from society, and we have not, of course, advertised our troubles. But we have been slowly liquidating what we can. That is why my father sold Ari to you."

"I see." It was nothing. He cared not about settlements. But her sweet, disinterested honesty in revealing this to him made him realize what a prize she was. He wanted to kiss her, buy her everything she could ever want, and spend the rest of his life trying to make her as happy as she deserved to be.

Lydia swallowed. "And now that you know the letter told the truth, does it change your opinion of me?"

"I hope, in addition to believing this recent defamation, you do not also suspect me of fortune hunting." His eyes were smiling as they sought out hers.

Lydia's lips pursed with the effort not to grin. "Not of fortune hunting, certainly, but most people would think my family's turn of fortunes a material consideration. I think it would generally be considered in the realm of prudence, rather than avarice."

"If you had advertised your misfortunes, you no doubt could have dissuaded Mr. Delacroix from his infamous conduct. But my intentions are honourable, and have nothing at all to do with money. You shall not dissuade me." How he longed to take her in his lap and kiss her.

But Aldley knew that he should not take liberties in this situation. There would be time enough for lavishing her with affection when she felt more secure, when they were engaged. Hopefully that would be soon, if only he could get her to stop throwing up maddeningly pointless objections that only made her seem more adorable and perfect.

Lydia felt such a relief at Lord Aldley's—*Thomas'* words, that she hardly noticed when the carriage slowed to make a turn.

Aldley opened the carriage door and leaned out. "Where are we?"

"We have just turned west, my lord. Our carriage is larger, and we must take our turns more slowly. I still have an eye on him. This is the way to Bristol—though I know not where he is destined."

"Keep tracking him." He slid back into his seat.

"Are you very sure your mother was in that carriage?" Lydia could not help remarking on the way his lithe muscles shifted in concert as he slid in and out of the seat. It stirred something inside of her and warmed her cheeks.

His brow creased. "Yes. But now that we have solved the mystery of the letters, I am even more in the dark about my mother's abduction. I only wish we could catch them."

"I am sorry. You must be very worried."

"It is a great comfort to have you here." He almost took her hand again, but stopped himself. "And it is not as if my mother is a young maid, so..."

"Yes." She could not help remembering her own abduction.

"I only hope she does not struggle and give them reason to harm her."

They were quiet for a few minutes. Then he spoke again, "They have to stop some time, but I wish I had packed some provisions, for we did not even stay at the ball long enough to dine, and I think it may be a long journey. I hope you are not expiring from hunger."

"At the moment my stomach is too nervous for food."

"You have nothing to fear, dear Lydia."

"You have not heard all of my confession, Thomas."

"Indeed? Now you intrigue me. What else can an angel like you have done?"

"I have kept something from you—not by design but because there has never been a good time to broach the subject."

"I suppose we could not have many better times than now."

"Yes." She drew a breath. "Perhaps you might recall a trip that you made some time ago, before you went to Paris, to a pleasure garden in the countryside."

He smiled. "I most certainly do. I was rescued from yet another scheming young woman by a most unusual and fascinating dryad. I have always wished to find her again, to thank her, but I never got her name and I did not see her face."

"I was the scandalous tree-climbing maid. I recognized your voice when I first met you at Lady Goodram's ball. I have never forgotten the encounter, either. I have often wished I had been less of a coward, and had walked with you back to the hall. It amazes me that we ever should have met again." She was blushing, but searched his face for understanding.

He took her hand then. She smiled, so he moved a little closer to her. "Indeed it is a miracle. I admit, I had my suspicions when I heard gossip about your tree-climbing. But far from being a dark confession, you cannot imagine how happy it makes me that it was you. It is as though we were destined for each other."

He kissed her hand. "My dearest dryad. What a joy it is that you are here with me."

Her heart beat quickly. He leaned toward her. His mouth was mere inches from hers.

"Wait." She was breathless and did not sound convincing.

But he stopped, and cupped her chin in his hand. "What is it, my dear? I hope I am not frightening you. This is not a dalliance. I am quite in earnest."

"But you have not heard the rest of my confession."

He leaned back into the seat. "Surely you are tormenting yourself over nothing."

"I must proceed." She should much rather be receiving his kisses, but she did not trust her resolve to continue, if he should kiss her.

"Very well." He squeezed her hand. "What other egregious sins have you to enumerate?"

She swallowed. "As I have told you, my family's circumstances are less easy than they would seem. I wanted to do something to contribute to our recovery, so I decided to start investing the pin money I had saved, through a lawyer."

"That is not so very bad."

"I admit that I rather enjoy the excitement of it, but I have been further enticed."

He raised an eyebrow. "Do tell."

"I have come up with a business idea—a good one—but still, if my proposed partner agrees, I shall in essence be in trade."

"Good Lord! Well, that will no longer be necessary. You must give up any such venture as soon as may be, and never speak of it. I think we can conceal it entirely if you abandon it now, but you must give the scheme over immediately."

Lydia shook a little. It was too much.

After all the strain her nerves had taken this evening, in the recent days; after all the ways in which her *unladylike*, unconventional behaviour had saved her and his friend, and even him, from the unscrupulous behaviour of people with very undeservedly elevated status among the ton, for him to look down upon the means she had found to save her family because of mere appearances was intolerable.

By what right did he reprimand her, order her about, and try to put her back into the petty little hypocritical cage to which proper society had relegated her?

CHAPTER 42

*T*illy wrinkled her nose as the fine hairs of her mink coach blanket tickled it. She pulled the fur more closely about her, stretched out her legs across the carriage seat until she was in a proper slouch, and settled in for yet another lengthy voyage.

Although adventures and intrigues were diverting, all the bouncing around in cold carriages was insupportable.

She smiled at Mrs. Carlton, her patient and mercifully deaf companion, whom Tilly compensated well enough that the woman put up with almost any imposition, including being dragged out of a warm parlour and hustled into the carriage for an evening voyage.

Tilly had only stopped home briefly before embarking on this most recent journey. She was forced to be satisfied with biscuits and cold sandwiches, hastily constructed by one of the many servants whom she had ordered about so as to be on her way as quickly as possible.

She knew she must look a fright, but at least she was no longer wearing a servant's costume.

Tilly was destined for Essington Hall. It would seem that Aldley had ordered his brother-in-law returned to the countryside, without his wheelchair. There was definitely a story there.

She could not help laughing at the charming society Miss Delacroix was no doubt enjoying. However, Tilly could not countenance even a trouble-maker like Miss Delacroix being physically accosted, and she suspected that his lordship's only restraint would be his physical limitation.

Go she must, and make such a rescue as she could contrive. She would require some help however, and had written a few quick notes before she left. Do it as she shouldn't, she also scrawled off one unsigned note to that luscious Mr. Rutherford. He would know who it was from.

It was fortunate that her parents were away in Amsterdam. They were quite accustomed to their daughter's irregular mind, and in general were too self-absorbed to pay her much attention. But even pretending to accommodate an imaginary parental concern with pro forma explanations would add precious time to her travel plans.

She hoped she would have a chance to see Rutherford again, soon. Assuming he was still at Nesterling Lodge, he was not so very far out of the way.

She wondered, with a smile, if he still kept to his bed. With such thoughts for relish, she finished her sandwich and drifted off to sleep amid the rocking motion of the carriage.

CHAPTER 43

*L*ydia squared her shoulders and met Aldley's gaze with a look of such fury that her eyes almost glowed green in the gloom of the carriage. "I see. So your lordship disapproves."

"Please, darling, call me Thomas. Do not be so. Surely you can see—" Aldley's plea was cut off by the imposition of Lydia's raised hand.

"Permit me to tell you a few other things, then, *my lord*. I was raised in the countryside, where I learned to climb trees with the local farm children. And I learned to fight, to ride astride—even bareback—and to find all the little shortcuts which got me places faster, but with torn and dirty clothes. I was not raised a lady, nor do I desire to emulate the supreme hypocrisy and unjustified self-congratulation that is the essence of behaving like a lady."

Lydia drew a breath and gave the earl a look that made him abandon any hope of interrupting her, then continued, "You should know that much of my *unladylike* conduct has been my salvation in escaping the clutches and thwarting the schemes of so-called *gentle folk*, my lord. In saving your friend from dying at a *gentleman's* hands, for example, and in saving you from the clutches of that *gentleman's* sister. Yet she is a *proper lady* by the reckoning of the ton. And she is not the first woman whose schemes I rescued you from, as your lordship may recall."

"How could I forget? You were magnificent. But—"

"I am still, and will remain, the person who does what needs to be done expeditiously, albeit with metaphorically torn and dirty clothes —or wine stained ones, for that matter."

It seemed to him that she was sort of babbling. He wondered if she had come down with a fever.

She swatted his hand away from her forehead. "I am perfectly well, and I mean to tell your lordship that I shall not abandon my venture, nor shall I be ordered about. I can see now that my heart has misled me. My true destiny is to be a self-made woman."

"You need not be so adamant. I am sorry to have given offence, my dearest Lydia. True, I did not mean to make you angry. This is perhaps not the time for either of us to be discussing such matters. We do not need to resolve everything right this moment."

"I do not know what *you* have left to resolve, my lord." Her chin jutted out.

"Call me Thomas, please." He could not help being a little aroused by her anger. She was gorgeous and imperious. She would make a proper countess.

"But I have already made my resolution," she said with finality.

"Lydia." He was reaching for her when the carriage lurched suddenly to one side and then to the other.

Objects slid about on the seats, and the light of the carriage lamps flickered ominously. He grabbed Lydia's waist to steady her.

Lydia screamed and slipped suddenly from his grasp, as the carriage lurched downward and violently turned over, flinging their bodies abruptly into the ceiling as they were plunged into darkness.

He opened his eyes, puzzled. Where was he? Why was his face wet? He swiped his hand across his cheek, but in the darkness could not see what the liquid was. He was in a carriage, but on the ceiling, for some reason. Recollection came flooding back to him.

"Lydia!" The carriage lamps had gone out. He felt around for her body in the darkness. His hand grazed warm fabric. He grasped instinctively before realizing it was her breast. No response.

A cold sweat crept up his back. "Lydia, dearest, wake up now. The carriage has over-turned. Do not be afraid, but wake up, my darling."

Where were the servants? He pounded on the door, though his right arm hurt him. "You there! Come help us!"

He tried to reach up above his head and find the door latch, but his arm gave him such a jolt of pain that he withdrew it. If it was broken, he would be utterly useless to help her. What if the servants were dead or so badly injured that they could not lend assistance?

"Lydia?" He touched her again, aiming for where he imagined some more neutral part of her body to be. He found her head and stroked it. It was wet. No, no, no.

Just then the door rattled and the little tiger who had been riding on the back opened it. Aldley became aware of the smell of smoke. "My lord, are you injured?"

"I am well enough, but Miss Norwood is bleeding and senseless. You must get us help. Don't worry about getting us out, we can wait in here, it will be warmer. Are the others injured?"

"Bigsby has a smarting eye and an ankle what will need looking at, my lord, but Pilch and me and the horses is fine. There's a fire in the area. Smoke spooked the team, then we hit a deep pothole and rolled into the ditch. But I don't think the fire is terrible close. Can't see it, at any rate."

"Then perhaps there will be someone about to put it out. We shall wait with the carriage. Go get help. Only for the love of God hurry, lad!"

CHAPTER 44

*S*ometime in the wee hours her carriage slowed. Tilly stirred and stretched in her nest of fur. They had finally pulled up outside of Essington Hall. She threw off the blanket and rushed out before the servant could open the door for her.

Hurrying over to the Aldley carriage, she arrived just in time to intercept the dishevelled and harassed person of Miss Delacroix, who spilled out of the coach like a sack of onions falling off a cart.

Her wig had tumbled off and bits of hair clung to her face where they had wound their way out of the hair net. A horrid stench wafted out from the carriage behind her. The young lady collapsed on Tilly's shoulder.

"Oh Miss Ravelsham. Thank God you are here. I have been trapped in that carriage with such a ghastly man. He was drunk and vulgar, and he said the most horrid things," Miss Delacroix sobbed.

"There, there. You are safe now, Miss Delacroix. I shall convey you to Dunston Hall, immediately. True, you are quite safe now."

She led the distraught young lady to her own carriage, just as the servants began to carry the struggling, cursing and extremely drunk Lord Essington out of Lady Aldley's carriage.

The reprobate halted in his litany of oaths and bruising speculations about the servants' parentage just long enough to look over to Miss Delacroix and call out, "At least the bastard was kind enough to supply me a game pullet for the journey."

He was swinging her red wig around on his index finger. "Adieu, my darling. Next time we meet I shall be ready for you, I assure you, for a slicker bit of herring I scarce can recall."

Then he laughed and burst into song.

"He took this maiden then aside,

where they never would be spied,

And told her many a pretty tale,

And gave her well of Watkins ale..."

"You filthy beast!" Miss Delacroix seemed about to charge him, but Tilly hurried the distraught young lady into her carriage before the exchange could further escalate.

When they were safely on their way down the drive, Tilly handed Miss Delacroix a bottle of warm wine. "It will steady your nerves."

The girl drank meekly and looked apprehensively at Mrs. Carlton.

Tilly introduced them, then added, "Mrs. Carlton is quite deaf, Miss Delacroix, so you must forgive her not contributing to the conversation."

Miss Delacroix nodded. She sipped her wine for a few minutes, while Mrs. Carlton nodded off.

"He was utterly vile." Miss Delacroix shook her head violently as if to dispel the memory. "Oh, Miss Ravelsham, it was dreadful. You really cannot imagine."

"Just so. I really cannot imagine such a horror. It is very unfortunate that you should have been trapped in the carriage with such a man."

"He terrorized me. He tore my dress."

"And spilled wine on it, I see." Tilly's nose twitched.

Miss Delacroix hesitated. "Yes. He was mad drunk, and kept drinking more and more, like a man possessed."

"He did not...assault your person?"

"No. Thank God he is a cripple, so I could fight off his advances. Vile little worm. But he... soiled himself. Right there in the seat." Miss Delacroix burst into tears. "And he laughed about it."

Well, well. Tilly wished she could be there to see Lady Aldley's face when she discovered Essington's calling card in her best carriage.

She stifled a chuckle as she patted Miss Delacroix's arm and put a blanket around her shoulders. "There now, have another drink. That's right. Just calm yourself."

"The stench was revolting. I thought I should die." Miss Delacroix paused and breathed deeply. "Is that lavender?"

"I like to keep my carriages well-aired and scented. I find lavender quite soothing." Tilly gave the sprig muslin sachet an affectionate squeeze.

"Yes." The stunned woman took another deep drink between sobs. "Soothing."

"There now. You will be safely back in the care of your brother in no time." Tilly patted Miss Delacroix's arm. "He will decide what is to be done. Not to worry. He will handle it all."

Miss Delacroix stopped crying and seemed to be thinking intently. She took several more drinks of wine. "You mean, I suppose, that something *is* to be done about it?"

Tilly nodded. "I assume, yes, that the head of your family will have to make plans for your future."

"You mean, to defend my honour?"

"I... well, it will be entirely up to your brother, of course. But if I were he, I should prefer not to call out an already married, crippled man and draw attention to the fact that he had spent the better part of an evening locked in a carriage drinking with my sister."

"But that was not how it was. I was there against my will." Miss Delacroix sounded almost as though she believed her own protests.

"Lord!" Tilly exclaimed. "It is worse than I thought. Someone forced you into that carriage?"

"Yes." The distraught girl raised her chin.

Tilly pretended to contemplate this revelation. "It could not have been Lord Essington. Who was it?"

"It was... Well, I was not exactly forced. It was more that I was lured."

"Someone lured you into the carriage?" Tilly's brows raised in theatrical surprise. "Who?"

Miss Delacroix took another drink. "I do not wish to say."

"Very well, I shall press no further." Tilly smiled consolingly. "But I do not think that this sort of explanation will really help, do you?"

Tilly waited patiently while Miss Delacroix sank into silent tears and continued to drink for a quarter hour. Finally the weepy girl roused herself from the rumination. "How on earth did you come to be waiting at Essington's estate just as I arrived?"

"I happened to be outside the Aldley ball. I witnessed your stepping into the carriage, and its immediately departing in great haste—though it appeared you were wearing a wig at the time. But I digress. I could see that it was Lady Aldley's carriage, and I had just seen Lord

Essington lifted into it before you arrived. I knew there had to have been some mingle mangle."

"Yes. That it was, a mingle mangle." Miss Delacroix nodded readily.

Tilly continued, "I have had a brief and unpleasant meeting with Lord Essington, which was enough to persuade me that his manners are less genteel than one might expect, so I had my carriage follow. I am glad I did, for I see that my instincts were correct."

"I am glad you did, too. I should thank you, Miss Ravelsham, for putting yourself so far out of the way in order to rescue me. Indeed I do, from the bottom of my heart." She hiccuped, and wiped a tear from her eye.

"Miss Delacroix," Tilly paused for effect, as though fighting with her scruples about broaching the subject, "we do not have to speak of this if you do not wish to, but I think it would be greatly preferable if as few people as possible knew of what happened tonight."

"Most certainly. But surely the servants will talk—even if that vile man does not," Miss Delacroix sneered.

"I may be able to help your situation."

"How could you help me?"

"It will depend entirely upon whether or not you wish to keep quiet, to pretend that the events of tonight never happened, and create a plausible story quite to the contrary." Tilly's face was a study in deceptive innocence.

"Of course I do." Miss Delacroix rubbed her eye.

"And how far are you willing to go to achieve that end?"

The tipsy young lady drained the last of the wine. "Why not try my resolve, Miss Ravelsham?"

Tilly handed Miss Delacroix another bottle.

CHAPTER 45

*A*ldley halted in his pacing across the wooden floors of the inn to stare out the window onto the desolate roadway of the tiny hamlet below. Lydia had not wakened. He pulled at his hair with his fists. God help him, he could not bear that she was hurt. It was his fault.

They had been situated at the inn for days—long enough for his valet and three other house servants to arrive. Still she hardly stirred. She drank small amounts of water when prompted, but she never opened her eyes.

The doctor had come and put Aldley's arm in a sling and examined Lydia. His was but a sprain, and would likely heal quickly. Her injuries were much more severe.

The doctor believed her neck to be uninjured. The blood from her head was merely a flesh wound, but the blow had been severe. He did not know if she would awaken, but said that she should not be moved.

So Aldley had sent for a special physician from London, and sent word to her father, who was no doubt on his way. Aldley knew he would have a great deal to account for with Mr. Norwood.

He had also sent word to Rutherford, begging him to come if he were well enough, to give Aldley company and support. And he wrote to an acquaintance in the home office whom he knew would be discreet, enlisting him to take up the hunt for his mother, as the earl had hopelessly lost any possibility of doing so himself.

He made contact with his secretaries, that they might direct important correspondence to him at the inn, or pressing business matters to his solicitor. He knew not how long he would be there.

He had also attained a special license. The moment she awoke, before she had a chance to remember how he had ruined everything, he was going to ask her, implore her, to relieve his misery and become his wife.

He hoped to enlist the influence of her father, who, though he could only be incensed at the turn of events, would doubtless come to see the necessity of their wedding expeditiously.

If Aldley had his way, they would marry immediately. He knew she might have apprehensions, but at this point he was willing to use whatever means were legal to prevail upon her to marry him—as he should have done already.

But for now Aldley had run out of things to do and people to correspond with. So he paced and fretted and stared out the window.

He cursed himself for becoming a creature of regret and retrospection, always realizing each new installation of his idiocy after the fact, and remaining blind to the fresh foolhardiness of the path he was treading.

But this time he was making plans. She would wake up. She had to wake up. And she would forgive him and marry him. It was the only outcome he could bear to contemplate.

Aldley's rumination was interrupted by the arrival of Mr. Norwood and Rutherford. Rutherford greeted him warmly. Mr. Norwood bowed, but did not smile.

"Take me to her. I shall talk to you later, Aldley."

Mr. Norwood had never referred to the earl as *Aldley* before. Aldley did not mind the familiarity, but it was an ominous sign. When the worried father was in Lydia's chamber, safely out of hearing, Aldley collapsed in a wooden chair with his head in his hands.

Rutherford sat down beside him. "There has been no improvement?"

"No, but also no worsening of her symptoms. Her heart is regular and her breathing is normal. There is no sign of a fever."

Rutherford stood up again and paced a bit. "What the ruddy hell were you thinking, Aldley? After everything she has already been through, making off with her *in a carriage?*"

"Do not berate me, Rutherford. I cannot forgive myself for putting her in harm's way, but events of the evening had been so peculiar. I simply could not let her out of my sight. I wanted to propose immediately, but my mother had been abducted. I had to chase after them."

"This abduction is very strange timing, may I just say. Did Miss Norwood accept your proposal?"

"I... we did not get a chance to directly discuss it." Aldley looked sheepishly away.

Rutherford threw his head back and shook it in disbelief as he stared at the heavens. "Oh. Yes. I understand completely. I mean, you had been so determined to propose that very evening that you absconded with her in your carriage rather than let her out of your sight. But once you were on your way, what was the hurry, really?"

Aldley cleared his throat. "I did not abscond with her. She consented to come with me."

"Well, I am glad you got around to asking that much. No, really, you have done very well, for she will be obliged to marry you now. You might get a wife without taking the trouble of asking at all."

351

"I shall ask her father as soon as may be." Aldley stood again to pace with Rutherford.

"You may ask me now, if you like. But I should warn you, I am not inclined to encourage my daughter to marry a man who would take such risks with her well-being and reputation." Mr. Norwood looked weary and extremely unhappy as he stepped out of his daughter's room.

"Forgive me, Mr. Norwood. This whole mess is my own doing, I know it. True, I am in misery, which is just what I deserve. But I want nothing more than to marry your daughter—well, what I want most is to see her well again. But then I hope she will consent to be my wife, though I do not deserve her. Will you forbid it?" Aldley looked hopefully at Lydia's father.

Mr. Norwood seemed slightly mollified.

He sat down heavily. "I suppose not. It is entirely up to Lydia. If she does not choose to marry you, I shall not impose my will upon her— nor will I let you do so, and make no mistake. I shall expect you to hush this matter up entirely, whether she consents to marry you or not."

"Of course." Aldley walked a few paces.

He turned again to Mr. Norwood. "I hope you realize I never intended to put her in a position where she would be forced to accept me. My actions were selfish, impulsive and ill-conceived. My only defence is that I was acting with my heart, and in great haste, and I truly believed no harm would come of it."

Mr. Norwood's bushy brows knit together. "I should also tell you that my intention is to make her settlements entirely her own—a trust to her exclusive benefit, to which you will have no claim."

"I understand. I should not have it any other way."

"And when she inherits, it shall also go into a trust for her. You may challenge that all you wish, but I assure you my lawyers are very adept."

"I do not doubt it. And I should not dream of challenging your testamentary arrangements. Mr. Norwood, I assure you my interest is entirely in your daughter. True, I care nothing about settlements, or family fortunes. I love her, that is all."

Aldley was overcome by emotion and had to fight to regain his composure. They were all still for a while.

"Is there nothing to drink, man?" Rutherford broke the silence. "My shoulder still hurts from being stabbed, you know—and thank you for asking."

"Of course." Aldley's laugh was a little forced. "Look at us, two peacocks with wounded wings, eh?"

He was so thankful that Rutherford was here to support him, even if he was harder on Aldley than Mr. Norwood was.

He walked to the door and hailed the servant outside. Perhaps brandy would help.

CHAPTER 46

*T*illy sat contentedly drinking tea and eating biscuits in a quiet parlour at Dunston Hall. She was very well pleased with herself.

It had been a busy few days, but her work was done. She had unfortunately missed Rutherford, who had left Nesterling for London with Mr. Norwood just hours before she called there.

That was unlucky, for she enjoyed looking at him in his loose-fitting night shirt. Occasionally catching sight of a nipple gave her pleasant thoughts, and she enjoyed flirting with him mercilessly. He was not at all a prude and was a great deal of fun to tease.

She wondered if perhaps he might be interested in a little discreet affair. She would be certain to catch up with him later.

She smiled to herself and dusted biscuit crumbs off her frock. All in all, things had turned out pretty well.

She had begun making arrangements which she thought would prevent Lord Essington from spreading any gossip. Hopefully she would have time to finalize them in the afternoon before heading back to London.

She took another sip of tea and wondered whether Lydia might by now be well on her way to the altar. She doubted that the earl would delay long, considering the unchaperoned carriage ride.

Still, Tilly had received the day-old London papers. She had been scanning them for days looking for an announcement, but nothing appeared.

A servant entered with a letter. It was addressed from Lydia's father to her home in London, but a rider had delivered it to Dunston.

Dear Miss Ravelsham,

I am sorry to write of this so abruptly, but I need to inform you that my daughter has been in a carriage accident and has been gravely injured.

I know how close you two have grown. I hope that gathering as many familiar and beloved voices around as possible might help wake her from her deep sleep.

Moreover, I know she will want to see you when she awakes from this slumber. I believe your company will cheer her and speed her recovery.

I am only just arrived, myself, but already I can see it has become a bit gloomy with just three men loitering about and waiting. Mr. Rutherford and Lord Aldley are also here. I fear it is an imposition, but I implore you to come as soon as you can.

I leave the direction below. Lord Aldley has taken all the rooms in the inn, so there will be comfortable chambers for you and any companions.

I hope we shall have the pleasure of your company soon.

Sincerely yours,

Charles Norwood

P.S. If you can lay your hands on any books that might interest Lydia, please bring them, as there is no library here and reading will be a pleasurable way to pass the time while she heals.

Tilly's thoughts raced. Injured in a carriage accident. Deep sleep. This was all her fault.

She should have gone after her friend instead of concocting plans and making bargains with Miss Delacroix—who had her fair share in the blame for the way things went the evening of the ball.

But there was no point in trying to redirect the guilt. Miss Delacroix was much more interesting than Tilly had originally thought and had some natural talents, but a strong conscience was not among them.

No, she must not try to slough off her own blame in the affair by pointing fingers. Then again, how could she have prevented the accident?

At least she could have been there to assist, instead of leaving them stranded in—she looked at the directions in the letter again—the middle of God knows where. She might have to find a Delacroix servant who knew how to get there.

No. She would go to London first, for it was almost on the way—she looked at the envelope again—probably almost on the way. And she still had business with Mary Wheeler in the evening. She could travel to be with Lydia after that, though it would be slow going at night.

She hailed her servant, scrawled off a quick note, and then went to take her leave. Her tea and biscuits sat abandoned on the table.

CHAPTER 47

When Lydia opened her eyes, she was confused. It seemed to be night, for the curtains were drawn and a candle was lit, but the room was not her own. There was a strange woman sitting on a chair in the corner. Lydia could hear the rasp and whistle of her breath as she slept.

Lydia's mouth was dry. There was a cup and a pitcher on a table beside the bed. She reached for the vessel. A pain shot through her right arm, and she cried out involuntarily.

The woman in the chair stirred sightly, but did not wake. Should she awaken her? She had no idea where she was, or whether this woman was one of her captors. She could not remember much, only that she had been arguing with Lord Aldley in a carriage.

Had he tried to abduct her? Surely not. But why did she have recollections of being pawed and molested. Why did she remember the glint of a knife blade and a leering smile, and being told not to struggle? Had she been compromised?

She reached out with her other arm to pour a drink clumsily. She took a long quaff. Barley water. She refilled her cup with a more steady hand. She was monstrously hungry, so she picked some bread from the loaf beside the water pitcher and stuffed it in her mouth.

She sensed that she was in danger, but could feel that her body was in no condition to flee, and her head ached. She thought it better to go back to sleep. Yes, she would sleep now, and then feign being senseless until she sorted out exactly how much danger she was in.

CHAPTER 48

"The barley water was spilled!? Oh thank God!" Lord Aldley rushed to the door of Lydia's chamber. He would see for himself.

In the gloomy light of the curtained off windows, he could see the water pooling on the rough wooden surface of the bedside table. The chipped clay pitcher stood beside the spillage, half full. She must have drank in the night. He was overjoyed.

He could hear her steady breathing. Her eyes were closed as he leaned over to look at her. Her long, thick lashes rested serenely just above her fine cheek bones. He had to restrain himself from reaching out to stroke the tiny mole beside her eye.

How he longed to call out to her, see her open her eyes and look up at him. But the doctor insisted that no one try to wake her.

Still, she had awakened in the night. There was hope. He suppressed his wrathful thoughts about the nurse who had slept through her awakening and spilling water trying to serve herself. There was no point in taking out his anxiety on the servants.

He kissed her hand and turned to leave the room. The doctor should be summoned and Mr. Norwood must be informed of the good news.

He stepped out of the room just in time to catch Rutherford entangled in an embrace and deep kiss with Miss Ravelsham. He quietly returned to the sickroom and opened the door very noisily before stepping out again. When he emerged they were innocently greeting one another.

"Miss Ravelsham. How good to see you." Aldley was sincerely pleased.

"My Lord." Miss Ravelsham beamed at him. "I am also glad to see you, though I suppose we could both wish for better circumstances."

"Very true, but I am so relieved that you are come." Aldley ran a hand over his neck.

"May I see her?"

"Yes, of course. She is still sleeping and we are not to wake her. However we have had good news." Aldley grinned like a madman. "She apparently awoke in the night and drank some water, for the servant found spillage and the pitcher is half empty."

Miss Ravelsham sighed in relief and smiled. "That is good news. I have been so anxious about her."

"As have we all. But I am so grateful that you are here now. I know it will be cheering for us to have some female company." Aldley's eyes flicked briefly to Rutherford. "And what could be a better tonic to Lydia than to have her good friend with her?"

"What, indeed, except perhaps a small collection of books." Tilly held up the large bag she was carrying to show her literary bounty. "Only the most licentious and high flung novels would do. Nothing serious at all, for we do not wish to injure her head further."

"No, indeed." Aldley smiled.

"Surely those are too heavy, Miss Ravelsham." Rutherford took the bag from her. "Where is Mr. DeGroen? He should be carrying these for you."

"He is delayed and will join us later. If Lydia does not regain her health soon enough to remove back to London, we shall see him within the sennight."

Aldley could plainly see that the delay did not bother Rutherford, who did not even try to conceal his grin. He hoped his friend would not make the situation with Mr. Norwood even worse by carrying on scandalously with an engaged woman. He would have to have a word with him.

"Why do you not go see Lydia, Miss Ravelsham?" Aldley suggested. "Rutherford can see to the books. She will not be needing them quite yet."

"Thank you, my lord. I believe I shall." She disappeared into Lydia's room.

Aldley crossed his arms and looked at his friend. "Out with it, Rutherford."

"What?" Rutherford shrugged slightly.

"I saw you two kissing before. Do not bother to deny it."

"I have no reason to deny it." Rutherford grinned. "The woman drives me mad. I know she likes me, too. But she insists on going through with the wedding—though it is to be a *long* engagement."

"You have proposed marriage?" Aldley was taken aback by how far things had progressed.

"Of course. Not everyone is as beef-witted as you."

"I shall not dispute it." Aldley pursed his lips. "But it is not quite the thing to propose to another man's fiancée."

Rutherford waved the comment aside, as though swatting a fly. "It is her prerogative to change her mind. I cannot stop thinking of her, and now she is within my reach for several days with nothing but a rather inattentive duenna to interfere. I have no intention of letting Miss Ravelsham marry that DeGroen fellow, who could not even be bothered to escort her here, as you heard. I shall take her away from him and make her mine."

Aldley scoffed at his friend. "She is not a horse, Rutherford. You cannot just steal her."

"Call it whatever you like. I care not what means I must use." Rutherford waved his hands about a bit madly. "I shall woo her, I shall turn her head, I shall even seduce her if needs be. I shall do whatever it takes to make her break off this ill-conceived engagement and marry me instead."

"Normally I should not care about your seductions, Rutherford, truly. But at least try to be discreet. I do not need anything else to make Mr. Norwood think the better of permitting the marriage."

"I do not mean to sound stone-hearted, my friend, but your failure to be engaged to Miss Norwood is entirely your own fault." Rutherford inspected a finger nail. "You have neglected to seize your chances."

"I cannot deny that you are right, but you need not throw it in my face."

"But what else should your best friend do?" Rutherford sat down again, sprawling his long legs out and slouching until Aldley feared for the life of the wooden chair.

"In any case," he continued, "I am now presented with this fantastic opportunity, and unlike you, I shall not let it slip through my fingers. However, I shall try to be discreet before Mr. Norwood. He is a decent chap, whom I like a great deal, and he has enough on his mind at the moment."

"Thank you, best friend. You are most obliging. However, I shall not let you darken my mood. I am so elated at this improvement. Oh, but I almost forgot. The doctor must be fetched." Aldley dashed for the door. "And I must call for some more barley water—and gruel, in case she awakens hungry."

CHAPTER 49

*L*ydia was aware of being carefully examined. Her bandage was unravelled and replaced. Someone bent close to hear her breathing.

She surmised that it was a doctor, but she kept her eyes closed. She was not yet certain of her surroundings, of her situation, and in any case she did not feel so very far from sleep. She allowed herself to doze.

It was night again when she next awoke. The servant was gone. Lydia reached out, this time using her left arm, and carefully poured herself some barley water. She drank greedily, then tested her limbs.

They were all mobile, but her right shoulder hurt a great deal. There was gruel. She ate it all within a few moments and wished there were more.

Carefully she moved her legs to the bed's edge and sat up, resting part of her weight on each foot. They seemed normal. She stood and walked a few steps. Her head felt a little light and was aching. She felt bruised all over, but at least she was capable of walking.

She was wondering if she should try to escape or wait until she had healed up a bit more, when she heard movement outside the door. She hurried back into bed and feigned sleep.

Someone—two people, she thought—entered the room and were silent for a time.

"Is she sleeping?" It was Tilly's whispered voice.

Lydia restrained herself from calling out to her friend. Who was with her? She could not risk opening her eyes, for surely they were both looking at her, trying to ascertain if she were awake or not.

"I believe so." It was Rutherford.

What were they doing here? Had they come to rescue her? Why else would they be here in the middle of the night? Her question was answered when she heard the strange sounds, and peeked through one eye to see the two of them embracing, kissing.

She should be embarrassed by the display. Tilly was an engaged woman. If she had feelings for Mr. Rutherford, she should end her engagement.

Or at least, that is what Lydia should think, but in her heart, she found herself surprisingly ambivalent about it. The situation was confusing and bizarre. Where was she, why were her friends behaving this way, and why did she find it enticing rather than shocking?

"Mm… darling, you are delicious." Rutherford's voice was a breathless half-growl. "I need you. Relieve me from my torment and marry me."

"You are rather tedious for someone who is so ravishing. We have already discussed this. I have no intention of breaking off my betrothal to Mr. DeGroen."

"But what of us? You cannot tell me you feel nothing for me."

"Oh I feel." Tilly pressed her hips against his. "But unlike you, I am not romantic about marriage. Marriage is not concerned with love or passion: it is only a question of property and status. When Mr. DeGroen and I marry our fortunes, we shall be among the ten richest families in England. And what you and I do on the side will have no effect on that. We must only be discreet."

"Discreet? You mean you expect me to sneak around like I have something to be ashamed of? My passion for you is undeniable, but my love for you is pure. I want you to be my wife, not my mistress."

"I am sorry, then. But perhaps it would be better if we do not see more of each other. I do not want to cause you pain, but I *am* only looking for a mistress. Oh very well, a *mister*, if you will."

There was a shocked silence for several moments. "You mean to say that you—*your* intentions are not honourable?"

"Not in the least. I assure you that they are quite as filthy as you can imagine—and perhaps filthier."

This last comment was, apparently, more than Mr. Rutherford could bear. He began to undo Tilly's bodice, all the while guiding her to the small bed ordinarily used by Lydia's nurse.

He dropped his pantaloons and lowered her onto the surface. "Perhaps this will change your mind," he said, as he hiked up her skirts and kissed his way down to her womanhood.

Tilly began to make little moans and gasps, as he ministered to her in this strange way. Lydia knew that this was not something she should be watching, but she could not stop.

Her own body responded to the movements of the two lovers. When Mr. Rutherford finally emerged, positioning himself over Tilly, and thrusting himself into her, Lydia could scarcely restrain herself from moaning along with her friend.

Tilly and Rutherford were clearly trying to be quiet, but could not help making such sensual noises that Lydia was in no doubt about their mutual enjoyment, until, at their climax they both stifled vocal exclamations.

If this is what married couples did, Lydia had been missing out. And perhaps unnecessarily, too, for if it were as simple as Tilly made it sound, she need not even be married.

She waited until Rutherford sneaked out of the room, and then spoke up. "Right, Tilly. I do not know where I am, or why you are here, but you simply must teach me how to do *that*."

Tilly sat up. "Lydia! Oh thank God you are awake. The doctor said you might never—but never mind that." She rushed to her bedside. "You cannot know how worried I was."

"Well, not so worried as to prevent you from taking advantage of my unconscious state."

"Ah that. I am sorry, my dear friend. We did not think we should be disturbing you."

"Well I am disturbed—disturbed that my education has been carefully crafted to omit any real understanding of carnal knowledge, in order to instil a notion of virtue which is apparently entirely fictional. As you have proven yourself utterly shameless, you must teach me."

"And I shall." She smoothed Lydia's hair. "I shall only be too happy to corrupt you thoroughly, as soon as you are better. Only for now, you must not over-tax yourself."

"Fine. I am a little sleepy. But before I drift off, tell me where we are. Did you rescue me?"

"Rescue you?"

"From Lord Aldley, when he abducted me."

"Abducted? He did not really abduct you. You got into his carriage and went with him willingly when he gave chase to his mother. His *mother* was abducted."

"No, he abducted me," Lydia squinted at her friend's stupidity, "and Rutherford came to save me, only he was injured—though apparently not as badly as I had thought."

Tilly pursed her lips. "He is quite recovered enough for a little light exercise."

Tilly examined Lydia's face for a moment. "But you are confused, dearest. It was not Aldley who abducted you. Delacroix abducted you some time ago, and Rutherford did come to rescue you, and both of them ended up injured.

Lydia tilted her head.

Tilly pressed on, "Do you not remember making that contraption to haul Rutherford behind his horse? Then we met you at the main road. And we had to make up a story, and go call on Lord Delacroix on the pretence of checking on his convalescent brother. Surely you remember that."

Lydia's brows knit together. What her friend was saying did make a sort of sense to her, but she could not help persisting in the belief that it was Lord Aldley who had abducted her. She shook her head. "I do not know."

"Do you recall the night of Lady Aldley's ball?"

"I believe so. I wore a white dress."

"And do you recall that Miss Delacroix spilled wine on you."

"Yes, that is right! And she arranged to have me abducted by her brother, only it was Aldley in the carriage. He abducted me instead."

A look of profound worry crossed Tilly's face, as Lydia's eyes drooped. "My dear friend, you need to rest. We can talk of this more in the morning. Only know that I am here and I shall not let anything bad happen to you. You are quite safe." She stroked a stray lock of hair off of Lydia's face.

Lydia wondered, as she drifted off, if Lord Aldley had done things to her like Rutherford had done to Tilly.

CHAPTER 50

*W*hen Aldley entered the room they all used as a breakfast parlour, Tilly was already seated, drinking a cup of tea, her brow furrowed. She stood as he entered and they greeted one another.

"Good morning, my lord. I am glad I shall get a few moments to speak to your lordship alone." Her face looked very troubled.

"Good morning, Miss Ravelsham." Aldley sat down across the table from her. "Is there something the matter?"

"Indeed there is. Lydia awoke in the night, and we spoke." She sipped her tea pensively.

"But that is wonderful!" Aldley was elated. "She is recovering. Thank God."

Tilly nodded. "Yes, of course, it *is* wonderful. Only she is very confused."

Aldley waved his hand. "The doctor said that was to be expected at first."

"Only the thing she is principally confused about seems to be you, my lord."

"Me?" Aldley leapt from his chair. "What did she say?"

"Put succinctly, she believes your lordship abducted her."

"What?! Oh no." Aldley's face collapsed and he sat down again. This was a catastrophe upon a catastrophe.

"Yes." Tilly continued, earnestly munching on a biscuit. "She seems to be confusing events on the evening of the ball with the occasion when Delacroix attempted to make off with her."

"So she thinks me a villain." His shoulders slumped. "Just when I thought things could not get worse."

Tilly sighed. "I do not want to worry you unduly, my lord. We may still persuade her of the truth. Only, I thought you should be prepared for the fact that you cannot see her yet, my lord."

"Cannot see her? But I must. I have to clear this matter up. She must know I have not done this horrid thing. I have to propose to her, as I should have done ages ago."

"I understand your feelings, my lord." Tilly fidgeted with the table cloth. "But imagine how much worse it might make things if your lordship were to force his presence upon her while she is still afraid."

Aldley's jaw dropped open for a moment. "Did she say she was afraid of me?"

"It was clear from her demeanour. In fact, she asked me if I had come to rescue her. She seems to have thought that she was still in captivity." Tilly's eyes were full of compassion for Aldley's situation.

"I hope you corrected her view of things."

"I did, and then she fell asleep. It is hard to be certain whether or not she accepted my version of history."

Aldley stood again and began to pace the creaking floor boards. "You cannot understand how it plagues me that I have let things go as far as they have already without making her an offer of marriage. And that she has come to harm under my care—it is an endless source of torment."

"I can imagine it, truly, my lord." Tilly frowned. "I, too, have been pondering what I should have done differently."

"What could you have done?" Aldley thought that she must be merely trying to commiserate.

Tilly shook her head. "I only mean that such thoughts are common when someone you care about is injured. But in my view, we must all put aside our personal feelings and focus our efforts on helping Lydia."

"What do you propose?"

"When Mrs. Norwood arrives this afternoon, she, Mr. Norwood and myself should speak with Lydia, to tell her what really happened. If she hears it from the people closest to her, she may eventually get things straight in her mind. But until then..." Her face was resolute.

"I know you are right, Miss Ravelsham. It does not make the prospect any easier. I cannot stand to think that the woman I most love in the world is lying under the same roof as me, believing that I abducted her."

"If that is what she says happened, I am inclined to believe my daughter." Mr. Norwood had heard them from the hall. His lips were pressed in a hard line.

Aldley passed a hand over his troubled face. "Mr. Norwood, I know you have reason to question my judgement, given recent events, but surely you do not question my character, my intentions."

Mr. Norwood thought for a few moments. "Perhaps not. But I am also unwilling to question my daughter's word." He made for the door to Lydia's chamber.

"Wait. She is sleeping again." Tilly rushed to him and put her hand on his arm. "And if you heard her speak of it, you would know her mind is befuddled. She is confusing Delacroix's attempt to abduct her with the night of the Aldley ball. The doctor told us some disorder of the mind is to be expected."

"Aye." Mr. Norwood sighed, and diverted his course to the parlour window, where he stared out for some time, before continuing, "But as you have spoken with her, Miss Ravelsham, I assume that means she is spending more time awake."

"We spoke for several minutes last night, but she could not stay awake longer. However, it is a very good sign." Tilly smiled encouragingly.

"Yes. We must all rejoice for it. It will be a relief to give Mrs. Norwood some good news when she arrives." Aldley was, in fact, relieved, for he envisioned an even frostier greeting from Lydia's mother than he had received from her father.

"Indeed. My poor wife must be beside herself." Mr. Norwood sat down at the table.

Just then Rutherford entered. "Good morning. I see I am the last up."

"Did you sleep well?" There was not a hint of innuendo in Tilly's voice.

Aldley had some idea of how things might be between them, and decided to interrupt lest they give themselves away before Mr. Norwood. "Rutherford, we have had some good news. Miss Norwood has awakened in the night again."

"Ah, really?" Rutherford was less the master of his face than was Miss Ravelsham, and Aldley could see some small disturbance before he recovered himself. "Well, that is wonderful news!" Rutherford turned to Tilly. "Did you speak to her, then?"

"Yes, for some minutes." Tilly smiled. "Then she fell asleep again. It seems that she is recovering, only she is a bit confused about events leading up to her injuries."

"That is to be expected. But she will make progress. True, this is excellent news... but why does everyone look so serious?" Rutherford looked with bewilderment around the room.

It was Miss Ravelsham who informed him of the trouble with Lydia's mind. And her face betrayed no inkling of her involvement with Rutherford, so much so that Aldley began to doubt what he thought he had seen on Rutherford's face earlier.

For surely if there had been some further dalliance between the two, the maid's cheeks would be the first to flush. And yet her countenance betrayed only concern for her friend and determination to see her well again.

After a few moments of silence, Mr. Norwood stood up. "The nurse will be here soon. I shall go check on my daughter."

How Aldley longed to be the one who looked in on Lydia.

Nemesis was punishing him for taking too long in declaring his feelings. He had been so assured that he had all the time in the world, that it only required his deciding to marry her for the matter to be decided. How he now suffered for his arrogance.

He needed her. There had to be a way to clear Lydia's mind and make her his wife.

CHAPTER 51

*T*his time when Lydia opened her eyes it was light out. The heavy rust-coloured curtains were half drawn, but a ray of sunlight crept in to illuminate her mother's face, and reveal the dark circles under her eyes.

Both her parents were seated near her bed. She was confused, for she was still in the same place. Surely they would have removed her. Was she too injured to be moved? Her head, at least, felt better.

"Mama, Papa, you are here!" Lydia was relieved, even if puzzled, to see them.

"Oh thank the heavens!" Her mother was at her side immediately, pressing a kiss to Lydia's cheek, before her father pulled her back.

"We must not crush her, my dear. Remember she is still delicate."

Her mother's laugh extended to her misty eyes. "Of course, I was carried away by my feelings. But if there is one thing our daughter has never been, it is *delicate*."

"That is true." He laughed. "Lydia, my dearest girl, we are so relieved that you are awake. How are you feeling?"

"I am glad to see you both, and my headache is gone." She put a hand to her empty stomach. "But I am very hungry."

They had soft food brought in on a tray immediately. Lydia began to eat, somewhat inelegantly. Her mother did not even register this with a turned cheek, but sat smiling happily.

When Lydia had eaten most of her meal, she continued, "But where is this place and why am I still here?"

Her father replied, "We are in an inn, some place north-west of London—or *just outside of God knows where*, as Miss Ravelsham calls it."

"So beyond the reach of grace, then." Lydia's smile cracked her dry lips.

"Precisely." He grinned. "But we could not remove you back to civilization, for the doctor said you were not to be moved or even awakened."

"But Lord Aldley says a special doctor from London shall arrive soon." Lydia's mother looked hopeful.

"Aldley? Is he here?" Lydia felt the panic rise in her. Why was everyone acting as though Aldley were not an abducting fiend?

"Yes." Lydia's father gave his wife a withering look. "But he is not the danger that you think he is. He knows what you think of him and has agreed not to come to you unless you ask for him." Her father put a reassuring hand on her arm.

"That is not likely. I hope never to lay eyes on him again. He is an abductor." It wasn't entirely true, for even as she feared this man who had abducted her, her body warmed at the thought of him.

She had memories of his scent. A secret little part of her wished he might sneak into her chamber at night to have his way with her. It was hardly something Lydia wished to admit to herself, however, much less mention in front of her parents.

"He did not abduct you." Mrs. Norwood ignored the warning look from her husband

"But he did, you were not there. Miss Delacroix arranged the whole thing." Lydia could not comprehend why no one believed her.

"Miss Delacroix?" Her mother was incredulous. "That little minx tried everything to get an introduction to the earl, and as I have been informed, threw herself in his path. Do you really believe that when she finally got an invitation to the Aldley ball, she spent her time contriving that someone *else* would be compromised by him?"

Lydia had never heard her mother speak as directly or honestly about disliking a member of their acquaintance. Though, when she thought it over, there was one other person her mother had berated, but at the moment Lydia could not remember whom.

Still, it was unusual to hear her mother speak so plainly. Her mother's logic was sound. Lydia knew, better than her mother did, just how ruthless Miss Delacroix was in her pursuit of the earl. There was simply no reason for the scheming little witch to arrange Aldley's abduction of anyone other than herself.

"But what about the carriage? And why did she spill her wine on me, then?"

Her parents did not know what Lydia was talking about, but they patiently described the events surrounding Delacroix's attempt at abducting her.

"Do you not remember that, now?" Her father squeezed her hand.

"Yes, Papa. What you are saying is familiar. And it was all Delacroix, you say?"

"Certainly. The night of the ball, you got into the carriage with Aldley, voluntarily. Just when he had finally located you, someone made off with his mother in another carriage. You both leapt into his carriage and pursued them as fast as you could. Hence the accident. And although I should not mind laying a whipping on the earl for taking such risks with you, I believe his intentions were honourable."

"Yes, that is just what Tilly said. So why do I remember him threatening me with a knife, and trying to… take liberties." She hoped her more salacious thoughts on the topic did not register on her face.

"Do you not think that you are confused from your head injury?" Her mother took her hand. "For it sounds as though you are muddling up the two events."

"Perhaps." There might be something in what they were saying, for she also had a memory of Lord Aldley forbidding her from starting her business, as if he had the right. She had thought, at the time, that it was the end of things.

Such thoughts, and in fact the entire conversation, would be completely absurd if conducted while Aldley attempted to rape her at knife-point. "And I suppose Lord Aldley did not really have a motive to abduct me, did he?"

"No, indeed. Both your mother and I had made it quite clear that we approved of his courting you. And, although I am not happy with you for it, it appears that you told him of the downturn in our fortunes. I can think of no other motive for his interest than love, and no impediment to his marrying you more expeditiously by special license than by abduction. In fact, from everything we have seen of his character, it defies credulity that he would attempt any such compromise. Do you not remember how he purchased Ari so that he could leave the horse in your care?"

"Yes. I do remember." Lydia began to be convinced that she had been confused, that Aldley was perhaps not perfect, but he was kind, and certainly not the monster she was recollecting him to be.

"I think you are right. I must be confusing things." She sighed. "It is very hard to be in doubt of one's own senses. If you do not mind, I need to speak with Tilly. Is she is still near?"

"Of course. We shall send her in." Lydia's father kissed her cheek lightly, followed by her mother.

When Tilly arrived, she could not restrain her joy. "I see you have eaten. It is marvellous to see you so well. Let me pour you some more barley water."

"Thank you." Lydia accepted the cup and drained it. "My dear friend, I believe my mind is playing tricks on me. I need to get my thoughts in order. Will you relate to me, in as much detail as you remember, everything from the day of the ball?"

Tilly complied, also filling in the details of her conference with Miss Grey and discovery of Miss Delacroix's plot to impersonate Lydia, culminating in Miss Delacroix's rolling off in the wrong carriage, locked into a lengthy trip with the boorish Lord Essington.

Lydia laughed with cold, vindictive glee at the fate she supposed Miss Delacroix to have suffered. "Yes, I remember that now. So she got her comeuppance. I suppose I shall require no further vengeance."

"Your being happy with the earl will be the best revenge." Tilly's smirking mouth seemed the wrong messenger for such pious advice.

"As to that, I am not certain we shall suit."

Tilly sighed. "But surely you no longer believe he abducted you?"

"No. I cannot help feeling some fear, still, but my reason is persuaded that you all have the right of it. I am sure that my nerves will calm themselves with time. My body is another matter. And now that I know of your own conduct with Mr. Rutherford..."

Tilly lifted an amused eyebrow, but did not so much as blush.

Lydia licked her lips. "I do not mind admitting to you that I should not object if Lord Aldley tried to ravish me now. However, he has expressed some views which make me believe him highly unsuitable as a husband."

Tilly looked amused. "Such as?"

"He forbade me from starting the hair pomade business." Lydia crossed her arms.

"You told him about that?" Tilly wrinkled her nose in disapproval.

"In general terms, not specifics. When we were in the carriage together, I foolishly decided that it would be better to tell him everything he did not know that might change his mind about me." Lydia could no longer understand why she had thought that necessary at the time.

"Well, I can tell you that *his* mind is not changed. His heart is yours. He is chastened by the experience of almost losing you, and then having your mind so effected that you thought him an abductor. The man is quite beside himself. You could probably make any condition you wish before accepting him." Tilly's face betrayed a deep sympathy for the earl.

"Well, if it is as you say, then there is some hope." Lydia sighed a little bewildered sigh. "I am sorry he is suffering. It is very odd. I think I loved Lord Aldley, before. And before the accident I already wanted to experience *congress* with Lord Aldley. I did not know quite how that was to come about, however."

She paused to think. "And although I have had recent reservations about his character, I longed for him more than ever. Since the accident I feel much more free to pursue my physical inclinations. I only wish they could awaken my feelings again, for my heart is a little befuddled."

"Oh dear. Well, it may be a consequence of the blow to the head." Tilly laughed. "But be careful, my dear, or you will turn into me."

"And whatever would be wrong with that? You are beautiful, brilliant and rich. You live your life in freedom without shame, and apparently without any shade upon your reputation. I should very much like to turn into you—except that I should be better at riding horses and climbing trees."

"Climbing trees?"

"Yes." Lydia shrugged in surrender. "I suppose there is little point in hiding that from you any longer, seeing as we now share much more scandalous secrets about one another."

"Well, actually I had already heard a rumour about that particular oddity." Tilly tilted her head equanimously.

"Really?" Lydia feigned a look of shock. "And you did not sever all ties with me? I am most grateful."

"Think nothing of it." Tilly pressed her fingertips together to form a saintly steeple. "It makes you slightly more interesting. And, as you say, climbing trees pales by comparison to our other secrets. I have no pretences in that direction, or about equestrianism, but I believe I may lay claim to being better at gathering useful resources around me."

"Very true. Some day you will have to tell me all about that." Lydia hoped it would be soon, for she was extremely curious about Tilly's mysterious side.

"I believe I shall. Some day. But at the moment we have more important things to discuss."

Tilly always said things like this, Lydia remarked. Even if it happened to always be true, it was suspiciously evasive. Lydia sat up straight. "Indeed we do. I want to start building my business as soon as might be, assuming Miss Grey will agree to it."

"I think she will. We shall have to arrange a meeting when we return to London. You will find you have a great deal more freedom, once you are an engaged woman."

"Assuming I am engaged. And assuming the man I am engaged to does not try to constrain me." Lydia shifted her right arm to a more comfortable position.

"You will find him very pliable, I am sure. Indeed, the man is smitten and truly contrite."

"If that be the case, I think I shall have him. It is an excellent match, after all." Lydia smiled wickedly.

"I do not believe I have ever heard you speak of *excellent matches* before."

"Yes, but I see things more clearly now. I am altered, and I am not so disinterested as I once was." Lydia was thoughtful. "I do not mean I am now hungry to become a countess or secure his fortune. But I can see now that marrying him will have its advantages. Is that so very bad?"

"You are asking a fallen woman," Tilly reminded her. "However, although I should never think you mercenary for taking the material prospects of your suitor into consideration, I do not think your *heart* is as disinterested as you make it appear."

"Perhaps," Lydia shifted uncomfortably, "but I am having difficulty discerning what my heart might say from my immense attraction to him. Even had I decided not to accept him, I think I should have tried to have him as a—well a *mister*, in the way that you have Mr. Rutherford."

"Recollect that an engaged woman is in a different position from an unengaged woman." Tilly laughed. "I knew I should one day corrupt you, but I had no idea of the extent, or that it should take such a direction. Or, for that matter, that the mode of the corruption would be voyeurism."

"I do not think I shall allow you all the credit. And do you like me better now that you have discovered my vice?"

Tilly cocked her head. "I am not sure. I believe I should find it more diverting if I did not harbour the suspicion that it proceeds from your illness."

"It does not." Lydia thought for a few moments. "I can only attribute to the accident a certain sense of liberty. It is natural that one should come to a few new realisations after a series of near-disasters, is it not?"

Tilly nodded thoughtfully.

Lydia now knew that life gave you what you were willing to squeeze out of it. One simply could not be too squeamish about the means one used to beat away the obstacles to happiness.

She snorted. "If I should have to deal with another Miss Delacroix, henceforth, I should knock her down, and lock *myself* in the back room with Lord Aldley.

"Well then," Tilly laughingly conceded. "If I may give you some very prudent advice, I suggest that you try to conceal these internal urges. If you decide to act upon them, be wily. Let Lord Aldley believe he is seducing you."

"I think I shall have to, as I do not at all know what I am doing."

"That is best. He has an over exaggerated sense of propriety, but he is mad for you." Tilly smirked. "I doubt he will be able to resist temptation."

Lydia recollected the earl's strong shoulders and sweet maddening scent. She swallowed. "I am not certain I shall be able to, either."

"These feelings you have are quite natural, but you must keep them concealed. Hypocrisy is an indispensable tool."

Lydia smiled. It was not the first time she had heard Tilly say as much. Experience told her that her friend was quite right.

She would be discreet. But she needed to explore carnal knowledge with Thomas. She hoped it would help her to understand her heart, for she could remember being in love with him. In truth, no matter how altered she was, she wanted to get those feelings back.

"Let me change the subject. I have something to show you." Tilly walked to a small table near the window and retrieved a stack of papers. "Here are some sketches of a piece of property that has come available in London." She handed them over.

"You mean as a shop front?" Lydia gazed with some scepticism at the sketches of a dowdy looking building.

"My brother found it. At the moment it is not much to look at. But the structure is sound, I am assured, and there are good back rooms where the product could be mixed and jarred."

"But I do not think this looks like a place that would appeal to the customers we are hoping to attract."

"But look at these." Tilly handed over some more pictures. "Frederick drew them."

"I had no idea your brother was so accomplished." Lydia was impressed with the beautiful drawings and the fine detail.

"Indeed, he is—though I admit as a doting sister, I might be a little biased. But you can see he has contrived to expand the windows, and to create interest with a colourful, but tasteful façade."

"I am beguiled. But will it not cost a great deal to make these alterations?" She still had a lot of money concerns to work out.

"It will. And there will be improvements needed in the inner space as well. However, I see this as the next step. You will have already sold many pots of pomade by the time you start work on the shop."

"You have put a great deal of planning into this venture, I almost feel I should hand the entire thing over to you."

"Not at all. The idea was yours, and it was a good one. I have my own projects to attend to." Tilly chortled happily. "Now that we are sharing our mutual shames, I do not mind telling you that I love business. Of course I conduct mine discreetly, as I suggest you also do.

"Still I feel you have done a great deal." Lydia twisted the fabric of the bed sheet. "And we do not even know that Miss Grey will accept my offer."

Tilly shrugged. "If there were no risk, it would not be as exciting. I am sure the property will go up in value soon, for it is just outside of Knight's Bridge, but has been passed over and forgotten. Even if you merely hold it for a year and sell it, you will make money. But as for Miss Grey, she strikes me as a smart young woman. Your offer is good. She will no doubt accept."

"Oh! I am so tired of lying in bed." Lydia fidgeted. "I want to get back to London and start working on things."

Tilly smiled and squeezed Lydia's hand. "Only do not tax yourself too soon. There is a special doctor coming today. Talk to him, first, before you climb out the window and into the mail coach."

"I shall listen to you, Miss Prudence, but only because I can feel how sore my body still is." Lydia wrinkled her nose. "And I have no wish to suffer another prolonged headache."

"Speaking of prolonged headaches," Tilly leaned back in her chair, "I believe there is a pending question of your plans for marriage. Lord Aldley has formally asked your father's permission to propose to you, you know."

"Has he? And what did my father say?"

"I have it from Rutherford that, although your father was still angry about your being embroiled in a most inappropriate carriage chase which almost killed you, he consented."

"I am not surprised. He must be even more desperate for me to make a good match now that I appear to have been compromised."

"Even more desperate?" Tilly's brows perked up.

"Never mind that." Lydia tried to wave her hand as Tilly always did, but was prevented by the pain in her right arm. "It is my father's business."

"Very well." Tilly's nose twitched. "But it seems your father did make the clear stipulation that he would not compel you to marry the earl, if you did not desire it. Nor would he allow Lord Aldley to use your apparently compromised position to press you into marriage."

"He truly said that?" Lydia was impressed. She had the best father in the world.

Tilly chuckled. "You have it third hand, but yes."

"Times like these show who your truest friends are. You, for instance." She smiled at Tilly. "And my father—a wonderful, true-hearted man."

"Yes, yes." Tilly's eyes only betrayed a little sentimentality. "But I hope you will not go maudlin on me now—I was just beginning to enjoy your new found fortitude."

"I am as strong as ever. And I am ready to speak to Lord Aldley."

"Very well. You seem to know what you are about." Tilly stood. "I shall send him in, but first let me lend you my lady's maid. You may have to be firm with him, but you needn't frighten the poor man out of his wits."

CHAPTER 52

*L*ord Aldley had just returned from taking a walk along the few rudimentary paths that ambled off the main road running through town. It was not the most scenic location, but he needed the fresh air and exercise.

All the sitting about in the clean, but depressingly under-decorated, rooms of the inn had tested his nerves to their utmost. The knowledge that Lydia's parents had told her what really happened made his condition worse, for he could not stop wondering why she did not summon him.

He knew he should be more understanding. It was quite natural that she would wish to speak to her best friend, but he could not help feeling slighted and a little jealous of their closeness. Such thoughts were unmanly and beneath him. Aldley knew it.

He tried to dispel them. He reminded himself that Miss Ravelsham was probably his best advocate—aside from Lydia's mother, who, against all expectation, seemed not to blame him in the least for her daughter's present condition.

But if more neutral than Mrs. Norwood, Lydia's closest friend was likely more influential. That was the hope he must cling to.

The door opened and the lady's maid was summoned. He ran his hand over his face and could not restrain an audible groan.

"Do not fret, my lord." Mrs. Norwood came to his side and patted his arm. "She just wants to look presentable for you. It is a very good sign."

Although his recent exposure to Mrs. Norwood had shown her to possess an optimism that bordered on delusion, he could not help feeling a little cheered by her words. Surely it was a good sign, was it not?

"This female preening always takes some time," Mr Norwood added. "Perhaps when Rutherford returns from the village, we can all sit down to a hand of whist."

Mr. Norwood was also apparently feeling sorry for him. Aldley winced. It was mortifying that he cut such a pathetic figure, and yet he could not help but hope that with both her parents in sympathy with him, his suit had some chance.

"Thank you." Aldley nodded. "That is a good idea."

It was a mere quarter hour before Rutherford returned, but he declined whist, saying, "I have a bit of news that will no doubt put cards out of your mind, my friend." He opened a day-old London paper to a certain page and handed it to Aldley.

It was an announcement of the wedding of Sir Gerard Beauchamps to Lady Elizabeth Aldley (nee Halton), formerly The Right Honourable, The Lady Aldley.

Aldley squinted at the announcement. "Good Lord, how can this be? Has that man forced her into an elopement?"

"My Lord, whatever is the matter?" Mr. Norwood inquired.

Aldley handed the paper over to Mr. Norwood, and Mrs. Norwood peered over her husband's shoulder. Lord Aldley settled into a sullen silence as they read.

After they had finished, Aldley took back the paper and folded it, as if to put matters back in order. "I suppose now you may both reconsider allowing your daughter to marry a man whose own middle-aged mother has no scruple but to throw her family into disgrace with an elopement."

"Quite the contrary, my lord," Mr. Norwood demurred. "I have read no news of an elopement—that is to say, the paper only reports that Lady Aldley has wed a respectable gentleman. In any case, our daughter's own situation must make your mother's wedding entirely moot."

"I see your point, and I thank you for your kindly interpretation of these events, but excuse me if I am angered by the situation." Aldley frowned.

He then did not scruple but to launch into an airing of his familial grievances. "I thought I was beyond ever again being astounded by my mother's unequalled hypocrisy. But after all her talk of appearances and stellar matches, she has eloped to Scotland with this Beauchamps character, whom I have met for all of five minutes on the eve of her elopement. I mean, if she wanted to marry the fellow, why not do things properly?"

"Perhaps she thought your lordship would oppose the match." Mr. Norwood meant to be helpful.

"And if I did? She is not a fifteen year old maiden. She may legally marry whomever she wishes. She hardly needs to run off to Gretna Green."

"Now, now, Aldley, we do not know that they went to Gretna Green. Perhaps they favour the fine old churches in Edinburgh." Rutherford slapped Aldley on his good arm.

"Well, eloping to Gretna Green is sort of romantic, really." Mrs.

Norwood's voice was a little dreamy. "Perhaps neither of them ever had the chance to be young and irresponsible."

"Perhaps. And I could wish them happy, if I knew for certain that my mother were a willing participant in the scheme." Aldley found that it was true. He really could wish them happy, as bizarre as circumstances were, if it were a love match. Recent experience had taught him how impulsive love could make a person.

"You still think that she may have been forced into the marriage?" Rutherford looked sceptical.

"It is a possibility." Aldley shrugged. "But I am now in doubt. I have been wondering how anyone could extract her against her will from her own home while she was hosting a rather grand ball. An elopement seems more likely. I shall write her a letter this afternoon to be certain."

Aldley turned to the Norwoods. "But I cannot forget that your daughter has paid the price for their caprice."

The pleasant distraction of this rant was soon followed by a more sombre mood. Aldley took a few moments to write to his mother and summoned a servant to post it. He was then startled out of his brooding by the emergence of Miss Ravelsham and her lady's maid.

"Well, my lord, Lydia is asking to see you." Tilly smiled encouragingly.

"Thank God!" Aldley passed a hand over his face. "But how does she seem?"

"I think you will find she is a little altered, but as charming as ever."

He swallowed. What if Lydia meant to refuse him? His nerves were already frayed and he did not think he could endure it. Aldley patted his neck cloth and stepped into Lydia's chamber.

CHAPTER 53

*L*ydia was sitting up in bed, supported by a cloud of pillows. Her beautiful hair was coiled back into a loose chignon, with a curl adorning each temple. She was dressed in a cream afternoon dress with mauve ribbons at the sleeves, which her mother had apparently brought.

She appeared less pallid than she had before, and her green eyes glistened with a new energy. His breath caught. Even in this weakened state, she was so beautiful. She had a little lace shawl around her shoulders, which she set aside, as she looked up at him.

"Lord Aldley—Thomas. Please come in and sit down. And lock the door, if you will. I believe we have some things to discuss, and I do not wish to be disturbed."

He locked the door and moved a chair close to her bedside, pressing her hand. "Lydia, I cannot tell you how relieved I am to see you better. I have been so plagued by thoughts of our last conversation, by guilt that my pointless pursuit of my mother brought you to harm."

"Please, do not trouble your mind about it. You could not have known that the carriage would overturn. We were not even travelling all that fast, as I recall."

"Fast enough." He grimaced. "To make matters worse, it appears my mother has actually eloped with the man, and was not abducted at all —although I shall have to wait for confirmation from her own account."

"Eloped?" Lydia tried to repress a smile.

"Indeed, her *lately married* found its way into the London papers a couple of days ago. They have it that Sir Gerard Beauchamps is the lucky man."

"Beauchamps! Really?" Her jaw dropped a little, then she recovered herself.

Aldley squinted at her. "You sound as though you know something about this."

"It was a piece of gossip I had heard some time ago. I had almost forgotten about it."

He stiffened. "Well, please do not hold back with me. I should greatly prefer not to be in the dark about my own mother."

"I do not consider it such a great scandal, but apparently the two are not strangers. Mr. Beauchamps was a cousin of your mother's girl-hood friend—when she lived in Warwickshire. They fell in love, but your grandparents opposed the match, as at the time he had little fortune and no title." She paused.

"I can see you are concealing something, please do not feel the need for delicacy."

"Well, one hears that she was either abducted or they attempted an elopement—recent events would suggest the latter. Her father caught up with them, removed her to London and covered the whole mess up. After a year in London your mother was safely married to your father. I suppose it should be *shocking.* I am sure it is an uncomfortable piece of family history for you, but I admit, I think it is a little romantic that they have found each other again, after all these years."

"I suppose it is." Aldley sighed in resignation. "And I suppose it might also explain their choosing to marry in Scotland."

"Making good on their first attempt at marriage? It is rather sweet, really." Lydia privately thought it was also a little silly, but nothing to get upset about.

"You can say that, when the timing of their folly has cost you such an injury?" Aldley could not believe it.

"It was a strange set of circumstances that led up to that accident." Lydia shrugged. "I cannot blame it entirely on your mother's wedding plans."

"You are more forgiving than I." Aldley was relieved.

"I doubt that, but recent events have made me realize how important it is to focus on the things that matter and let go of pointless aggravations." Her smile was tranquil, but he thought he saw some more smouldering feeling register in her look.

"Indeed." He swallowed. "Just so. In fact your wisdom brings me right to the point. I should have told you this long since, and let all the other distractions go to the devil, but I shall tell you now."

He kissed her hand, then looked deep into her eyes. "I love you. I do not deserve you after all my idiocy, but you see before you a man who will come undone if you do not elevate him to the elysian fields by consenting to his proposal. Will you please, please marry me, you maddening, beautiful creature." Aldley's blue eyes willed her to agree.

Lydia's heart was stirred as well as her body. She remained silent, but continued to stare into his eyes as she stroked his hand, letting her finger tips travel up his arm to the *cubital fossa*, where she tickled his delicate skin with tiny butterfly strokes.

He gasped slightly and straightened his cravat with the other hand.

"God, you do not know what you do to me. Dearest, please tell me you will be mine. I want to marry you as soon as may be. I love you so."

She put a finger to her lips. "Shhhhh. Then she played with her lower lip a little, before leaning in toward him slowly and pressing her lips against his surprised, but ready mouth.

He was overcome for a moment and shifted himself onto the bed, so that he could grab her waist as he kissed her firmly.

When he came up for air, she pulled him back again, prodding his mouth gently with her tongue. He answered by pushing his tongue into her mouth, caressing her own.

His body responded, and they were both aware of it. Soon he was lying beside her, pulling her hair loose from its coil, running his fingers though it, kissing the exposed skin around her delicate collarbones.

"You know," she whispered, "I think this dress is a little too tight for an invalid. Perhaps you could loosen it a little."

"Are you sure you would like me to do that, dearest?" He was panting lightly, his voice a bare growl.

"Yes, please."

His hands flew to the cords. When he had sufficiently loosened them, she stretched her torso upwards, so that the top of the gown slid down. "Oh." She assumed a surprised facial expression.

Only her chemise stood between him and her breasts. He could see her pink nipples through the translucent silk. And she could see his erection, which would not be suppressed by the fine cloth of his pantaloons.

"You are killing me, my darling," he groaned.

"Tell me what you want."

"I want all of you."

"You want these?" She traced her fingers around the edges of her rosebud nipples and their hardening was visible.

"Oh yes."

She let her hand pull the material slightly down, as if by accident. Her left breast was fully exposed.

"Mmm." He pulled the other side down and was upon them in a moment, kissing, teasing, licking.

She moaned quietly. "Oh yes. More."

He continued his attentions, until he had to stop himself. He sat up, swallowed, and said "My angel, I am yours, you have my heart. But this is pure torture."

"What can I do?" Her voice was barely audible.

"I—I cannot ask it of you."

"I hate to see you suffer."

"I want you naked under me."

She gestured at her very loose dress. "You want to take this off?"

"Oh yes, I do. But I should not." He let out his breath in a huff of frustration and ran his fingers through his hair.

She reached out and gently pushed his hair back in place, stroking his ear before letting her hand fall back to her lap. Her voice was the faintest of whispers. "You know, I am having such strange feelings." She traced her fingers over her pubis. "Down here. Is that normal? What should I do?"

"God help me." He lifted her as though she were a feather, pulled off her dress, and then more gently lifted her chemise over her head and threw it aside.

He sat for a moment and stared at her naked body, then traced her line of symmetry with his fingertips. Her nipples were flushed and erect.

"You are so beautiful." He was beside her on the bed again, kissing her naked skin, touching her gently between her thighs. "Here?"

"Oh yes. And further up. It is very wet. Is there something wrong?"

"Oh no," he said, finding the right spot with his finger, and suppressing her little squeal with a kiss. "Everything is very right. Oh, you are so wondefully wet." He stroked her randomly a few times, then settled into a rhythm, following the undulations of her body. "Do you like this, darling?"

She nodded, speechless and gasping.

"God how I love you." He kissed her deeply, then sat back to focus on the task of playing with her.

"That feels so amazing. What else do you want to do?" She reached a hand down and grazed his massive erection, as if unintentionally "Maybe you should take these off."

He responded by moving down to position his head over her warm mound and redoubled his efforts using his tongue, relentlessly teasing her, until he could feel how close she was, and then he came up. "I think you are not quite ready for that, my love."

"You have seen me. Do you not wish to show yourself to me?"

"I want more than that," he growled.

Her eyes were wide. "Then show me. Give me more."

"You are maddening, but I do not want to hurt you. Besides your parents are in the next room—and we are not married."

"I shall be quiet. Just satisfy my curiosity."

He took off his clothing. His chest rippled with muscles, and his manhood was protruding. It was very large now. It seemed to strain at her and pulse. He lay down by her again, and she touched him.

"It is marvellous. What should I do?" She petted it lightly, and it responded by growing harder still.

"That is nice, would you like to feel it, down here?" He stroked her a few times with his finger.

"Yes."

He complied, moving his member around to stroke her as he had done with his tongue and finger. She moaned quietly.

"More?"

"Oh yes."

He did it a little faster, and then dipped the very tip of his manhood down a little further, just to the entryway, and pushed it in ever so slightly. She knew instinctively what she wanted.

He moved it back and continued massaging her with it, dipping it back into her chasm on every forth beat, gradually getting a little bit deeper, a little faster, then dipping it in every third stroke, but never going all the way.

∾

SHE COULD FEEL herself getting closer and closer, until finally she grabbed his hips and pulled him inside of her, almost screaming as she convulsed with pleasure. That is what she wanted, him inside of her, and more. She wanted more. She wanted him to feel as she did.

Waves of pleasure continued to course through her, as he plunged into her faster and faster and then stiffened suddenly. She could feel a warmth spreading into her, and his member was spasming as he gasped and kissed her. "Oh, my angel. Oh God yes! I love you."

They lay together silently for a few moments, kissing and stroking each other's skin, holding onto one another. When he finally slid himself out of her, his member was already swelling again.

"I should feel sorry for what I have just done," Aldley whispered, kissing her forehead. "But I do not. I love you so, and I cannot but treasure it. You are so beautiful, so enticing and fascinating. You are my everything."

"That was the most beautiful thing I have ever experienced." Lydia sighed happily. "I do not feel sorry in the least. Do it to me again, please."

He laughed. "I suppose that means I did not hurt you. I was worried. I am told it is often painful the first time."

She looked at him a little mischievously. "You were very gentle." Then she laughed. "Or perhaps it was all that riding astride instead of using a side saddle, as the old matrons always harped about. Had I known how much pleasure I should get from riding you, I believe I should have started sooner. Let us do it again."

He laughed. "You will be the death of me, I can tell. Shall I take that as a *yes?*"

"*Yes* what?"

"You are maddening! *Yes, Thomas Aldley, I love you. I shall marry you and make a respectable earl out of you.*"

She thought for a moment and smiled. "You may take it as a *maybe.*"

His jaw dropped in disbelief.

"But I do love you, Thomas Aldley."

CHAPTER 54

*R*utherford reclined in his bedchamber at the inn and coiled a curl of Tilly's hair around his finger, admiring the multitude of nuances within its golden tone. She sat up and straightened the rumpled sheets of his bed.

"So will you marry me now, Miss Ravelsham?" He kissed her shoulder.

"No. Please consult the minutes of our previous meeting."

"You are as maddeningly inscrutable as your hair colour." He flopped back onto the pillow.

"I am blonde."

"Only superficially." He stared admiringly at her. "There are so many brilliant little hues strewn like gems beneath the surface of that gold."

"You are very poetic." She smiled and kissed him lightly on the cheek. "But you make me out to be more complex than I am. I believe I have been as direct, plain and unambiguous as is possible. If you refuse to take me at my word, it is at your own peril."

"Your words say one thing but your touch, your kiss, your body all say quite another."

She lifted her chin and gave him a pert little smile. "I shall not be made responsible for your wilful misinterpretation of my physiological interest in you. Though I like you a great deal, it is, as I have explicitly told you, purely carnal."

"Oh yes." He pulled her back to him and kissed her deeply. "You have been very explicit, indeed. It is one of your many, many charms."

"Before we get too carried away, I believe the family Norwood and your earl-friend will be returning soon enough. We must make ourselves presentable." She stood up to escape his advances.

"We should not be forced to steal moments if you would just marry me."

"Tedious man. Speaking of which, I understand our mutual friend has not yet accepted Lord Aldley. How is he taking it?"

"The two of you seem bent on toying with your true loves' hearts."

Tilly rolled her eyes and began re-pinning her hair.

Rutherford straightened his pout into a more manly expression. "Well, at least *she* has not refused him outright. She bears that much dissimilarity to her cruel, cruel friend. However, Aldley is smarting, I can tell. He tries to put a brave face upon it, but I know he was hoping for a better answer than *maybe*. I can see his disappointment—but I myself only dream of someday getting a *maybe*, so I cannot feel entirely sorry for the fellow. Still, I hope this has not been the product of *your* influence."

Tilly scoffed. "I have not told her outright that she should accept him, but I believe I have been, at least, encouraging. She has been through a great deal, you know. I think it is wiser for her to take a little time to make such an important decision, although it is clear that she adores him."

Tilly slid up her corset and began to do it up lightly in the front.

"Yes, that is obvious. And it is reciprocal." Rutherford grimaced. "Frankly, I find his mooning about like a love-sick puppy slightly revolting."

Tilly laughed at him. "I know precisely what you mean, Mr. Pot. Mr. Kettle *is* looking rather burnt about the arse. At least Lydia is not so boring, we have plenty of conversations about other things."

"Indeed?" He was a little distracted by watching Tilly twisting the corset round again so the laces were in the back, then shifting all the pinched spots back into place. She threw on her slip and stepped into her dress.

"There I am done, will you fasten my dress in the back, now?"

He sighed heavily, but complied. He wished she had asked assistance with the corset, as he tied the looser constraints of the day dress.

He kissed her shoulder and said, "I am sure he will get a hold of himself when he is back in town and engaged in his regular activities. Out here he scarcely has anything else to dwell upon."

"True, and that may be soon. The London doctor said Lydia may be removed to town in a few days, if it is done slowly."

Rutherford frowned. "I cannot say I am thankful. What will happen to our little tête-à-têtes when we leave this place?"

"You are a single man with a large house in London." Tilly straightened his hair. "And I am an engaged woman living in London with significant resources. I am sure we shall get on quite well. Now, can you not put some trousers on, my darling stallion?"

CHAPTER 55

*A*ldley sat in the gloomy light of the breakfast room. It was a rainy, grey day. The dome of his head was cracking like the egg of some hellish beast. And the fledgeling claws of a headache were scratching about inside his skull. Sleepless nights were taking their toll.

He was glad to think they would all be leaving after breakfast. A return to London would at least distract him from his suit of Lydia, which was proceeding ambiguously. What was worse was that she seemed entirely unromantic, and focused solely on the business side of the marriage.

According to her father, Lydia was adamant that the settlement of fifty thousand—a much larger sum than he had expected—should become available to her immediately upon their marriage. Aldley had not the least objection. But why was she so insistent?

Lydia entered the breakfast parlour and she smiled so brightly at him that he thought the sun had finally come out. "Thomas! Good morning."

"Good morning, my angel. Did you sleep well?"

"To be honest, no. I find my sleep quite disturbed." She lowered her eyelids slightly.

"I suffer the same fate, I am afraid. But you could improve things if you would just consent to marry me, instead of leaving me hanging."

"I am sorry to hear of your discomfort. My own sleep disturbances proceed from an entirely different quarter." She cocked her head and smiled at him.

"Oh really?"

"Yes. I cannot stop thinking about our little *discussion* the other day, in which you were not *left hanging* at all, except perhaps at the very end of things." She sniffed at a weedy looking flower in a vase on the table, and looked up at him over the petals.

"Careful, my dear." He could feel himself hardening at the mention of it. Though he was, in part, thankful that they had not had much time alone since, he was also frustrated by it. They would have a very enthusiastic honeymoon, if he could just get her to marry him.

"I do not want to be careful." She gave him a mischievous smile. "I want to further explore the topic of our conversation."

He stepped close to her and put an arm around her waist, pulling her in for a deep kiss. When they both emerged, breathless, he thought there would be no way of concealing his arousal should someone enter the room.

He tried to mentally calm himself. "I think you know what you have to do if you want to peruse the finer details of that topic."

"Marry you."

"Yes. And honestly, why not? You know that you must, now, anyway."

"I do not think I *must*, exactly. And in any case, clearly it is possible to indulge in such subject matter without matrimony." Her smile was now openly wicked.

"This is a scandalous line of talk." Aldley tried to suppress his own grin. "I hope you are not proposing—"

"A counter offer? Not exactly. I was just pointing out your false assumption. In any case..." She played with the hair around his collar. "There really is only one impediment to our marriage, from my perspective."

"And what would that be?" He stared into her eyes, searching.

"I am not certain that you would be willing to give me the freedom I need."

"I have no wish to oppress you. Surely you do not think that of me."

"I mean the freedom to conduct my own business."

He rubbed one temple with his thumb. "You mean to engage in trade."

"More or less, yes. I do not plan on running the shop myself, but I do intend to own one, at a distance. And I shall be directing the business, but discreetly. Can you accept that?" Her green eyes sought out his own, and fixed him with a look of earnest inquiry.

"I do not know why you are so stubborn about this point." He gave her nipple a little stroke through the fabric of her dress. "When we marry, you will have a large settlement that you may invest, and extremely generous pin money, above and beyond your personal expenses. I shall give you anything you ask for. It simply is not necessary for you to begin hawking wares on the street."

"You assume I am doing it out of a desperate motive, but I am not. It may be hard for you to understand, because you are a man and you have always had your freedom. But try to imagine what it is like to be a woman, to be expected to sink your time into pointless activities to show your merit, instead of being able to prove yourself on the same playing field as others—as men. Would you not find that frustrating? Would you not long to build something for yourself?"

He kissed her hand. "I can understand your motives. I even see them as quite elevated. But you would be the wife of an earl, hopefully the mother of an earl. Society is just not ready to accept that the upper classes, particularly women of the nobility, should engage in certain activities."

She lifted her chin. "I reject the chains they would put me in."

"Then they will reject you." He shrugged.

"I do not care for their acceptance, but you are assuming I am incapable of being discreet. If I am a rich countess, and the business is conducted by my trustee, will anyone look too closely?" She raised a brow. "Will they not prefer to be on friendly terms with us?"

"No doubt, but everyone has enemies. You should also consider how your actions might affect the prospects of your children." His hand moved involuntarily to her stomach.

"I am thinking of them. How many noblemen do you know of, who scarcely can keep their fires burning and their household supplied with candles, because of their parents' mismanagement, and because they lack the wherewithal, and the gumption, to earn anything for themselves?"

He sighed. "I know enough of them. But our children," he pulled her close again and looked into her eyes, "one of which you could now be carrying, I might add, will never want. I have not frittered away my fortune. In fact, I have added to it."

"So you see?" She looked up at him, hopefully. "You know what it is to engage, perhaps even a little too closely for the ton's liking, in making your own money. You are not one to rest on your laurels. Can you not understand why I should want that for myself?"

"I can." He kissed her hair. The smell of violets made his heart pound. "And if anything it makes me love you more, for you are a true rarity. You are so precious. All I want to do is to take care of you, to protect you, to love you and our children. But I can see you will have your own way. And since I clearly cannot resist you," he took in the curve of her breasts with his gaze and gave her bottom a squeeze through frustrating layers of fabric, "I suppose I must comply with your most unreasonable demands."

She rewarded him with her most dazzling smile. "Good."

"But this having your way with a fellow and then refusing his proposal is bargaining in bad faith, you know. I cannot risk my child's future, after all." He patted her belly.

"I think you are leaping to a wild surmise that there is any such offspring to begin with. But as long as you will give me my freedom, I am willing to comply with your most reasonable demand."

"Are you saying yes?"

"Yes."

He crushed her into him and kissed her for several minutes.

"Pardon me. I thought this was the breakfast parlour." Mr. Norwood stood in the doorway with one bushy eyebrow raised and a paper tucked under his arm. Rutherford and Tilly appeared behind him.

Aldley beamed at Lydia's father. "It is the room in which your daughter has made me the happiest of men."

"Oh thank God!" Mr. Norwood and Rutherford said at the same time.

"Indeed!" Tilly kept a straight face, but her eyes twinkled at Lydia. "After a kiss like that, you had better be getting married."

CHAPTER 56

*W*hen Lydia was finally returned to London, she found herself stupidly busy with matters she considered unimportant.

If she was not being fitted for her trousseau, her mother dragged her off to this and that parlour to call on what seemed like their entire acquaintance, so that they might partake in the joyous news.

She had always found such calls tedious, but they had become even less interesting since her accident. She knew her mind had changed, and her tolerance for boredom was now quite low. But she also knew that she needed to master this internal dissatisfaction.

When she became a countess, social calls would be an important part of her future—though she would principally be receiving them, at first.

It was not something she was looking forward to, but on the other hand, as a countess and mistress of her own household, she would be much more able to be 'not at home.'

And there would be other benefits to marrying Thomas that would quickly chase away the ennui of receiving guests. She wondered how long they might honeymoon for.

Thomas and she had gone to call on Lady Goodram almost as soon as they arrived in London. They wished to give her the earliest news, to thank her for introducing them, and to personally hand her the invitation to their wedding, which was to be the following week.

Lady Goodram expressed her joy and announced that she would not ·miss the wedding for all the world, though it meant a tedious carriage ride to Nesterling, where the two planned to be married in the estate's small chapel.

But now, with all the social calls completed, Lydia intended to get down to business. She had a lot to accomplish before the honeymoon that would take her away from London. Tilly and she had planned an outing–though the true intention was a meeting with Miss Grey and their lawyers.

Tilly was right, one of the advantages of being an engaged woman was that she had more freedom. This was especially true because, having acquired for her mother an earl as a future son-in-law, Lydia could now do no wrong.

She could slouch, sigh, drink red wine or brandy and even openly discuss business matters with her father. Her mother only smiled sweetly and caressed her daughter's hair, giggling gleefully to herself. It was mostly pleasant and only faintly disturbing.

When Tilly arrived, Lydia was full of energy.

"You are looking radiant, Lydia. I believe engagement agrees with you." Her friend was also looking especially fetching in a pale blue day dress and matching bonnet.

"I find it is rather good for the circulation. And the most trying part is over. I believe we have now finished calling on or entertaining anyone in London with whom we have the least connection."

"Not quite. There is one more person you should call upon." Tilly gave Lydia a mysterious look.

"Is that so?" Lydia was accustomed to her friend's love of the dramatic.

"Yes, but I shall keep you in suspense, for we must be off immediately if we are to be on time."

When they were tucked into the rose and lemon-scented carriage, Tilly continued. "So do you wish to know who we should call upon on our way home?"

Lydia looked perplexed. "I have been trying to guess and I honestly cannot imagine."

"It is my brother—mostly because we should talk a bit about the plans for improvements to the shop."

"Yes, I suppose it is not too soon to discuss it with him, though I should like to have the builder present so we can discuss costs." Lydia knew she would be coming into a great deal of capital soon, but she meant to be wise in her expenditures.

"Next time. The second reason we should call on him is so that you might wish joy to him and his new wife." Tilly looked merry.

"New wife? He has married? Good Lord! A lot must have happened while I was sleeping."

"If only you knew." Tilly wiggled her brows.

Lydia shook her head in bewilderment. "Indeed, I did not even know that he was engaged."

"It was a brief engagement, though the lady is someone whom he has admired from afar for some time. I believe he thought the case was hopeless and should never have proposed at all, except that an opportunity presented itself."

"This all sounds quite romantic." Lydia tried to keep a dismissive tone out of her voice. She still loved romance in her heart, but after much thought on the topic, she had decided that it often disguised a trap, especially for women.

"Oh it is, really." Tilly squirmed happily in her seat. "They were married in the same little chapel where she was baptised. Is that not sweet?"

"Yes. As you know, that is also my plan. So I assume it was an intimate ceremony, then."

"Quite, but I know such things bore you to tears, so I shall not beleaguer you with lengthy descriptions." Tilly was very forbearing. "Suffice it to say that Frederick is radiantly happy and cannot believe his good luck."

"So what was the nature of the opportunity which presented itself so propitiously?" Lydia could not help being curious.

"Well, I shall tell you, only you must promise never to breathe a word of it to anyone—in fact even we two should not speak of it after this, just to be safe." Tilly's earnest face only inflamed Lydia's curiosity.

"Is it really as secret as that?" Lydia laughed. "But, very well. I shall add it to our growing collection of things to keep concealed from society. Do go on."

"She was, you see, in a most difficult situation, having spent a great deal of time alone in a confined space with a man who could not marry her. Although nothing happened, if word of it had got out, she would have been ruined. But Frederick happened to be quite willing to ask for her hand to pre-empt any gossip and to save her reputation. Her brother, who is the head of the family, was also quite pleased with Frederick and found his easy circumstances a bounteous addition to an already compelling argument for their marriage." Tilly looked a little too pleased with herself.

Lydia squinted suspiciously. "And is she happy? Was she willing to accept him?"

"Yes, only too willing. You know, a great deal of the consideration must have been expedience and prudence, but on the other hand she would not be the first young lady to find herself in love with a man who stepped in to rescue her when she thought all was lost."

"You have a point, there." Lydia nodded. "A great deal may be built upon a foundation of gratitude."

"That is just what I think. In fact that is why I believe that cultivating gratitude by helping people when they least expect it, or are most in despair, is a very good way to develop one's personal resources."

"I suppose." Lydia was not entirely convinced. "So is this lady some mysterious heiress he met in the Lowlands?"

"Not at all. In fact, you are acquainted with Mrs. Ravelsham, nee Delacroix."

Lydia's face blanched. "Now I know you must be toying with me. You cannot mean that snake has married your brother."

"Indeed she has," Tilly raised her hands in a calming gesture, "and your reaction is why I thought it best to discuss it somewhere where we would not be overheard."

Lydia glared accusingly at her friend. "You waited until we were locked in a carriage so I could not storm off. You planned this match. You were the only other person who knew about her carriage ride with Essington. This marriage is entirely your arrangement. Admit it!"

"I might have assisted Miss Delacroix out of her embarrassing situation. Oh come now, I could not just leave her with that beast of man. Who knows what might have happened to her?"

"Essington is crippled." Lydia scowled.

"Nonetheless, the ordeal and the risks were very real. As awful as Miss Delacroix was to you," Tilly conciliated, "you cannot wish *that* upon another woman."

"No, not wish it upon her." Lydia scowled. "But I believe I should have been content to leave her to the fate that she brought upon herself by trying to destroy my happiness."

"I do not think she was trying to destroy yours, so much as craft her own. That is a very different thing. I know that she did wrong, but in a way, she is the reason you are about to marry Lord Aldley. Can she not also have some small happiness?" Tilly's voice was pleading.

"No, she cannot."

"And what of my poor, lovesick brother? Should he also have lost his chance at happiness?"

"I see you are trying to prey upon my sentiments, but it shall not work." Lydia raised her chin. "I cannot believe that you have chosen that conniving witch over your best friend."

"I did not choose her over you." Tilly raised her shoulders as if to shrug off culpability. "I simply helped her out of a difficult situation that would have ruined her. And I helped my brother at the same time."

"And he really loves her?"

"To hear him speak of it, he is absolutely besotted and extremely happy."

Lydia pressed her lips together. "And I suppose you have not told him how she ended up in that carriage."

"I thought it better for her to explain it in her own way." Tilly played with a ringlet.

"In other words, with a lie. Well that is a sound start to any marriage. Still, none of it is your brother's fault."

"He is only guilty of falling in love." Tilly bobbled her head in a *c'est la vie* sort of way that made Lydia wish to squash every single one of her bonnets.

"I shall be civil to her only for your brother's sake, and because I expect he and I shall be working together quite a lot during the improvements, for I love his ideas for the shop. Do not ask more of me." Lydia frowned at her friend.

"What more could I ask?" Tilly beamed. "I am so glad. You will not regret it, my dear friend!"

"I only hope *you* do not someday regret inviting that lady viper to slither into your family."

"She is forever in our family's debt." Tilly waived a hand. "And in yours too, for she must have surmised you have puzzled out her plot against you. She is also indebted to you for keeping quiet about what you know."

"I suppose that cannot hurt, but I shall not assume she is finished scheming against me. She seems quite up to anything."

"I think now that she is married to a very rich man who gives her whatever she wants, she will be content. True, I believe all will be well." Tilly patted her friend's hand.

Lydia made no reply but gave her mouth a doubtful twist.

The meeting went perfectly. Miss Grey, having decided to accept the business offer, was highly energetic and quite ready to start immediately. This suited Lydia very well.

The business decisions would appear to come from her lawyer, so that it was never apparent that Lydia was directly involved in the business. They threshed out the first steps and immediately made plans to procure ingredients and other supplies.

Tilly was given the task of selecting the crystal jars, as she was so strongly in favour of their being irresistibly opulent. Though Miss Grey was scandalized when she heard the approximate price, she did not violently object, as it was Lydia's investment.

All seemed fair and ready, and the papers were signed. They were prepared to start making *Miss Grey's Exquisite Hair Pomade*. Initially, Miss Grey would sell it to the ladies she coiffed, for they would inevitably enquire after the product when they saw the handsome crystal pots.

When they were into profit, they would start thinking about other products they could sell, and make the improvements to the store. Lydia was in such a good mood when they left, that she thought nothing could dampen her spirits.

"Shall we drive by the property on the way?" Tilly suggested.

"Yes, I should like to see it in person." Lydia stared out the carriage window, smiling to herself and imagining the improvements to her new store.

Tilly interrupted her thoughts by announcing, "I have an idea for an assistant to you."

"Who would that be?"

"Well, I do not suppose you remember Mary Wheeler?"

Lydia thought the name sounded familiar. "I can remember hearing the name, but I am not sure where."

"I suppose that might be just as well. However, I think you would remember her face, so I shall tell you. She is the hench-woman that my new sister-in-law hired to take your dress and lock you in a disused room on the night of the Aldley Ball."

"Yes. I certainly remember her." Lydia shook her head in dismay at her friend. "I suppose you are just bent on darkening my mood, is that it?"

"Not in the least. Only think how motivated she will be to do a good job."

"I can just imagine. She did a bang up job for her former mistress."

"Well, she did more or less fulfil her duties, with some modifications."

Tilly assumed an air of sympathy. "You must consider that she only agreed to do it because she needed money for her sick mother."

"I see." More of Tilly's saintly redemption schemes. "I do not suppose you have another brother you can marry off?"

Tilly raised her open palms to her shoulders and said, "Alas, I have exhausted my supply of marriageable brothers."

"So you must turn to me for a fresh victim," Lydia scoffed. "And have you met this ostensible mother?"

"I have been a bit busy attending my brother's wedding and visiting with my invalid friend in the middle of God-knows-where." Tilly paused to assume a look of martyrdom.

She recovered her worldly sense shortly, and continued, "However, I have had someone look into it. The woman exists. She was on the point of losing her tenement, for she was too sick to work. Wheeler has now moved her mother to a more wholesome location and cares for her on the money she got from Genevieve and me."

"Genevieve, is it?" Lydia spoke through clenched teeth.

"You cannot expect me to call her *Mrs. Ravelsham*."

"Surely you could use something less formal, but still appropriate, like *nasty little piece who tried to steal my friend's fiancé?*"

Tilly placed a finger to her lip and paused for thought. "Too long to be practicable."

"How about *shit-face?*"

"I think it might be badly received. Perhaps *dearest sister* would be more *pro forma*," Tilly suggested, helpfully.

"So long as you are thinking *shit-face* whenever you say it."

"That would, I am persuaded, also be *pro forma*."

Lydia shook her head. "And what am I to do with this Wheeler woman?"

"Hire her to work for you at the shop. If you are pleased with her, she can also run errands and act as your agent in things. She can be your secretary."

"Can she read?"

"No," Tilly raised an interjecting finger, "which will be advantageous, if you do not trust her."

"I do not." Lydia huffed. "But I do not know who would hire a secretary who cannot read and write. And I am beginning to seriously question your judgement."

"You must take my word for it. People you could send to the nick, but whom you nonetheless have given decent employment, make excellent workers. They are extremely loyal and will do almost anything you ask."

"I think I should prefer to hire only people who have never attempted to forcibly confine me." Lydia shook her head. "Perhaps I am too nice about qualifications." She was not sure she liked this strange other side of Tilly.

When they arrived at the location, Lydia felt too disheartened to disembark. She merely peered out the window. "Good Lord, it is hideous. And even filthier and more run-down looking than the sketches indicated."

"A lot of the impression derives from the surrounding buildings. And from the dust, too, but it comes from construction. Look, that one is under improvements." Tilly gestured to a store front two doors down, with a crumbling façade, a missing front window, and a ladder propped against it. "A good sign is it not? Remember things must get worse to get better."

"I suppose. Do you think there is a general intention to improve the area?"

"Perhaps not *general*, just yet. But I believe two shops on the street making improvements is a good start."

"I shall come back to look inside another day when I am dressed for it. In the meantime, let us go call on your brother and his snake-wife and get it over with. I must be home early enough to dress for dinner. My betrothed is to join us." Lydia licked her lips.

"I myself have plans for the evening," Tilly looked demure. "So we shall keep the call mercifully short."

When they entered the sitting room, it was apparent that the new Mrs. Frederick Ravelsham was making extensive use of her husband's money.

She sat in a gleaming gold gown which was technically a day dress, but whose level of ostentation was only exceeded by that of the lady's jewellery. Thumb-nail-sized rubies, Lydia noted to herself, should not be hauled out for tea.

After they had made their greetings and felicitations, Genevieve, as they were now to call her, rang for tea. The peacock plumes dangling from her cap bobbed insanely around her face as she shook the bell.

"My husband will be with you shortly. But I am so glad we have a chance for a snug little chat amongst ourselves." She giggled. The woman seemed manic.

"Your ring is exquisite, Genevieve." Tilly leaned over to inspect the proffered hand. "I was so disappointed not to see it before the wedding, but my brother showed me the design. The craftsmanship was worth the wait."

"He spoils me so." Genevieve fluttered her lashes.

"Such a large diamond," was all Lydia could add before her mouth became dry.

"Oh indeed. It positively hurts my hand." Genevieve smiled and turned the ring this way and that to watch it glisten. "But I love to look at it and think about the wonderful man who gave it to me."

"Oh yes, the sentimental value must be the greatest thing." Tilly kept a straight face, but Lydia knew her friend was trying to make her laugh.

"I understand you are also soon to be wed, Miss Norwood. And to the earl, too! And even his mother none the wiser, you sly thing. Though it turns out that she had her own wedding plans." Genevieve gave them a sidelong glance.

"Indeed." Lydia wondered how the woman could possibly broach this subject with her, of all people, and pretend to be all innocence. Such gall was unparalleled. "There are others much more sly than me. I do not think our engagement came as a surprise to *everyone*."

"Certainly not a surprise to you two sweethearts, in any case." Genevieve contrived to giggle at this comment. "Still it was rather sudden—are you not to be wed next week?"

"Yes we must wait that long. We do not have the planning mastery that you and Mr. Ravelsham possess, or we should have contrived to get married before we had even met." Lydia meant it as a barb, but in a way it was true. She had experienced a singular attraction to Thomas before she had even seen his face.

"Yes, well, it is true we did manage rather a miracle. I must thank you for being such a help, Mathilde." Genevieve's voice was syrupy. "I could not ask for a sweeter, more attentive sister."

Lydia had to consciously extend her fingers so as to avoid forming fists of them.

"It was my pleasure, but you have already thanked me, *my dearest sister*." Tilly turned her face and winked at Lydia on the side that Genevieve could not see.

Then Tilly addressed Lydia directly, "And how shall you like being a countess, Miss Norwood?"

"I suppose I shall like it very well." Lydia was satisfied to see a little vein bulge in Genevieve's pallid, stiffening neck. "It is generally reckoned pleasant to be of the nobility, is it not? But it was not my reason for marrying Lord Aldley. He is handsome, accomplished, brilliant, and has the most charming manners. How could I avoid loving him?"

Genevieve played with her earrings, and forced a smile. "Quite."

"Oh indeed. You are marrying for love, no matter how advantageous the match might be." Tilly said it in exactly the same tone as she had spoken of the sentimental value of Genevieve's horse-choking diamond.

Was her friend making a sly criticism? Lydia faltered. "Indeed, I... I do not know of any other good reason for marrying."

The tea arrived and Genevieve rallied. "Well, that is very romantic! I wish I were offering champagne now instead of mere tea, for truer words have not been spoken."

She lost her words, then added suddenly, fidgeting with the table cloth, "Oh, but why should we not have champagne?" She giggled. "My husband has a whole cellar full of it—we have so many wine cellars. Why, I could bathe in champagne if I wanted. Mills, bring us a bottle and glasses."

"Yes, indeed." Tilly raised her tea cup. "Well, until the champagne arrives, here is to marrying for love!"

She knew that Tilly was savouring the spectacle, but Lydia could not understand why. This woman was married to her brother, and she had arranged it, though it was obvious that the pretty viper only cared about his money. Lydia was extremely glad when they left.

When they were settled in the carriage to leave, Lydia said, "You seemed to be enjoying yourself."

"I admit it. Those earrings! Oh and ordering champagne for tea time!" Tilly cackled. "Utterly grandiose and vulgar. And we are the *nouveau riches*, mind!"

Tilly chuckled to herself a few moments. "But I adore champagne, and thoroughly enjoyed the hypocrisy of indulging my own bad taste under the guise of being polite to the hostess. Gave it a little extra sparkle. Marvellous! Genevieve supplies me with endless diversion."

Lydia's lips formed a disapproving line. "I do not see how, when it is clear she only loves your brother's money."

"But he believes a deeper connection is possible in time." Tilly massaged a scented sachet, and inhaled the fragrance. "Why should not I? After all, we have been given to understand that many a good marriage has been built on less."

Lydia snorted. "I think we both know that is just another fairy story made up by society."

"Perhaps," Tilly gave her head a philosophical tilt, "but they are both happy for their separate reasons. Who are we to judge?"

Lydia supposed she was not in a position to judge. She had seduced her fiancé before she had the intention to marry him. Viewed strictly in the light of what was correct, or even tacitly permissible, and what was not, these newly-weds were in the right, and she was in the wrong.

But she did not accept society's way of thinking. She felt no pang of guilt. If anything, the thought of it made her want more. If they had a chance before the wedding, she would gladly do it again.

Lydia sighed. "Now that this first call is over with, I hope I shall not have to see her again often."

"I suppose it will be possible to avoid seeing her every time you wish to speak to my brother. But that is not what you were thinking of just now. I recognize that look. You were thinking of your betrothed." ⬗

Lydia smiled. "Yes, I was. I admit there is really nothing that drives him entirely from my mind. I do not know what I should do with myself if I were not marrying him."

"I am sure you would sort it out." Tilly grinned wickedly. "Speaking of which, I have a gift for you." She pulled out a small block wrapped in paper.

"What is it?"

"It is a manual, of sorts. Be very careful with it and only unwrap it when you are somewhere that you will not be disturbed."

"A book? Is it seditious?"

"In a manner of speaking." Tilly wiggled her brows. "If you get caught with it, you must say that you found it in the rooms at the inn where you convalesced. You did not receive it from me, and I know nothing about it. Agreed?"

"Certainly. But what is it?" Lydia was puzzled.

"Do you recall when you asked me to teach you about certain things?"

"Yes." Lydia did not even blush.

"This is your primer. If you have any questions you can ask me, or perhaps your future husband, if he is not too prudish."

"He appears at first glance to be frustratingly proper. But upon further acquaintance, I do not believe I should call him prudish." Lydia smiled slyly.

"Is that right?" Tilly's eyebrows almost disappeared into her bonnet. "Well, well."

Her friend was chuckling as they rolled up to Lydia's home. Lord Aldley was waiting and opened the door to the carriage.

"Ah there you are at last, my darling. It is most unkind of you to keep her from me for so long, Miss Ravelsham." Aldley paused and looked at the two broad smiles. "You two look like the cat that got the cream."

They both burst out laughing.

CHAPTER 57

*A*fter dinner that evening, Lydia's parents decided to let Thomas and Lydia go through to have their brandy alone, for Mr. and Mrs. Norwood *had some important matters to discuss* and would join them shortly.

"This is one of the great advantages of being engaged." Thomas stroked one of her nipples through her gown as he planted a kiss on her lips. "People will actually contrive to leave us alone."

"Not for long enough, unfortunately. I suppose my parents wish to keep things as proper looking as possible, given the amount of scandal we have only just evaded in this past month."

"Yes, but it is not unheard of for an engaged couple to go out to see their future home together." He played with her hair. "Would you not like to see Alderwick Manor before we are married?"

"I believe that would make for a pleasurable trip."

"Oh yes. I could make it very pleasurable. And, after all, the future Lady Aldley should get a little taste of what is to come."

"Yes." Lydia was breathless. "She should get as much as she can. There are some things she would very much like to taste." She brushed her hand over his member. "And after all, getting acquainted with everything in advance will better prepare her for her wifely duties."

"Mmm. I think there is something I should prefer to this brandy."

"Indeed? Do tell. You know as your fiancée I should be most attentive to your desires."

"Is there somewhere more private we could discuss my desires?"

"That closet over there is rather large. Would that be acceptable?"

He smiled. "It will do. Never let it be said that I am inflexible." He pulled her close to him and kissed the entire length of her neck, then took her hand and steered her toward the closet.

In the darkness he kissed her deeply.

"We do not have much time, so we shall have to be much faster than I should like to be, my love."

The sound of his beautiful voice in the darkness made her shivery. She lifted up her skirts, and guided his hand to her womanhood. She was already wet.

"Oh you dear, dear goddess. You are a fountain of ambrosia."

"I have been thinking of you all through dinner. What do you propose to do about it?"

He began to stroke her. She gasped. "Oh God yes."

He dropped his pantaloons and guided her hand to his member. It was hot and fully erect. "I propose that I thrust this into you repeatedly until you scream—but not too loudly."

"I believe that is one proposal I can accept immediately."

The possibility of being discovered made it more exciting, as he continued to tease her, and then began to stroke her with his throbbing manhood.

"Oh yes, give me more!"

He lifted her up by the waist and pinned her to the wall, thrusting his cock into her part way. "Are you all right, my angel?" he gasped.

"I shall be even better when you give me all of you."

So he did, thrusting into her slowly at first, and when she moaned with pleasure driving her a little harder, a little faster, until he was sure the whole household must be able to hear the thumping on the wall.

But he didn't care. She was so hot and wet and beautiful, he could smell the sweet honey scent of her hair and he had to hold back.

She began moaning and gripping his buttocks to pull him closer, deeper inside of her. It was all he could do to hold on until he heard her stifled scream, "Oh Thomas, God yes!" and felt her shudder with pleasure.

Then his whole mind turned to steam and he let himself go, thrusting so hard and fast that her head shook.

"Oh God! I love you!" He thrust deep inside her, filling her with his heat until he had no more.

He held her there for a while, and then they both collapsed, giggling, onto the floor.

"Shhhh. We must hurry, my love." He kissed her. "Let us get ourselves straightened before your parents come through."

CHAPTER 58

*B*eams of morning light filled the chapel at Nesterling Lodge as the happy couple left through an archway of ivy ornamented with white roses. Lydia wished that she felt more sentimentality about the wedding.

She loved the wedding present her father had given her before the ceremony. It was a fishing rod from his collection, the one he had lent her when he tried to teach her to fish before her second season in town.

"Something borrowed," he had said. She would never forget the tears glistening in his eyes as he gave it to her. She had kissed his cheek and promised him they would go fishing together every summer.

Yes, her heart was moved by the cluster of family and friends who assembled to see them wed and wish them joy, but she could not help feeling a little sad that she no longer had that sense of romance about it.

The wedding was merely another obstacle in the excruciatingly long process of getting to be alone with Thomas, to having his luscious body all to herself. No more stolen moments. White dresses and floral arrangements be hanged.

Tilly and Rutherford walked behind them. Her dear friend kissed Lydia before she was handed up to the glistening coach, now sporting the Aldley colours. "I wish you great joy, Lady Aldley," Tilly whispered. "Although it be entirely unnecessary for me to do so."

"Thank you, my good friend, but I am always Lydia to you. And I could not be happier, now that this blasted wedding is finally done with."

"I doubt that. You will go from bliss to ever greater bliss." She gave a little quirk of the mouth.

Lydia put a hand on Thomas' shoulder, smiled at him and then drew Tilly aside, where they would not be heard. "You have equipped me well for blisses. I must thank you, again, for that book, and for explaining so much to me. But tell me, truly, some of those positions are simply impossible, are they not? The authors must have been having a lark."

Tilly pulled a face and said, "The one on page forty-seven absolutely must be, I think. But who knows? With a contortionist anything might be possible."

Lydia laughed. "And do people actually talk that way during bed sport?"

"That and worse," Tilly assured her. "Or better, depending upon how you look at it. But as you are now married for better *or* for worse, I suppose you may say whatever makes you happy."

Lydia sighed, "I am already very happy."

Tilly looked mischievous. "Perhaps I could augment that happiness just a little by telling you that it appears a grave misfortune has befallen your enemy."

"Whatever can you be speaking of?"

"Mr. Delacroix has been abducted."

Lydia squinted in disbelief. "How is it possible?"

"He seems to have been not entirely unwilling," Tilly's lips curled. "For he stole all the jewellery and half of the silver in his brother's home before the event."

"But who on earth..."

"Miss Dervish, if you can believe it."

"Miss Dervish!" Lydia shook her head for several moments. "Now I think I must be dreaming."

"You are a countess now, so I shan't make free to pinch you. You are not dreaming, but it seems that the young lady's circumstances are not at all what we were led to believe."

"No?"

"And what is better," Tilly laughed, "Mr. Delacroix will soon discover they are not what *he* was led to believe either. He thinks he has pulled the wool over her eyes by selling off his brother's property so as to appear flush with blunt. He thinks he is marrying an heiress."

"But she is not?" Lydia prompted.

"She is a common swindler. Well, an uncommon swindler, if we take her beauty into account. She simply does not look like a commoner. Nor does she sound like one, so I think she must be quite clever. But she was found out and had to leave London hastily, but made a stop at Dunston. Mr. Delacroix has disappeared, whisked off in her carriage. Genevieve is quite beside herself, but my brother has consoled her by letting her pick out a wardrobe of fur capes."

"No doubt she will exercise all the elegant restraint of good taste." Lydia pressed her lips together. "But was Delacroix not still too ill to travel?"

"I suppose if he were well enough to rob his brother's house, he is sufficiently recovered for a little travelling. In any case, it is hard to say where he will show up, but even if she were an heiress, she could never marry him."

"Why not?"

"Because the man posing as her father is actually her husband!" Tilly broke out laughing loudly, then remembering where they were, hushed herself. "Is that not perfect? I suppose swindling people is the family business. But why do you frown so? Is this not highly diverting news?"

Lydia crossed her arms. "I am just wondering if you are planning on chasing after him and marrying him off to one of your cousins."

"You are tiresome harping on about that. But not at all, I assure you. Mr. Delacroix is beyond my redeeming. He is what we do-goods call *incorrigible*."

"I am greatly relieved to hear you say it." Lydia smiled and kissed her friend's cheek. "I believe I may permit myself to be diverted now."

"Well, then, off with you. You have an heir to conceive." Tilly wiggled her brows for good measure.

"I believe I shall need a good deal of practice first." Lydia smiled at her friend as though butter would not melt in her mouth, and then returned to the carriage to let herself be handed in.

Aldley was drumming his fingers as she entered. "Well, I seem always to be waiting for you, darling. You are very cruel." He drew her into his lap and wound a ringlet of her hair around his finger.

In reply, she only kissed him very deeply.

When they were safely across the threshold at Alderwick Manor and locked into their chambers that evening, she pulled a book out of her trunk and handed it to him. "It is my wedding gift to you."

"A book?" He began to leaf through it, and a flush came to his cheeks.

"Not the book so much as the contents of the book." She pulled the pins out of her hair.

"Oh really? You are familiar with the contents of this book?" He reached out and assisted her until he was rewarded by cascades of thick red curls tumbling wildly about. A stupid grin spread over his face.

"I have been diligently doing my research so that I might be a good wife." She gave him a chaste little smile.

"You are so dutiful. I might call it pious, if it did not make me want to rip this wedding dress off of you and tie you up with it."

In reply she turned to expose her lacing to him. "By all means. I shall not be needing it anymore."

He removed her dress and under-things a little more roughly than he intended, but it seemed to spark a fire in her, for she began hungrily unfastening his pantaloons.

When they both stood naked, he gently grazed his finger over her skin, skimming her nipple before tracing her womanly curves down to the pert muscles of her buttocks. He massaged them for a while, then he grasped her hips and turned her over so suddenly that she gasped.

He bent her over the bed, spreading her open, rubbing the tip of his member into her, then moving it in a circular motion until she was dying of anticipation.

"So wet. Such a naughty little countess."

"Oh yes, very naughty. You cannot imagine the thoughts I have been having. And in the chapel, too."

"Shall I punish you?"

"Oh most certainly. You should apply the rod to me mercilessly. For I deserve it."

"Oh yes, yes you do." His voice was hoarse, and his cock grew even harder.

She could feel the heat between her legs respond to the hardening of his member, boiling over with wanting all of his length and force inside of her.

"But you also deserve this." He reached his hand around to massage that spot on her to which he always resorted. It seemed he could find it by instinct.

She moaned with pleasure. "Oh please, give it to me."

"You mean this?" He entered into her about half way.

"Oh yes please."

"You want me to fuck you, my countess?"

"Ride me hard."

He thrust into her then, so hard and deep that she gasped.

"More."

"Patience, my darling." He pumped her slowly and massaged her fast.

"Oh god, yes. Fuck me faster!"

He did not restrain himself further, thrusting into her harder and faster, moaning out loud.

She screamed a feral sound of ecstasy and he entered once more throbbing and spreading his seed inside her.

"Oh god, yes, yes, give it to me."

He could only grunt in reply. Her warmth and her wetness made him want more. His member began to get hard again while he was still inside of her.

"Oh my angel." He kissed the back of her neck. "You drive my body mad. Are you comfortable down there?"

"Exceedingly."

"Good. Don't move." He began thrusting into her again, and massaged her so vigorously she made little jumps and shrieks, then he began pounding into her so hard she could feel her wetness and his flying around in the air where they conjoined.

When he shot his seed into her the second time, she screamed along with him. He lay still for a while, panting and shaking. Then slid out of her, picked her up and lay her gently on the bed, kissing the entire length of her body. "I love you. You are a goddess."

She sighed happily. "They will have to burn these sheets, you know."

"I do not care. Tomorrow I intend to destroy this bed entirely while having congress with my beautiful wife. But for now I am exhausted." He wrapped his arms around her, and fell asleep.

She would let him rest for a while, she decided. But she was not waiting until morning to get astride him. He would wake up to the ride of his life.

CHAPTER 59

*T*he carriage rolled down the well-kept road to Alderwick Manor, as the Earl and Countess of Aldley returned home from their honeymoon. Lydia peered out the window to enjoy the view of the vast forested lands of which she was now mistress.

She could see smaller paths running within the trees, sometimes joining up with the road, sometimes disappearing into the deep shadowy greens of oaks and firs. It would be glorious ride Ari over such long runs.

Though she supposed she would have to give up that amusement soon, at least for a time. In fact, she was very grateful for the excellent suspension of the vehicle, for even on good road she found that her body registered the jouncing motion of the carriage much more than before.

The honeymoon on the continent had been everything she imagined, but it was good to be returning to her new home, where she was sure she would continue to enjoy her husband as much as ever.

"Are you glad to be coming home, my darling countess, or shall you miss travelling?" Thomas played with one of her curls.

"I have enjoyed every moment of our trip, but I admit, I am looking forward to settling down and seeing friends and family again." She stretched her legs. "And I miss Ari."

He nibbled her earlobe. "Well, at least he will be pleased that you have stayed in practice with your riding while you were away."

She smiled. "Your riding skills are also improving. But I think I am still a little better at it than you."

"You are my idol in all things, so I shall not contradict you." He pulled her into his lap, so she could feel him growing hard against her buttocks. "But I guess that just means I need more practice, you wicked little filly."

"Mmm. The wicked little filly could eat your carrot before we reach the manor."

"I love the way you think, darling, but perhaps we should wait until we are home. I should rather you emerge from the carriage with a face that is radiant, not glistening. The servants are well trained, but we ought not try to shock them."

"Very well. But in the future, we shall have to train the servants to mind their own affairs."

"They are very good at that, I assure you." He grinned. "I shall give them instructions to serve dinner covered in the rooms annexed to our bed chamber. We shall dine privately at our leisure, and ring for them to clear."

"A sensible arrangement. We need to keep up our strength, after all."

"Oh yes." He looked as though he were about to pull her in for a serious kiss, when the coach turned onto the long driveway of the manor. "Well, my love, it appears you will have the luxury of a softer surface than these coach seats when I take you for a riding lesson."

"Oh indeed!" Her tone was prim. "You cannot tousle me just anywhere now, you know."

"Hmm?" He ground against her buttocks. "Are you going to become prudish now that we are back from the continent?"

"Not at all. If anything, more demanding. But in the near future I may not be quite as flexible as I have been."

"Really?" He tilted his head. "May one enquire why?"

"One may. It is because I am greatly of the suspicion that your child may not be so obliging as I am. Taking after the father, it would seem."

"Are you saying? Are you sure?" His face gleamed with hope.

She shook her head. "Of course I am not sure, but I am late, and when I consider our marital amusements for these past months, it almost seems impossible that I should *not* be with child."

He embraced her, stroked her hair, kissed her head and put his hand to her belly. "You marvellous creature! Just when I thought I could not be any happier! This is wonderful. I only wish we could announce it right away. Of course we cannot, but I admit I should like to hire a herald just to parade around the village shouting of our happiness."

"That would be very bad form, and also bad luck," she laughed. "I am glad you are happy. So am I. But calm yourself. And stop petting my belly. It is far too soon for that."

"Do not be so prickly. You cannot know how my heart is pounding." He practically bounded out of the carriage as the door was opened, then turned to lift her out, holding her across his arms. "Decorum be damned, I am going to carry you, Lady Aldley."

"Silly man, put me down. You will embarrass the servants."

"Oh, now you are concerned?" But he obliged her and put her down exceedingly gently.

Then kissed her head, took her arm and walked with her to Alderwick. A large grin of pride spread across his face at the thought of bringing his beloved countess and his future child across the threshold of his ancestral home.

Lydia smiled up at Thomas and felt a great internal contentment that she was making the man that she loved so happy. Joy filled her heart at the sight of his handsome, beaming face, and she knew he would be a wonderful father.

Her plans to get back to business in London could wait a few days.

AFTERWORD

Dear reader, if you enjoyed *Three Abductions and an Earl*, why not give it a review on Amazon, i-Tunes, or Goodreads?

With just a few moments and a couple of clicks, you can help to share Thomas' and Lydia's romantic adventure with others.

Thank you, in advance, for your review: it makes such a difference to new authors like me, and it helps readers find new books to love!

All the good karma to you, and I'll see you in Book 2!

ALSO BY TESSA CANDLE

Mistress of Two Fortunes and a Duke, Book 2 in the *Parvenues & Paramours* series
—coming very soon! Sign up for updates at http://eepurl.com/cIzyVr. I will
be sending out a cover reveal...

Accursed Abbey, a Gothic Romance—coming soon! Sign up for updates at
http://eepurl.com/cIzyVr. Everyone on the Tessa Candle Updates list will be
offered a free copy when it is ready for release!

Three Abductions and an Earl, audio book, as read by the author—coming soon!
Sign up for updates at http://eepurl.com/cIzyVr.

Or you can sign up at www.tessacandle.com.

ACKNOWLEDGMENTS

Three Abductions and an Earl would not have been possible without the hard work, encouragement and support of many people.

If you passed eyes over this book, or its cover, or had to listen to me chatter on, pepper you with hundreds of questions, or bewail my piteous lot, thank you.

You know who you are, and you are wonderful.

ABOUT THE AUTHOR

Tessa Candle is a lawyer, world traveler, and author of rollicking historical regency romance. She also lays claim to the questionable distinction of being happily married to the descendant of a royal bastard.

When not slaving over the production and release of another novel, or conducting *research* by reading salacious historical romances with heroines who refuse to be victims, she divides her time between gardening, video editing, traveling, and meeting the outrageous demands of her two highly entitled Samoyed dogs. As they are cute and inclined to think too well of themselves, Tessa surmises that they were probably dukes in a prior incarnation.

Those wishing to remain apprised of the status on her patent for the *Rogue-o-matic Self-ripping Bodice* should subscribe to Tessa Candle Updates on her website.

Visit Tessa Candle's website:
www.tessacandle.com

Made in the USA
Middletown, DE
13 March 2019